HER WICKED HIGHWAYMAN

THE LEAGUE OF ROGUES

BOOK XIX

LAUREN SMITH

To you, the woman who feels the need to linger on a quiet country road, embracing the pull of the shadows and the mystery of the trees beyond, and senses that perhaps a highwayman had once passed through the very spot you are standing on. To you, the woman who wishes you could have met him on a moonlit night and seen the flash of that smirk beneath a mask and felt the gentlemanly caress of his gloved hand over the column of your throat as you tremble, torn between fear and desire. This story is for you.

The wind was a torrent of darkness among the gusty trees.
The moon was a ghostly galleon tossed upon cloudy seas.
The road was a ribbon of moonlight over the purple moor,
And the highwayman came riding—
Riding—riding—
The highwayman came riding, up to the old inn-door.

He'd a French cocked-hat on his forehead, a bunch of lace at his chin,
A coat of the claret velvet, and breeches of brown doe-skin.
They fitted with never a wrinkle. His boots were up to the thigh.
And he rode with a jewelled twinkle,
His pistol butts a-twinkle,
His rapier hilt a-twinkle, under the jewelled sky.

- *The Highwayman* by Alfred Noyes

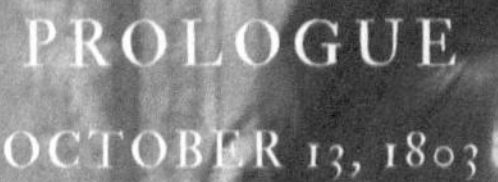

PROLOGUE

OCTOBER 13, 1803

"Malcolm please! Don't go, I beg you!"

Rafe shut his eyes against the sounds of his parents quarreling. He held his breath as he prayed he would go unnoticed in his hiding place at the top of the stairs. But he was no longer a tiny child, able to tuck himself away in a wardrobe or a cupboard. At ten, he was too tall, too lean, and too large to hide himself behind the railings of the stairs. Rafe forced his eyes open, reminding himself that he was old enough to face the truth—that the deep love his parents had once shared was withering away like flowers after too much sun and too little rain.

The Lennox townhouse was nearly dark, the candles and lamps extinguished for the night. The servants were already abed, and they knew it was not their place to interfere in such quarrels. Only the grandfather clock dared to chime in the midst of such an argument.

His father stood in the marble entryway, the light from the open parlor door showcasing his aristocratic nose and the ice of his blue eyes. Rafe's mother stepped toward Malcolm, one hand clasping his coat sleeve to halt him.

"Let me go, Reggie, damn you. I have debts to settle, and I must handle them tonight!" Malcolm hissed. Regina paled, drawing back from her husband as though he'd struck her. He had never hit her, but ofttimes words could be just as brutal. As could a callous disregard for those one was supposed to love.

"More debts? How much more? Malcolm, we cannot afford—" Regina's soft voice quavered. His mother had always been a commanding force, and now she was afraid. Rafe wanted to go downstairs, to stop this, to put an arm around his mother's shoulders and tell her all would be well. But he couldn't. He couldn't get between them and defy his father, a man he loved just as much as his mother.

"Don't you understand? I lost it all. We can afford *nothing*," Malcolm said, his voice rough with emotion. "I've been a bloody fool, and now . . . it's too late."

What did he mean? Rafe's stomach dropped and his mind blanked with dread. Whatever it was, it couldn't be good.

Regina covered her mouth with her hands for a moment. Then she tried to calm herself. "But my bride price . . . My father put it in a trust for me to use if we had need of it. We still have that—"

Malcolm gave a harsh and broken laugh, and the sound dragged invisible claws over Rafe's spine. He had never heard his father sound like that before.

"I wagered that too. I was sure I could win this time, Reggie. But Lord Caddington cheated. The bastard won every shilling. I've already withdrawn the money from your trust."

Regina's lips parted and her face drained of color. The silence between them, albeit brief, could have frozen the entire world.

"How could you? It requires my approval," she said.

"I forged your signature, and your solicitor and trustee believed it to be genuine."

"You . . . you stole my future, our *children's* future! Malcolm . . ."

"Reggie," he said and reached for her this time.

His mother slapped his father across the face and then, clutching her hand, fled the entryway, leaving his father to stand there alone, his shoulders hunched.

Malcolm stared in the direction that Regina had fled. Then, with a sigh so weary that it seemed to carry the weight of his every sin, Malcolm walked out the front door.

As the door closed, Rafe's stomach clenched. He was going to be sick. He bent double, his belly cramping, and he struggled to breathe until he calmed. Was it true? Were they without *any* money? Surely his father hadn't spent everything in the gambling hells. Surely he couldn't have . . .

Suddenly, Ashton exited their father's study and rushed down the stairs, looking the way their mother had gone and then toward the front door. Then he looked up toward the stairs, seeing Rafe as if he'd known as he always did where Rafe liked to hide.

"What happened? Where's Father? I heard shouting." Ashton was only fifteen, but he already held an air of command. Rafe knew his brother could fix the break between their parents—Ashton could do anything.

"He left—he and Mother quarreled about money again."

Ashton cursed softly. "Stay here, you understand? I'll bring him back." Then Ashton grabbed his cloak and rushed out into the night.

Gripped by a need to help his elder brother, Rafe raced down the stairs and out into the night. Ashton walked ahead of him, and their father was just beyond them, barely visible in the gloom, his pace brisk, his head bowed.

Rafe followed his brother and father along Half Moon Street as they wandered deeper and deeper into a part of the city he knew they should not go. The streets grew narrower, the muck on the road thickened, and the mingled smells of fear and despair emanated off the walls of the hovel-like structures they passed. Where was his father going? Surely the people living here were not anyone he would or *should* know. Yet without a backward glance, his father strode toward a tavern, unbothered by being in such a place as this.

His father disappeared into the building, whose faded sign read, "Devil's Spear." A minute later, Ashton carefully crossed the road and entered the building as well. Rafe kept a watchful eye on the men around him who passed through these cramped streets. The men who lived in this part of London had hard and dangerous faces. Rafe had always been able to read a person by their expressions, even the most minute ones, and he could usually read a person's intentions. These men would slit his throat without a second thought.

Rafe stepped deeper into the shadows of the mews across the street until he could decide what he should do. He cursed the light hue of his hair, fearing the shine of it might reveal him in the dark just as his bright-blue eyes so often did. If his father or Ashton saw that he was here, he would never hear the end of it.

Rafe squared his shoulders as he crossed the street and took hold of the door handle to the Devil's Spear. When he opened it, he found a boisterous taproom filled with gambling tables and drunk men. The building was a ramshackle maze of rooms and corridors so crowded that it was hard to see where his elder brother had gone.

Women with bared breasts sat atop the laps of several men as they offered tankards of ale. Serving wenches wandered through the room with trays, handing out yet more ale. At one table, in full view of everyone, a man had a woman's skirts up over her bottom and was . . .

Rafe's face flushed at the unexpected intimate sight. Where the devil was his father and Ashton?

He wove his way through the chaotic din of rooms, seeking the familiar faces of either his father or his brother in the crowd. Finally, in the farthest corner of the room, he spotted a square table with three men speaking, their voices drowned out by the din. One of the men was his father. Letting out a sigh of relief, he decided to risk his father's displeasure and show himself and beg him to come home. Rafe navigated his way through the room, feeling the menacing stares of the men and the wistful smiles of the wenches. One woman even grasped his arm as he walked past.

"My, my, ain't ye quite the lad . . ." She batted her lashes at him and leaned forward, letting him see her bountiful bosom.

Rafe's face flooded with heat as he pulled away from the woman. He was frightened by the way she looked at him.

The men around her sneered, and laughter broke out as one man slapped the woman's bottom hard. She yelped, but then she started laughing too. Rafe took the opportunity to escape and moved even more quickly toward the table in the back.

When he reached his father, he stood behind him and placed a hand on his shoulder. Malcolm flinched and whirled, as if expecting a fight. He gaped when he saw it was Rafe.

"What the devil are you doing here?"

"I came to take you home, Father." Rafe didn't dare look at the other two men, but he could feel their eyes on him. He didn't mention that Ashton was somewhere in this awful place—that might well make his father even more furious.

"I'm in the middle of something important, Rafe. *Go home.*" His father's voice held a warning that terrified Rafe. His father was a strong man, and Rafe had always believed he could do anything. Now, for the first time in his life, he saw a different side to the man he had idolized.

"Go home, my boy, *please.*" His father grasped Rafe's arm, giving it a hard squeeze. "Take care of your mother and sister. I will be home soon."

Rafe wished desperately that his elder brother was there. Ashton always knew what to do, what to say. Where was he? How had he not found their father as quickly as Rafe had?

Rafe finally summoned the courage to look at the other two men at the table. One was stout but looked strong. He wore the fine coat of a gentleman, but cruelty lined his features in deep grooves. The second man was massive, a brute with a heavy, pockmarked face. He sneered at Rafe.

This was the sort of man one would never dare wager against in one of those underground boxing rings he wasn't supposed to know existed.

The gentleman eyed Rafe with frighteningly dark eyes. "Introduce us to your welp, Lennox."

"I . . ." Malcolm hesitated, but finally relented. "Rafe, this is Lord Caddington and his associate, Mr. Phelps." His tone was so full of woe that Rafe immediately feared what lay between his father and this man.

Caddington swept a cold gaze over Rafe. "How old are you, boy? Ten, twelve?"

"Ten, my lord." Rafe's tone was steady, even though he was shaking inside. Something about this man felt terribly wrong. Rafe couldn't read him like he could other people. He had no tells, no quirks, no slight expressions to indicate what he was thinking or feeling. The man's eyes were *empty*.

"Pretty lad, aren't you, boy?" Caddington mused and stroked his chin. "Lennox, perhaps your boy can work off your debts by attending me in my household."

Malcolm shot to his feet. "No!"

The bellow was so loud and unexpected, the entire room quaked with the rumble of Malcolm's shout. A hush fell across the drunken crowd until they resumed their activities like nothing had happened.

"No, Caddington," Malcolm said more quietly, but with no less menace in his tone. "You have the necessary papers to acquire the funds I owe you, and that should be enough. My son has nothing to do with this."

Caddington toyed with his glass of brandy as he assumed a contemplative expression.

"It may be enough for now, but you can't avoid the

tables forever, Lennox. We both know you will be back. And when you are, I will claim that boy as payment." Caddington flashed Rafe a grin that promised dark and terrible things should he and Caddington ever meet again.

Rafe backed up a step. He wanted to leave, he wanted to turn tail and run, but he was a Lennox. He wouldn't abandon his father to this man.

Malcolm grasped Rafe's arm. "It's time for you to go home, son." They both headed for the door of the gambling den and stepped outside into the night.

"I'll call a hackney for you," his father muttered, refusing to look his son in the eye as he raised his hand and called a coach to come toward them. When the driver stopped before them, Malcolm paid the man and gave him the address of the Lennox townhouse.

"Aren't you coming with me?" Rafe asked his father in a quiet, scared voice.

"No, there is something I must do . . . I will be home by morning." His father's voice had an odd sound to it, and Rafe didn't like the strange look upon his father's face.

Rafe shuddered and glanced back at the doorway of the tavern and gambling hell. A dark shadow blocked out the light coming from the open doorway. Rafe recognized the shape of the man. It was Mr. Phelps.

"He wants the boy, Lennox," Phelps said. "Give him to me."

"Never," Malcolm snarled. The beast of a man started toward Malcolm, a dark, glinting object in his hand. A knife.

"Father, look out!" Rafe cried out.

Malcolm spun and placed himself between Rafe and Phelps. His father, once a prizefighter at Jackson's salon, swung and planted a facer on Phelps's chin, catching the man off guard. The man grunted and then swiped the blade at Malcolm's chest. Malcolm dodged back. The men swung at each other, punches landing on flesh in sickening sounds. Rafe was forced to step back to stay out of the way. It was clear his father was winning the fight—Phelps was outmatched, even though Malcolm smelled strongly of ale.

"Get in the coach now, son!" Malcolm shouted at Rafe and pushed him into the waiting hackney his father had summoned. Rafe fell back against the stiff coach cushions as the hackney started to move, but he didn't want to go home alone—he wanted to bring his father back with him. Before the coach could pick up any more speed, Rafe opened the door facing the opposite side of the street and jumped out onto the ground, his feet sinking into the dirt and muck upon the road, momentarily catching him in place.

A sharp clatter of hooves and a coach driver's sudden shout startled Rafe. He had stumbled into the path of a passing carriage. He couldn't move, couldn't think, couldn't breathe as the horses bore down upon him.

Something slammed into him and Rafe hit the ground, rolling over and over until he landed on the other side of the street. His head collided with hard stone, and everything went dark.

MALCOLM CURSED AS HE WATCHED THAT BASTARD PHELPS stalk back into the tavern. It had been a close one tonight, but Phelps couldn't win and they both knew it. Rafe was bound for home, he was safe . . . for now. But that wouldn't always be true. Malcolm had made the mistake of tying his fate to Andrew Caddington's when he'd started losing money to him, but he'd never dreamed that it would put his young son's life in danger.

Caddington had a dark side, a side that liked to hurt people, especially young men. He had a fondness for beating men senseless, and it was rumored he'd killed more than one young man at his estate through his love of brutality. He was a devil, a devil whose darkness knew no limits, and now he'd set his sights on Rafe.

But Malcolm was sober enough tonight to know that he had a choice—let his child's life be in danger, or do the thing that would damn his soul forever but would save his child. When he viewed the situation from that perspective, he knew there was but one course of action to take.

He must kill Caddington. Even if it brough ruin to his family in society, even if he faced the gallows for the murder, it must be done. Caddington could not be allowed to live. Malcolm stepped back into the Devil's Spear and glanced around, seeking out Phelps and Caddington.

"What now, dearie? Care for a ride?" one of the whores who frequented the brothel in the back asked him as he stepped inside. He'd made the mistake more than once of taking them to bed, when he should have gone home to his beloved Reggie, but he couldn't bear the shame of seeing her pain, her disappointment in him. So he sought solace where he could, with who he could.

"No, not tonight. Where is Lord Caddington?" he asked the woman, knowing she would be well aware of where one of the good "marks" were in the establishment.

"Lord Caddington is in the back. Want me to show you?" She hooked her arm through his and led him past the main gambling room. They stopped at the door to one of the rooms at the end of the corridor and she opened it. "He's just in there . . ."

As Malcolm stepped inside, something struck his head hard from behind. He stumbled and caught himself on the edge of the empty bed in the room. Everything in his vision spun wildly and he collapsed onto the bed, trying to catch his breath. He was vaguely aware of the whore searching his pockets for money. When she pried his pocket watch from his chest, he struggled to get it back but she shoved him hard and he fell back onto the bed, clutching his head.

The door to the room slammed shut, leaving him in darkness. Then the door suddenly whipped open and someone was rushing toward him.

"Father!" Ashton's voice came through the haze too late as Malcolm struck out, hitting his son across the face.

"Leave me, boy!"

Ashton put a hand to his face, and Malcolm hated the look of hurt in his eldest son's eyes. He had never struck his son before.

"Father, please," Ashton begged. "Come home. Mother needs you. We all need you."

Lord Lennox stumbled to his feet. "Damned whore took my coin purse." He patted his pockets. "Pocket watch too."

"Father . . ."Ashton still touched his face where he'd been struck, but Malcolm wasn't listening.

He left the room, tripping over his feet into the hall. He had to find Caddington, had to make sure that man never had a chance to hurt Rafe or anyone ever again. Ashton hurried after him, dodging the gaming tables.

Several men shouted and cursed as Malcolm bowled into them. The blow he'd taken to his head was doing far more damage to his balance than the alcohol he'd consumed.

"Careful, man!" Someone shoved Malcolm toward the front door, trying to get him out of their way.

Have to find Caddington . . . have to . . .

Malcolm's thoughts abruptly stopped as he reached the curb to the street and spotted something on the sidewalk across from him.

Rafe . . . his dear, sweet boy was sitting on the sidewalk, covered in street filth and holding a hand to his head as though he'd been hurt. Had Caddington tried to get to him again? *Please, God, no . . .*

"No," Malcolm gasped and started across the street toward his younger son.

"Father!" Ashton's shout from behind him came far too late.

⚜

AFTER WHAT FELT LIKE AN ETERNITY TRAPPED IN darkness, Rafe opened his eyes. His body hurt everywhere, and he lay on the stone walkway beside the road, his head throbbing.

Where was his father? Rafe struggled to sit up and looked around in confusion.

His father was across the street staring directly at him, shock and fear on his face. There was no sign of the frightening Mr. Phelps he'd been fighting with. Rafe stared back at his father as his father took a step off the curb and entered the street, not seeing the coach bearing down on him. Everything seemed to slow down, and Rafe could not move, could not blink or even cry out.

Horses screamed and Rafe lifted his head to see them frantically treading upon a lump in the road before the carriage wheels followed, thumping over the shape and crashing back down. A woman who'd been walking down the sidewalk by Rafe screamed, pointing a trembling finger at the mass upon the ground.

"Father!" Ashton's shout caught Rafe's attention as he saw his elder brother running after their father, who'd stepped into the street.

"Dead! The man is dead!"

The woman's words caught Rafe's heart in an icy grip and squeezed, making it impossible for him to move, to breathe.

Ashton raced down the steps and skidded to a stop a few feet away from their father's crumpled body.

"Who is it?" the driver demanded as he climbed down from his perch on his coach.

Ashton cleared his throat, but the word still came out broken. "He's my father."

"He *was* your father," a dark-haired young man with a cane said as he stopped by Ashton, along with others who'd been near the tavern and witnessed the accident. "Drunken fool." The man walked back into the club, but Ashton remained still, staring at their father, his face utterly white.

Rafe stood up, brushed his bloody scraped hands on his trousers, and walked on shaky legs toward his elder brother.

Ashton lifted his head and stared at Rafe for a moment, his eyes unseeing, then rage and fury filled them.

"What the devil are you doing here? What have you done, Rafe?"

What had he done? Rafe's lips parted, but he didn't know what to say. He couldn't remember. They'd been ready to leave, his father had been sending him home, and then that terrible man Mr. Phelps had come after them, and they'd fought. But Father had been winning the fight, hadn't he? *Hadn't he?* Rafe's mind ached and he shut his eyes briefly, trying to think, but he couldn't remember.

"I . . . don't know . . . Ashton. I don't know . . ."

"You've killed him, that's what you've done, because you couldn't stay home where you belonged," Ashton snarled. "You *killed* him . . ." The last words choked from his brother as Ashton looked at Rafe in a way he never had before. With scorn—with hatred.

"No, he can't be dead. Father . . ."

Pain throbbed in Rafe's shoulder and head, where he'd fallen against the pavement. But none of that mattered. He knelt down and lifted his father's head, trying to cradle it on his lap. Blood coated Malcolm's lips and his body was bent at unnatural angles. His eyes were open, but his expression was dazed. Rafe didn't want to think about how much pain his father was in. He'd broken his arm once, falling from a tree a few years ago, but his father was . . . beyond repair.

Malcolm licked his lips, his gaze slowly moving between Rafe and Ashton, who'd knelt down next to Rafe. Ashton's face was white as marble. His lips were parted but he didn't speak, didn't move—it was as though he was frozen.

Rafe turned his focus back to his father. His hands shook as he gently touched his face. "Father."

"My boy." The words escaped Malcolm's lips like a soft sigh, and then the glimmer of life in his eyes faded away.

Rafe held his father's head in his lap, tears streaming down his face as he met Ashton's gaze. His older brother didn't move, he simply stared at their father . . . utterly broken.

"Someone help us! Anyone! Please!" he shouted at the bystanders who looked on with mingled sorrow and pity. But there was no help, not for Lord Malcolm Lennox. It was far too late. Not even his elder brother could help their father now. He was gone—and Rafe had been the cause of it.

Rafe wiped at his eyes, a strange numbness creeping through his limbs as he saw Mr. Phelps and Lord Caddington staring at him from a short distance. They were more wraiths than flesh and blood. Rafe's eyes burned with a hatred so strong that, for a moment, it filled the emptiness that his father's death had left. They were responsible for this.

Someday he would kill them both. Even if he had to wait a lifetime. His steel would taste their blood and his father would be avenged.

⚜

REGINA LENNOX STARED AT THE BURNING EMBERS OF THE fire in the drawing room. Every bone in her body ached as her worry for Malcolm deepened. She pulled her plaid shawl tighter around her shoulders. They had quarreled before, but never like this. And she'd never struck him before. But he'd done the unthinkable. He'd betrayed her trust in a way he'd sworn he never would.

That money, the dowry her father had given her, was to be a gift to their children someday. And he'd gambled it away without a thought . . . because he hadn't bothered to think of her at all as he'd lingered over those tables full of vice. Her throat tightened as she struggled to keep herself from crying. Tears would do no good. She had to be strong, for herself and for her children.

It was two o'clock in the morning and still Malcolm had not returned. A hard clacking of the front door's brass knocker pulled her from her thoughts. *Malcolm!* She abandoned her seat in the drawing room and rushed into the entryway, flinging the door open.

"Malcolm, where have you—"

Her voice died as she saw a stranger on the steps facing her. The man removed his hat and held it in his hand, his face solemn.

"Lady Lennox?"

"Y-yes." She could barely speak. Her throat closed as a sudden inescapable weight pressed down on her chest, threatening to choke her. She knew what this was. She knew.

"I regret to inform you that your husband has died."

A ringing started in her ears as she saw two figures step out from behind the man speaking to her. Rafe and Ashton. Their faces were ash-white, and Rafe's clothes were covered in mud. When had her sons left the house?

"My lady?" the man asked. "Did you hear what I said? I said, your sons witnessed the accident."

"Accident?" Regina had never fainted before, but right then the world spun dizzily around her. Her legs gave out.

Rafe dove to catch her, but Ashton shoved him out of the way and held their mother tenderly to him. "Mother!"

"How . . . how did it happen?" Her voice was breathless, but the man still heard her.

"He was run over by a carriage, my lady," he said as he knelt close to Regina. "I was the constable on duty. I will need to ask you some questions about your husband's movements this evening and—"

Regina stopped listening to the man. She stared into her sons' faces and read the pain in their eyes, the pain and . . . in Rafe's face, *guilt*. Her beautiful little boy's face was twisted with grief. Ashton shot Rafe a look of pure rage that Regina couldn't understand. Her sons loved each other, they never fought . . . they never . . .

Something had happened tonight to change that.

She clutched Ashton's arms, her heart shattering and her voice breaking as she stared at her youngest son.

"Rafe, what have you done?"

CHAPTER 1

Excerpt from the *Quizzing Glass Gazette*, October 13, 1822, the Lady Society column:

Lady Society has become aware of reports of a dangerous highwayman who hunts for jewels and coins on the road in the country throughout Hampshire. While Lady Society usually focuses on scandalous gossip of the goings-on of the ton, this tale was simply too delicious to ignore.

By all accounts, this highwayman is dangerous only to those who dare cross him. He holds the men at bay with a pistol in hand, while kissing the rings off the ladies with the other. He is without question a scoundrel of the highest order, but one can't help but embrace the romantic imagery he evokes. Lady Society wonders what lies beneath the domino and the black cape. Who is this man who cries, "Stand and deliver!" as he collects his prizes? Perhaps he will move his hunting territory to the streets of London so that the ladies of the ton might feast their eyes on this handsome devil.

. . .

DIANA FOX PULLED HER SHAWL TIGHTER ABOUT HER shoulders as she stared bleakly out of the coach window. She would be home in a few hours, but as much as she was glad to be returning, she had no good news to bring with her to those servants who had loyally stayed with her after her father died.

Foxglove Hall, her beloved family home, would soon belong to creditors if she could not find a steady source of income for the estate. They had the farming tenants, of course, but she could not take what little money they were able to earn. She'd spent the last three weeks in London, meeting with her father's solicitor and doing her best to sort out the mess his passing had left her to deal with. At least now she had a complete list of the debts she must pay and the amounts. The solicitor had persuaded the banks to give her a month's time to come up with at least half of what she owed. The problem was, she was without a means to earn it.

Wind whistled against the windows of the coach. Its chilliness permeated the cracks in the frame, freezing the interior of the coach, along with its passengers. Three others traveled with her on this stagecoach, two men and a woman. They were huddled together for warmth on one side of the coach, while she kept her distance on the opposite side. She had learned during their brief discussions that the other occupants were a family, with a father, a mother, and their son, Claude, who was around Diana's age of twenty-three.

She had politely put off the young man's attempts at small talk when it became clear he was interested in her.

She had neither the time nor the inclination for romance, let alone the patience to entertain a restless young pup like this young man. He was nice enough, even pleasant looking, but his attentions only stirred a frustration deep inside her. She'd given up on love and marriage years ago, when she'd begun caring for her ailing father.

I barely have time to care for myself. How could I possibly stretch myself thin for yet another man?

It was a question she wearily voiced in her mind whenever a pang of loneliness struck her more deeply than usual. As always, she'd pushed the loneliness down, buried it so deep it could not easily claw its way back to the surface.

Other women might have married for security, but she couldn't stomach the thought. A marriage as an agreement or contract would put Diana at a disadvantage—and ultimately at the will of the man she married. Should their relations sour, she would be the one who stood to lose everything.

Therefore, it made no sense to marry someone unless it was for love, a lasting love and friendship that would not devolve into a war of wills she would ultimately lose because she was a woman and therefore her husband's property. If she married, it would be for love. It would be because her heart simply could not beat another second without the man she loved in her life. But that kind of man was nothing but a girlish daydream. Her home and the well-being of the servants who lived there were all that mattered to her now.

The coach dipped a little as the wheels fell into a rut on the road. Diana braced herself against the side of the coach, wincing at the jarring distraction.

Only a few miles down the road, the coach would stop in front of a pair of carved stone foxes on pillars that abutted the entrance to Foxglove Hall, her family's home.

A bitter ache stirred in her chest as she reminded herself that she no longer had any family.

I'm all that's left of the noble house of Fox.

Her mother had died when Diana was fifteen, and her older sister had run away from home to get married not long after. And then her father had passed from a stroke less than a year ago.

"Shouldn't be long now," Edwin, the older gentleman, pronounced to his wife. "Good thing to be home. A storm is coming. I can smell the rain."

His wife nodded primly, as if she took her husband's words as gospel. "We don't want the road too muddy. If the coach becomes stuck, we would have to spend the night on the road." She glanced at Diana, trying to include her in the conversation. "Do you have very far to go, my dear?"

Diana tore her gaze from the window. "Perhaps another two miles?"

"And where are you bound, Miss Fox?" Claude asked eagerly. "Perhaps I could escort you there?"

"No," she gasped out, then calmed herself. "I mean, no, thank you. I will be quite fine. My staff will be waiting for me. My groom usually waits for me near the road."

It wasn't exactly a lie. Her groom, a wonderful though somewhat ancient fellow named Nelson, always insisted on riding out to meet her at the gates and escorting her home, but today he didn't know *when* she would be coming home. But the last thing she needed was yet another man trying to woo her with his courtly gestures. She'd been through all this before and had seen where it ended—with a man believing he could take liberties, or force her hand into marriage. And it *always* started with a polite escort home.

He deflated instantly at her rejection. "Oh."

The coach slammed down into another rut and the woman shrieked, clutching her husband's arm.

"Miss Fox, you can hold on to me, if you like," Claude offered with a hopeful look upon his face.

"I'm quite fine, I assure you." She adjusted her white-knuckle grip on the faded pink curtains of the travel coach.

A crack of thunder, sharp and clear, forced the coach to a jolting stop. Diana grunted as her head bounced off the glass of the window she'd been peering through. She rubbed her forehead and looked for any sign of the storm that had suddenly descended upon them.

"That was rather close thunder," Diana muttered. She hoped the storm would not come yet. It might be a long walk in the rain to the house, and she was already cold.

A shout outside the coach was partially muffled, but the words *"Stand and deliver!"* were clear enough for everyone to hear.

Edwin straightened, his face paling. "That wasn't thunder. That was a pistol shot."

His wife gasped. "Edwin, what are we to do? It must be a highwayman!"

"Unfortunately, that is likely," Edwin agreed. "Claude, my boy, you must do exactly as we are told. No foolish heroics, do you understand? These scoundrels will shoot a man for the slightest insult."

Claude puffed out his shoulders, but then gave his father a solemn nod. "Miss Fox, I will protect you."

Diana offered him a wan smile. This boy couldn't defend her, and she didn't expect him to, not against a highwayman. And given her current mood, she was far more likely to be able to defend herself than any man, even against a highwayman. The last few months had been among the most wretched of her life, and if he dared demand a thing from her, Diana would make sure he regretted it.

More shouts came from outside the coach. The horses whinnied and the coach rocked back and forth.

"You bloody scoundrels!" the stagecoach driver shouted from above.

"Come down, now!" came a voice that carried a sharp air of command that stilled Diana's rapidly beating heart.

The door next to her was wrenched open, illuminating them in moonlight and silhouetting the figure staring at them. A masked man peered inside the coach, his pistol raised at the occupants. He wore no billowing cloak, but a trim black wool greatcoat that sparkled with rain droplets.

"Good evening, ladies and gentlemen," the highwayman said. He had a Scottish burr that rippled across Diana's skin. She frowned at the unexpected reaction. Perhaps it was just the rich timbre of his voice that she admired?

Admired? Was she going mad? She didn't admire this man. He was a petty thief—there was certainly nothing to admire about that.

The highwayman grinned, the domino he wore concealing all but his mouth and eyes.

"Please kindly step outside and form a line. If ye cooperate, this will go smoothly and I willna hurt anyone. I request that ye remove all valuable coins and jewels from yer persons." He waved the pistol at Edwin. "Ye will exit first."

Edwin climbed out of the coach and helped his wife

down. The poor woman was trembling so hard she nearly fell.

The highwayman pointed his pistol at Claude. "Ye go next, laddie."

"You vile thief!" Claude puffed his chest out but made no move to reach for the man's gun. "How *dare* you rob us!"

The thief chuckled and spoke over his shoulder to two other riders, also wearing masks, who waited nearby, their pistols raised and ready to shoot.

"Ach, I'm wounded. The laddie thinks we are vile thieves!"

The other highwaymen laughed, unbothered by the insult.

"All right, laddie, ye've proven ye're brave. Now be at ease, young pup."

Claude reluctantly climbed down and stood beside his parents. He turned to assist Diana, but the thief nudged him aside with the barrel of his gun.

"Well now," the man purred as he spotted Diana. "What a bonnie wee thing ye are." He held out a gloved hand to her.

Diana scowled at him. *Bonnie.* She wasn't unkind in her appraisal of her looks, but she was well aware that she possessed an impertinent chin and a slightly upturned nose that made her look more mischievous when in good spirits and quite harsh when she was in a bad mood. And right then, she was most assuredly in a foul mood.

"I do not require any assistance, nor any of your false flattery." She braced herself on the side of the door and used her free hand to lift her blue velvet skirts out of the way as she stepped through the coach's doorway. She'd worn her best dresses while in London, hoping to remind the bankers she was still from a noble family, and now she regretted that choice. If it rained now, her dress would be like lead weights upon her skin.

"Ye will let me help you, lass. I insist." The man reached forward, curling one arm around her waist and lifting her off her feet.

She slid down the front of his body, all too aware of every hard, muscled inch of him, like a marble statue. She clutched his shoulders in surprise at the way her body warmed in response to his. She gazed into bright-blue eyes that seemed like clouds shot through with moonlight. As he set her down, her shawl slipped and she released his shoulders, intending to pull it back up.

"Allow me," the Scotsman said. He took the shawl and wrapped it back around her, but his gaze lingered on her breasts as he tucked the opposite ends of the shawl into her shaking hands.

"Exquisite," he said, his gaze still focused on her chest.

"I beg your pardon!" she hissed and covered herself.

The man's low, rough chuckle scraped over her skin in a most erotic way, sending a flutter of heat through her. "I was speaking of yer necklace. Although, I could say the same of yer beautiful breasts. They are *also* exquisite."

"How *dare* you speak to a lady thus!" Claude shouted. He took a step toward the thief.

Rather than feel challenged, the highwayman seemed only amused by the young man.

"Every lass likes to hear her beauty praised, laddie. Best to learn that lesson before ye start bending women over, eh? All women deserve a bit of wooing before the loving." The Scotsman's gaze never left Diana as he brushed the backs of his gloved fingers over her cheek and then down to the column of her throat.

She should have slapped his hand away, but she was caught still by his gaze. She'd never felt like this before. This man's eyes held her pinned like some poor butterfly beneath a pane of glass. She was powerless before him, but why? No man had ever made her feel like this. His sinfully lush lips parted, and she tasted the sweetness of his breath as he continued to watch her. Their faces were so close now that he could almost kiss her. He seemed to realize the startling effect he had on her, and his grin grew wistful.

"Ye're too sweet for a man like me, kitten," he said, his lips curving into a charming, crooked grin. That singular grin unfurled a river of sweet heat that licked through her veins.

"On that, you are quite wrong," she replied. Some of the fire came back into her blood. Fire she could use. Fire she understood. "I am anything but sweet. I spew fire and I rage," she warned. But the words came out more breathless than she had thought they would. She was angry, wasn't she? Why didn't she sound angry?

"Lucky for ye, lass, I quite like to be burned." The way he said the word *burned* sent a thrill through her. What could he mean by that? Were there other ways to burn other than from anger?

One of the other highwaymen spoke up with a light Irish lilt. "Come now, Tyburn, collect our winnings so we can leave."

Had these men come from all parts of the kingdom? Joined forces to rob Englishmen and women? Given how the government had treated the Scots and the Irish in the last hundred years, she couldn't blame them. A moment later, she realized that she'd learned the dashing Scotsman's name.

Tyburn.

Rather fitting, since he would someday hang at Tyburn for his crimes.

"Verra well," Tyburn said as he stepped back from her and removed a leather pouch, opening it with one hand while keeping his pistol aimed at his victims. "Ye heard him. Pocket watches, jewels, and any coins, if ye please." He started with Edwin and his wife, who dropped their money and jewelry into the pouch. Claude reluctantly surrendered his money and pocket watch. When the highwayman held out the bag to Diana, she poured the meager contents of her coin purse into the pouch with great regret. She *needed* that money, blast him! He cleared his throat and stared at her expectantly.

"I gave you all the money I have!" she practically spat.

"Ye forgot yer necklace, my lovely fire drake."

Her hand shot instinctively to curl around the large freshwater pearl that hung from the gold chain around her neck. It was the only thing of her mother's she had left that she hadn't sold to help her keep possession of her home. It was the one thing she couldn't part with. Her father had given it to her mother the day she'd given birth to Diana. Unlike many men, he hadn't cared that they'd had no male children. He'd been overjoyed to have a second daughter, and that pearl was a representation of his love for his wife and their new child.

All the fire inside her left. "*Please,* I must keep it," she begged. If she had to grovel to keep the necklace, she would.

Tyburn's lips twitched. "Alas, love, I canna show favoritism to ye or my reputation will be ruined." He reached up, most likely intending to break the chain in order to remove it from her.

"Wait! Let me do it." She reached up to undo the clasp, then she cupped it in her gloved palm. He raised the pouch up for her, but rather than drop it into the pouch, she blew out a fast breath, which created a small space between her breasts and the bodice of her gown. She dropped the necklace into the valley of her bosom, then inhaled, preventing the man from being able to reach the pearl.

"Why, ye little—" The thief halted at whatever insult he'd intended and scowled, his blue eyes frosting like a lake in winter. "That wasna a clever thing to do, lass."

"There is no way you can get to it now," Diana declared.

"Ye think so, lass? Now ye've gone and tempted me." He eyed her clothes with a measuring look that took her by surprise.

Oh dear Lord . . . She'd made a terrible mistake. No gentleman would have taken that as a challenge.

"But you are a gentlemen! You wouldn't dare." She'd read about highwaymen in the papers. They were often men of noble or gentle birth who had fallen upon hard times or circumstances that forced them to resort to thievery. The ones she'd read about were not callous murderers, and they hardly ever forced themselves on women.

"My friends may be gentlemen, but *I* am not, lass. I *will* have that necklace, even if I must strip every inch of clothing off yer body to get it." He reached up and grasped her throat with a gloved hand. He didn't squeeze, but held her trapped between his powerful fingers. A shot of wild heat ripped through her body and she gasped, but not from fear. His possessive, dominating hold on her neck should have terrified her, but rather it only excited her.

I must be mad . . . truly mad, she thought.

His hand moved to the nape of her neck as he forced her to walk away from the others.

"What are you doing?" Edwin and Claude both shouted. "You cannot abduct a lady!"

"'Tis exactly what I'm doing," Tyburn growled as he pushed Diana toward his horse. The moment he reached the steed, he picked her up and tossed her over the saddle. She scrambled to catch hold of the reins and briefly envisioned riding off, but he quickly mounted up behind her and seized the reins from her hands. He tucked his pistol inside his coat, well out of her reach.

"Keep a watch on them, Oxford. Then take the third route back to our meeting place," Tyburn ordered. The man he'd called Oxford nodded. When Tyburn and the third man urged their horses forward, they reached a full gallop after only a few moments.

Diana clutched the horse's mane, trying not to fall, but Tyburn wrapped an arm around her tight and jerked her back against him. He seemed to be quite used to riding with a hostage in front of him. His long legs settled against her own, his thighs pressing in against hers. She could tell he was laying a hard path to follow, given the varied terrain he took them over, which was far from any roads. It would be hard to track them.

Oxford, she realized, would leave yet another trail to confuse anyone who might come searching for them. Still, Diana did her best to memorize everything she saw.

Although much of the countryside looked the same to her, there were places she felt she could remember if pressed.

They rode for half an hour, then slowed their horses in the middle of a field and stopped.

"Why have we stopped?" she asked.

"Cambridge, the blindfold, if you please." Tyburn pointed to the third man's waist. Cambridge removed a strip of black cloth from a pocket in his greatcoat and urged his horse next to Tyburn to hand it to him.

"No!" She tried to duck and slide off the horse's back, but Tyburn held her still with his iron band of an arm. Cambridge manhandled her until he had a grasp on her head and neck. His touch then gentled as he wrapped the blindfold over her eyes. Then her wrists were bound together with another bit of cloth. She wanted to fight, but she wasn't a fool. If she fell now, bound and blind, she could be trampled by their tall, powerful horses. It was better to bide her time and pretend she was compliant. Once she found out where they had their hideout, she would develop a plan for escape.

The two men were silent as they rode for another length of time. This was harder for her to measure because she was unable to see her surroundings. All she had was the heat of Tyburn's body behind her and the sound of the horses' hooves pounding upon the ground.

The rain finally came in driving sheets that soaked her to the bone, but she made no protest. She still had her pride. Still, she couldn't stop herself from shivering. Her captor seemed to feel it because Tyburn pulled his coat close around her. But it wasn't large enough to cover them both.

"We havena much farther to go, lass. I'll warm ye up when we are inside," he murmured in her ear. She found herself nodding, and her teeth began to chatter.

When they finally stopped, he slid off the horse behind her and helped her down. He then swept her up in his arms as though she were a child and carried her across a threshold, where the rain became muted and ceased to pelt down on her skin. He settled her onto something warm, which she sank back into. An old overstuffed chair, perhaps? The scents she breathed in were clean, no hint of must, nor did she hear the sounds of other people around save for herself and her captors.

The blindfold was removed. Diana blinked as her eyes adjusted to the dim light around her. It appeared to be some sort of hunting lodge, given the rustic look of the furniture, including the chair he'd set her down on. It was cozy and felt lived in, but most certainly by bachelors. It had no feminine touches, no draperies, nor matching fabrics.

The two highwaymen moved to a corner of the room and spoke in low tones while stealing glances at her. Then, the one called Cambridge nodded and left the lodge. She saw him through one of the windows as he walked the horses to a nearby stable.

"Now, lass, what am I to do with ye?" Tyburn mused as he came to stand in front of her. She shrank back in the chair, then despised herself for showing such fear, so she raised her chin and met his gaze with a stubborn glare of her own.

Tyburn was tall, and his pale-gold hair turned to a burnished filigree with the rain. His domino still concealed most of his face. In this light, she could see clearly that his eyes were a piercing blue and those sensual lips were too lush for a man's mouth.

"You shouldn't have taken me. The others will send the authorities after you." She tested the restraints that bound her wrists. It only pulled tighter at her struggles.

"I suppose they will. But until they come to yer rescue, I plan to have that necklace, kitten, and ye will give it to me one way or another." His gaze rolled over her body, and she trembled. "Lucky for me, getting ye out of those wet clothes is to yer advantage. Let no one say ye caught yer death in my arms." He chuckled as if at some private joke.

Then he leaned over and braced his palms on either side of her chair, staring down at her. She stared back, refusing to flinch this time. She was not some shrinking violet. She was as rough and hardy as a dandelion.

Tyburn reached for her wrists, removing the binding and rubbing them to soothe the red marks that Cambridge had left when he'd tied the rope hastily around her.

"Do ye have a husband waiting for ye at home, lass?"

"Yes."

He grinned. "So ye arna married. What about brothers?" He removed his gloves and tossed them onto a nearby table.

"A dozen," she said. "Rather large and angry ones. They will destroy you if you dare touch me."

"Another lie, kitten. You seem to be as alone as I am in this world." His Scottish burr came out in a seductive purr.

"I am *not* alone," she argued, even though the flash of old pain at the truth stung. She'd never let him see that, never.

The Scotsman pulled her to her feet, so they were standing before each other. "Ach, but that's the biggest lie of all, lassie. Ye are alone. Like calls to like, ye see. There is a deep longing in yer lovely brown eyes. Looking at ye makes me feel warm." He reached up to stroke her arms, as if to warm her, not seduce her, and she realized she had started to shiver again. "But it seems ye are still half-frozen."

Tyburn released her and knelt by the fireplace to start a fire in the hearth. She stared down at his bent head and wondered if she could find something heavy to knock him out with, perhaps one of the logs in the iron stand beside him? No, she'd have to reach past him to get to it. Before she could locate a different weapon in the room, he was standing again and had taken her hand, lifting it to his lips.

"There's only one way to get ye warm, lass. It's time we get ye out of these clothes." He kissed her hand and then removed her soaked shawl, letting it fall to the floor in a damp heap. The cool air around her shoulders and neck made her shiver even harder.

"Please . . . ," she begged as he unfastened the front of her gown. This was one of her easier dresses to travel in— the blue velvet could be done up the front and required no maid. But it left her feeling vulnerable to stare at his masked face as his fingers delicately slid buttons through slits.

"I willna hurt ye," he said, sounding both amused and exasperated. "I havena forced a woman to my bed yet, and I willna start now."

"You are a man," she whispered. "It's in your nature to hurt women."

His hand stilled. "Have ye been hurt before, lass?" he asked, his voice holding a hint of quiet rage that she didn't understand.

Flashes of memory filled her head. Hands touching her, clawing at her clothing. After her father had died, a number of local men had believed her easy prey, either for rape or ruination so that she would have to marry them. But she'd avoided falling into either trap.

He caught her chin and turned her face so that he could see her eyes again. "Who hurt ye? Give me a name, lass, and I'll put a bullet through the bastard's heart." His voice was a low growl, so full of a menace that she hadn't expected that her eyes flashed wider with fear.

"I wasn't hurt. I wasn't," she insisted when he seemed to doubt her. "Most women aren't raised to defend themselves, but for me, it's second nature to swing a fist." She thought back to the man who'd tried to assault her as she rode home from the market one afternoon. She'd punched him so hard he'd fallen right off his horse and lay stunned in the road as she'd ridden off.

"Ye havena flung a fist toward me yet, lass," he said with a smug smile.

"Give me a good reason, and I certainly shall."

Unbothered by her threat, he grinned back at her, the silence between them charged with something too strange and exciting for her to name. The moment was broken when her teeth started to chatter again. He cursed under his breath and grasped her shoulders, pushing her toward the fire he'd started. When her back was to the warm flames, heating her body, he resumed unbuttoning her gown until it draped away from her. She clutched her arms to her chest. Without a word, he gently pried her fingers away, and the velvet cloth of her dress dropped down over her hips to the floor. He tugged at the ties that kept her petticoats fastened until they too fell to the floor. She now wore nothing more than her chemise and stays.

"These are too wet for ye, lass. They'll need to come off as well."

He gently turned her around, letting the front of her body feel the kiss of the fire's warmth. His fingers touched the laces of her stays.

"Please don't take my necklace," she said as the stays around her breasts loosened.

He slid a hand down her collarbone from behind, then moved his hand past her breasts and into the valley of her bosom until he found the necklace just below the undersides of her breasts, where it rested against the stays that hugged her lower ribs. She flinched as he lifted the necklace out from beneath her clothing. He didn't try to grope or touch her; he simply held on to the pearl and its chain as he pulled it out from her clothing.

"What value does it hold for ye?" he whispered, his breath tickling her neck. The sensation washed over her and lit a fire inside her before she reminded herself what was at stake. He held the necklace between them, and her breath caught at the sight of something that mattered so much to her.

"It was my mother's."

"Ahh . . . ," he said. "I'm sure she can give ye another one."

"No, she can't. She is dead, and I sold everything of hers except for that necklace." She nodded at the pearl resting on his palm.

Tyburn was quiet. His sparkling blue eyes were unreadable in their intensity.

"Verra well, I will let ye keep it."

She reached for it, but he pulled his hand back.

"On one condition."

"What condition?"

The wicked gleam in his eyes was her only warning as to what he would demand of her.

"Ye give me something ye've given no other man."

CHAPTER 2

"Y*e give me something ye've given to no other man."*

It took Diana a moment too long to fully comprehend his meaning. He wanted her to give herself to him . . . That was the only thing he could possibly mean. His gaze was still wicked, but there was an underlying warmth that had never been there with other men who had attempted to take liberties with her. She was both affronted and curious, because she was not repulsed by the thought of kissing this man, nor indeed doing anything else with him. He was intriguing, perhaps too much so, but she'd always loved a mystery. Her mother had warned her as a little girl that curiosity could be dangerous.

But wasn't life supposed to be full of discoveries and explorations? Wasn't curiosity meant to be satisfied? She licked her lips and challenged him.

"You would ask that of me?" She raised her chin and met him with a defiant stare.

"Aye, I would, lass. And I wager ye are brave enough to agree, are ye not?" he challenged with a sinful smile.

Diana was standing on a precipice. Her next step might send her spiraling into a world she wasn't ready for. But not to move, not to take a step in one direction or another, was impossible.

This man before her took up the entire room with his presence, making the hunting lodge seem so very small, so very closed in. Yet she didn't feel dwarfed by him. She felt . . . drawn in, if that were possible, like when a small flame touches tinder and reaches out, bleeding its heat into another tiny flame.

He was a stranger, yet something in her blood felt a . . . connection, like she was staring at herself, only in another life, another body, another gender.

Two sides to the same coin. It was a strange and eerie feeling to look into this man's eyes and see herself reflected in their piercing stormy depths.

"I promise ye will feel great pleasure," he said softly. "I am a stranger, but if ye trust me tonight ye willna have regrets." He held the pearl necklace out to her, and she curled her fingers around it. Was this how Persephone felt when she sank her teeth into the juicy pomegranate seeds, knowing that she would forever belong to the lord of the underworld? For this highwayman was surely Hades himself, disguised in black breeches and a domino.

How could she even *consider* doing what he asked, let alone agree to it? A decent lady would rather die than give herself to a man like this. But she'd stopped feeling decent the moment her father had died and she'd had to do whatever she could to keep her home and her servants—*her family*—together. What was one more transgression against the rules of polite society, that same society that had failed to help her when she needed it most?

Her grip tightened on her mother's pendant, and she swallowed past the lump in her throat. She nodded. She would do just about anything to keep her mother's necklace. She had a feeling that being with this man might not be a hardship, that she might actually enjoy it. The way he watched her made her feel that was certainly possible. She'd heard whispers that the best lovers were often the most wicked, and this man was certainly that.

"I will do it," she agreed.

Tyburn lifted her hand to kiss her fingers. His lips were soft, warm, and the gesture was oddly tender rather than seductive. "Then let us retire to my chamber."

He led her into one of the rooms within the lodge that held a cozy little bed just big enough for two to share, leaving no question as to what would be happening this night. There was a washstand in one corner and a little armchair that had seen better days, with its faded blue cushions that had been crudely stitched back together in places. Tyburn kept a hand upon her lower back, the heat of his palm surprisingly welcome. It made her feel connected to him, as though they were together in a way that went just beyond what they would share in bed. It was the sort of gesture a gentleman did with a lady he was in love with, a lady he had the right to touch in a possessively tender way.

Heavens, when had she become so sentimental as to crave something like that? Diana shook her head, but it didn't dispel the highwayman's effect on her. Even the way he moved about the room, with slow, sure strides, and how his clothing fit him so perfectly as to reveal his slender hips and broad shoulders had her rapt attention. The man held her in his thrall by simply *being*. A flush rushed to her cheeks as a sudden noise from the outer room had her turning to the open door. She'd forgotten about the other man. Would he want to have her as well? Would Tyburn share her? She shivered with a new fear.

"What about your companion?" she asked as he closed the door, sealing them inside the little room and silencing the noises from the outer chamber.

"Cambridge willna disturb us," Tyburn promised. Strangely, she trusted him. She relaxed, but only a little.

She turned to face the bed. Hesitation made her put her mother's necklace on the little side table. She straightened and breathed deep, steeling herself. But he hadn't grabbed her and thrown her down on the bed to take what he wanted. She let out a breath of relief.

He lounged against the closed door, a reminder that they were not to be disturbed, but also that she had no escape. While lust glowed in the man's eyes, she also saw something softer there. Deeper. A melancholy born of longing. Her lower belly stirred with rebellious butterflies as she stared at him. He seemed so relaxed, so confident, whereas she felt as though a single breeze would knock her down.

I shouldn't be frightened. He hasn't hurt me, and I do not believe he will.

But Diana had never liked not knowing what came next. She liked to plan and strategize, and this wildly hasty decision to sleep with a stranger was now overwhelming her. How many other young maidens had stood where she was, seeing this man's place of solitude and knowing they would share his bed?

"Do you often bring women here?" She asked her question a little too loudly as she tried to cover her anxiety. She focused on the sharp line of his jaw and what little she could see of the shape of his nose, which wasn't much. She wanted him to remove the mask, to see if the rest of his face was as beautiful as his eyes and mouth promised him to be.

"Never," he said as he slid his black greatcoat off his body.

"Truly?" That stunned her. She imagined he would have a great many women ready to come to his hideout with him and taste the dark magic of this man's seductive powers.

"I wouldna lie to ye." He shot her a sinful smile, but she strangely believed him.

Beneath his coat he wore a black waistcoat with a white shirt with billowing sleeves and fine lace cuffs. He cut quite an enchanting figure that no decent woman could deny. His hips were lean and his shoulders broad, and when added to his height, she could feel the physical strength rolling off him. His pale-blond hair and leonine smile gave him the grace of a jungle cat, with corded muscles barely concealed beneath his well-tailored clothing.

Diana shivered at the thought of taking such a body between her thighs. She had never made love to a man, but she knew enough about the act to know what to expect. Her housekeeper had told her of what occurred between men and women back when she'd been ready to debut. She had believed it was her duty to impart such knowledge since Diana's mother had died. Still, knowing the generalities of what would take place, she couldn't calm her sudden flush of nerves. She returned her focus to their conversation, trying to remember what she'd asked him.

"You've *never* brought a woman here?" She raised her brows as he began to unbutton his waistcoat.

"Too much of a risk, lass," he replied. He slid off his waistcoat and draped it over the back of the single armchair in the little bedchamber.

"Then why risk it with me?" Her voice was breathless as he removed his cravat and tugged his shirt free of his black trousers.

"Because I believe ye to be the sort of woman a man would break *every* one of his rules for." His words were spoken softly, yet with honesty rather than seduction. He held her gaze and she saw the words he hadn't said.

Tyburn was lonely, just like her. She understood then why she'd agreed to this and what the desire between them could give her. She would share one night with him before they both returned to their own worlds. He would ride off into the mist and become a mere memory, one that she could draw upon during cold winter nights, and perhaps for a few hours she could banish the chill in her bones and the ache in her chest for things that were destined never to be.

He bared his chest and she stared at him, stunned by the sight of so much skin and the hard lines of his muscles. There was a knotted pink scar on his shoulder, yet it didn't mar the perfection of his body. Without thinking, she reached up to touch it, then pulled her hand back.

"I'm sorry, I didn't mean to—"

He caught her wrist and placed her fingers on the scar. "'Tis fine, lass. 'Tis an old wound. It feels better to have yer touch upon it." He rubbed her wrist with slow, seductive touches of his fingers, which soothed and excited her all at once.

"How did it happen?" she asked.

His full lips thinned as if he meant to stay silent, but then he spoke.

"I stopped a coach a few years ago and robbed a woman rather like ye, lass. She was a little hellion and had a pistol hidden upon her. I didna expect a lady to travel armed, so after I took my prizes from the passengers, I rode away and she shot me. The bullet passed through the front . . . here." He pressed her index finger to the scar. She moved around him to see the other scar on the back of his shoulder where the bullet had exited.

"Did you let the woman tend to you?" A prickle of an emotion she'd never felt so strongly before slithered under her skin, making her feel uncomfortable and oddly cross.

Tyburn chuckled and caught her chin with his fingers, grinning down at her. "Let the hellion tend me? Certainly not, lass. I rode away as though the hounds of hell were upon my heels. If I had stayed near her, she would have put another bullet in me."

The green tint to Diana's vision faded. He hadn't desired that other woman, then, but did he desire Diana? She needed him to truly *want* her—it was the only way she could agree to this.

As if he could read her foolish thoughts, he leaned down until his mouth was an inch from hers.

"Ye are the only woman I've ever been tempted by, lass. So much so that I made an excuse to *steal* ye."

Her breath caught. "I thought you wanted my necklace?" Her gaze dropped to his mouth. Lord, she wanted him to kiss her, wanted it more than anything in her life. And she was fully aware of how mad that was.

"I dinna need any more bonnie jewels, lass. I have hundreds here in this very lodge. No, when I took ye tonight, it was because I wanted ye. *Ye* are the only pearl I crave. From the moment I saw ye, I had to have ye. I'm risking my life and that of my friends, ye ken. Do ye sense the power ye wield now? Ye hold my fate in yer hands, lass," he murmured an instant before his lips touched hers.

Her eyes fell closed as a fire blossomed to life within her. It was as though she'd lived in some cave before, watching shadows play upon the wall, and now for the first time she was stepping into the light, feeling its intoxicating burn. That was what it meant to kiss this man. It was to be reborn in fire and see a world that she could have only imagined before.

His lips gently urged hers apart. She tasted him and moaned in shocked surprise as his tongue thrust between her lips and flicked against her own. He threaded his fingers into her hair and cupped the back of her head, making her a tender prisoner to his lips. A sudden pulsing grew between her thighs, creating a fierce ache that drove her to clutch his shoulders and cry out when the sensations became too great. His lips left hers and he curled an arm around her waist, holding her up when her knees buckled.

"Are ye all right?" he asked.

"I hurt," she breathed out in shameful confession. Her housekeeper had never mentioned this, the pain in her body, the pain from *needing* a man.

"Where does it hurt, lass?" He slid a hand up her chemise along her outer thigh, his fingers powerful, firm, commanding as he then slid them between the juncture of her thighs and touched her bare sex where it ached most. His exploring touch was light, a whisper of a caress. "Here?" His voice was rough, yet there was a gentleness to it as well.

"Yes, there . . . *Oh!*" She jumped as he slid a finger into her. The sudden invasion, however gentle, was entirely unexpected. Her body felt like a keg of gunpowder that was sitting dangerously close to a sparking fire. Diana shuddered as he sank that finger even deeper into her, thrusting in and out in a rhythm that felt at first terrifying and then . . . *wonderful.* Her body responded to his touch with a sudden rush of slickness that made her flush with mortification.

"I . . . I'm sorry," she whispered, and buried her face against his chest.

"For what, lass?" he asked, continuing to stroke her. He seemed unbothered by the wetness that was now coating his finger.

"I . . . am wet," she confessed, and then shut her eyes, closing herself off from the deepening mortification.

"'Tis a good thing, darlin'," he breathed in her ear. "'Tis natural. The wetter ye are, the easier and better I will enter ye. 'Tis a sign that ye desire me, lass."

She lifted her face to gaze at him in scandalized wonder. "Truly?"

"Aye," he chuckled. "For a fire drake, ye sure are innocent of flames." He lowered his mouth to hers, kissing her softly, and she melted into his arms with a moan.

"My God, ye were made for pleasure, weren't ye, lass?" His voice was thick with passion.

Diana found it difficult to think, let alone hear his words. Her blood pounded in her ears as she rocked against him, seeking something she didn't understand. She knew only that she wanted to keep moving, to press herself against his body with his hand between her thighs.

"I do love it when a woman takes what she wants,"

Tyburn growled as he added a second finger inside her, thrusting them deeper, *harder*, into her until she was squirming and whimpering. An explosive need for more built up until she was almost *there*—but then he pulled his hand from between her thighs, and she plummeted with a physical disappointment so strong she nearly shouted in frustration.

A moment later, she was raised up and placed on the edge of the bed. Tyburn took her chemise off her body and placed a hand on her chest, pressing her gently back so that she lay down on the bed, spread out naked before him.

"Ye are a bloody goddess, woman, a bloody beautiful goddess," he groaned as he stared at her.

His words set her free in a way she'd never imagined she could be. This stranger had made her feel as if she was truly special. Tears pricked her eyes, but she fought the urge to cry with quiet joy.

His eyes flashed with fire beneath the mask he wore. Then he cupped his hands on her inner thighs and pushed her legs farther apart. She expected him to fall on her right away, but instead he knelt before her, his head bowed. A halo of candlelight illuminated his golden hair. He pressed his lips to her center and kissed the most sensitive part of her body. She was not one to believe in angels, fallen or otherwise, but damned if this man didn't make her wonder if he'd once had wings, because he knew how to make her fly.

He dragged his tongue along the wet folds of her sex, and Diana screamed. She threw her head back and clutched at the bedding as he cupped her bottom and thrust his tongue into her. The sensation of pleasure was so strong that her body unleashed a flood of wet heat. She couldn't form any words as she wriggled in encouragement.

"Lass, ye taste like honey," he murmured in approval as she lifted her hips, eager for more of this most sinful kiss.

"Don't stop!" Tears were streaming down her face. She had to have more, had to have it *all* with him. There was nothing in her head except that she wanted *more*.

"Beg me, lass. Tell me to ravish ye. Command me to take what I want from ye," Tyburn growled before he tasted her again. His carnal words only made her burn hotter and her lower belly clench tighter.

"Oh God!" she screamed. "*Please.* Take what you want!"

"Say the words, lass. Tell me to ravish ye."

Why did his words make her feel as though she would never quench this desire raging within her? How could he send her spiraling so far out of control that she would bend to his will and beg him to take her?

"Give me the words," he commanded again, and her control finally broke.

"I want you to ravish me. Take what you want, *please*!"

Before today she never would have begged a man for anything, but now with this man, the begging, the desperate hunger for him to possess her, made the fire in her belly swell into a blaze. She wanted to be under his control, knowing he would fly her to the heavens with pleasure and that she would give him the same in return. It was a unity of purpose, one that now set their decadent desires on a path to collide.

Tyburn stood up and unfastened his trousers, letting them drop far enough to expose his cock. She admired the length of him, surprised at its size. Curiosity got the better of her, but when she reached for it, he caught her hand with a wry chuckle.

"Lass, if ye touch me now, I'll not be able to satisfy ye. I've not been so tempted by a woman since . . ." He trailed off, his gaze darkening with desire as his eyes roved over her bare body.

"Oh . . . I'm sorry, I didn't . . ."

He released her hand and she lay back again, trying to calm her racing heart.

"I dinna wish to hurt ye, but I canna avoid this."

She gave him a little nod. She knew enough to expect a little discomfort, and she was already aching for him. What more could her body take if she did not have him satisfy the hunger?

Tyburn grasped her hips, tugging her closer to the edge of the bed so that she lay open right in front of him. She stared down the length of her body at his massive shaft.

She had never seen one except on statues in museums, and those had never jutted upward nor had they looked so rigid. Before she could get a better look, he grasped her hip with one hand and used his other hand to guide himself inside her. He thrust in hard, deep, and the pressure of his sudden presence within her body caused a flash of pain. It was too tight, too hard to breathe, too much of everything. She whimpered at the discomfort. He bent over her, his gaze on hers as he held still, letting her handle the pain without causing more.

"That's it, lass, *breathe* with me," he crooned.

She drew in a breath at the same time as him, and together they repeated breathing together twice more. The pressure began to ease.

"There's a good lass," he said, and then kissed her

hungrily. She welcomed his mouth on hers, and this sense that he was just as out of control as she was. This thing that burned between them was so much bigger than either of them.

She whimpered again when Tyburn moved inside her, but this time with stunned pleasure rather than pain. He kissed her a moment longer, then lifted his head and captured her wrists, pinning them on either side of her head. She was helpless, but rather than feeling afraid she was thrilled. He held her, grounded her when she would have flown away and been lost.

"Ye're mine, my bonnie fire drake, ye ken?" he growled softly against her lips.

Yes—he owned her very soul in that moment.

Diana wasn't ready for what came next as Tyburn began to drive himself into her. She lost herself in his blue gaze that cut clear to her soul. They became one beating heart, one breath, one burning fire as he thrust into her over and over. They were an unstoppable inferno, their shared desire an intense conflagration.

A delicious madness carried the old Diana off into the night, leaving behind a changeling creature she did not recognize. His grip on her wrists eased, but he didn't let go. Instead, he surged deeper, his hips hammering so hard against her the bed creaked violently beneath them. It was animalistic, primal, an ancient rhythm that defied the dictates of polite society, and she wanted to laugh with the sheer joy of defying the rules that had curled such weighty anchors around her. She was breaking free, running deep into the lovely, dark woods where no one would follow, no one but this beautiful stranger.

His lips were moving, and it took a moment to realize

he was whispering the word *mine* over and over as he gazed down at her.

She lifted her face and breathed the word *mine* back at him, which made his eyes glow like a warm lake reflecting the noonday light in brilliant flashes.

"Aye, lass, yours," he agreed roughly. "*Always.*"

No man had or ever would own her like this man owned her now. There would only ever be this stranger for her, in this moment, and in their memories forever afterward. She would never be truly alone. Tyburn would always be out there somewhere, dreaming of her as he removed his mask and laid his head upon his pillow each night. As if that realization was all she needed, the building pleasure shot even higher and she came apart, her mind blanking as her body bowed beneath him and she cried out.

He pounded into her even harder until he shouted hoarsely with his own release. His hips jerked reflexively, and Diana caught a flash of vulnerability in those cunning blue eyes. For a brief instant, the walls of Tyburn's inner castle fell and she saw him, *just* him. It did not matter that he still wore a mask. She saw what she needed to see, a glimpse of the man he truly was. It was burned forever in her memory.

He rocked his hips slowly now in and out of the cradle of her thighs, and she felt the surge of a new softer heat begin. She clenched her legs tight around his hips, wanting to hold him within her forever. Diana didn't want to lose that connection, and it seemed neither did he.

He feathered his lips over her cheeks, and she realized he was kissing away her tears as they streamed down her face. She was crying, but she couldn't say why. She wasn't in pain, but she felt cut open, raw down to the bone, as if he held her beating heart in his hands. No one had ever had that much power over her. It was terrifying and thrilling.

"Did I hurt ye, lass?" he asked after a moment. "Sometimes 'tis best not to be gentle the first time a man enters a woman. Better to break through the maidenhead quickly than too slowly."

She shook her head. "It was uncomfortable, but only for a few moments," she admitted.

"Stay still," he warned as he gently pulled himself out of her. She winced at the soreness in her sex and then ached more with the loss of him.

He pulled the covers back from the bed, then lifted her up and settled her in the center. He removed the rest of his clothing. Once he was completely naked, he crawled into the bed beside her and blew out the candle. He still wore the mask, and it was almost impossible to see him in the darkness. He pulled her weary, sated body against his own, clutching her to him as if he feared she would vanish in the middle of the night. One of his hands gently cupped a breast, and the feeling was strangely comforting.

She wasn't sure how long she lay in his arms, the comfort of the warm bed and the darkness wrapped around them while the rain tapped on the windows and roof of the lodge. Diana thought of nothing but the drifting peace of being skin to skin with this enigmatic highwayman. A man who had given her a gift rather than stolen one from her. And it was something she would hold on to as long as she could.

"Tomorrow morning, I shall escort ye to within walking distance of where ye were traveling to. I trust 'tis not far from where we stopped the coach?"

Her heart shuddered against her ribs at the thought of leaving. But she couldn't avoid the discussion.

"It's not more than three miles," she guessed.

"Use my arm as a pillow, if ye wish." He held out an arm, and she nestled her head against his biceps.

How strange that she would sleep so close to a complete stranger, and a brigand at that. She had let Tyburn take what she'd never planned to give anyone. A proper lady would've never done that, and if she had been that kind of lady, she would be filled with regret and shame. But Diana was so weary of the toll that society had placed upon her that she no longer cared what they thought.

All she cared about was her home and the servants who had been loyal to her and stayed to make a go of whatever they could with her.

Every offer of marriage she'd had in the last year had come from men who'd sought only her lands and money because they believed she was an heiress, which in a way she was. She'd turned down each, but she feared that someday she would face the choice between a loveless marriage or losing her home and the family she'd worked so hard to keep.

Why did men never suffer such impossible situations? Her father would have reminded her that life was not fair, but shouldn't people want to fight to make it more fair? What was the point of anything, if one did not fight for fairness in the world?

Tyburn, seeming aware of her restless thoughts, made a soft shushing sound and pressed his lips to her forehead. His other arm draped around her waist, holding her.

"Whatever ye are thinking about, ye can think on it tomorrow. Tonight, my little fire drake, ye have conquered me. Ye should enjoy yer rest and bask in yer triumph."

She had conquered him? Diana couldn't see how that was possible. He had abducted her, ravished her—willingly, yes, but ravished all the same. She had been the one conquered, hadn't she?

"Will you take off your mask and let me see you?" She reached up to touch his face and found the edges of the mask and began to slip her fingers under it, along the line of his jaw.

"Nay, lass. I've made enemies that wouldna be troubled at the thought of torturing my identity out of an innocent woman. The less ye see, the less ye ken, and that is better." He grasped her hand and pressed a kiss to the inside of her wrist, which sent flutters of fresh excitement through her sated body.

"But I know your name," she reminded him. "And I know that you are Scottish."

"Am I, lass?" He chuckled. "Or am I something quite different?" He now spoke with an Irish accent.

"Your name isn't Tyburn, then?" Startled, she lifted her head to stare at him in the darkness, where she could only see the faint moonlight that seemed to condense in his blue eyes.

"I am *any* man," he now said with a Welsh accent. "I am *every* man." This time with a Yorkshire voice. And it wasn't just the accent that had changed. He was able to completely change the sound of his voice, so that it didn't sound like the man she'd come to know in the last hour.

Diana wanted to know his name, wanted to see his face.

She deserved to know the real man, the one who'd taken her virtue and given her such forbidden dreams. She deserved to know who might have left the quickening of new life inside her. She stilled at that sudden realization.

"I have a right to know who you truly are," she said. "What we've done tonight . . . it might result in a child."

To her surprise, this gave him pause. He was quiet a long moment, as if he realized he had not thought of the possible repercussions until just now. But what did she expect? He was a marked man, doomed to hang if he should be discovered. It was foolish to think he could take responsibility, even if he wanted to. Which was why his next words shocked her.

"I will meet ye in two months' time, at the same place I leave ye tomorrow. If ye are with child, we will discuss what we shall do. Now lie down and sleep. I want the comfort of ye in my arms." He nestled her into his embrace and pulled the sheets up close to their chins, keeping them warm.

Even though he burned like a fire in the deepest winter of her soul, new fears now spread like cold, insidious shadows between the flames. What would she do if she bore this highwayman's child? He was a thief, a villain, a disreputable scoundrel. Their child would be beautiful and mischievous, of that she had no doubt. She would love that child with every fiber of her being.

But she could not weather the scandal of bearing a child out of wedlock. It could cost her what little she still had. Tyburn placed a hand on her belly, tenderly stroking her as he curled his arm back around her waist.

Diana's heart shuddered. A child of her own, a child born of pleasure and sweet, glorious fire. Oh, that child would be loved fiercely. Diana let out a breath and closed her eyes, savoring what few hours she had left to ease the loneliness in her soul—and wondered who the man beneath the mask truly was.

CHAPTER 3

Diana was in a cozy sitting room, a book resting in her hands, the lazy sun making her skin glow with warmth. Her father's voice was a gentle rumble as he read aloud from one of his favorite novels. Purple wisteria draped over the windows outside like feathered plumes. Colorful butterflies wove among the petals. The sound of a piano echoed down the hall as Eleanor practiced scales, then she began to play songs she'd composed herself.

The smell of freesia filled the air as her mother carried a vase filled with them into the room and set it on a nearby table.

"Those are beautiful blooms, Mama," Diana said. Her mother's face shone as she smiled at Diana.

"Everything the earth makes is beautiful," she replied. "Every ephemeral cloud, every bit of everlasting stone."

Eleanor began to play a new song. The melody was one Diana had never heard before, yet it was familiar.

Something was not right. She felt . . . strange. Not quite

herself. Diana set her book down and went to the tall gilt mirror that hung in the sitting room. The door next to it opened. Eleanor slid past her as she entered the room and joined their parents. The feel of her as she passed was more ghostly than real.

Diana's gaze moved from her family back to her reflection. The others were seated at the table, speaking softly and smiling as they had so often done . . . years ago.

That was it, that was what made no sense. The woman looking back at her in the mirror was too old—she should be thirteen or fourteen, not three and twenty. She glanced over her shoulder and saw the table was now empty. The sunlight, once so bright in the room, had begun to fade. Her family had vanished . . .

She spun back to the mirror and gasped. Her family was still reflected in the perfect morning light, but only in the flashing silver of the mirror's world. With a trembling hand, she reached up and touched the glass. Her foolish heart broke the moment she realized she wouldn't be able to pass through the mirror and into the life she wanted to reclaim. But the mirror only vibrated beneath her touch, as though the rising despair in her heart and soul seemed to be strong enough to fracture this moment that existed only between time and space.

"Mama!" she called out. "Eleanor, *please*!" She pressed her palm flat on the mirror, trying to push herself into their world. Tears rolled down her cheeks as they ignored her and went on with their happy day. She felt like she was dying. Why couldn't they hear her? Why wouldn't they let her in?

She beat upon the glass, trying to break it, trying to find some way into the world of the looking glass. The darkness around her grew as the candles burned low, until only twilight reigned around her. But she did not look away from the world in the mirror. In the reflection, her parents and sister stood up to leave. They were leaving her . . .

"Let me come too," she begged brokenly. "Please! Let me come with you. Do not leave me!" Her mother and father passed out of sight into a sunny corridor far out of her reach, her sister not far behind.

She screamed her sister's name. Eleanor halted, one hand on the doorframe. She turned to look at Diana over her shoulder, and their gazes locked.

"You must wake up, Diana," Eleanor said. "You must wake up *now*!"

Diana heaved a sob as she jolted upright in the darkness. It was night, and she was no longer in the sitting room. Her family and the cursed mirror were gone. Gasping for breath, it took her a moment to realize she was not at home at Foxglove. She was in a strange bed. She shifted and flinched at the soreness between her thighs. A stranger lay beside her, one arm draped over her waist. The shadows made soft grooves in the lithe, muscled arm that loosely held her.

Tyburn . . . the highwayman.

Tyburn slept on. She covered her mouth, hoping he wouldn't feel her shake, nor hear her weeping. The dream still fluttered at the edge of her memory, like the wings of a butterfly kissing her skin. It had felt so *real*, as if she'd actually been with her family again.

But her mother and father were dead, and Eleanor was likely dead too. That was the truth she constantly tried to deny, that something had happened to her sister. Why had Diana felt their presence so strongly in that dream? Why had it felt as if she could have joined them, if she'd only found a way to pass through the looking glass?

She wiped her eyes and carefully slid out of Tyburn's arms so she could sit on the side of the bed. The thief lay facing her, his mask still in place. A pale hint of the coming dawn glowed faintly at the edge of the window where the curtains had been pulled back.

Her hand reached out, almost touching Tyburn's face, but she halted just short of his cheek. She could remove the mask and see his face, but something made her stop. Perhaps he was right. It was best not to see him. Best not to know him. Keeping this night a mystery would be better for both of them.

Determined to banish both the remnants of her dreams and her desire to curl back into Tyburn's arms and sleep, she squared her shoulders and reminded herself to breathe. She slid out of bed and retrieved her clothing, then quietly dressed. She found the door to the outer chamber unlocked.

Tyburn still didn't rouse at her exit, and the rest of the hunting lodge was quiet. That meant the other two brigands, Oxford and Cambridge, would be sleeping in the other rooms. She explored the main chamber while she clasped her mother's necklace back around her neck. Spotting a row of chests against one wall, she knelt and tested the lid of one. It was unlocked, so she lifted it and stifled a sound of surprise. Jewels and coins winked at her from inside. Hundreds of banknotes were nestled among its treasures. This must be where the thieves kept their prizes. What she wouldn't give for this kind of money!

Diana stilled as a plan hatched in her mind. She did not have to wait for Tyburn to take her home. She could take one of their horses and some of this treasure and go home on her own. If she left now, she might ride fast enough to lose them even if they pursued her. She recalled passing a stream on the way here; she could ride in the water for a time to disguise her trail before she continued home.

That way, her newfound money could not be taken back by Tyburn and the others. She frantically searched the lodge's small kitchen, where she found two burlap sacks with twine ties. She hastily moved as many of the banknotes as she could into the two bags. She left the coins behind since she knew they would jingle too loudly, and silence was crucial.

Diana paused by the doorway to the chamber where Tyburn still slept. An invisible tie seemed to hold her still. If she left now, that tie would break. What she did now didn't come from a place of greed, but survival. However, she doubted Tyburn and his friends would see it as anything but betrayal. It would be best to cut all ties with this man.

And yet she could not. Part of her wanted him to know what she had done wasn't about gaining wealth, and the only way she could imagine that was if she gave up that which was most precious to her now.

She reached for her mother's pearl necklace, and with a sudden pang she knew she must leave it behind. Her wicked highwayman needed a way to remember that he was not alone, that for however brief a time, they had shared each other and eased that ache within their hearts. She only hoped he would understand, even if he could not forgive.

She undid the clasp of her necklace and crept back into the chamber. Tyburn still slept soundly. She carefully lifted his hand to twine the necklace around his wrist, then redid the clasp to turn the necklace into a bracelet. The pearl gleamed like a drop of frozen dew upon the highwayman's wrist. She hoped he would keep it, that he would want some small vestige of her to carry with him.

Lord, she had become foolishly romantic. All because she'd given herself to a man whose true name she didn't even know. Her gaze drifted from the pearl that rested on Tyburn's skin to the man's face. She had to leave. It was time to leave all that *could have been* behind.

She retrieved the bags and carried them, one in each hand, out the front door of the lodge.

The stable was only a short distance away. She found six horses inside, ranging from black to snowy white, each with different markings upon their noses and hooves. Six horses and three men, at least one of whom could change his accent at will. Now she understood how Tyburn and his friends had not yet been caught. She couldn't help but admire the man's cleverness. They were quite good at this.

And I will have stolen from them, she thought with guilt. Tyburn had treated her well, hadn't taken anything from her that she hadn't freely given him, and she was betraying his trust. Still, she had to take the money. Everyone who lived on her estate was counting on her to protect them, to see them through these tough days and into a time of financial security. Tyburn could steal more, and likely would soon to cover this little loss. Even though her chest ached at the thought of leaving, she had to focus on her own future and the future of her servants.

She chose one of the brown mares and quickly saddled her, then strapped her burlap bags on each side and guided her out of the stable. The mare was a patient creature, allowing Diana to use a footstool to mount up and sit astride. The thieves would be short one horse, but she could not think of a way to return the mare.

Mist cloaked the dawn landscape as she rode far from the hunting lodge—and the highwayman who'd changed her life forever. She pushed away thoughts of last night, of how she'd felt when he'd first touched her and how she'd felt when she'd woken in his arms, weeping for a life that was long gone.

When her sister had left, she'd had to surrender the moonspun dreams of her girlhood. She'd become the master and mistress of her home after her father died. She had no time for love, no time for the foolish dreams that her heart once called out for. She was practical now, because she had to be.

As she got farther from the lodge, she felt confident she knew where she was, even though she'd been blind-folded. She knew this part of the country well since it wasn't far from Foxglove. She had a good sense of direc-tion, and after a short while, she found her way back to the road where she had been taken. There was no sign of the family she'd shared the ride with nor the coach, but that was to be expected. The highwaymen would have let them continue on their way after enough time had safely passed.

It took her two more hours to finally reach the gates of Foxglove. She was halfway down the path to the manor house when Nelson, her old groom, came to meet her. He rode one of the estate's draft horses, a lovely beast with a pale-gray coat and large feathered hooves. A steady and reliable creature for the older groom, who wasn't as spry as he'd once been.

"Miss Fox!" Nelson swept his cap off his head as he greeted her.

"Good morning, Nelson," she replied, hoping to hide any signs of weariness. They rode the rest of the way toward the house together. When they reached the steps to the front door, he dismounted and took the reins of her horse.

"You were supposed to be here yesterday," the old groom chided. "We've been worried sick, we have. Especially Mr. Peele and Mrs. Ripley. I was just about to ride to the next coaching station to find you."

"I'm sorry to have worried all of you. But I'm all right, Nelson," she told the groom.

"Was it carriage trouble, miss?"

"You might say that. It's a long story."

"Well, I'm right glad to have you back." Only now did he realize she was sitting astride a horse that didn't belong to Foxglove. "Who is this beauty, eh?" He gave the mare an affectionate pat.

"She will be one of our new horses. I collected her on my adventure back home."

Nelson's eyes narrowed. "Sounds like you don't want me asking questions about it, miss?"

She chuckled. "Fear not, Nelson, the owner is not in a position to demand where she's gone off to—or in a position to find me."

Nelson gave a gruff laugh. "You *are* your father's daughter."

"I take that as a compliment." She smiled. Her father had been a man who could do anything he'd put his mind to, up until he died. He'd once been quite talented at rubbing two shillings together to make several pounds. If their estate had poor crops one year or the tenant farms had trouble with livestock, her father had always had enough to keep his family and his tenants afloat. Diana was happy to think that she might have inherited her father's skills, even in a small way.

"What's in these?" Nelson asked, pointing to the two burlap sacks slung over the back of the saddle.

"Our salvation," she replied.

He raised an eyebrow but asked no other questions as he removed the bags.

"Thank you." She took the bags from him and he left, walking the mare and his draft horse back to the stables.

She shouldered the bags full of banknotes and climbed the steps just as the door opened and a tall, thin, but strong middle-aged man with dark gray-streaked hair came out to meet her.

"There you are!" Mr. Peele exclaimed. "Where is your valise, Miss Fox? Heavens, what happened to you?" The butler grasped her shoulders the way a concerned father would. "You look as though you've been out all night in the rain."

"In a way, I was. 'Tis a long story, and I'm so very tired. Would you please find Mrs. Ripley and meet me in my study? I would speak with you both about something rather urgent." She nodded at the bags. "I shall take these with me." She went directly to her study.

She paused as she entered the room. The study had once been her father's, and it still carried a hint of cigar smoke, something that always struck her heart when she'd been away from the room for a few days.

Since her father's passing, she had tidied up his haphazard papers and rectified his disorganized system of records until she had a system that worked for her. Diana had perhaps a little more of her mother in her when it came to organizing. She went to the oak desk in front of the windows that faced the back gardens of the house. Towering bookshelves lined the left wall, and to the right was a fireplace where portraits of her parents hung on either side. After her father had died, she'd moved the paintings from the great hall to this room. She felt comforted to see them whenever she worked on matters for the estate.

The artist had captured them so perfectly. A young Florence and a young Stephen Fox, captured in the bloom of their youth with love and vigor warming their cheeks and illuminating their smiles. A lump formed in her throat as the vivid images from her dream flashed through her mind like quicksilver. Her hands clenched as she remembered trying to shatter the mirror to get to her family. Why had last night been so different from all her other dreams? Something about letting her walls down with Tyburn had resurrected an old heartache. Diana rubbed a fist against her chest and blinked away the burn of fresh tears.

Stop crying, you ninny. You have too much to do.

The weight of the two burlap sacks had grown a little heavy due to her own weariness, so she set them on the desk. She turned to face the door just as Mr. Peele and Mrs. Ripley entered. The butler closed the door behind them.

Mrs. Ripley breathed a sigh of relief. "Miss Diana, thank goodness you're all right."

Even though Eleanor had been gone for years, Mrs. Ripley still called her *Miss Diana* rather than Miss Fox, since she was now the oldest daughter and the lady of the house. But this didn't bother Diana at all. In fact, she took comfort in what remained the same after losing so much over the last few years.

Mrs. Ripley took in Diana's appearance. Her dark hair was a terrible rat's nest, and her velvet dress was stiff from dried rainwater. "You look quite a fright. The stagecoach didn't stop here yesterday, and we've all been worried sick. Nelson waited four hours for you in the rain. Mr. Peele had to command him to return to the house for tea and a hot bath so he wouldn't catch his death."

Diana felt a stab of guilt knowing the old groom had waited so long for her while she'd been experiencing her first taste of passion in a highwayman's arms. She'd been warm and safe—relatively speaking—and her poor groom had been waiting in the rain for her to come home.

She sighed and gestured for them to sit in the two armchairs that faced her desk. "I'm afraid my coach was waylaid by three highwaymen."

"Highwaymen?" Mrs. Ripley's face paled. "Miss Diana, what happened to you? They didn't harm you, did they?"

"No, no, they did not," she rushed to assure them when she saw Mr. Peele's eyes harden. "As hard as it might be to believe, they were, in fact, gentlemen."

"But you've been gone so long," said Mr. Peele. "Did the coach break a wheel after the highwaymen left?"

"No, that is not the reason I was delayed. I was forced to accompany the thieves to their hideout because I refused to give them my mother's necklace. One of them was quite insistent on having it. So they left the other passengers and the driver on the road with the coach and took me with them."

"The brigands kidnapped you?" Peele almost snarled. "Why, I'll kill—"

"They didn't hurt me," she reminded her protective butler. "Please, just let me tell you the rest of the story."

The butler and housekeeper exchanged worried glances, so Diana continued.

"When the storm came, the men gave me shelter." She stopped herself from reaching for the necklace that was no longer there but left behind, tenderly tied around her mysterious lover's wrist.

"And then?" Mr. Peele prompted.

Diana found the will to smile despite her exhaustion. "I woke early, before they did, and found *these* while I searched their lodgings." She opened one of the sacks and poured its contents onto the desk. Banknotes and fine jewels tumbled onto the oak surface.

Mrs. Ripley covered her mouth. "Good God."

"Miss Fox, you *stole* this from the highwaymen?" Mr. Peele's quiet voice held a deep tone of concern.

"I know that it is not the action a lady would take, but we need the money. I believe this will cover the debts we have to the bankers in London. Once I've had a chance to rest, I should like to collect all the paperwork on our debts and arrange for payment as soon as possible. I can take it back to London myself and have the solicitor handle the rest."

"This is good news, but there is still the matter of our future expenses," the housekeeper said. "We would need something like this coming in at least four or five times a year if we want to improve the house and finally be able to provide the staff with decent wages."

"I agree. The tenant farmers have been keeping us afloat, but I want them to be able to keep more of what they earn and for the house and its staff to be less reliant on tenancy income." Diana leaned back against the desk and crossed her arms. She was stiff from the tension of the previous night, her head ached a little, and her stomach reminded her that she hadn't eaten in more than a day. But she could eat after she'd told them her idea.

"This ordeal has given me an idea, a rather mad one, but perhaps it will save us. However, I don't want to put anyone at risk for my actions without their explicit agreement to participate. Until we decide what to do next, you are the only ones who can be aware of my plan. If we are discovered, it would mean prosecution and possibly death as my accomplices."

"*Accomplices?*" Mr. Peele uttered. "Just what is it that you are proposing?"

Diana lowered her voice even more. She trusted everyone who worked in this house, but she would not put them in harm's way if she could help it. She did not want to risk anyone who happened to be walking past the door overhearing even part of the conversation.

"What if I were to become a highwayman myself? I will keep this estate running and food in our bellies until we find another means of support."

Her butler and housekeeper stared at her as if she had gone mad. "But they *hang* thieves. Men *and* women," Peele muttered. "You cannot do this. You are a gentle-born lady. Your father—"

"My father would want me to do something about our situation, even if it meant taking a great risk."

"Risk?" Mrs. Ripley said sharply. "This is not a simple risk you suggest taking. It is your life in your hands, and ours if we agree to help. This isn't the way, Diana." Mrs. Ripley's voice turned soft, full of motherly concern.

It struck Diana then how much these two had come to mean to her in recent years. They'd become surrogate parents, ones who cared about her and handed out good advice when she needed it. Her heart swelled with love for them both, but her idea held merit, and if she did it well, they would be well off for a few years until she could sort out a better solution, like investing the extra money in funds in London with someone in the city who knew his way around investments.

"I know it is not proper, but it is the only solution we have at the moment."

"Assuming we agree, how would you go about it? Dress up as a man? Act like one? What about help? Many coaches have not only a driver but other men who might try to fight you. What happens then? Will you be armed?" Mrs. Ripley asked.

Diana had given this situation quite a bit of thought during her flight from the hunting lodge, and she was convinced she knew what to do.

"Reports of highwaymen are easy to read. The *Morning Post* carries accounts almost daily of various robberies committed. I will read up on those and I will pretend to be like the men who stopped me yesterday. There were three of them. They used nicknames and had at least six horses that I believe they use interchangeably. One also spoke with different accents at different times. I can do that, and if I take two men with me, it should be easy enough to manage. The travelers we stop will think that we are those other three men. We will have to carry pistols, and I am prepared to use them if necessary." She was a decent shot, had to be, since they'd often hunted for pheasants, rabbit, and even some deer on her lands when winters were leaner.

"I hope to save up enough to invest the extra money so that we can live upon the dividends," she added after a moment.

They both stared at her before Peele spoke. "What men could you trust to do this with you? Surely no strangers? The authorities always offer steep rewards for highwaymen, and I'm sure they would give you away in an instant."

"I thought I might ask Matthew and Luke."

"Our footmen?" Peele gaped at her. "But they are barely over twenty. Smart lads, yes, but they still run about like young pups when overexcited. You couldn't possibly keep them under control during such a dangerous activity. You'd risk their lives?"

"They are both strong, good riders, and I believe the danger of the situation might help them focus. More importantly, they are also loyal to this house. I will offer them a fair percentage of what we take in order to make up for the added risk. It will be entirely their choice. I will not force them, and I will remind them of the inherent risks that come with such a decision." She sighed and rubbed her temples with her fingers. "We can discuss this in more detail later. I desperately need a bath and some breakfast. We also need to hide this new wealth in a safe place."

Peele eyed the bags thoughtfully. "I have a place in mind."

"Good," Diana replied. "Take the bags. I need to find the list of accounts we owe for the solicitor."

She left her butler in the study with the burlap sacks and went up the grand staircase that led to the rooms in the east wing. The bedchambers were all empty now except for hers. She'd tried to convince the staff to move out of the servants' wing, but they had refused, insisting it wasn't proper. Mrs. Ripley had offered to move Diana's things into her parents' bedchamber, but Diana had declined. The house still held the lingering presence of gentle spirits within those lifeless rooms, and Diana couldn't bear to chase those spirits away by changing anything.

She entered her bedchamber and closed the door, leaning back against it. The velvet day gown she wore was stiff and heavy on her skin, making her feel even more weary than she had moments ago. Perhaps it was because she was home, and she was alone, and no one now would see her crumble and cry. She covered her mouth with one hand as tears crept into the corners of her eyes and she stifled a sob. She was so tired, so very weary of everything she'd had to face these last few years. What she wouldn't give to have just *one* moment that wasn't driven by fear, anxiety, hunger, or despair?

Wiping away her tears, she faced the room and squared her shoulders. Morning light crept through the gossamer curtains of the tall bay windows, muting the light a little. The pale-blue walls were painted with branches bedecked with flowers, birds, and bees. As a little girl, she'd begged her mother to live in the garden behind the house. Her mother had politely told her that young ladies did not dwell in gardens like fairies, but she would see to it that

Diana's room felt like a garden. She'd gotten out her paints and her brushes, and for a full two weeks she'd painted the floral elements along the base of the walls. Her mother had added woodland creatures like foxes, hedgehogs, badgers, and rabbits. The beasts were so wonderfully lifelike, even after all these years. Diana never wanted to sleep in another bedchamber, not when her mother's touch of magic was everywhere.

Diana unbuttoned the front of her gown. In the quiet bedchamber, she finally let herself feel what her body had gone through in the last day and night. She could still taste Tyburn's kiss, like a ghostly presence whenever she dared to let herself think about him. She was still sore between her thighs, and she blushed with the memory of how she'd come to be so. She had been loved, *well loved*, last night, and she had loved him back the only way she'd known how. She had given herself to a stranger with no regrets.

Diana curled her fingers around her bare throat, missing her necklace and missing Tyburn even more. She placed her other palm against her abdomen, wondering, *hoping* that perhaps she would have something beyond her memories to carry forward in her life. Her bearing a child would be impossible to hide from the families who lived on the lands around them, but she would gladly suffer the scandal to have a piece of that wonderful night that she could cradle in her arms. Her best memory would have a name. It would have adorable chubby cheeks and a laugh that would banish the storms and bring out the very sunlight.

Only time would tell if she had such a life within her womb. Tyburn would never know her name or if she had a child. She couldn't meet him again in two months, not after what she'd just done.

Diana dropped her hand from her throat. It was time to put aside her emotions. It was time to protect her future. Tyburn and his friends had shown her the way. She would not let her servants, *her family*, down.

CHAPTER 4

"Tyburn, wake up!" someone snarled. "We've been robbed!"

Rafe shot up from his bed, a pistol held ready in his grip. He always kept one under his pillow, lest he was set upon in his sleep. It took him a moment to comprehend the words that had woken him, and to realize that the bed he lay in was empty, save for himself. The bewitching beauty he'd bedded was nowhere to be seen. Where had his fire drake gone? He had to find her.

He surged out of the bed, tangling his legs in the sheets and nearly tripping.

"What the devil?" Rafe struggled to free himself of his bedclothes and bolted for the door, gun raised, but a man blocked his way out of the bedchamber and politely reminded him he was stark naked. It was William Amberly, known as Oxford when they were out robbing coaches.

"Put on some clothes, would you?"

Heart pounding against his ribs, Rafe slowly lowered the pistol.

"What's happened? Where's the woman?" Rafe dragged his hand through his hair as he shook off the vivid dreams he'd been having about the woman he met last night when they had stopped that coach. He didn't even know her name . . .

Dear God, had that been a dream? Or had he really taken that dark-haired beauty back to his hideout and seduced her? He glanced around the bedchamber, seeking any sign of her clothing strewn about on the floor.

Perhaps she was in the outer chamber, waiting for him?

"You don't seem to understand," said William. "That chit you abducted last night is gone . . . along with almost all the money we've seized from the coaches. She bloody robbed us! And take off that mask. She's gone." Will stomped into the main sitting room of their hideout with a growl.

"What? When did she leave?" he called after Will. Then he realized something was tied around his right wrist. A necklace with a beautiful freshwater pearl.

She'd left her mother's necklace for him?

His chest tightened with a sudden warmth, but that warmth froze over when he heard Will's reply, reminding him of their dire situation.

"How should I bloody know? I tracked her a quarter of a mile before I lost the trail. She's been gone for at least an hour," Will snapped. "There's no trace of her."

Rafe walked back to his bed and collapsed on it, tossing the pistol onto the bed linens. Then, with shaking hands, he removed the mask from his face. Had she dared to look at him last night as he slept? Did she know what he looked like now? *No.* If she had, she wouldn't have taken the time to put the mask back on him, and beyond that he felt a strange sense of trust given that she'd left the only thing of her mother's with him. That meant something existed between them, didn't it? Something that neither of them could deny had been born last night between them, but now it was over, she'd vanished just like the morning mist.

He could hear Will tearing through the lodge, making a racket as he muttered curses loud enough to carry all the way to Rafe's chamber. It reminded him of the very real problem that should be at the forefront of his concerns at the moment.

The feisty little creature had robbed him . . . That damned wench! He scowled, fresh rage burning within him. But the rage soon began to fade against the utter hilarity of the situation. His intended victim had turned the tables and robbed him instead. He supposed there was a level of ironic justice to it all, but damnation, he and his friends had fought for every bit they'd saved up these last few months.

The real problem was, as far as he was concerned, this wasn't *his* money. It was meant for another. The first time he hadn't been acting for selfish reasons, and some chit had just come along and stolen all his hard work away.

The sweet scent of the woman, mingled with last night's storm, still lingered in the air, which only muddled his conflicting emotions. He wanted to be furious with her, but he had to admit he was also impressed, and he wanted to tell her that . . . after he'd kissed her senseless.

Last night had been both a mistake and a gift. He smiled as he realized this was typical for him. His life was always vastly complicated. He'd wanted just *one* night of pleasure and connection with a woman, one moment where he could ease the loneliness that grew deeper and deeper in his soul, and it had backfired spectacularly.

Rafe had but one bright spot in the darkness and that was a little Scottish orphan, Isla, whom he had taken as his ward. She'd started to call him Papa, and damned if that didn't make him feel like some foolish knight protecting a young princess from the dragons of the world. He would do anything for that child. And he would start by tracking down his mystery woman and retrieving his money. Emboldened by fresh resolve, Rafe jerked his clothes on, blood pumping hard through his body.

He met his companions in the main room, who waited for him to explain himself. He hated admitting to when he'd made a mess of things, but he never avoided making such admissions. He studied the faces of his friends carefully.

Will Amberley was the darkest-haired of their trio, and his amber eyes currently blazed with frustration. In contrast, Rafe's other friend, Caspian, Viscount Falworth, sat patiently, waiting for an explanation and a plan for what to do next. Where Will was dark, Caspian was fair, with golden hair and sky-blue eyes. The two often played the roles of devil and angel when it came to Rafe's decisions. Will was always ready to leap into danger, whereas Caspian would always weigh the odds first.

He'd known both men since they'd been at Eton, and when they'd decided upon this life, they'd also chosen nicknames for themselves. Rafe had selected Tyburn, Will had claimed Oxford, and Caspian had chosen Cambridge. He trusted them with his life, and they had always trusted him with theirs. Now he'd put them all in danger.

"Exactly how much of our stash is gone? You said almost all?" Rafe joined his friends near the four chests they had nearly completely filled with loot. The chests were more than half empty now. The bottoms still glinted with coins and some jewelry, but the banknotes, the money that held the highest value for them, were gone.

Will growled as he kicked one of the chests. "We had more than two thousand pounds here to split between the three of us. Now we have just a handful of coins and a few bloody necklaces."

A pit formed in Rafe's gut as the reality of how much they'd lost hit him. All that they'd worked toward had disappeared, and all because he hadn't been able to resist the temptation of a pretty woman's sorrowful eyes. He was a fool.

"Six months of work for nothing." Caspian sighed and crossed his arms as he met and held Rafe's gaze.

"Was she worth it?" Will asked bluntly. "Because she had better be for what we've lost."

Rafe wasn't accustomed to guilt or shame. Over the years, he'd developed a distant relationship with those less amusing emotions, but at that moment he was plunging beneath the surface of both and it felt like he was drowning. He had made a terrible mistake in bringing that woman here, and he didn't even know her name or where she lived.

But the memory of her lips on his, her little gasp as he had sunk into her body that first time, her look of fear turning into one of trust as he had made love to her . . . that was imprinted on his soul. Of all the women he had seduced over the years, this one, an untried virgin with the fire of a lovely dragon in her soul, she alone had tempted him to be reckless with his life and the lives of his friends. He couldn't regret what he'd done, but he did regret the consequences and his own lack of foresight. All three of them had needed the money they'd been saving to pull their lives out of the spiral they were in.

"Yes, she was worth it," Rafe admitted. "You two shall split what is left. I think it best that we abandon this lodge for a few months. We can move to the cottage in the south."

"I agree," Amberley said. "She had to have ridden off before dawn, because I was in the stables at daybreak and that's when I realized we were missing a horse. One of yours, Rafe." He checked his pocket watch. "She has at least an hour head start. She could already have a search party headed this way. It isn't safe to stay here."

But Rafe wondered if the pretty little thief would go to the authorities. Surely she wouldn't be so foolish, given that she'd just stolen already stolen money, but he couldn't take the chance of guessing what she would do. Clearly, the little fire drake he'd seduced was not predictable in the slightest. He wouldn't make the mistake of thinking he could control her or guess her plans a second time.

Caspian agreed with Will. "We should take a few weeks off and see what the local authorities do."

Will would ride to the north and return to his crumbling estate, Amberley Hall, and Caspian would return to his bachelor's residence in London. Rafe would remain in this region and send them a summons once he believed it was safe to begin their activities again. They had a coded language they used in correspondence whenever the law was homing in on them, as it was now.

The three of them packed their travel bags and made sure nothing of a personal nature was left in the abandoned lodge. Will and Caspian rode off, along with their spare horses, in different directions. Rafe had only his white mare, Nimbus. He took a road that edged around several farms and a small village before he let Nimbus step back out onto a proper road. For several hours, he did his best to try to track the woman and the horse she'd stolen from him, but he couldn't find any trace of where she'd gone. Finally, as the afternoon gave way to dusk, he knew he needed to let his horse rest. So he headed for his brother's estate.

It was probably time for him to rest too, Rafe reflected. He had been gone for three weeks already and was missing Isla terribly. The little girl had unlocked the rusty door to his heart and pushed her way in. The child was absolutely beautiful, with russet hair and big blue eyes. He could hardly believe she would be seven soon. What he loved most about her was the strength and depth of her ability to love. Her mother and father had perished from illness in Edinburgh. Rafe's brother-in-law Brodie Kincade and his wife, Lydia, had rescued the girl from grave robbers, who were notorious for killing easily forgotten people when no fresh cadavers could be found and sold for autopsies.

From the instant Isla had come into Rafe's life, the child had gravitated toward him, the unmarried scoundrel who had no idea how to care for himself properly, let alone a small girl. But when she'd first held out her tiny arms, he'd lifted her up and something in him that had been out of place for as long as he could remember slid back into place.

This new state of accidental fatherhood had put restraints on him that hadn't been easy to adjust to. For the first time in his life, he didn't want financial assistance from his elder brother, Ashton, yet he needed money now more than ever. Not for himself, but for Isla. He'd hired a nanny last month now that Sabrina Talleyrand, the young woman who had been Isla's temporary governess, had gotten married. The child was in constant need of new clothes, books, toys, and all manner of things that children required. It was not the best time for Rafe to grow a conscience . . . of sorts. He would rather take money from strangers than his elder brother. He'd spent too many years begging Ashton for funds, but damned if he'd do that now. He had to support Isla on his own. He owed that to her as her father.

He adjusted his hold on the reins as memories of the past crept up on him. It was one of the reasons he despised being alone. When he had naught but his own thoughts to keep him company, that was when the past began to whisper dark things in his ear. The memories that surfaced burned his chest like the very devil himself had thrust a fiery spear into him.

The day his father had died in his arms, Rafe had gone from a boy who'd had a golden future at his fingertips to a life without sunlight. His mother had never been the same, losing the man she'd loved since she'd been a young woman. His eldest sibling, Thomasina, just seventeen at the time, had turned into a second mother to Rafe and Joanna. Little Joanna had cried for months and had been so frail for nearly a year because she had refused to eat. She'd only been three, and while she understood death by its definition, she had not understood what it meant in truth. She'd kept expecting their father to come home.

Everything had changed between Rafe and Ashton after the accident, as he'd blamed Rafe for their father's death. Rafe's wonderful elder brother, the young man he'd looked up to all of his life, had only been fifteen at the time. It was Ashton who had been forced to shoulder their father's debts. He'd had to cut costs, reduce their staff, and close their country estate for two full years, all the while working to earn enough to reopen it. Being burdened by their father's debts had made Ashton coldhearted, but he'd saved the family. They'd even been able to afford a decent debut for Thomasina the following year. But Rafe had lost his brother and his own soul in the process.

In time, the family had climbed out of the looming threat of debtors' prison and back into society's good graces. Thomasina had made a brilliant match, Joanna was happily married now to a wild Scottish lord, and Ashton had married that man's sister. His siblings clearly had a love for Scots.

Even I fell in love with a Scot. Rafe chuckled as he realized he had the same fascination, given that little Isla was Scottish.

But despite his siblings' happy marriages, there was still tension in the family, and Rafe was the cause of it. Though Ashton had become more cordial over the last year, he hadn't completely escaped his brother's judgments or censure. And Joanna, who had always loved Rafe, still did not trust him the way she did Ash, despite the fact that he'd taught her how to fight and had supported her when she'd run off to Gretna Green with her future husband.

And then there was their mother. She could not look at

him without the past shadowing her eyes. She was the hardest one of his family to face, so he avoided her whenever possible.

"Rafe, what have you done?" Those words had held pain, fear, and fury as she'd collapsed in his arms that night so long ago.

He could only reply, *"I killed Father . . ."* Because he had. Had he not left the coach that his father had put him in to go home, he wouldn't have been injured and his father wouldn't have crossed the street to rescue him and been trampled to death. Whenever his mother looked at him, she saw her husband's death, not the son she'd once loved.

A painful lump formed in his throat, and he tried to swallow. Rafe pulled his horse to a stop and glanced back down the long, winding road he had come from. A shiver flitted beneath his skin as that grim question he so often faced rose once again in his mind.

What if I turned back? Simply rode away and never came home? Would anyone care?

Isla's face flashed across his vision, and he could hear the echo of her giggles.

"Papa! Come play with me!" she would cry as she sprinted about the lush lawns of their family home. Rafe would give chase until they were both laughing as they fell into the grass and lay there side by side just staring up at the clouds.

His daughter needed him. He could never leave his darling girl, not even when this bleak despair threatened to drown him. Rafe urged his horse forward once more and he pushed the shadowy thoughts away, focusing instead on how happy he would feel when he got home, lifted Isla into the air, and spun her around.

It was close to twilight as he rode into view of the

Lennox estate. The large Palladian-style home gleamed in the glow of the setting sun. The emerald of the trees was richly illuminated, and the pale golden stones looked warm and inviting on an evening like this.

Home. Of course, it really belonged to Ashton now. As the eldest brother, *everything* belonged to Ashton. As the second son, Rafe was entitled to nothing.

He came down the long path to the grand house, where merry lights winked in several of the windows. Everyone would be ready to have dinner soon, including his little mite. He met one of the Lennox grooms at the stables and handed Nimbus off to him. He collected his saddlebags and handed them to Sam, a footman who'd spotted him as he'd arrived and followed him to the stables.

"Thank you, Sam. Is everyone preparing for dinner?"

"Yes, sir, it will be served in about an hour." The young man shouldered the two bags without effort.

"Excellent. Could you please have a bath drawn for me?"

"Of course, sir." The footman rushed back toward the house ahead of him.

Rafe's muscles were damned sore from the past several days of chasing down coaches. Most people who were robbed gave over their jewels and money quietly, but every so often there was one man who tried to be a bloody hero. Rafe was usually the one to put a stop to the foolish heroics with a single punch, but every now and then he'd had to tussle until a coach passenger playing the hero was subdued.

By the time Rafe reached the house he was ready for a bath, a meal, and bed, but he knew he would not get to bed as early as he wished.

The butler, Mr. Cheaves, greeted him at the door. "It's good to see you've returned, Mr. Lennox. You've been sorely missed."

"Have I?" He chuckled as he glanced around the empty entryway. He hadn't expected a welcome party, but it would have been nice to see one person glad to see him. Sometimes he thought Cheaves just tried to be polite because he was still a Lennox.

Cheaves smiled back. "Oh yes, Miss Isla has been staring out the windows waiting for you to come home every day, sir. You chose to come back the one day she wasn't allowed to. His lordship has been keeping her busy today."

"Oh?" He couldn't deny the warmth that blossomed in his chest at the thought of at least one person missing him.

"Of course, she adores you, sir. She said—"

A booming voice cut off the butler. "Rafe!"

Rafe winced at the sound of his elder brother's bellow.

Ashton appeared at the top of the stairs, his fierce blond-haired Viking appearance somewhat softened by the young girl he carried in his arms. Rafe's girl. Once upon a time, it had been said that he and Ashton looked like two sides of the same coin, both tall and fair-haired with bright-blue eyes. Ashton had let his hair grow longer, and Rafe had kept his trimmed shorter per the style of the day. It was strange to think that Ash looked more like a barbarian warrior and Rafe the polished gentleman, given who the true pillager of the family was.

"Good evening, brother." Rafe managed to grin at Ashton as he came down the stairs.

Isla stared at him, her eyes wide as she blinked away tears on her rosy cheeks. Had his wee mite been crying?

"Let me take her." Rafe held out his arms, his body aching to have the comfort of her light weight in his hold.

Ashton passed her over, but his fierce blue eyes shot an accusation at him.

"Three weeks is far too long," Ashton said. "Rosalind and I've had to take turns sleeping in her chamber nearly every night. She cried whenever she woke up from bad dreams and you were not there to comfort her." His brother's tone was gruff, but quiet, so as not to worry the girl. "I hope you have settled whatever business you had in London and can now stay here for a time."

"For now," Rafe assured him, but the lie was bitter upon his lips.

Ashton could never learn that he was still robbing coaches. He would be furious to know Rafe was risking not only his life but his family's reputation, and an angry Ashton was not something anyone wanted to face. The man could throw a punch strong enough to fell an elephant.

"Perhaps we should speak about it?" Ashton offered.

"Could we discuss it later? I am weary and want to spend time with my little Scot." He gave Isla a playful sway in his arms, and she squirmed with a little giggle. "And speaking of Scots, where's your hellion?"

The stony expression on his brother's face softened to one of a lovestruck fool. "She's dressing for dinner. We had a long afternoon together in the gardens."

"Did you, now?" Rafe teased. He knew just what his brother and his sister-in-law would have been up to in the gardens, assuming they were left alone.

Ashton's wife, Rosalind, was a dark-haired beauty who enjoyed the world of business as much as his brother did.

The two made a fierce yet perfect pair. Rafe couldn't deny the pang of envy he felt. To have someone he trusted like that, a woman who rivaled him in cunning and matched him in sensuality . . . He desperately wanted what they had. But a lady who was a man's perfect match was as hard to find as a shooting star across the night sky. One could wait a lifetime and never see that flash of brilliant starlight.

He blew out a soft breath as memories of last night filled his head. Now that woman had been a comet, bright and bold, moving across the heavens far out of his reach. But he'd reached for her, and for a moment, he'd almost touched heaven itself.

"We shall talk later this evening," Ashton said, and placed a hand on Rafe's shoulder. "See to Isla and change for dinner."

Rafe carried his daughter upstairs to her nursery, where the plump nanny, Mrs. Chesterfield, sat in a rocking chair, darning a small white pinafore with a tear in it. Isla must have been climbing trees in the garden again. The nanny's white ruffled cap covered her silver hair, but she had a quick mind and seemed to need very little sleep, which, when it came to watching a busy little child, was an invaluable trait.

"Mr. Lennox!" The nanny rose with a smile and set aside her darning. "Isla has missed you." She looked lovingly at her small charge, and Rafe felt that bittersweet ache in his chest once more.

If only he could give Isla a mother, so that when he was away she had another parent to love her. Her previous governess, Sabrina Talleyrand, had been the closest Isla had to a mother, but she had married another. Rafe had approved of the match, of course, but when he had seen Sabrina walk down the aisle, he realized he could have married her, that he could have been glad for a female companion, a permanent one. They would have been happy enough together, and perhaps one day that easy affection could have grown into love. But her heart had belonged to another, and he could not stand in the way of that.

If only his little fire drake had stayed through the morning. He had planned on waking her up in a most satisfying way. Then he would have gotten her to tell him her name and he would have escorted her home. But he knew logically that because she'd taken his money, she wouldn't have wanted him to know her name or where he could find her for that very reason.

If he was being honest, part of him had hoped to learn that she was with child, that there was some tie between them that would keep her in his life. But he had no name, no idea where she'd gone . . . and no way to learn if their union bore fruit. Had they both chosen another path, Isla could have had a sibling. The thought turned his hard heart into a soft mess. He could feel the hidden pearl necklace still wrapped around his wrist, a constant reminder of what he'd lost.

God's teeth, I suppose my rakehell days are coming to an end, he mused as he sat down on Isla's bed. He was taken up more and more with the thought of love and wanting it for himself and Isla. But to find a love that matched what his siblings had, a love that made one's lifetime seem to stretch into an infinite summer . . . that seemed an impossible dream. Lightning had struck three times for the Lennox children. What were the odds of a fourth? Yet he'd been close to grasping that dream last night, he was sure of it. What a damned fool he was.

He glanced at the bed he'd bought for Isla. It was made of white poplar and was intricately carved with fairies and flowers on the headboard. The first few nights he'd put her to bed at the Lennox home he had shown her the fairies and had her trace the carved shapes with her tiny little fingers. He'd whispered tales of the fae folk until the little hand curled around his at last loosened as she'd fallen asleep. It had become a ritual for them, to share tales of magic and beauty before bed. Isla had known such loss in her short life and still carried so many fears. It was his duty to care for her and show her that life could be beautiful and safe. That she was loved and cared for and would never be left alone again.

"Will you dress her for dinner, Mrs. Chesterfield?" he asked. It was quite unusual to have children at dinner, but Rosalind and Ashton enjoyed having Isla dine with them, and Rafe was glad. He liked the sprite's company immensely and missed her whenever she wasn't able to dine with them when Ashton and Rosalind had guests.

"Of course, sir." The nanny bustled to the dresser that held most of Isla's clothing. Rafe's stolen money had bought those gowns, but someday soon he would find a way to earn money without stealing. He would speak to Ash tonight. It was time he swallowed his pride. He would not ask for a loan, but he would seek his brother's counsel about investing. Once he'd collected enough, he could invest it smartly. He settled Isla firmly on his lap and lifted her chin with gentle fingers.

"Papa?" she breathed.

"Yes, kitten?"

"I thought you might not come back." She shut her eyes and buried her face once more against his chest.

"Nonsense, I would never leave you in the dastardly clutches of Uncle Ash," he teased.

She giggled, but her face turned solemn again. "But my first Papa and Mama, they did."

Rafe shot a glance at the pair of small painted portraits of Isla's birth parents on the side table by the bed. He didn't always have them out on display, but when he left Isla for any length of time, he made sure her parents were watching over her. The portraits had been among the possessions they'd collected from the room where Isla's mother had been staying. Her father had dark hair with kind, serious eyes. Her mother had a gentle face with a hint of mischief in her eyes. He mourned their loss as much as Isla did, even though they were strangers to him. They had been the ones to bring this child into the world, and he would never stop thanking them for the gift that he'd been given, though it had come at the cost of their lives.

He took a moment to find the right words.

"You understand that they didn't want to leave you, don't you? And I will do everything in my power to always come back to you." He kissed Isla's russet-colored curls and held her just a little bit tighter. Ash was right, three weeks had been far too long to be away.

Isla let out a sigh that threatened to fracture his heart. How could she sound so world-weary at such a tender age? His poor child was destined to carry the soul of a woman a century old, not a wee mite in the bloom of life's youth.

"Go let Nanny dress you for dinner, and then you and I shall sit together at the table. I will read you a story tonight before bed. And if we are *very* sneaky, we might steal some apple tarts from Mrs. Gibbs down in the kitchen." He kissed her forehead again and set her down on her feet.

"Now I must go bathe, kitten. Uncle Ash will be displeased if I show up at dinner smelling like horses."

Isla brightened as she gazed up at him. "You *do* smell like horses," she agreed. "But I like the smell."

He chuckled as he surrendered her to her nanny and left the nursery.

His chambers were two rooms away, and he was glad to be home. The hunting lodge was comfortable enough, but he missed the comforts of hot baths and softer beds than the hay-filled mattresses of the hideout. He carefully removed the pearl necklace from his wrist and set it into a silver jewelry box on the mantel above the fireplace.

A copper tub in his dressing room was already full of steaming water, so he stripped out of his clothes and eased into the bath. Lord, he was getting too bloody old to go gallivanting around the countryside for weeks at a time. He'd been so close to leaving thieving behind, until that dark-haired vixen robbed him. He was still furious for being played a fool by the woman, but he had taken her virginity. She had taken the money he'd intended to invest with Ashton. Perhaps that was a fair price to pay—his future for the gift of her trust.

He closed his eyes and leaned back in the bath and smiled. Despite it all, he could not stay mad at her. However, he imagined all the ways he would torture her with pleasure when he found her again, how he'd make her regret stealing from him by tying her to his bed and teasing her until she begged to be taken and taken again. For every banknote she'd stolen, she'd pay in kisses; for his horse, she'd pay by riding *him* until she came so hard she lost her voice.

He might be willing to sell his very soul to steal one more night with that lovely little thief—his fire-breathing dragon, his luminescent pearl, his shooting star streaking across the night sky.

CHAPTER 5

Cold water splashed around Diana. Sputtering, she flailed at the edge of the bathtub that she'd fallen asleep in and slipped beneath the surface. The now-tepid water seeped into her skin and deep into her bones, chilling her.

"Miss Diana, you must come at once!" Her butler's panicked whisper came through the closed bedchamber door.

She blinked and wiped water from her eyes. "What is it, Peele?" She reached toward the little stool beside the bath and grasped a clean cloth to dry herself. As she stood, her body shuddered from the chill of the air. Water sluiced down her skin and she shivered as she wiped the cloth over herself as quickly as possible.

"You must make haste. The magistrate has come to see you, and he has two gentlemen with him. They claim to know you were abducted by the highwaymen and demand to see you." Mr. Peele's usually calm voice held a note of fear. "I told them you were not receiving visitors today, but the magistrate was firm in his demand to speak to you."

A flash of panic shot through Diana as she dug in her dresser for clothes. If Peele was shaken, this must be serious indeed. She had never met the local magistrate and wasn't even sure she knew his name. She'd stayed out of social circles in the country, except for her best friend, Rachel Merton.

She threw on a pale-lilac day gown that buttoned up the front and braided her damp hair into a coiled knot before tying a ribbon around it. She wasn't as put-together as she could be for such a meeting, but it would have to do.

Diana squared her shoulders and left her bedchamber, mentally readying herself to meet the gentlemen below. Gentlemen turning up at her home when she lived alone, unmarried and without a proper chaperone, could cause quite a bit of trouble. While her land was not entailed to any male heir, it was buried in debts, and there was always the fear that those debts might be bought at any moment by a gentleman with no honor. She could be turned out on her ear, and her servants might lose their home and jobs as well. So she had to keep up appearances as best she could. It was why they had kept the front rooms, where she would entertain guests, as newly decorated and furnished as possible, while the rest of the house was in a far worse state.

Peele escorted her to the largest sitting room. She paused at the sight of the three men standing there. Two she recognized at once—the father and son from her coach ride yesterday, Edwin and Claude Fellows.

"Miss Fox, thank goodness, are you well?" Claude rushed over to her and reached for her hands in a way that was far too familiar for their brief acquaintance. She shied back, yet he did not release her fingers.

"I am well. Thank you for inquiring, Mr. Fellows."

The third man now spoke, his voice cool and his gaze appraising. "Miss Fox, I am Lord Caddington, the local magistrate. I was informed that you were abducted from a stagecoach two days ago?"

"Yes, my lord, I was." She could feel Lord Caddington's gaze move over her, assessing her. What was he looking for? Or rather, what was he *hoping* for? Because he was clearly seeking something.

"Did you suffer an assault on your person?" Caddington asked. Then she saw it, a lightning-quick flash of excitement in his eyes as he examined her. Did he *want* to learn she had been injured in some way?

An eerie chill ran down Diana's spine. This man liked pain. She wasn't sure how she knew that, but she was certain of it. She had always been able to read people, even as a girl, and the time she had spent working with her servants, trying to keep their home alive, had honed that ability. Caddington was well dressed, well spoken, held a title, and no doubt possessed a fair-sized estate, along with his magistrate's powers. It would be easy for most people to place their trust in such a man and learn too late he was not a good man.

"I was not harmed, Lord Caddington, but I appreciate your concern for my welfare." She kept her tone polite. "I was fortunate enough to make my escape and find my way home on my own, but thankfully I was not harmed in any way."

Please let this be the end of his questions, she prayed.

"But that scoundrel threatened you!" Claude insisted, still holding on to her hands. "When you would not surrender your necklace, he said he would remove your clothing to get to it," the young man declared, his face flushed with rage and embarrassment on her behalf.

She delicately pulled her hands free of Claude's grasp. "The thief said that, yes, but it was a mere boast. He did not carry out his threat."

"But he *abducted* you!" Claude continued. "He might have done anything to you."

"And yet I tell you he did not harm me. I am fairly certain I would remember if he had."

The father spoke up. "If you can recall, Miss Fox, where did the highwayman take you? We informed Lord Caddington of all that we know, including the general direction he and his companions took. We would have come sooner to see to your health and safety, but we were not positive we knew the location of your residence. We live several miles away, you see. It wasn't until one of the servants in our household mentioned that she knew of your estate that we were able to inform his lordship of where you lived."

Diana deeply wished that servant hadn't said anything, but she no doubt thought she was being helpful. Diana would have to be careful about what she revealed to Caddington from this point on.

"I was carried blindfolded at first to a little glen perhaps a mile away from where our coach was halted on the road. I am so wretched with distances," she lied. "And directions. I believe they took me westward? The sun was setting in the east . . ." She touched her fingertips to her temples as if in pained recollection.

"The sun sets in the *west*, Miss Fox," Caddington said. "So did you ride in the direction of the setting sun or against it?"

She fluttered her lashes, ready to feign a fainting spell. It wouldn't be the first time she'd had to play the role of a delicate lady. The last time had been at a ball two years before, and she'd been desperately trying to avoid dancing with the vicar's son. The young man simply had too many hands, and those hands had a tendency to wander where they weren't welcome.

"Please sit, Miss Fox." Claude pulled her toward a settee and sat down beside her. She inwardly bristled at the young man who had the audacity to offer her a seat in her own house.

"Think hard, Miss Fox," Caddington ordered. "Which way did you go, toward or away from the setting sun?"

"It was toward the setting sun, I am certain of it." Tyburn had, in fact, taken her east, but she wasn't about to give that information to Caddington or any other authorities.

Of course, her protection of a lawless criminal wasn't entirely based on a secret desire to shield her mysterious lover from the hangman's noose, though that did play a small part. Truth was, if Tyburn was caught, he might tell the authorities that she had robbed him of most of his loot. Then she would also be facing the noose.

"Tell me your account of the robbery," Caddington said. "What happened when you were stopped in the woods?"

He walked to where she sat and stopped just inches from her so as to loom over her, no doubt expecting her to wilt in his presence. She reminded herself that she had to keep playing the role of the helpless female. She preferred men who underestimated her.

Diana cleared her throat, letting tears shine in her eyes. "I was so scared at first. There was a loud crack, which we thought was thunder. Only it was a pistol shot. A man in a mask came and forced us all to leave the carriage. He demanded that I surrender my necklace to him. I refused and hid it in a place I thought he would not attempt to retrieve it from. I was wrong." She reached up to touch her neck to feel the pearl that usually hung there, but it was gone. She prayed it was still fastened around Tyburn's wrist. "He took me on his horse far from the road and made it clear I had no choice in the matter. Thankfully, I was allowed to remove it from my hiding place without the men watching. I gave it to the thieves, and they showed me mercy."

"Mercy? Ha!" Caddington snorted. "That trio of bastards has robbed me of more than four thousand pounds just this year. Whenever I get close to finding them, they go to ground."

Ah . . . Diana thought with grim understanding.

Now she could see why Caddington was interested in her story. He wanted to catch the clever thieves who had robbed him repeatedly. If she were to ever see that seductive—er, dreadful—Tyburn again, she might just kiss him because he had caused so much trouble for such a foul man.

"Lord Caddington," Claude warned, "we are in the presence of a young lady. I advise you to remember that."

"I will not censor myself in front of anyone, not even a *lady*." He said the words as though he thought her quite the opposite of a lady. He pressed on with his interrogation. "What did they do when they let you go? Where did they take you? Did they bring you back to this house?" He threw his questions at her like barbed spears, looming ever closer, invading her space as an almost manic energy seemed to pour off him.

"Heavens no." She shook her head, widening her eyes and pretending to be truly surprised. "They simply rode off and left me alone in the woods. I wandered around for a few hours, got turned around, and when I found the main road I was able to walk back here yesterday morning."

"You walked all night?" Poor, sweet Claude looked devastated at the thought.

She patted his hand. The last thing she needed to deal with was a weepy young lad. "I slept for several hours in a field. It was not so terrible," she said.

"A field?" Claude nearly squawked. "A gentle lady sleeping in a field? It's not to be borne," the young man growled, trying to communicate his protectiveness to her. Diana nearly laughed. Claude's little growl might as well have been a mew. She had a different growl burned into her memory. A growl of pleasure and satisfaction as a particular masked man sank deep into her body.

Her face flamed at the wild, scandalous memory of how she'd given her body and soul to him. Could anyone blame her? Tyburn's rumbling voice, made rough with that rich Scottish brogue, had captivated her. And the way his blue eyes had gazed upon her as though she were his entire world? No woman could resist that sort of seduction.

"*No* woman should be made to sleep in a field, gentle-born or not," she said. Claude blinked at her, clearly not understanding what she meant. "My back is no more deli-cate than a scullery maid's."

Claude's lips parted and his brows rose. "Surely you jest, Miss Fox? It's just that a lady such as yourself could not be . . . That is, you are not used to that which a scullery maid might . . ."

Good Lord, did he truly think gentle-born women were different than other women?

"Shall we return to more *important* matters?" Caddington shot the poor lad a quelling look. "Now, Miss Fox, can you tell us anything about these men? Their faces, their accents, their names perhaps?"

"I . . ." She didn't want to say anything, but she was going to have to say something because Claude and Edwin had heard the men use names.

"As I told you, Lord Caddington, my father and I heard two of the men were called Tyburn and Oxford," Claude said proudly. "I believe Tyburn is a Scot, based on his accent, and Oxford might be Irish."

"Yes, that sounds correct," Diana agreed. "You must forgive me—I forgot such details. I was simply so frightened, you see, that my mind quite blanked."

Caddington narrowed his eyes. "Yes, it is regrettable that females are so delicate." The way he said *delicate* made her skin crawl. She shuddered to think what had made him form such a low opinion of women, given that most women she knew were strong in both mind and body.

"If I recall any other details, where should I write to you, Lord Caddington?" She had no intention of writing to him, but she had to play the charade correctly; otherwise, he might sense her deception.

He handed her a calling card with his name and the name of his estate. "You may write to me here." It was about ten miles from Foxglove, and she was thankful it was no closer.

"Well, since the young lady is not injured, we should leave her to her day." Edwin cleared his throat and gave his son a meaningful look. "You're to call on Miss Appleyard this afternoon, remember?"

Claude's face fell as he shot a sheepish look at Diana. "May I call upon you tomorrow, Miss Fox?"

"Oh, that isn't—" she began, but she was cut off by Edwin.

"I'm *sure* Miss Fox has much to do, and you have made your promise to another young lady." Edwin cleared his throat.

So she was not an appropriate lady for Edwin's son? Diana was both relieved and insulted. She may be penniless, but the Foxes were a noble line that went back more than three hundred years.

"Father . . ." Claude almost sounded like a whining child.

Edwin sent a stony look at his son, then turned to Diana. "We are relieved you are well, Miss Fox, but we really must take our leave."

Diana rose and lightly curtsied to him. "Of course, Mr. Fellows. I understand." She let Claude's father know in her tone that she had heard his warning.

Claude reached once more for her hand. He bowed over her knuckles as he kissed her fingers. He stilled and frowned.

"Are these calluses?" he asked. She pulled her hand away, shame heating her cheeks. Damnation, she wasn't supposed to let anyone see. Now she had to come up with yet another bloody lie.

"What? Oh yes, from riding. I often forget to wear gloves." She was building a cathedral of lies, and she feared for the day when they would crumble around her.

A typical day for Diana included carrying buckets of water and coal. She scrubbed the floors on her hands and knees alongside the maids. She broke her back almost every day to keep this house—*her home*—working.

"I see. You must remember to wear gloves, Miss Fox. It is so very important to have smooth hands. You wouldn't want any gentleman courting you to think you are working in the fields." Claude admonished her as though she were a child. If only he knew what she did every day. She'd wager she was twice as strong as he was after all of the work she'd done these last few years.

It made her want to cuff the lad's ears for his presumption, but instead she once again summoned up a pleasant smile from the depths of heaven-knows-where.

"You're quite right, of course. I shall endeavor to do better, Mr. Fellows. Please allow me to escort you to the door." She kept her smile in place as they exited the sitting room. Mr. Peele opened the front door for them, and her grooms already had their horses waiting.

Mr. Fellows ushered his son out of the house. Lord Caddington lingered in the doorway. His presence continued to make her skin crawl.

"Should you remember anything, you would do well to inform me at once."

"Of course, Lord Caddington. I've kept your card, and I shall not misplace it." She flashed the card for him to see.

Glaring at her, he lowered his voice but didn't hide the menace oozing from it. "Anyone harboring knowledge about fugitives of the law will be put to death, even pretty young ladies like you." He smiled at her, the expression showing far too much teeth.

"I certainly would not wish to support *fugitives*, my lord," she replied seriously. Diana waited patiently for him to leave, with a bland expression upon her face.

He pulled on his riding gloves before he leaned in and whispered, "You might believe you are clever, Miss Fox, but I assure you, you are nothing more than a vessel for men to slake their basic lusts upon. And I would have no qualms reminding you of that." With that, Caddington walked down the steps to his horse, as if he hadn't just threatened to rape her.

Diana held still, heart slamming against her ribs. Peele came to stand beside her.

"I could shoot him and bury him in the back gardens," the butler suggested, his tone icy. He must have heard what Caddington had said. Peele was excellent at hiding in the shadows and not being noticed unless he was needed, and Caddington was not the sort to notice servants.

"I am tempted to let you," Diana said as Caddington rode away. She had a terrible feeling that she would see far more of him than she would like. And then a rather wicked thought entered her mind. If Caddington had too much money on his hands, then perhaps she would relieve him of some as well. That was certainly a man she would feel no guilt about stealing from.

"Please tell the footmen to meet me in my study. It's time to formulate our plan."

I will show Caddington just how clever I can be.

Rafe sat on the large settee in the Lennox library. Isla was cozied up beside him as they feasted on a tray of tarts they'd nicked from the kitchens. Most likely, Mrs. Gibbs had left the tray unguarded on purpose for them. She did so adore spoiling him, and now Isla as well. The dear old woman.

"What say you, kitten? Is cherry better than the apple?" He stretched an arm over the back of the couch. His little girl licked her fingers and grinned up at him. The tray they'd stolen had a mix of both apple and cherry tarts.

"Cherry is much better, Papa," said Isla. "Apple is sweet, but I like the tartness of cherry." Her adorable little brogue made his heart clench.

He stroked a lock of hair back from her face. "Spoken like a true connoisseur."

She yawned and leaned her head into the crook of his arm. "What is a con—ah—sir?"

"It means you are an expert judge in matters of taste."

"Hmmm . . ." Isla burrowed closer to him. "Are ye a connoisseur, Papa?"

Rafe considered her question. "I suppose I am a connoisseur of fine ladies and sparkling treasures," he answered with a chuckle. He'd been plagued all day with thoughts of that little vixen-turned-thief he'd abducted last night. Her eyes had certainly sparkled as bright as any of the finest jewels he'd ever stolen.

Isla raised her little face to look at him. "Will ye find me a new mama?"

"A new mama? What's all this now?" Rafe brushed his thumb over her little cheeks.

"Uncle Ash says I need a good mama, but he thinks . . . he thinks ye dinna ken how to find one."

"Uncle Ash is a busybody," Rafe muttered. "And I do know how to find a mama for you, but I haven't found the perfect one yet. And you deserve the best mama, don't you think?"

"I suppose . . . if she is verra kind and verra smart," Isla murmured. "And if she likes to tell me stories and would eat cherry tarts . . . with us." She yawned as her lashes fell onto her cheeks.

"All right, kitten, time for you to be in bed." Rafe took her into his arms and stood. He carried the girl up to the nursery, and under her nanny's care, she was soon ready for bed. She clutched the doll that he'd bought her in Edinburgh as he tucked her in and pressed a kiss to the girl's head.

"Ye must kiss Mrs. Crumpet," she demanded, and held out her doll.

Chuckling, Rafe pressed a kiss to the doll's forehead as well.

"Good night, kitten. And good night, Mrs. Crumpet." He stroked Isla's hair back from her face.

But Isla was not quite done fighting off sleep. "Ye willna go away again?"

"Not for a while," he promised.

Isla rubbed a fist against her eyes. "Not ever!"

"I can't promise that," he said sadly. "But when I come back, I will bring you wonderful toys."

"I dinna want toys. I want ye to stay here," she whimpered. He leaned over, pressing another kiss to her brow.

"My my, how fierce you are, my little tiger. I shall not leave ever again unless you allow it?" He would have to find a way to convince her to let him leave when the time came. She may have him wrapped around her little finger, but he could still charm her when he needed to. Satisfied with his promise, she snuggled deep into her blankets and fell right asleep.

"Oh, to be that young and to sleep that soundly," Mrs. Chesterfield mused from her rocking chair nearby.

"Only the truly innocent can sleep like that," Rafe said sadly. His thoughts suddenly stilled. That wasn't true. Isla's life was not untouched by tragedy. Far from it. She had seen both of her parents die, yet somehow she'd found a way to peace, to trust and love again.

Why couldn't he do the same? Was he incapable of healing? Was he broken?

The grim thought slithered into his chest, coiling like a black viper around his heart, warning away all those who would try to seek access. Only Isla had been able to slip beneath the viper's scales.

He stroked an index finger down his daughter's nose and stood.

"I must retire," he said to the nanny. "It is quite late."

She nodded and resumed her knitting. "Good night, sir." The soft clicking of needles in the quiet nursery was oddly comforting.

Rafe stepped into the hall, only to have that sense of peace he'd had shattered. Ashton leaned against the wall just outside the door. Rafe's heart jolted from the sheer shock of this surprise.

"Ready for that talk, brother?" Ashton asked.

"Bloody hell, Ash, you mustn't lurk like that. If you are trying to kill me, at least have the decency to use a pistol or a sword. Frightening someone to death seems hardly sportsmanlike. It's unbecoming for a baron," Rafe replied.

"I didn't wish to miss you before you retired. I can see

that you are weary, but weary from what, I wonder? Did you spend several weeks carousing in London so much that you look dead on your feet? I thought those days were behind you?"

The accusation, although one that would have been correctly applied to the Rafe of years past, still stung.

"They are behind me." Rafe gently closed the door to the nursery and headed for his chambers. Ashton kept pace with him, shoulder to shoulder.

"Oh? Then what business were you settling in London? Mother was there, and she wrote to me saying she did not see you."

Damnation, he hadn't thought of their mother. "I did not stay at your townhouse. I stayed with Caspian." He should have remembered that Mother liked to spend the fall in London at the primary Lennox residence, but he'd been so intent on his work with Will and Caspian that the matter had slipped his mind.

"Falworth? How is he?" Ashton asked.

"He's been better. His father's death has made for some financial complications," Rafe replied. "He and I were out seeking investment opportunities. That's what has made me weary."

"Investment opportunities?" Ashton's eyes sharpened and he stroked his short golden beard.

"Christ, you really do get aroused by talking business, don't you?" Rafe teased.

"What arouses me is none of your concern, little brother."

"On that, we agree," said Rafe. "That's poor Rosalind's duty, not mine."

Ashton's growl was more playful than threatening. "Hush, pup."

Who knew marriage could tame his lion of a brother? When Rafe had tricked Rosalind into playing and then losing a game of chess against Ashton, which had resulted in her having to marry Ashton, Rafe's only desire had been to punish the Scottish minx for shooting him. He certainly hadn't planned for the pair to fall in love and make each other happy rather than miserable. But did Ashton ever give him credit for playing Cupid? Of course not!

"Tell me, Rafe, what do you want to invest in? And why didn't you come to me first?"

They were at Rafe's bedchamber now. Rafe gestured for his brother to join him inside and walked over to the drink cart in one corner of the room. He poured them both a glass of scotch, and they settled into a pair of chairs by the fireplace. Some thoughtful servant had come by and lit the fire, and he was damned glad for the warmth of the flames. Ashton leaned back in his chair, waiting for a response to his earlier question.

"Because you've made it clear in the past that you did not wish for me to come to you for help."

"Rafe, that isn't true. I would have helped you, but I didn't want to simply toss money at you when you were younger and more reckless. I didn't want you to end up like . . ." Ashton cut himself off, but Rafe knew what he meant to say.

"Like Father," Rafe replied, his voice hollow. "Let's not talk of the past, Ash. I've had enough of it as it is."

"I agree. You've changed over the last few years, especially since Isla has come into your life, and I want to help you. Tell me what you're thinking of."

There was no avoiding this talk—Rafe knew his brother too well. He let out a sigh. "I wish to invest in something, but to invest smartly," he began. "Something that will produce a reliable income for myself and for Isla. I also wish to put some money aside each month to create a dowry for Isla. Not that I will ever allow her to marry, no man is good enough for my child, but she could use the money as she wishes when she's old enough."

Ashton sipped his scotch and studied the fire, thinking on Rafe's words.

"Well, we could put some money in the consuls to start, but you would need a fair amount to invest to expect solid returns. How much do you have ready to invest?"

"Not much at the moment, but by the end of the year I hope to possess a thousand pounds?" Rafe estimated he could steal that much if he, Will, and Caspian spread their territory wider and worked even harder. They'd mastered their system over the years to target wealthy travelers by paying tavern maids and stable boys for information. Maids and stable hands were always ignored, and yet they saw everything, especially casks of gold coins or fat purses. As long as they continued in their good sources of information, he and his friends could acquire more money again.

"A thousand? How will you acquire such funds?" Ashton braced his arms on the sides of his chair and leaned forward. "Would you take out a loan, or bring in another investor?"

"I think loans are a terrible idea, as is bringing in another investor," Rafe replied. He knew Ashton too well. If Rafe said he wanted either of those, Ashton might well browbeat him into taking money from him, and he was done with that. Not that he'd ever been given much to begin with, but Ash had been pushing funds at Rafe ever since he'd taken Isla as his ward. Rafe had reluctantly agreed to take a little money early on for a few dresses and some toys, but now he wished to care for his daughter all on his own as he found that his pride would not let him take another shilling from his older brother.

"I will find a way to raise the funds. When I have them . . . would you counsel me on how best to invest it?" It wasn't easy to ask his elder brother for advice, but he knew Ashton was the best man for it.

Ashton nodded. "Of course, but Rafe, you *could* have the money. I would give it to you at once."

Rafe shifted restlessly in his chair, old painful memories resurfacing. Ashton shouting at him, slamming doors, demand letters from the butcher, the modiste, the tailor tossed at him in a shower of unpaid bills.

"No," Rafe said firmly. If he'd learned anything in his life it was that the people he loved thought he took advantage of them when all he'd ever needed was a little help and a little trust. His mother, Thomasina, Ashton, and even young Joanna had all given up on him or turned him away when he needed them most. As much as his mother's rejection hurt, he could at least understand the reasons behind it. But Joanna had been too young to remember why she didn't trust him, and she'd never understood why she still instinctively shied away from him. Ashton had never once let him explain, never once gave him a moment of compassion. Until now . . . and now it was simply *far too late*.

Ashton let out a heavy sigh, finished his scotch, and stood.

"Very well, but my offer stands. If you do acquire the funds you wish to invest, I will be here for you."

"Thank you," Rafe said, his throat unbearably tight.

I will be here for you. Those words might have saved his soul once upon a time, but now they had come too late. He was stuck with the man he was, not who he might have been, and it was up to him to work his way to something better. Even if it was through the unwilling purses of others.

He waited until he heard the bedchamber door close, then leaned forward and braced his elbows on his knees, covering his face with his palms. He started to shudder. Tears dampened his palms as he tried to rein in his emotions.

He did not cry. Not now. Never again.

He was not a boy anymore. He was a man . . .

He dashed the tears away and got up to pace back and forth by the fireplace. After a moment, he removed a small silver-covered box from the mantel and opened it. There amidst the precious keepsakes of his life lay the freshwater pearl pendant he'd hidden a few hours before. He cupped the pearl in his palm and closed his eyes. He recalled how the pearl's owner had looked as she turned in his arms, almost bare of clothing, moonlight illuminating her skin as she gazed at him with innocence and trust. She seemed now to be more dream than reality.

She'd been alone, so *very* alone. He had seen it in her eyes. That quiet despair, that hunger for a gentle touch, that desire for any sign of affection or desire. Lord, he had seen his own soul in her eyes. He'd felt no prick of Cupid's foolish arrows, but rather the piercing agony of having his own soul laid bare to hers and surrendering all to a stranger he could not even name. If he were to live a thousand years, he knew with bittersweet certainty he would not know such beautiful anguish as belonging to *her* ever again.

Rafe sighed in the dark and placed the pearl back in the box of keepsakes, nestled beside his mother's locket and a small pocket watch that had once belonged to his father.

He had hidden both away when his mother and brother had insisted on selling everything of value in the weeks following his father's death. It was sentimental of him to hold on to such things, he knew, but it was all he had left of life before. The life where he had killed his father.

CHAPTER 6

The full moon was like a heavy pearl hanging amid low-lying clouds. Moonlight played with the shadows upon the open road. It was a *perfect* night to rob a coach.

Diana held the reins of her horse, the same one she'd stolen from Tyburn, and glanced at the men on either side of her who waited for her signal. Matthew and Luke, her two loyal footmen.

"Ready?" she asked them. Her heart swelled with a fierce, sisterly love. When she'd asked them to be a part of this scheme to save Foxglove, they'd agreed without a second thought.

"Oxford reporting for duty," Matthew said with an Irish accent that honestly could use a bit of work. His smile shone white in the darkness of the trees where they lay in wait.

"Cambridge is ready to follow you to the gates of hell." Luke, on the other hand, sounded quite perfectly Welsh. They would use the same names Tyburn and his crew used in the hopes the people they robbed would assume they were the same men.

"Then let's move into position." Diana pulled her domino down over her face and adjusted the wig she'd had made to help disguise herself. Her men put on their own masks, then moved their horses closer to the road and waited as the coach came around a distant bend, headed straight toward them.

Diana was quite certain this coach had three wealthy, *very* drunk men and one woman who was the mistress of one of the male passengers. Diana had waited two hours at the nearest coaching inn, listening, watching, choosing her first prey carefully. She'd spotted the men and their female companion dining and drinking to excess. That had helped make her choice. Drunken men were less likely to put up a decent fight if they chose to defend themselves. When she'd heard the men call for their coach to be brought around, she, Matthew, and Luke had raced to the stables, mounted up, and rode ahead to lie in wait.

Diana's heart pounded like the drums of war as she gave the order to ride. She led the charge, pistol raised, as she stopped her horse in front of the coach, blocking its path on the road. The coach driver jerked at the reins and halted the coach.

"Stand and deliver!" she bellowed in her deepest voice, trying her best to imitate Tyburn's Scottish accent. Even the blond wig was fashioned after Tyburn's windswept style. It itched a little, but it did give her the look of Tyburn from a distance. Only her brown eyes and shorter height would give her away if anyone looked too closely. She'd decided she would stay on her horse whenever possible.

"Stay where ye are, driver, and stand up." Matthew kept his gun aimed at the coach door. He nodded for Luke to join him. Luke slid out of his saddle and tapped the barrel of his pistol on the coach door, then flung it open, giving the occupants no time to resist.

"You four, out, *now*," Luke ordered.

Three very drunken, confused men stumbled out. Luke offered his hand to the sole female passenger. She stared wide-eyed at the trio of thieves and trembled, her face paling.

Was this how I looked? Diana wondered as she stared at the woman. Unlike her male companions, she seemed to realize the danger they were in.

"Remove yer money and valuables," Luke instructed, holding up leather pouches in front of the men.

"I say!" one of the drunken gentlemen began. "You have no right to take our money." He pointed a finger at Luke but wavered on his feet due to the influence of his drinking.

"The presence of our guns says otherwise," Diana replied, moving her horse closer. The height and natural strength of the beast made the men reflexively take a step back.

With muttered grumblings, the men surrendered their money and pocket watches. The woman, a rather pretty creature perhaps in her early thirties, surrendered her jewels without a fuss. As Diana maneuvered her horse back a little, the woman suddenly spoke to Diana.

"Are you him? The one Lady Society writes about? The charming highwayman?" There was a hint of feminine interest in the woman's voice.

Diana almost laughed. Her plan to pose as Tyburn was apparently working.

"My lady, I am simply a common scoundrel. I sincerely doubt anyone would bother to write about me." She shot a glance at her men. Matthew and Luke were ready to leave. They'd split the two pouches between them and tied them to the saddles of their horses. That way, if one of them was captured, it would prevent all the loot from being lost.

"Coachman, ye shall wait a quarter of an hour before ye continue on yer way. Someone will be watching." With a quick nod to her men, she angled her horse away from the coach. Each was to take a different route home.

Diana rode into the darkness, diving into the woods out of sight of the coach. She headed east, whereas the coach would go north. Matthew would go south, and Luke would head west. They would each ride straight for a mile or so before they arced back toward home. She prayed she'd thought of everything, but only time would tell. Once they were confident in their performance, she would feel more comfortable adjusting their strategy, but for now, she was nervous enough that her stomach kept pitching south.

Diana rode for the full mile, glancing over her shoulder again and again until her neck ached. No one was following her. She turned toward home and marveled at the beauty of the night, the clouds and the hint of stars that the moon swallowed up during their progression across the sky.

The pit of dread in Diana's stomach eased into a nervous fluttering. Finally, she drew in sight of Foxglove. She did not take the main road, but instead cut across the fields. She knew the paths back to the house better than anyone. She had shed blood on these lands. She had wept tears into the soil as she worked beside her tenant farmers. She'd given all but her life for this place and the people who dwelled here. She refused to think about the fact that she'd just stolen money that didn't belong to her. What was one more sin if it took care of these people and the home she loved? She couldn't give up, she just couldn't.

The stables were lit by a single lantern, which drew her in like a beacon. Nelson was there waiting for her.

"My lady," the elderly groom said as she rode into the meager patch of light at the entrance of the stables.

"I'm here." It was so very quiet outside that she dared only whisper her next question. "Did the others make it back safely?"

"Yes, both lads have gone inside for the night. They wanted to stay out here, but I wouldn't let them. Too many chances to be seen dressed black as night as they were. Let me take this beauty." He grasped the mare's reins, and the horse nickered softly and nudged the old groom's shoulder with clear affection. Every beast, even the pigs, loved Nelson.

"Thank you, Nelson." She slid out of the saddle and kissed the old man's cheek. "Did the grooms have any trouble tonight?"

Her other two grooms had split duties pretending to be footmen while she and the others were away. She didn't want any visitors, like Caddington, dropping by unannounced and noticing that she had lacked footmen in the house. He seemed the sort of man to notice a detail like that.

"No, my lady. It was a quiet night."

"Thank heavens."

Nelson patted the horse's neck affectionately. "I'll put this lady in her stall."

"Then you must go to bed yourself," she reminded him before she left the stables.

Just inside the front door, Mr. Peele and Mrs. Ripley were waiting for her. The housekeeper squeezed her in a tight hug.

"You made it! The lads arrived before you, and we feared the worst." Mrs. Ripley covered her mouth with a trembling hand. "I didn't know you meant to come back separately. You mustn't do that again."

"We feared you had been captured," Peele added.

"I took the longest route, the easiest one to follow. I didn't want to risk Matthew and Luke more than I risked my own life."

Her butler gave a huff of disapproval but didn't argue with her.

"Where are Luke and Matthew?" she asked.

"In the sitting room waiting for you," said Peele. "I now realize that, if we continue this, we shall need a proper place to hide you when you return, in case you are followed and discover that fact too late. Perhaps the wine cellar? It has an old priest hole that runs into the woods behind the stables."

Diana nodded. "Yes, that is an excellent idea. We shall look into that tomorrow." She pulled her mask, wig, and gloves off and gave them to Mrs. Ripley, who rushed away to hide them.

Diana retired to the sitting room and found her accomplices still dressed in their black trousers and black waistcoats as she was. Peele was right. They would need a place to change clothes and hide their highwayman disguises before returning to the house. Dark-haired Matthew was seated, while the fairer-haired Luke paced back and forth by the fire. They looked like young lords of light and dark. The two jolted to attention when she entered and closed the door behind her.

"Well? Did anyone try to follow you?" she asked.

"No," Matthew replied. "I watched the coach. The woman seemed to insist the gentlemen stay put like we instructed."

Luke chuckled. "We made an impression on her, no mistake. The lass looked both terrified and fascinated, especially by you, my lady."

Diana snorted. "Put a woman in a wig and she'll look as handsome as any man," she retorted.

Matthew and Luke both laughed. "She *did* think you were that Tyburn fellow everyone is talking about. I suppose that means your plan worked out very well, my lady."

In truth, she wasn't proud, she was just . . . relieved. Relieved that no one had been hurt, captured, or killed.

Luke retrieved the pouches from by the fireplace and handed them to Diana.

"Shall we see how we fared?" She poured the contents onto a nearby reading table, then separated the jewels from the coins and banknotes.

"Here." She gave the men each their agreed share of coins and banknotes. "I shall have Peele fence the other items and pay you your hazard fees once I receive the money for them. The rest goes to the estate."

The two men gratefully accepted their payments.

"You must be sure to hide your money," she warned in a low tone. "No one can know where it is. Do you understand? Do not hide it in the servants' quarters."

"My lady?" Luke's brows rose. "Do you believe someone who works here will steal it?"

"No, of course not. Not anyone in this house. But if anyone suspects us, they will search this house, especially your quarters. Being found with too much money will bring you under suspicion."

"Ah," Matthew sighed in understanding. "Because we are *servants*. They will suspect us first."

"Unfortunately, they will," Diana agreed. "But my financial position won't be hidden for much longer. I may face a similar level of scrutiny. No one would suspect me of riding out with you, but they may suspect that I have hired others to steal for me. I will be hiding my portion as well."

A gleam of excitement filled Luke's eyes. "When do we ride again?"

"We must wait and watch for a few days. I want to see how the authorities handle the situation. That will tell us how our next . . . acquisition will go. Now, 'tis late and you both need rest. Off to bed."

She shooed the footmen out of the room, then retired to her own bedchamber and stripped out of her black clothing, which she would need to see carefully hidden away on the morrow. She was too exhausted after the anxiety of that first robbery to worry about it tonight.

Mrs. Ripley had thoughtfully left out a nightgown for her, for she had no lady's maid. After her father had died, a number of the servants had sought employment elsewhere, and her maid had been one of those she'd had to bid a tearful farewell to. Once she'd donned the nightgown, she hastily brushed her hair out and collapsed into bed.

Diana lay there, unable to sleep, watching the moonlight move in slow patterns across the walls. It took several long moments for her fears and the tension of the night to finally bleed out of her. Perhaps this mad scheme would work after all.

A lady highwayman.

What a shocking notion indeed. She tried not to think about what her parents would have said had they still been alive. Instead, her thoughts drifted back to the mysterious Tyburn. Had he taken advantage of the moonlight to conduct his own nefarious robberies as well? Had he stopped another woman passenger and had he looked at her with desire as he had Diana? Would he kiss that other woman? Or was he lying alone in a bed, wondering about her and where she was? Could he be dreaming about her?

Three weeks had passed since her abduction, and in that time she'd had her monthly courses come and go, leaving her disappointed. No child was to come after all. That seemed only to heighten her secret longing to find Tyburn again, even knowing how impossible and dangerous such a thing would be. He'd probably want to strangle her for taking his money. But that didn't stop her from missing his touch . . . his kiss.

Her fingertips touched her lips as she drew up that now-sacred memory of the highwayman's kiss. How his lips had moved over hers, how his hands had roved over her body, and how it had felt to lie beneath his muscled form and feel the strength of him beneath her fingertips. His body had held the heat of the sun, and it had unfurled her deeper, sweeter dreams, the way flowers opened beneath sunlight.

She could still hear his shuddering breath in her ear as he came and remembered how her body had lit up as she'd scaled that beautiful mountain, and how a vast universe of pleasure had exploded through her.

With a sigh, Diana rolled onto her side and gazed at the empty spot in the bed beside her. Two words echoed bittersweetly in her chest.

If only . . .

DIANA SAT BACK ON HER HEELS AT THE EDGE OF THE back gardens, where she was pulling out weeds from the once-pristine tended lawns. The gardens would never be as perfect as her mother had once had them, but if she could keep them free of weeds, she would be satisfied enough. Of course, if they were ever able to afford a team of gardeners again, she might just manage to make them as beautiful as they once were. Lost in fanciful thoughts of what she'd do with all of the extra help she could hire, she didn't hear her butler speak until he cleared his throat.

"There's a rider coming down the road, my lady," Peele announced as he approached her, stepping around a box of gardening tools she'd left on the path.

"Oh?" She wasn't sure if this was something to worry about or not.

"It appears to be Miss Merton," Peele added.

A delighted grin curved her lips as she removed her gardening gloves and straightened her soil-stained apron that protected her sensible lilac-colored day gown. "Rachel?"

"Yes, Miss Diana. Judging by her speed, it would seem she's anxious to see you." Peele collected her gloves and garden trowel from her as they returned to the house together.

She came in through the back terrace and heard Rachel's voice echoing through the halls. It was a most welcome sound. She found her dear friend deep in conversation with Mrs. Ripley just inside the entryway.

Rachel Merton was a brilliantly beautiful dark-haired woman with stunning brown eyes that radiated the warmth of her very soul. They had known each other since they were six, and everyone who spoke to her felt they were welcomed into the woman's confidence, and that extended to the servants as well. Mr. Peele and Mrs. Ripley both thought of Rachel Merton in the highest regard.

Rachel turned to see Diana and almost gasped. "Heavens, Di, is that dirt upon your cheeks? What on earth have you been up to?" There was delight rather than censure in the question.

Diana beamed at her friend. "Digging to China, what else?" It was an old joke between them. When they'd first met, Diana had been beneath the base of a large old cypress tree, carving a path around the vast system of roots. She'd been covered in dirt and completely forgotten by the adults watching her. Then along came Rachel in her perfect little dress, eyes bright, and she'd knelt right down beside Diana to join in the dig without a care in the world except aiding Diana in her goal to reach the Far East by way of a tunnel through the center of the earth.

"Truly? May I come with you?" Rachel swept the train

of her dark-blue gown out of her way and came over to take Diana's arm, unbothered by the bits of garden debris clinging to Diana's sleeve.

"Of course you shall come! What would I do without my second-in-command?" Diana teased.

"Well then, what will my duties be in the depths of these tunnels?" Rachel giggled, a sound that always made Diana feel like dancing.

"You shall be chief of bucket emptying." Diana said this with such a serious tone that Rachel burst out laughing. Diana's heart leapt again with joy. She had deeply missed Rachel. Her friend had spent the last six months in London. Her mother and father were still trying to see her married off, even though she was three and twenty, just like Diana, and past the age when most men would take her as a serious candidate for courtship.

"Well, that sounds infinitely better than sitting in a stuffy drawing room waiting to see if some gentleman will come calling. I only had a few callers who held any real interest this season. Mama kept praying I would receive even just one posy before some of the balls we attended. But alas, I received none."

Rachel did not sound terribly upset about this, but Diana knew that Mrs. Merton wished desperately for grandchildren. Rachel was an only child, a radiant beauty, and quite the wealthy heiress, which should have drawn any number of gentlemen to her. But Rachel had a cunning way of putting men off with her quick wit and brilliant mind. Few men were interested in a wife who could not only talk but think circles around them. And Rachel was adamant not to settle for someone who would feel threatened by her.

"Such fools, these so-called gentlemen," Diana declared, and gave Rachel's arm a squeeze.

Rachel sighed dramatically. "Indeed. Now catch me up on all of the adventures I've missed since I left for London."

"Well, as you can see, my gardening skills have not improved much," Diana said as they entered the library. Matthew brought in a tray of tea and some cucumber sandwiches before he quietly withdrew.

"Dear, are we *that* dull now? Have we nothing else to gossip about?" Rachel mused sorrowfully.

Diana almost told Rachel about her daring moonlight ride disguised as a highwayman, but the confession died upon her lips. Tyburn's warning about hiding one's identity came back to her, and it was echoed by Lord Caddington's open threat. Rachel was her truest and dearest friend, but she could not endanger her life simply to have someone to talk to. There was no way she could risk telling her about her plans. But she could tell Rachel about her own robbery at Tyburn's hands.

"Sadly, we must be that dull. I've done nothing but fret over money and work . . . and I was robbed by a highwayman."

"What?" Rachel gasped. "When?" She took charge of the tea service and poured them each a cup as she waited for Diana to continue.

And just like that, she told her best friend everything that had happened, meeting Tyburn and even being abducted. She let out a deep breath and made her final confession.

"I . . . shared his bed, Rachel," she whispered.

"You . . . you slept with this Tyburn gentleman?"

Rachel's cheeks pinkened and she leaned forward a little. "What was it like?"

"Wonderful," Diana confessed. "It was as wickedly wonderful as you could imagine. No wonder they won't let debutants run off into the gardens with men. I can understand the danger now. Once he kissed me . . . I quite lost my head."

Rachel signed and smiled dreamily. "Now that is far better than digging to China. It's a pity you likely won't see him again."

"Yes," she agreed. Even though she could tell Rachel wanted to discuss it more, Diana had other things she wanted to speak to her friend about.

"I did go to London for a few days," Diana added. "I paid a call on my father's solicitor to see about the estate's debts. What I want . . ." She halted and considered her words carefully before continuing. "What I *wish* is to invest some money in a few months, but I fear it would be a small amount. I would need a banker who would take me seriously."

Rachel nodded in understanding. "And I assume no man will talk to you?"

Diana took a sip of her tea. "That is what I'm afraid of." She had not visited with any bankers on this particular trip, but she knew well enough that they would not speak to her about investing if she had.

"Di, have you considered an idea that might be a bit . . . unconventional?" A gleam lit Rachel's eyes and she leaned forward in her chair. "Like perhaps a female banker?"

Diana blinked. "A what?"

"A *woman* banker. They exist, you know." Rachel

grinned over the rim of her teacup. "And you happen to live not too far from one."

"I do?" Diana set down her teacup as her hand began to tremble. She was thirsty, overworked, and now excited. That was not a very good combination if she wished to preserve the integrity of her teacup.

"Lady Lennox."

Diana's brows drew together. "Regina Lennox isn't a banker."

"You misunderstand. Not Regina, the dowager baroness, but *Rosalind*, Lord Lennox's wife."

"Oh . . ." Diana's face flamed with mortification. "I'm afraid I have not attended any social events these last few years. I do remember hearing of a hasty wedding with Lord Lennox and a Scottish woman, but that is all."

"Well then, you are in luck. That is one of the reasons I came over this evening. You are invited to our ball tomorrow. We would have sent an invitation sooner, but it's been a bit chaotic returning from London. Mama sent all the invitations out from London, and when I reminded her about you, she was quite upset that she'd forgotten."

"Your mother is a dear. It is easy to forget me. I have not been out since my father died. Tell her not to be distressed on my account."

Rachel tapped Diana's teacup with her own in a toast. "Drink up and have dear Mrs. Ripley ready your best dress. I will introduce you to Lady Lennox, and you can ask her about investing. I have a feeling she might be the answer you've been seeking."

Buoyed by a wellspring of hope, Diana abandoned her teacup and got up to hug Rachel.

Rachel chuckled as she patted Diana's back. "Goodness, you *are* glad about this, aren't you?"

"You haven't the faintest idea how much," Diana confessed. "You are an angel, heaven-sent."

At this, Rachel let out a devious giggle. "Do not call me an angel, for they have far less fun."

Diana returned to her seat, finished drinking her tea, and listened to Rachel's tales from London. For the first time in more than a year, the cold hearth in her heart once more held the burning embers of small sparks of hope.

CHAPTER 7

"You have a lot of explaining to do, brother," Rafe declared. He sat down beside Ashton at a table on the back terrace that faced the south lawn of Lennox House. A footman stood in attendance and offered Rafe refreshments, which he politely declined. If he and his brother were going to argue, he didn't want to be full of tea and cakes.

Ashton continued to peruse his newspaper and didn't even look at Rafe as he turned the page.

"What, pray tell, must I explain?" Ashton asked after a moment of silence.

"It seems that dear old Uncle Ash has been suggesting to Isla that I find a mother for her." Rafe watched his sister-in-law, Rosalind, playing badminton with Isla on the bright-green lawn in front of them. The pair batted the shuttlecock about with no real intention of the rules being followed, laughing all the while. Rafe thoroughly approved of that. Rules were made for fools.

The newspaper that blocked his brother's face wilted,

exposing Ashton's usual solemn face, but today there was a hint of mischief behind it.

"And if I *had* suggested such a thing?"

Rafe arched a brow. Two could play this game. He knew he looked like his older brother so much that they were often mistaken for twins, which meant he could usually read his brother's expressions because it was like reading his own face in a mirror.

"Then *I* would suggest you take your meddling elsewhere."

Ashton's lips twitched, but his unshakeable self-control prevented any smile from showing.

"Well, in that case, I'd have to regretfully inform you that I've been tasked with such meddling by our dear mama."

"Mother? What has she to do with this?" Rafe dropped the hypotheticals. What had he done to attract his mother's attention? There was no way this would end well. When Ashton had been caught in their mother's sights, she'd tried to match him with every eligible woman within fifty miles.

"She believes that because you are now a father, you need a suitable young lady to marry. She says Isla will need a mother figure in her life. And even more unfortunate for you, Rosalind especially agrees with her. She grew up with a cruel father, and while her brothers are fine gentlemen, they certainly weren't motherly. There was no one who understood what her struggles were, especially when coming into womanhood. She would have given anything to have had a mother during such pivotal times in her life."

Rafe's gaze strayed to Rosalind, who had tossed her racket away and was chasing a squealing Isla about the well-cut lawn. Finally, she captured the little girl and swung her up in her arms. Something clenched in Rafe's chest, and his fisted hand pressed against his heart as if somehow that would ease the pain there.

"For a man who loves to gamble, you certainly cannot hide your feelings well." Ashton folded his paper and set it down on the table, a sure sign that Ashton was committed to this uncomfortable discussion.

Blast and damn. Rafe turned away from him. Damn the man for being right. Rafe *did* want a woman in his life, as a wife, as a lover, and Isla needed a mother. It took him a moment to compose the thoughts that ran about in his mind before he spoke.

"It cannot be just *any* woman, Ash. Whoever it is, she must be exceptional. Brilliant, beautiful, kind, brave, and loving."

"Expecting perfection is a dangerous thing," Ashton warned.

"It never stopped you." Rafe's shoulders dropped. "Besides, I don't desire perfection. Heaven knows I don't deserve it. You and I know that few people can offer you everything."

And I offer so little as it is. The grim thought made his world bleaker than he knew it should feel given that it was a bright and sunny day.

"True enough, but you must also ask yourself what you would offer this woman in return? A good marriage is a marriage between equals. If you find this truly exceptional woman, what will make you worthy of her?" And there it was, Ashton, ever the soothsayer reading Rafe's deepest, darkest, most shameful thoughts.

"Never good enough, am I?" Rafe muttered, unable to

hide the bitterness in his tone. "No title, no money, no home of my own. Perhaps you and Rosalind should take Isla and—"

"Rafe," Ashton growled in frustration. "You and I both know that Isla is your child—she could not live without you. And as to the matter of possessing a title or money, none of those things matter to the *right* woman. What she needs are the very same things you desire of her—bravery, kindness, and most importantly, love." His brother's eyes softened. "You will know the right woman when you meet her. Perhaps not love at first sight, but you will feel something beyond words, something that pulls you into her. Even when Rosalind and I were fighting over shipping companies when we first met, there was this wild spark that made it impossible for me to stay away from her. I could not erase her from my mind. Some men mistake lust and obsession as the signals to look for, but it must be deeper than your body's impulse to possess her. It is the difference between simply wanting to bed a woman and wanting to be there for her afterward, eager to listen to her whispers as she shares herself, her thoughts, her dreams, and her hopes with you."

How insufferable it must be to always be correct about everything, Rafe thought. He saw Rosalind and Isla collapse onto the grass. Isla raised her little hand, pointing at the clouds above their heads. It made Rafe's thoughts drift back to that night in the hunting lodge, to the woman who had given him her trust and held her soul in her eyes.

He'd wanted to tell her his name, wanted to tell her about Isla, about his family, about everything. He'd wanted to ask her a thousand questions about her own life. He'd craved to know her, but he couldn't. The more they knew about each other, the more dangerous it was for both of them, and he could not risk that young woman's life. His little fire drake . . . his cunning little thief. He couldn't help but smile.

"Now that is something I haven't seen in quite a while," Ashton mused.

"What?"

"You smiling with, dare I say, mischievous delight?"

Rafe leaned back in his chair. "I smile. I smile quite often."

"Yes, you have smiles for Isla, smiles for Rosalind, and even a smile for me on occasion. But that *particular* sort of smile . . . It's been years since I've seen that. Since before . . ." Ashton paused. "Since before Father died."

Rafe said nothing. Thinking about who he used to be before that terrible night was too much to bear.

"Right, well." Ashton cleared his throat. "You can begin wife hunting tomorrow evening."

"Tomorrow evening?" Rafe didn't particularly like his older brother's amused expression, or the fact that he'd come to this conversation prepared for the outcome.

"Yes, we've been invited to a ball. I have accepted your invitation on your behalf."

"Ash, I am *not* in the mood to put on bloody knee breeches and run about fetching drinks for young chits for several hours on end."

His brother's brows rose. "Would you prefer to hunt for someone in London? I could easily send you off to stay with Mother. I'm sure she would be *more* than happy to take charge of such a noble mission herself."

Rafe shot to his feet, scowling. "Good God, man! You are a heartless devil."

Ashton's laughter followed him as he stalked across the lawn toward Isla and Rosalind, who were now examining a ring of toadstools at the edge of one of the flower beds.

"Look, Papa, we found fairies!" Isla proclaimed as she pointed at the ring of mushrooms.

He crouched down beside her, smiling. As always, his daughter had managed to restore the sunshine on his most cloudy days. "Well then, we must be sure to leave them a tea cake tonight, or else they will creep into your bedchamber and take you away to their magical realm."

Isla's eyes widened. "Please dinna let them take me, Papa!" Isla leapt up, exposing her grass-stained pinafore, and latched herself onto his leg.

"Hello there, what's this? My daughter's turned into a tiny little monkey!" He gasped dramatically and looked upon her with mock terror. "The fae folk have already bewitched her! Whatever shall we do?"

Rosalind tried not to laugh, her gray eyes sparkling with delight. "Oh dear, I think you must take the monkey to the kitchens and feed it tea cakes at once!"

Rafe carried his little monkey, still wrapped around his leg, for several steps before he pried the little creature off and swung her into his arms. They headed straight inside to find the magical cure of the tea cakes. Isla giggled the entire way, and the matter of a dreaded country ball was, for the moment, forgotten.

◈

ASHTON DRUMMED HIS FINGERS ON HIS FOLDED newspaper as Rafe carried the little orphan inside. He corrected himself. No, she wasn't an orphan any longer. Isla may not have been Rafe's child by blood, but she was *his* child in all the ways that truly mattered.

Ashton had been concerned when Rafe had returned from Scotland and declared his intention to adopt an orphan. Ashton assumed Rafe had found some wayward boy, but when Rafe had shared it was a girl and told Ashton the child's sad history, Ashton had been even more puzzled about his younger brother's fatherly response. Rafe had taken no interest in children before. But when Rafe asked to have Brodie and Lydia bring Isla to meet Ashton, he had finally seen what had so captivated Rafe's heart. Isla turned out to be bright, brave, and so utterly innocent that it was impossible not to adore her. Simply being around her had set off Ashton's already protective instincts. He'd become "Uncle Ash" to her nearly overnight.

Yet what had convinced Ashton to consent to Rafe's desire to adopt Isla was the moment the little girl had been reunited with Rafe. How she had clung fiercely to his neck, her face stained with tears. Her tiny nose had been red from crying, and Rafe had held her tight, one hand cupping her gleaming russet curls and his other hand supporting her little body as he closed his eyes and whispered something to the child that only she could hear. Ashton had seen something he'd never seen on his younger brother's face before.

Peace.

How could Ashton even consider denying his troubled little brother that peace? Lord knew that Rafe was owed it after all these years, given the demons that had haunted him. And damned if Ashton wasn't to blame for part of it.

"You're frowning," Rosalind said, joining him. Ashton curled an arm around his wife's waist and pulled her onto his lap. His Scottish wife gasped and clutched his shoulders. She was a strong woman, but Ashton took pleasure in making her feel precious and desirable. She especially liked his dominating side when it came to their intimate moments. Even though Rosalind had given birth to their son, Malcolm, earlier that year, the passion between them hadn't ebbed at all; if anything, sharing a child together had only deepened their love and their passion. As much as he adored his son, he was glad the babe was asleep for his afternoon nap so he could enjoy this moment with his wife.

"Wicked man," she said before she kissed his cheek. Heat flashed in her eyes and the fire in her kiss burned his skin. Christ, how had he lived more than thirty years without this woman in his life?

Ashton sighed and cradled Rosalind close. "I am wicked, and for once I am not proud of it." He couldn't avoid what had riddled him with guilt, but he knew he could speak with her about anything and get her advice.

She lifted her head and studied him. She was beautiful, with gray eyes and gleaming dark hair, loosely gathered at the nape of her neck and tied with a persimmon ribbon that matched her gown. But his wife's beauty on the outside didn't even come close to the beauty within. He tightened his hold on her and let out a slow breath. He was a damned lucky man.

"Tell me what's bothering you," Rosalind said. Her Scottish accent was lighter than little Isla's because she tried so hard to blend into English society. Perhaps that was why he wanted to protect Isla, because she reminded him of his wife. Both had experienced terrible tragedies at a young age, but Isla still had a chance for a happy childhood, and if he could give her that and see to his younger brother's happiness at the same time, he would do whatever he had to in order to help them both.

"I suppose I'm at that age where one looks back on one's life, and I only see my mistakes. They play before my eyes like a dreadful performance on Drury Lane."

Rosalind stroked her fingers through his hair. Falling in love with her had made him realize how cold and aloof he'd become over the years. Slowly, little by little, her fierce love had fired cannon blasts through the walls he'd made to keep others at bay. Someday his fortress would be nothing but dust and he'd be laid bare for the world. But Rosalind would be by his side, and he could survive anything so long as she was with him. She kept touching him, her love making this moment less agonizing.

"What mistakes have you made?" she asked.

It wouldn't be easy to tell her what he was feeling, but he had to try.

"I was just a young pup when my father died. I was dreadfully lonely, and the world was a cold and wretched place for me until I was able to leave for Cambridge. I was deuced glad that I met my friends at university."

"You mean the League?" Rosalind asked.

He smiled. "Indeed." If it hadn't been for his friends, Godric, Lucian, Cedric, and Charles, he would have been lost to his rage and grief after his father died. The League of Rogues had become his brothers even as he'd lost his connection with Rafe. "But it didn't change the mistake I made that night my father died. I let Mother think that Rafe was to blame, that it was his fault our father died."

"To blame how?"

"That he was the reason Father had been trampled. But I don't believe it was Rafe's fault. It was such a mess that night; I'd gone after Father to bring him home, but Rafe must have followed me. He was injured and across the street when Father and I came out of the gambling hell. Father had been struck in the head, and he wasn't steady on his feet. He just stepped out and . . . Christ, so much of that night is still a blur. When Rafe and I returned home with the constable, I was so angry, so . . . hurt that I didn't correct Rafe when he blamed himself, and Mother heard him take the blame. I should have said something to correct her impression, but I didn't. I was furious he'd followed me when I told him to stay home. And the next day, I learned our family was in dire straits. Worse than I'd suspected. We were deeply indebted to several banks, and everything was heavily mortgaged. It was . . ." He struggled for words but found none.

He couldn't describe the way panic had gripped his chest, and he'd had trouble breathing for months. He would go into shouting rages at Rafe just to find a way to clear his lungs so he could breathe again.

And his brother had taken all of that rage and absorbed it with quiet, pain-filled eyes, but Ashton hadn't been able to stop. He couldn't yell at his mother or his two sisters; they hadn't been to blame for his father's death. Rafe was the only one strong enough to bear it, but that hadn't made it right, even if Rafe was possibly at fault for what had happened that night.

"I took out all my anger on him, as did Mother. Thomasina, bless her, she never blamed Rafe the way I did. And little Joanna too often bore witness. She loves Rafe dearly, but she's never been able to trust him. That is most certainly my fault."

Rosalind kept silent, letting him puzzle through his feelings.

"The truth is . . . I was too much of a coward to ask Rafe what really happened that night with our father. And Rafe bore too much guilt for me to think him blameless. Mother still won't speak of it to me or anyone. She only said that Rafe was involved in the incident, and she only said it the night I returned to bury my father. After that, we used that silence as shields and flung barbed arrows over them.

"All I know is that my father was killed leaving a gambling hell, run over by a carriage. There's more to that night, but I cannot bring myself to ask either my mother or Rafe. I allowed my own weakness to break my family apart, even as I struggled to save it." Ashton held his breath, waiting for Rosalind to pass judgment. But his wife continued to run her fingers through his hair, soothing him.

"Rafe needs that little child in his life, but he is still broken," Ashton confessed. "I cannot see a way to fix him."

Rosalind smiled, the expression soft and tender. "You do not fix those you love. You help them heal. Tend to the wounds of his heart, Ash. Tell him all that you've told me. Apologize. Ask for his forgiveness. You might be surprised how far that alone will go."

Ashton pulled her head down to his, cupping the back of her head. "What he truly needs is a wife like you." He nuzzled her nose with his and then kissed her, letting her feel all that lay within his heart, a heart that belonged fully to her.

Rosalind made a little sound of pleasure against his lips

and chuckled. "Wicked rogue." She pressed her forehead to his. "You do realize how fortunate you are to have me?"

He laughed, showing her the smile meant for her and her alone. "I do. You are a gift I shall never deserve but will endeavor to earn every day."

She kissed him, her tongue flicking playfully against his in a way that always set fire to his blood. But he still had more to say.

"Does that mean you agree to help me play matchmaker?" he asked.

She bit her lip, pretending to consider it carefully. "We need to find a very clever, *very* bright young woman who can handle a former highwayman."

Ashton groaned. "Do not remind me. I am lucky you didn't kill him that night you first met."

"I certainly tried," she admitted. "And at the time, I was more than happy to shoot someone who I was convinced was you."

Damn that uncanny resemblance to Rafe. Despite the difference in years, they had been teased by many for being able to pass as twins.

"At least he's pursuing more respectable activities these days," Ashton said.

"Indeed."

Ashton's thoughts returned to matchmaking. "I was thinking. The Merton girl. Mother was always trying to match me with her. She might do well for Rafe."

Rosalind's dark brows arched in surprise. "Rachel Merton?"

"Yes. From all accounts, the young woman is intelligent, self-possessed, pretty, and possesses quite the fortune. I met her two years ago but didn't give a damn for marriage then and therefore I paid her little heed. Now I wish I had."

"Oh?" Rosalind arched a dark brow and gave him a mock frown.

"For Rafe, of course." He chuckled and squeezed her bottom.

"Hmmm." His wife finally smiled as if she approved of where his hand was and what it was doing.

Then Rosalind considered his suggestion. "I met her a few months ago when I was in London. She is very amusing, but kind too. I would certainly enjoy having her as a sister-in-law."

"Then it's settled. We will push them together at the ball tonight."

Rosalind stroked a hand down Ashton's chest, her lashes lowering. "Our son won't be up for another hour. I believe *you* can entertain *me* in the meantime, my wicked baron."

"Wicked wife," Ashton said with satisfaction as he kissed her again.

He stood and carried Rosalind into the house. He most certainly would entertain his little Scottish hellion, until she was hoarse from screaming his name and had left nail marks all down his back.

⁂

THE SWEET SYMPHONY OF SCREAMS WAS INTERRUPTED when Mr. Phelps opened the door to Andrew Caddington's private pleasure room.

Phelps's eyes were carefully averted from the young

man strapped to a rough-hewn cross with iron chains. "My lord."

Andrew scowled as he lowered his birch rod and waited for Phelps to explain his interruption. He knew better than to do that unless it was important.

"There's been another robbery. Three gentlemen were traveling on the same road where our coaches keep getting waylaid. It was by all accounts the same three highwaymen: Tyburn, Oxford, and Cambridge."

Andrew rested the birch in his palm and gazed at the labyrinth of pain he had carved in the young footman's flesh, allowing the pleasure to zing through his veins, soothing him when Phelps's news would have normally put him in mind to kill. There were already two graves deep in the woods because he had lost control. Too many more and people might start asking inconvenient questions.

"Back, are they? Double the guards on our next money transport to London," Andrew ordered. "And tell them to kill the moment they are stopped by anyone wearing a mask. I want those thieves dead."

"Yes, my lord." Phelps backed out of the room and closed the door, leaving Andrew to stare at his latest toy.

The young man had broken too soon, had wept at the first strike on his flesh. Tapping the cane irritably against his palm, Andrew closed his eyes and summoned up the image of the Lennox boy from so many years ago. Such a pretty young face, such strength and defiance in those blue eyes. Andrew had been filled with a desire to plunge a knife into the boy's chest, to see if he would wail or fight in silence up until the moment the life faded from those eyes. Was there nothing sweeter than taking a young, pretty creature and destroying it inside and out?

He had hunted the lad in his own fashion, but the boy had avoided the gambling hells that his father had frequented. Rafe had danced around every trap, every clever snare Andrew set. He'd left no debts to be bought. He was too quick to be abducted, although attempts had been made several times over the years. Rafe was harder to catch than any fox, but he was worth the hunt, because his pain was exquisite to see, and Andrew couldn't get Rafe's pain out of his mind.

Who could have known that killing the boy's useless father would have woven such a stunning tapestry of suffering? It was his dream to wound someone so deeply, and he hadn't even had to touch the boy. It made him want Rafe all the more, and what he wanted he always got, even if it took years. Like a spider perched at the far corner of his web, he couldn't wait to feel that first tremor as his prey stepped onto the sticky strings of his trap. The mere thought of it made him glow inside with excitement.

Soon.

CHAPTER 8

"Stop fidgeting," Ashton growled.

Rafe scowled as he continued to tug at the cravat at his throat, which had tightened around him like a hangman's noose. He *was* fidgeting, but he'd be damned if he let his older brother order him around, especially while trapped in the confines of a coach on the way to a ball he hadn't had the least desire to attend.

Rosalind sat beside Ashton, her arm entwined with his, grinning at Rafe from the seat across from him. "Rafe, 'tis only a little country ball."

Her light Scottish accent made him suddenly long to be back at home with Isla. She had wanted to come and see him dance tonight, but she was young, and sadly, it simply wasn't done for a child to attend balls. At least, not balls of this sort, the glorified mating rituals that adults put themselves through. Perhaps he could talk his brother into having a small family one so he could dance with his daughter. By now, she would be tucked away in her bed, sleeping while her nanny was on guard for the night.

"You're enjoying this far too much," Rafe muttered to Rosalind as he forced himself to stay still.

The coach hit a rut and pitched to the side, making him brace himself against the wall of the conveyance.

"Bloody hell, is the driver aiming for *every* hole on the blasted road? When are we going to arrive, anyway?" Rafe had asked that question three times already, and he wanted out of this coach.

Ashton shared a look with Rosalind, and Rafe's scowl deepened. They were amused at his expense.

Rafe stuck his head out of the coach window to see if the Merton house in the distance was any closer. Lit torches were stationed in a line down the long drive, and the light from them danced against the line of carriages ahead of them. He counted nearly twenty. That meant the ball would be packed to the edges with dozens of eligible women. He sank back into his seat and grimaced as he realized his brother and sister-in-law would force him to meet half of them tonight.

"We need not stay overly long, Rafe," Ashton soothed, but his tone was teasing. "*Just* long enough for you to find a wife."

While Rafe was fond of this new, softer side to his brother, he did not enjoy being on the receiving end of his teasing.

"If Rosalind wasn't here, I would plant a facer on you, brother," Rafe growled. His hands clenched into fists where they rested on his thighs.

"You would try," said Ashton.

"Oh, but you must think of Isla," Rosalind said. "There might be a wonderful young lady here tonight who would be the perfect person for you and your daughter."

Blast and damn. Rosalind knew how to sink a knife into his ribs with the truth. He must think of Isla, and she did need a mother. Still, he couldn't bring himself to accept the idea of marrying a woman just for his child. He needed to find someone who would suit them both, and he wasn't sure such a lady existed.

"I will look, but if I find none to interest me, I will leave, no matter how early it is." He crossed his arms over his chest and stared a little too petulantly out the window into the darkness.

"Dance with ten women and I will let you leave," Ashton said.

"Five," Rafe countered. Not that Ashton could stop him from leaving, but he did love a good haggle.

Ashton stared at him, steel behind his blue eyes. "Eight."

"Fine." The brothers shook upon the agreement, and Rosalind rolled her eyes, muttering something that sounded suspiciously like a Scottish word for fools.

When their coach finally stopped in front of the Merton house, two footmen helped Rosalind down and took her cloak and gloves. Ashton and Rafe followed her up the stairs and into the crush of the crowd.

Golden light filled the hall as they joined the queue of guests waiting to be announced before entering the ballroom. Once inside, Rafe took the measure of the Merton ballroom with a mild, somewhat jaded curiosity. Paintings in gilded frames hung on the walls and a string quartet played at the front of the room. It was certainly a ballroom that could challenge some of the best in London. Mr. Merton was rich indeed to have such a country house so well furnished and designed. The music drifted with a pleasant laziness through the room as people danced. For a moment, Rafe allowed himself to let go of his past and take in the present moment of merriment around him.

He had loved to dance, but the darkness in his soul had eventually drowned even the simple joys in life, such as a waltz with a pretty woman.

Ashton placed a hand on his shoulder. "*Eight women.* Surely there's one among these fine ladies who might be your destiny?"

Destiny? Until he'd abducted that pretty little creature and taken her to his lodge, he hadn't believed in such things. He fought off the urge to reach for the pearl necklace he'd wound around his wrist, which he'd tucked under his coat sleeve. He'd wanted to feel that pearl, the only piece of her that he possessed, brush against his skin. That woman had made him think destiny might indeed exist. But he couldn't marry a woman like that—a woman who stole, a woman just like him. Isla needed a mother, not a thief, because her father already was one.

Rafe swallowed a laugh and simply answered his brother with a nod. Then Ashton took his wife to greet their hosts, the Mertons, leaving Rafe to fixate on how quickly he could entice eight women to dance with him so that he could make his escape.

A familiar voice called out, "Rafe, what the devil are you doing here?"

He turned to see Graham Humphrey, the younger brother of the Earl of Lonsdale, who was one of Ashton's friends. As younger brothers to infamous members of the League of Rogues, Graham and Rafe got along splendidly whenever their paths crossed.

"Graham." He shook hands with his old friend. "I

didn't expect to see you here." Graham was much like Rafe and chose to spend his time with opera singers and ballet dancers or the latest actress who was taking London by storm. A ball with fresh-faced young women hoping for marriage proposals was the last place the younger Humphrey brother would normally be.

Graham shrugged. "I vowed to wife hunt this year, if only so my mother would leave me at peace for another season. What about you?"

"The same fate, I fear, though my mother has enlisted my brother to see me leg-shackled. How are the prospects tonight? Any chit worth a dance?"

Graham chuckled. "Well, the Merton girl is certainly worth a dance. I found her quite lively, yet with no silly stars in her eyes. A sensible creature with stunning curves."

"Which one is she?" Rafe vaguely remembered Rachel Merton growing up as neighbors. She'd attended family picnics and gone shopping in the nearby village with Joanna, but Rafe had paid so little attention to younger women back then. His sights had been set on the experienced courtesans in London, women who expected nothing but passion from a virile young man. Tonight, however, he would be dancing with young women who dreamed of finding a husband, which meant he had to be on his best behavior. Any sign of flirtation could be taken the wrong way and he could end up facing the father, expecting a request for permission to court her.

"Rachel Merton is the dark-haired beauty in the white-and-gold gown." Graham discreetly tilted his head, and Rafe followed his gaze across the ballroom.

An admittedly stunning creature was dancing with a gentleman. Her dark hair was pulled up in a fashionable style, with a diamond-studded gold tiara nestled in her tresses. Her dress was no less than the height of fashion, and her face glowed with animation as she laughed at something her dance partner had said.

"Quite pretty," Rafe admitted, but nothing in this woman enchanted him the way his little fire drake had when she'd defied him by slipping that pearl necklace into her bodice. Was he now to measure every woman against *her*? He let out a sigh of disappointment as he looked over the other guests.

A tingle shot across his skin, like the feeling of a coming summer storm.

There, in the shadows at the edge of the light, was a woman unnoticed by the men around her. It was little wonder, given how little attention she drew to herself. Her dark hair was pulled up in a simple style and she wore no adornments on her ears, neck, or brow. Her gown, clearly several seasons out of date, was a somewhat simple thing, yet somehow on her utterly striking at the same time. The dark-blue gown was covered with a sparkling silver netting that had hundreds of stars stitched into patterns of the constellations of the night sky.

When Rafe's gaze moved up to the woman's face, he sucked in a breath as he felt an invisible fist drive itself into his belly.

The clever little thief. The seductress he'd made love to in his hideout. The fire drake who'd stolen his loot and made him want to shake and kiss her all at once. It was *her*.

He grabbed Graham's forearm. "Who is she?" he said in a desperate whisper.

Graham glanced about, clearly confused as to who Rafe meant. "Who?"

"The woman just there. The one in the blue gown with silver netting."

Graham studied the girl for a moment. "I haven't the faintest idea. I saw her speak to the Merton girl and I believe they might be friends, but I haven't been introduced to her. She's been quite the wallflower this evening. So much so that I barely noticed her."

Wallflower? No, she was no trembling wallflower—she was ever-growing lush green ivy, covering the entirety of his dark soul.

"She is . . ." There were no words that could encompass what she was. She was as bewitching as the night sky that adorned her body.

"I imagine she's poor as a church mouse," Graham said. "Gown's too old. She's not even wearing paste jewels to pretend she's better off. You had better be careful, old friend. That parson's mousetrap might shut on you if you get too close."

Poor? Ha! That woman had stolen a fortune from him, Will, and Caspian. He couldn't help but wonder why she was playing a poor church mouse now. Was she clever enough to know that showing a sudden growth in wealth as a single woman with no male family members would be highly suspicious? Yes, yes of course she was. She was indeed far too clever, and the thought of her cleverness turned in the right direction made his blood run hot with lust. Oh, the things he could teach her, the things she would embrace with wicked excitement . . .

Rafe began to wind his way through the guests, stalking his prey. He had never imagined in a thousand years that he would stumble into her, let alone at a country ball.

All the fantasies he'd been having about her in the last

month, what he would do when he found her, flashed across his mind like a dazzling, enticing kaleidoscope.

The woman stared with muted resignation at the dancing couples, clearly at a loss as to what to do but not willing to draw attention to herself. She hadn't seen him yet, which gave him time to admire her. How could she not be drawing everyone's gaze? She was like a star in the night sky. Even without the artifice of candlelight, she shone. She needed no adornments, no jewels, but here she faded beneath the sconces and chandeliers, her celestial brilliance dimmed. But he saw her, and he would not let his shining star escape him this time. He would have her in his bed, and he would get his stolen money back.

His view was blocked as Rosalind and Ashton came to speak with her. Rafe shifted his position to get a better look and saw that the color had drained from her face, so much so that her skin had turned a worrying shade of alabaster. What was Ashton saying to her to make her look suddenly ill?

A hand clapped on Rafe's shoulder in greeting, preventing him from continuing in the woman's direction. "Ah, Mr. Lennox, how very kind of you to join us." He turned to see Mr. Merton beaming jovially at him. Rafe held in a growl. Damnation, he would have to talk to the host, and quickly, so he could get back to his hunt.

"Good evening, Mr. Merton. I thank you for the invitation." He summoned a smile and fought the urge to look toward his distant, shining star.

"We were delighted to hear from your brother that you would be attending. My daughter, Rachel, would certainly be honored if you asked her to dance." He waved at his daughter, who had just curtsied to her partner after finishing their dance. She floated across the room and accepted her father's arm. She smiled warmly at Rafe and seemed to instantly read the situation, most likely because her father had been throwing her in the path of gentlemen all night.

"Mr. Lennox, it's been a few years since we've met."

"It has indeed been a few years, Miss Merton."

"I imagine my father has asked you to ask me to dance?"

"I would be most delighted to ask you to dance." He offered his hand, hoping that she would accept. That would be one woman down, seven to go, and he could ply her with his charm and see if he could learn about her friend. At least, he *hoped* they were friends. He had to find someone who knew who the little thief was.

"Yes, of course." She gave her father an amused but doting look. No doubt her patience was being taxed as her father attempted to match his daughter to someone tonight, but she handled it with grace and humor rather than frustration.

She placed her hand in Rafe's, and he led her back onto the dance floor. The dance was a lively one, which meant he had limited opportunities to get close enough to speak with her.

"Thank you for indulging my father," she said as they twirled around each other, their hands clasped.

"It's my pleasure," he replied. She was a delightful dancer, he had to admit.

"I understand this is not your usual scene, Mr. Lennox," she said when next they came back to each other.

"You are quite right. Just as you are indulging your father, I am doing so for my brother."

"Ah, so he wishes to marry you off as well," she chuck-led. "It is a great pity we do not suit."

Rafe's eyebrow rose. "You do not even *pretend* you find me the most handsome and eligible bachelor in this room?" he asked, half-offended, half-teasing.

She giggled. "Handsome, most certainly, but rakes are *never* eligible. Any woman who assumes that has wool for brains."

"How right you are. I am most in love with my free-dom," he agreed, happy to be on such honest terms with a woman.

"As am I," she replied.

Rafe was stunned. "You truly have no desire to marry?"

She shrugged, her gesture effortlessly elegant. "I am content as I am. Should a gentleman come along who suits me, then perhaps I shall marry. But I have no aching loneli-ness, nor must I bend to any demand of familial duty to marry. My brother will inherit my father's estate, and he and I are good friends, not just siblings. Between my father's trust left for me and my brother, I will be well taken care of. With that weight removed, I am free to do as I wish."

Rafe pushed down the sudden flare of envy. What must it be like to have a brother who would support his sibling like that? Shoving that melancholic thought aside, he reminded himself he was pursuing the identity of his little thief. He could have her in his bed again, and his money back, if he was clever about it.

It all came down to what nature she truly possessed. Was she an innocent young creature who'd taken advantage of a situation? Or was she far more inventive and scheming than he ever could have realized? He was drawn to both versions of her, even as mad as it sounded. She fascinated him completely, and he had to know which one of those versions she truly was.

He returned his focus to the woman before him. "Miss Merton . . ."

"Rachel," she corrected with a chuckle. "We've known each other long enough as neighbors not to be so formal."

"Rachel, then. I saw a young lady this evening and was told that you might be acquainted with her?"

"Indeed? Has someone caught your eye, then, oh heartless rake?"

"It appears so," Rafe admitted, feeling that such an admission might win Rachel's assistance now that he knew she had not set her cap for him herself. "That woman there . . . the one in the dark-blue gown with silver netting." He nodded toward his little thief, who was still speaking with Ashton and Rosalind. The color had returned to the young woman's face, and she seemed more relaxed now.

"Who? Di?"

"Di?" he echoed.

Rachel corrected herself with a blush. "Diana Fox. She lives on the lands just past ours. Have you not visited Foxglove Hall?"

He had heard the name mentioned before, but he could not recall exactly in what context. This area of England had never been his home, his land, or his people—at least that was the way he'd felt since his father died. That was Ashton's privilege as the eldest son. Rafe had pushed away any desire to know the people who lived here. He didn't want to lose more friends when he eventually had to leave Ashton's home and support himself and his daughter. He wasn't sure when that day would come, but he couldn't imagine Ashton letting him live there forever.

"She lives on the estate just south of you?" he asked.

"Yes." Rachel's keen eyes shone. "What interest do you *really* have in my dearest friend?"

He heard the warning in her tone and knew he must tread carefully. He smiled at Rachel, being sure to make it one of his more charming ones.

"Curiosity, nothing more."

"Hmmm . . . a rake's curiosity often has dire consequences for the ladies who catch his eye. Let me offer you some advice, Mr. Lennox. Diana is not one to meddle with. She has things in her life that need her attention, and a man wishing to lure her to his bed for sport would be very foolish. She also has friends who would see such a man punished."

"Friends such as yourself?" Rafe asked. Perhaps it was the steel in Rachel's gaze or the ice in her voice, but he found himself taking the woman's warning seriously.

"Yes. Friends who would challenge you to a duel or have you driven out of England without a second thought."

Rafe quite believed Rachel would do exactly that. "She is fortunate to have you as a friend," Rafe said quietly, and he meant it. It was clear Rachel was a warrior in skirts.

Rachel softened a little at the compliment. "No, *I* am the fortunate one. Diana is one of the purest souls I've ever come across. She would do anything for those she loves, and she has suffered so much loss."

His chest tightened. "What has she lost?" He knew she had no one intimate in her life, no husband, no lover. He'd felt so clearly the ache within her when he'd been with her, but to learn that it was from loss . . .

"She lost her mother when she was just fifteen. Her dear sister ran away from home a few years later, and we are all quite sure she must be dead. They were so very close when they were growing up, but it's been several years since Diana's had even a letter from her. And last year, Diana's father passed away. She deserves no more sorrow, Mr. Lennox." Rachel paused. Her gaze cut straight to the heart of him. "I rather like you. It would be a pity to put a bullet in your heart for hurting my friend."

The dance ended, and she curtsied to Rafe before she left. His thoughts were churning. His little star was all alone, *his Diana*, and yes she was his. He'd had her once, and he would have her again and again. Yes, he needed his money back, and damned if he knew what he was going to do about that now that he understood Diana's situation more clearly. But first, he would have her before he went mad with desire. And when they were both sated so thoroughly from passion that neither of them could leave his bed, he would decide what to do about this woman who held him captive. Because letting her go was no longer an option.

◓◒

Diana stared up into Tyburn's face. He smiled warmly at her as he introduced his wife.

His wife.

Dear God, what a silly fool she'd been to think a man who stole money would have any honesty in him. But he'd never pretended to be truthful. He'd even blatantly told her that Tyburn wasn't his real name. Her chest tightened with sudden panic.

And what was worse? He wasn't some impoverished man running about the countryside, looking for someone to share his lonely nights with. No . . . Tyburn was Baron Lennox. The man who'd robbed her coach and stolen her virtue was a powerful lord who had no need for the money that he had taken.

She suddenly felt lightheaded, and Lord Lennox reached out to catch her. She swooned, and he held her up on her feet. But there was no rush of awareness between them when he touched her, no lightning charge filled the air as it had that night when they'd been together.

This . . . this couldn't be Tyburn. Whenever he touched her, there was a storm beneath her skin. This man's voice was a little deeper, a little more gravelly than soft and smooth. And he was perhaps an inch taller . . . Oh, how foolish she was to make an assumption so quickly on the man's eyes alone. She took a chance now to study him more closely.

Tyburn's hair had been shorter, and he'd had no beard. Lord Lennox looked more like a wild Viking, complete with a golden beard. A man couldn't grow his hair out that long in just three weeks. It must be the man's eyes that had convinced her she was seeing what she'd longed to see for the last month. She'd been searching for any hint of Tyburn whenever she met a man upon the road or when she went to the village with Mrs. Ripley. But he had to be long gone, likely fearing she would have told the authorities where his hideaway was. But still, she looked in vain for any sign of him. Such was the depth of her foolish longing.

Several men she'd met this evening had blue eyes that were vaguely reminiscent of Tyburn's. Lennox's eyes were so bright, so intense, so like Tyburn's. But now she was certain it was not him. This man's eyes were full of interest and intelligence, but they lacked that aching longing to share himself with someone that had so called to her heart that night.

I am seeing ghosts of him in everyone, and I must stop.

"Are you all right, Miss Fox?" Lennox still held her tenderly, gently, but without the intimacy that would have told her this was the man who'd changed her life forever.

"I'm terribly sorry, my lord. I'm afraid I did not eat enough before I came and—"

"Then I insist you let my husband fetch you some refreshment," Lady Lennox said. "Ash, please bring us some punch, along with anything small and easy to eat."

"Of course. I shall return in a moment." Lennox bowed and departed.

As Diana recovered herself, Lady Lennox linked her arm with Diana's.

"You certainly suffered a severe shock at the sight of my husband. Dare I ask if there is a reason he should frighten you so?"

"Frighten? No, as I said, I did not . . ." The words died on her lips. Lady Lennox had clearly seen something in her reaction that her husband had not. "He simply reminded me of someone." She allowed Lady Lennox to escort her away from the edge of the dance floor to a secluded alcove a safe distance from the boisterous dancers.

So this was the woman who Rachel believed could be her salvation. Rosalind Lennox had lovely, delicate features, yet she was also undeniably a formidable force. That garnered Diana's respect instantly. This was no wilting flower. This was a hardy woman who'd survived much.

"Rachel Merton mentioned that you were anxious to meet me?"

And the lady got directly to the point. Diana also appreciated that.

"Yes, I was hoping you might be willing to speak to me about some investment opportunities?"

Lady Lennox chuckled. "So she told you I was a banker, did she?"

"She did," Diana admitted. "I hope I've not caused offense, Lady Lennox."

"Not at all," Lady Lennox replied. "Please call me Rosalind. We are neighbors, after all, or so I hear."

"We are. I must apologize for not introducing myself sooner when I learned Lord Lennox had married." Diana drew in a breath. "I run my family's estate alone."

"Alone?"

"Yes, my parents are dead and I am unmarried. I've been kept busy managing the estate that they left to me as my inheritance, and my mourning for my father only ended a few months ago."

Rosalind squeezed her arm. "Miss Fox, you need never apologize for such things. Grief can take such a toll, especially when one is left to bear the burden alone."

"Please, call me Diana," she said. "I would very much like to count you as a friend."

Rosalind smiled, making her gray eyes sparkle. "Friends, certainly. Now tell me, what makes you need a woman banker?"

Diana was in the middle of explaining her dire financial situation when Lord Lennox returned and provided her with two cucumber sandwiches and a glass of punch.

"Eat those and I shall relay what you have told me to my husband."

"Oh, you need not burden him with—"

"Nonsense," Lord Lennox said. "I take any burden my wife desires me to share." He gave his wife such a lingering, deeply affectionate look that Diana's chest ached with a longing to have the same.

She ate the sandwiches quickly and prayed she would not get hiccups after she rapidly downed her punch.

When Rosalind had finished, Lord Lennox said, "How much debt are you currently in?"

"At the moment, none. I was able to clear my father's debts by selling everything I have of value aside from the land and the house." It wasn't a lie, if one didn't mind half-truths.

"And what about your estate's current needs? Do you have a way to handle those upcoming costs? What of the tenant farmers?" Rosalind asked.

"I have some plans, something that will take time, but I believe I will start coming into some money, which I would hope to invest at once. As for the farmers, I have been taking nominal rents because much of the cottages and equipment need to be repaired. The tenants have been handling the expenses for such things on their own. I am doing everything within my power not to have to sell my land or my house."

"I understand, Miss Fox. Dare we ask how you will be acquiring these funds?" Lennox's eyes narrowed slightly as he sensed she was withholding something.

"It's rather embarrassing and I would rather not say." Diana swallowed the lump in her throat. How was it that asking for help felt infinitely harder than robbing coaches?

"Ash, please do not press her for such details." Rosalind gave her husband a stern look. "I will be handling her investments, and I am choosing not to ask. Sometimes a woman does things she must in order to survive, and how she does it is her own affair."

The harshness of Lennox's features faded. "Very well, my heart. You shall do as you see fit." He winked at Diana, the expression teasing. She'd always thought the man so cold, at least from what she could remember of her few meetings with him in the past. He'd always been focused on business, but now his intensity was softened. Or rather, it had changed to an emotional intensity. It was a very pleasant change. Had she really thought this man to be Tyburn? It was silly now to think of her initial mistake, but in truth, she had no idea what Tyburn looked like. Only his eyes were fixed in her memory, his eyes and the way he spoke with that soft Scottish brogue. She couldn't imagine Lord Lennox ever donning a mask and changing his accent.

"Thank you, Rosalind, truly. And thank you, Lord Lennox, for the refreshments. It helped immensely." The punch and sandwiches had steadied her a bit. She had not been lying about not eating earlier. She'd avoided breakfast and lunch in order to make sure she could still fit into a gown that she hadn't worn in three years.

"Ashton, if you please," he said. "If you are on such intimate terms with my wife, then I must insist you include me."

Diana nodded. Even though Lord Lennox was only a baron within the peerage, he was by his nature and influence, financial and otherwise, one of the most powerful men in all of England. Even King George himself had been rumored to cower whenever this man entered the same room.

"I was sorry to hear about your father," Ashton said. "I apologize for not coming to your home myself and seeing to your welfare."

"Your mother and Joanna came to see me." Diana's face heated. She was not used to this kind of interest in her well-being, perhaps because she was so often alone these days. Other than visits from Rachel, she was quite a recluse. Except for her servants, she was out of touch with society. "They were so very kind." They had brought food and flowers and had stayed with her while she'd wept. She had never felt they wished to be elsewhere in that moment, which many people often do when they are present in times of grief.

"I am glad they came to see you. I know that the Merton lands separate us, but please know that you are welcome at our home at any time." Lennox's words were spoken with such clear honesty that Diana did not doubt that he truly meant them.

"Perhaps you would like to come for tea tomorrow afternoon?" said Rosalind. "We can discuss the particulars of your first investment."

"I would like that. I have some money ready to invest."

Rosalind nodded. "Wonderful. It was lovely to meet you, Diana." She turned to her husband and tilted her face up at him. "And *you* owe me a dance."

"Indeed I do." He bowed his head to Diana and whisked his wife onto the dance floor.

Diana sagged in relief. She'd accomplished what she'd come to do. There was nothing else here for her tonight. It was time to go home.

CHAPTER 9

Rafe cursed under his breath as Ashton nodded in the direction of yet another young lady, indicating Rafe should approach the woman for a dance. He arched a brow at Ashton in challenge, but his brother only smirked.

"Fine," Rafe muttered. The quicker he got through these dances, the sooner he could search for Diana. She had disappeared after he'd finished the quadrille with Rachel, and he could no longer see her in the crowd. Most likely she was hiding in some alcove, away from the crowds. And when he found her in the shadows, he would enjoy that moment with such pleasure that he could already taste her kiss.

Diana.

Her name was carved into his soul now, and each syllable tasted sweet upon his tongue. Tonight, he would hunt down his clever huntress. He found himself hiding a grin at the range of pet names he'd somehow managed to give this woman in so short a time. *Fire drake, thief, star,* and now *huntress*. She was all of those things to him, a fascinating blend of qualities that made him want to know more about her.

One fact hung most clearly in his mind, making it hard to think past it. She had been so close all this time. Just one property had separated them, and he'd never known. How had he never met her at any ball or dinner party before now?

Ashton came over to Rafe near the refreshment table and cleared his throat. "Rafe, Miss Coventry is ready for a dance. Do the young lady a favor, would you?"

Rafe shot Ashton a dirty look, then plastered a pleasant smile on his face. He headed toward a polite young woman with bright reddish-orange hair whom he'd learned was Amelia Coventry. She nearly fainted when he asked her to dance, but the brave young woman accepted and off they went to the dance floor.

He made conversation with her and found it wasn't as horrible as he expected. The girl was not as clever or willful as Rachel Merton, but she was a sweet creature. A group of young bucks had been watching him nearby with interest, but Rafe was used to being observed like this. Younger men wanted to emulate his reckless, rakehell nature. Perhaps this was one of those times where he could use his reputation for good rather than wickedness. Feeling charitable, he bowed once the dance ended and made an audible comment on what a delight she was to dance with and that she was just the sort of woman to tempt a man in the best sort of way.

He smiled as two young bucks argued about who would ask Miss Coventry to dance next. With the last of his required dances complete, he caught Ashton's gaze from a short distance away and held up eight fingers, four on each hand, wiggling them in a taunting way. Ashton rolled his eyes and, with an exaggerated wave of his hand, gave his reluctant consent that Rafe could leave.

But he wasn't ready to leave yet. He scoured the room, searching every alcove, every nook and cranny, and once, when no one was looking, discreetly peeked under the tablecloth of the refreshment table. There was no sign of Diana. He frowned and slipped into the gardens next, searching the winding rows of hedges and disturbing a few couples caught in scandalous embraces. There was still no sign of Diana. Like a clever fox, she'd escaped yet again.

He stopped just outside the entrance to the ballroom and lingered there a moment, watching the dancers as he considered his options. She lived nearby. He could take the coach home, then ride to Diana's estate. Yes, that's what he would do.

He returned to the front of the house and had the Lennox coach brought round. He informed the driver that after the man had taken Rafe home, he should return to the Merton house to pick up Ashton and Rosalind.

Rafe settled into the cushions of the finely decorated coach and let himself daydream about how he would surprise Diana tonight. Three weeks was simply too long to have to wait without her in his arms.

Diana, my little thief.

For the first time in what felt like forever, he felt a stirring of hope in his chest. But he dared not look too closely at what that hope might mean.

Diana was dead on her feet when she finally reached home. It had taken a full hour to walk back from the Merton house. She could have troubled Rachel for a ride in one of the Merton coaches, but she despised having to rely so much on others. Her household would have a fit once they learned she'd walked home in the dark, but she enjoyed the quiet and the solitude of a good walk. Besides, the cool autumn night had helped clear her head.

She'd made an excellent introduction with Rosalind Lennox and would see her tomorrow afternoon for tea. Things were going well, but she wasn't foolish enough to let herself become complacent. Lady Lennox could help her grow her accounts, but only if she had money there to begin with. There would be another full moon in a few days, and it would be a good night to conduct a second raid on some passing coaches. She'd been giving it quite a bit of thought. They needed someone who could stay at the coaching inns on certain nights and get word to them of coaches to target. They had been lucky last time, but this time, they needed a distinct plan.

She slipped back into the house through the green baize door of the servants' entrance at the back of the house, where she found Mr. Peele waiting up for her. She'd insisted that none of the staff wait for her to return home and that they should all go to bed since there was always much work to be done with such a small number of staff. But as always, her butler never went to sleep unless he knew she was back safe at the house.

"How was the ball?" he asked.

"Fine, quite fine. You look tired, Mr. Peele, please go on up to bed. I'm just going to fetch a little something to eat in the kitchens."

He tried to stifle a yawn and nodded at her before he left her alone.

She paused in the kitchen to steal some biscuits and a glass of cold milk. Patches of moonlight cut through the windows as she leaned against one of the kitchen counters, her mind now blissfully quiet and her body wonderfully tired. She hadn't realized how anxious she'd become since she'd begun her scheme to be a highwayman. She'd paid off her debts, yes, but without proper financial guidance she feared she might have to resort to robbery forever. The danger it presented terrified her. But now, with Rosalind's help, things were falling into place and the racing thoughts of her worried mind had begun to still.

After she'd finished her midnight treat, she climbed the servants' stairs to the main floor of her home. No one stirred and no lights were lit, but she knew the way to her bedchamber blindfolded. Once there, she opened the door and retrieved the rushlight from the small table by her bed. She lit the rush and placed it on an angle in a silver stand before clipping it securely into place. It would give her an hour or so of light if she let it burn all the way down, and she wouldn't have to waste any precious candles. She then reached up and unbound her hair, letting it fall loose down her shoulders and back. With the pins all neatly stacked on the table, she brushed the tangles out with her fingers and, with a sigh, turned toward her bed.

Diana choked down a scream and slapped a hand over her mouth.

A man sat in the chair on the other side of her bedchamber, a pistol pointed at her. For a moment, she thought perhaps he was merely a shadow, a figment of her weary mind. But he was real. His face was covered by a black domino, but the moonlight illuminated his pale hair, making her instantly recognize who it was.

Tyburn.

He sat in the chair as if he'd been there for hours, patiently waiting for her return.

"Good evening, lass." His Scottish burr sounded like soft, distant thunder. She'd always loved storms, especially during the summer when she could lie in a meadow and listen to the quiet rumbles of thunder several miles off and watch sheets of rain coat the countryside in gray curtains as the storm made its way toward her.

Thank heavens she hadn't screamed. The last thing she wanted to do was bring her entire household down to her bedchamber. Tyburn needed to be handled with the utmost secrecy.

"What are you doing here?" she asked, trying to put some steel into her tone.

"Visiting ye, of course. Or did ye forget that we might've made a wee bairn when last we met? Ye were supposed to let me escort ye home so that I would ken where to meet ye in two months' time." His tone echoed hers with a clash of steel, like two fencers' blades colliding and casting sparks.

"I hadn't forgotten, but you need not worry—my courses came last week. There is no babe to worry over."

"*Oh.*" He said the word so softly that she believed he had *hoped* she'd been with child. A lump formed in her throat. What would a highwayman do with a babe? Surely it was better for both of them that she wasn't in the family way?

"Well, given that I am not with child, you have no

reason to be here. You should show yourself out. And by the way, however did you find out where I live?"

He grinned in the dark. "I would be a poor thief if I could not find what I most desperately seek."

"I wish to retire, *alone*. So please leave." But the lie tasted bitter upon her tongue. She didn't want to be alone, she didn't want to banish the only man she'd ever felt anything for from her bedchamber. But she had to. If she didn't mention the stolen money, perhaps he wouldn't ask her about it. It was a feeble hope to wish that he and his companions had blamed one another for the missing money, but she knew Tyburn was no fool.

Hardness returned to his tone. "Ach, I think not, lass. We still have *much* to discuss before I can leave."

"We certainly do not," she argued, even though a pit of dread formed in her stomach.

A soft, sinister chuckle escaped his lips. "Oh, but we do, ye ken. Ye took something from me when ye left, and I must have it back."

Diana's lips thinned, but she refused to admit what she'd done.

"Give it back to me, lass, all of it, and ye need not fear this." He moved the pistol ever so slightly, reminding her he was armed. She'd quite forgotten that. She'd been shocked, delighted, and then dismayed to see him here like this, and the existence of that pistol had slipped completely from her mind.

I really have been a fool, she thought. She'd harbored such silly romantic dreams over their one night together that she'd forgotten who he really was. Of course he was more interested in the money. Tyburn slowly sat up, a subtle tension filling the lean lines of his body as he studied her.

"Don't tell me ye spent it, lass. On what? Gowns, jewels, a new saddle for my horse that ye stole?"

At that accusation, Diana flinched. She wasn't just a thief now, she was a horse thief too, something that would get her doubly hanged. She certainly didn't like him thinking that she was so foolish as to waste money on fine things when her survival was at stake. Not that she'd dare tell him—at least willingly.

"I didn't tell anyone about you, and I also didn't lead the authorities back to your lodge. I think it's quite clear you have nothing to fear from me." She hoped the change in subject would distract him. It didn't.

"Of course ye didna tell anyone, because then ye would have to turn over my loot to the authorities, lest ye be branded a thief yourself. I'll ask ye again, *where* is the money?"

Diana planted her hands on her hips. "*Gone.* It's all gone." Despite the dimness of the room, she thought she saw his eyes narrow beneath the mask he wore.

"Gone?"

"Yes. Every shilling went to pay debts. I haven't any—" She choked on the words she almost said: *"I haven't anything else to give you."* Instead, she turned away from him. "I left you the only thing of value that I had as a trade."

Had he sold her mother's necklace? The freshwater pearl was the only real thing of monetary value she'd had left of her mother. She'd never lied to him about that. She turned as she heard the chair creak, and she saw him pull back the sleeve of his black coat to reveal his wrist and the pearl necklace that was wrapped around it. Her heart gave a wild, traitorous thump at knowing he hadn't given away something so precious to her. Was it because of how he felt, or did he simply wish to taunt her?

She turned to face him, raising her chin. "I can give you nothing else, I'm afraid."

The devil smiled. "Ah, but ye can. Ye have in yer possession the softest skin I've ever touched, the sweetest lips I've ever kissed, and 'tis worth more to me than all the riches ye stole."

A flare of heat started in her belly and soon worked its way to the rest of her body. His words were scandalous, his intentions ruinous, but Lord help her, she was falling under his spell a second time.

Tyburn leaned forward, his gaze piercing, and his pistol swayed slightly as he gestured at her.

"Remove yer dress."

"What? No—"

"Ye stole all that I had and left me while I was still sleeping, yet now ye will not offer me even this bit of recompense? Ye wound me, little fire drake. And yes, ye also seem to forget who is holding the pistol. Strip, lass. *Now*." The deep command in his voice did something to her and she no longer could resist him. With trembling hands, she opened the hidden panel in the front of her gown to unfasten the laces and let the garment drop to the floor. She wrapped her arms around herself, though she still wore her underpinnings.

Tyburn let out a hiss of breath and adjusted his position in the chair. She noticed the bulge in his trousers and remembered how large and thick his cock had been. Heat seared across her as though she'd suddenly stepped into bright sunlight.

"Now the rest." His voice was almost smooth as he motioned with the pistol for her to continue.

With a flare of rage and desire in equal measure, she kicked off her petticoats and slippers, then removed her stockings and finally her stays.

"And the chemise, lass. I would have ye bare for my hungry gaze." His voice had lost some of its smoothness and was now rough, as though his control was fraying at the edges. Good. She wanted to torture him as long as she could as some small form of revenge.

She pulled the strings that gathered at her breasts and then let the chemise gape open at her neck before shimmying out of it. The night air drifted across her bare skin like a ghostly caress, yet it barely cooled her heated flesh, nor did it tame the fire in her belly. Tyburn studied her like a man desperate for water who'd come across a cold river in the Highlands.

"Come here." He pointed to a place just in front of him. She walked toward him, her body bare. He unfastened the necklace on his wrist and held it out to her.

"Put this on. I want ye to wear that and nothing else when I take ye."

Her thighs clamped together as his words painted a wild, erotic picture in her mind. Tyburn poised above her, still clothed, while she lay prostrate beneath him, a sensual sacrifice to the God of the underworld with only her mother's necklace at her throat for protection from the god's wrathful lust.

Tyburn looked upon her a long moment, his gaze like a tangible caress. He spread his legs a little and patted his thigh with his free hand.

"Sit here."

Diana would've bristled at the command, for she was no trained spaniel, but she ached to touch him. With no small amount of embarrassment, she eased down onto his lap. The soft black leather beneath her thighs was smooth and warm and somehow highly erotic. His body was hard in a way that made her delightfully dizzy, knowing that he could direct all that strength toward pleasuring her and taking his own pleasure from her. She held back a moan as she began to throb with forbidden desire.

He caught her waist, and she heard the pistol drop to the carpeted floor as he cupped the back of her neck. With a desperate growl, he pulled her down to meet him. His lips were angry as he captured her mouth. She gasped in surprise at the taste of his sensual rage, but when his tongue slipped between her startled lips, he softened his erotic assault. She kissed him back, hungry for whatever she could have of him. She dug her fingers into his hair. When Diana touched the black ribbons that kept his domino on, he jerked away.

"No, lass, *no*," he said firmly, though he was a bit breathless.

"But—"

"'Tis for yer safety. Ye canna be forced to tell what ye've seen if ye've never seen me."

"Is that the true reason?" she asked. His hair was thick and silky to her touch, and she trembled with a desire to see it bathed in sunlight. It would surely glow like a halo. "Are you scarred?"

"Scarred? Aye, but the scars are within. I have a fierce angelic beauty that would make ye weep to see me."

She snorted—it was clear he was teasing her. "So you are as common as I am in looks, then." She didn't care if he was scarred or plain-looking. The mystery of his looks mattered little to her. What she cared about was what he said, what he did, and how his kisses made her feel like she could breathe again.

His hand at the nape of her neck moved to slide into her loose hair, and she wondered if he was possessed by the same desperate need to touch her, to make fresh memories of what moments they could steal in the sanctuary of twilight.

"Ye are the farthest thing from common, lass. Never have I seen such beauty as when I look upon ye."

Diana wanted to call him out for false flattery, but his tone was honest, and he held a hint of reverence for her that set her to trembling anew.

"I'm not a beauty. I don't compare to other ladies."

"Lass," he groaned in exasperation and amusement. "If only ye could see yerself the way I do, ye'd never doubt yerself. Ye *shine*." He breathed in. "Like a distant star, so far out of a mortal's reach. I wonder what it must be like to glow forever in the dark, to burn on endlessly, giving a poor wretch like me the light to find my way home."

His words held an intensity that made her heart expand, filling it with such warmth that it actually *hurt*. She'd never imagined anyone would see her that way. What he saw of her was a version of herself that was not weary, had not been beaten down and crushed by life. His words gave her strength. He gave her what she needed most, but she dared not put a name to it. He'd come here tonight for her, he'd tracked her down, and yes, he'd carried a pistol and asked about the money, but all of that was but a side mission for him. That much was clear by the desperate longing in his lips and eyes. If she was perhaps truly a star, she felt like she was shining bright enough to lighten the darkest of nights.

"Kiss me, oh star, before I lose my way in the dark," he whispered.

She leaned in, giving her mouth to him, letting him teach her all the ways a kiss could spin new dreams on shafts of starlight. After what felt like stardust-coated centuries, their lips parted, and he rested his forehead against hers. She closed her eyes, her fingers clenching and unclenching in the folds of his shirtsleeves as she steadied herself. The entire earth had shifted beneath her. Nothing would ever be the same now that she knew this man's kiss.

Diana never could've imagined a kiss would have the power to make her soul so wonderfully dizzy. She was a young girl again, spinning in a meadow, faster and faster, and then suddenly falling down into the grass to stay still as the heavens whirled above her.

"My God, you are magnificent," Tyburn murmured between kisses. His mouth traveled down her throat, then to her collarbone, and finally to her sensitive breasts. He nuzzled one, kissing his way to its peak before taking the nipple in his mouth and sucking. Sweet lines of desire sizzled from her breasts all the way to her womb, and she moaned in the dark. In some distant part of her mind, she was aware of how mad this was, to be naked on a highwayman's lap as he suckled her breast. She'd never dreamed she would feel so wanton or so free.

"Please . . . ," she begged as his mouth moved to her other breast, giving equal attention to her other nipple.

He kissed his way back up to her mouth, making her lose her mind all over again. She gasped as he rose from the chair, carrying her with him. He placed her on the bed and followed her down, his mouth still hungry and insistent. She opened herself to him, whimpering as he moved down her body, his lips leaving a trail of sweet fire before he tasted her between her thighs. His palms kept her knees wide as his shoulders settled between them, and he licked and nibbled all of those forbidden places.

Diana felt treasured, desired, even cared for in a way that only made sense on an intimate and instinctive level.

"Tyburn . . ." She whispered his name as she came apart beneath him, the climax swift and sharp. She wanted to weep, knowing this moment with him would be over all too soon. And he would be gone once more.

Tyburn soothed her as he sat up. "Shhh . . . I'm not leaving ye yet, lass."

Diana grasped his wrist, holding desperately to him, still afraid this prince of moonlight would vanish before her eyes and she'd wake from a dream aching for him.

"Lass . . ." Heavy emotion layered in that single endearment, as if he understood all too well what she feared. "I'm *here*, 'tis no dream."

She released his wrist and gave him a nod of encouragement. Not that either of them could turn back. Someday she'd be brave enough to tell him what she needed from him.

He unfastened his breeches and freed himself. "I vow not to leave you, lass, not for a long while," he promised as he mounted her and entered her with a driving thrust that made them both share a moan of satisfaction. She was wet, her inner walls still clenching from the previous orgasm, which left her even more sensitive as he claimed her now.

She tilted her head back, writhing in pleasure as he withdrew and sank back into her. He nipped her throat, her chin, and her earlobe in playful bites before he captured her wrists, pinning them to the bed above her head. The pearl pendant at her throat seemed to hold the very starlight of her soul within it.

He made love to her with an almost harsh desperation, as if the deeper he sank within her, the more they would be one being rather than two. She wanted that, to feel that they shared one beating heart, one soul so full of each other that no loneliness could ever hurt either of them again.

She whispered hopeful, foolish, romantic things in the dark to this man whose true name she did not know as he took her to such heights of such joy that she knew she would never want another man as much as she wanted him.

Tyburn pounded against her as if by lasting just a few more seconds he could erase both the past and the future and capture this moment between them forever, and Diana felt all of that. It was as though she could somehow read his mind, such was their connection. His mouth sealed over hers, and she swore he whispered, "Love you, my little star," just before she came apart with a cry that he swallowed with a kiss of tenderness.

Heat blossomed deep within her, and Diana tightened her legs around his hips, holding him to her, desperate to do what they'd failed to last time.

Let there be a life born from this night. She sent the silent prayer toward the distant stars, then went limp, exhaustion creeping along her limbs.

Tyburn nuzzled her cheek and pressed a soft kiss there before he eased his weight off her. Using the last of her strength, she struggled to catch his arm.

"Please don't leave . . . *please.*"

"I'm only going to lock the door, lass. I canna have yer servants finding me here come the dawn."

He slipped from the bed and crossed the bedchamber to lock the door. Then he returned to the bed and tucked her beneath the covers. She watched him through half-lidded eyes as he removed his clothing and settled in beside her. With a chuckle, he pulled her close and tucked her up against his side, moving her until she had a comfortable pose cuddled around him, fitting perfectly. She wanted to stay this way forever.

She wanted to ask him how he'd found her and what would happen tomorrow, but being in his arms right now was such a relief and a quiet joy that those questions no longer seemed important. She quickly slipped into sleep.

RAFE HELD DIANA IN HIS ARMS, REFUSING TO MOVE OR breathe lest he wake her. The wan light of the moon made the pearl on her necklace shimmer like a dewdrop from the fae realm. The hold this woman had over him was nothing if not unnatural. Perhaps she was a fae, a princess from the seelie courts in those stories he always told Isla before bed.

"Oh princess fair, give me your laurel crown and show me the way to love immortal," he murmured in her ear. He'd forgotten, for the moment, to use Tyburn's Scottish accent, but she was too deep asleep to hear. He stroked the wisps of dark hair that danced along her cheeks, and something within him seemed to waken long-dead embers in his heart.

"Diana . . ." Rafe whispered her name. The very sound

of it seemed to cast new sparks of longing and desire into those embers, teasing it to a flame.

This beautiful, smart, resourceful, and brave hellion who dared breathe fire at a wicked highwayman was also such a fragile creature who doubted her own amazing strength and beauty. It made no sense. The light within her was so bright that it obliterated the darkness within him.

He'd played out a dozen fantasies he'd had about her tonight, but he still had a thousand more. He could bed this woman forever and a day and it still wouldn't be enough. He would have given his soul for such a gift. But alas, he was all too aware of how mortal he was, that he would not have forever with her. But he vowed to cherish every second life would give him with this woman.

My Diana.

Rafe dozed lightly, too afraid of the coming dawn to surrender fully to sleep. When at last he knew he could wait no longer, he left her in bed, nestled warm beneath the covers. He pressed a kiss to her lips, then he removed the pearl necklace from her neck and bound it back around his wrist. She had given this piece of herself to him, and he would never let go of it.

He gave little thought to the money she'd stolen now. He would steal more for himself and Isla. Because he had seen her face when she'd spoken of her debts, and he'd seen the shame and fear on her face that being without money had caused her. The last thing Rafe would do would be to press her for it, not when it was so clear that she truly needed it, perhaps far more than he did. He even left the horse that she had taken that morning from the stables. He had a few more, after all. What was one more left in Diana's care?

In truth, coming here tonight, finding where she lived, finding her, was all that mattered, not the money. He'd needed to see her, to kiss her, to see if the fire between them hadn't burned only for one night, and now he had his answer. She was in his blood, in his soul, filling every part of him with wonder and longing. He'd imagined nothing fantastical about what had happened between them a month ago—everything he'd felt that night was just as true as what he felt *this* night.

As he crept out the window and slipped down the vine-covered trellis beneath her window, he felt like a foolish Romeo, but he couldn't stop smiling. He found his horse grazing in the field where he'd left him, climbed atop the saddle, and rode for home.

CHAPTER 10

Diana had never been to the Lennox family home. In all the years that they had been neighbors, neither family had ever shared a meal or attended a ball at the other's homes. The deaths of the previous Lord Lennox and Diana's mother had dealt much grief to both families. She and her father had in many ways closed themselves off after her mother died and Eleanor ran away to get married. Perhaps it had been the same for the Lennox family.

She knew that the current Lord Lennox's mother entertained in London, but Lennox himself kept his country estate fairly quiet when it came to balls and parties. It was as though the Foxes and the Lennoxes had quite . . . *forgotten* each other.

Diana now had a chance to take in the Lennox home with fresh eyes. The lawns had been manicured, the flowers perfectly planted, and the hedges trimmed in marvelous patterns. It was the way Foxglove used to look before her mother died. Even though she worked as hard as the rest of her staff, the best she could do was keep her grounds from looking like a shambles. This estate, on the other hand, sang directly to her soul. That pang of longing for the past dug into her heart, but she could not step into the mirror world from her dreams and be with her family again. The only way now was forward.

She slid off the back of her horse before the groom could meet her.

"My apologies, miss," he gasped as he arrived and grasped the reins. He had practically sprinted toward her once he'd spotted her, but she was so accustomed to dismounting on her own that she had forgotten it was expected to allow someone to assist her.

"No, I am sorry. I was in such haste to go inside." She patted her horse's neck before she let the groom lead it away to the stables.

The butler guided her into the house. She let out a deep breath to steady her nerves. She'd had Mrs. Ripley prepare her best day gown, which was a sensible rose-colored muslin dress with flowers embroidered on the capped sleeves, hem, and bodice. Mrs. Ripley had cleverly concealed the wear and tear of the gown by adding such embellishments as bees and hummingbirds along her sleeves wherever the cloth had worn thin.

Diana pushed away her shame and lifted her chin. She was fit to be in this fine house with its new furnishings, expensive tapestries, and marble statuary. Her gaze drifted about the entryway, her curiosity piqued. She'd heard Lord Lennox was a cold man, but there was nothing cold about this house. Despite the fine feel of everything around her, it still felt warm and welcoming.

Perhaps that was because of Rosalind's presence. Lennox had been intense, but at the same time, very gentle and sympathetic when she'd met him at the ball last night. If either of them noticed her worn, old gown, she did not believe they would judge her too harshly. Rosalind had extended this invitation, after all, and she was well aware of Diana's situation after last night.

Diana was shown into a brightly decorated drawing room and left alone while the butler went to find his mistress. A tall portrait of Lennox and his wife hung on the wall opposite her, those blue eyes flashing, so reminiscent of the pair of eyes she'd taken to dreaming about nightly. It reminded her of how she'd woken and found Tyburn gone this morning . . . and he'd taken her necklace with him. She reached up and touched her throat, her fingers caressing the bare skin. Her gown suddenly felt overwarm and itchy against her sensitive skin as it longed to be touched by Tyburn's hands rather than cloth.

A blush warmed her cheeks as she recalled how it had felt to make love so wantonly to Tyburn last night, and how she had slept far better in his arms than she had in years. She'd felt freed in a way she'd never thought was possible. She'd done things that would have made the most trained courtesans blush, but she didn't regret a moment of it. She'd made herself vulnerable in a thousand ways last night and had been so eager to please him and to satisfy herself, but the experience had been more than physical. They'd *needed* each other last night, to hold each other in the dark, limbs entwined, their breaths mixing as they shared her bed.

When her hand had reached across the bed only to find a cold pillow, a part of her heart had ached. Was she always going to miss that mysterious stranger with such a deep ache? She rubbed her arms and wished she had thought to bring a shawl. She hoped her long sleeves would be enough if the weather turned colder.

She gazed out the tall windows, letting the sunlight warm her as she wondered what Tyburn was up to now. Was he sleeping in after the long ride back to wherever his new hiding spot was? He and his friends would certainly have abandoned the hunting lodge, which meant he was laying his head on a different pillow.

But not my pillow.

She gazed out at the dark-green lawns when an odd, prickling sensation tickled the back of her neck, like she was being watched. The door to the drawing room had been left open by the butler as he exited the room, but she saw no one standing there. Yet that sense of being watched had not left her. Careful not to spook her invisible watcher, she turned away from the window and walked to the book-shelves against one wall, pretending to study the titles.

A soft thud sounded behind her. She peered over her shoulder and hid a smile as she saw a tiny head adorned with russet curls duck behind the settee. A child. Diana pretended to finish her examination of the books and wandered toward the settee. She sat down, arranged her skirts, and let out a loud dramatic sigh.

"What a *pity* I have *no one* to talk to while I wait."

There was another little thud from just behind her, and a little voice whispered, "Mrs. Crumpet, she said she wants someone to talk to." The voice was Scottish and utterly adorable. Diana bit her lip, holding back a giggle. She waited very patiently until, out of the corner of her eye, she glimpsed a porcelain doll head rise up behind the settee just over Diana's shoulder as if it was looking at her. Then the doll dropped down out of sight.

"What did ye see, Mrs. Crumpet?" the little voice asked. "Is she a nice lady?"

More silence.

Diana couldn't hide the grin this time. The child was having a conversation with her doll. "I'm sure Mrs. Crumpet would tell you I'm very nice," Diana said to the back of the settee.

"Did ye hear that?" the girl whispered to her doll.

"If you come out, I would be most delighted to talk to you." Diana leaned over the back of the settee just as the child stood up. Diana stared transfixed at the most beautiful child she'd ever seen. Her solemn blue eyes stirred something deep within Diana, something that filled her chest with a tightness of both pain and a love that she could not fathom.

"Are ye here to see Uncle Ash?" the girl asked.

"Uncle Ash?" Rosalind had three dashing brothers, and all of them were married. This little angel must be one of theirs.

She offered the little girl her hand. "I'm Diana."

The girl stared at it before she grasped it with surprising strength. "I'm Isla."

Diana gave it a gentle shake. "Isla, it's a pleasure to meet you. Is that your friend?"

The girl glanced at her doll and nodded.

"Would you introduce me to her?"

Isla beamed at Diana and displayed her doll proudly. "This is Mrs. Crumpet. She's a fine lady . . . a duchess!"

"A duchess? Oh my. So we are in the presence of a lady of the realm! It is a pleasure to meet you, Your Grace." She bowed her head respectfully to the doll.

"Yer Grace?" the little girl echoed in confusion.

"Oh yes. When you meet a duke or duchess, you must address them as *Your Grace*."

Isla walked around the settee and then sat down beside Diana, placing the doll in her lap.

"Did ye hear that?" she said to her doll in amazement. "Yer Grace!"

Diana reached over and tucked the doll's fine blue dress back into place. "And I see she's dressed for a ball."

Isla nodded, then peeped shyly up at Diana. Something stirred in Diana with such a potent longing that her throat tightened.

"Do ye go to balls?" the child asked.

"I do, sometimes," Diana said. She stared at the girl's face, wondering why this child tugged at her heart so much. She was such a lovely little creature. Why was she here in this room and not playing with other children?

"Do you have any siblings?" Diana asked.

Isla shook her head. "'Tis only me."

"Oh, well, I am alone too." Diana didn't speak of her sister or her parents. She didn't want to burden this child with talk of loss and grief. Diana felt like an only child now in so many ways. The memories she had of her elder sister, even her parents, had become a very sad sort of dream over the last few years, rather than a reality.

Isla beamed at her. "Maybe we can be together. Ye, me, Mrs. Crumpet, and Papa."

"Not your mama?"

Isla sighed deeply for one so little. "She died."

"Oh . . . I'm so sorry . . ." Diana put an arm around the girl's little shoulders. One of Rosalind's brothers had lost his wife? It couldn't have been that long ago, and it must still be a terrifyingly painful subject. It would be best not to bring it up unless Rosalind did so first.

Rosalind swept into the room at that very moment. "Oh, Diana! I'm so sorry for the delay!" Then she spied the little girl and smiled.

"Ah. You've met Isla, I see."

"And Her Grace, Mrs. Crumpet." Diana winked at Rosalind, and the two women shared a knowing smile.

"Well, Isla, I'm afraid Diana and I must talk about very boring business things. Why don't you go wake your Papa? He's already slept half the day away. Then you can come back down and have tea with us if you wish."

Isla hugged her doll close as she slid off the settee. She rushed from the room with a happy squeal.

"I hope you didn't mind entertaining her. We have no other children here save for my little Malcolm, but he's only six months old. So poor Isla ends up running through the house on her own."

"She is a sweet child. I didn't mind at all."

Rosalind got straight to the matter of business. "Now, tell me about what you want to invest and what your fiscal goals are. I'm sure I can do something to help you."

Diana removed the banknotes she'd brought from her reticule. In total, she'd saved up a hundred pounds. It was quite a lot to her, but she imagined it had to be very little when it came to investments.

"I have one hundred pounds here . . ." She noted a concerned look on Rosalind's face and quickly added, "But I should have more in a few weeks. I was hoping to invest safely but still make a little money that I could use to support my estate. That would be my goal."

"Well." Rosalind tapped her chin. "The consolidated annuities provide a return of 3 percent, which is quite decent and safe, but I think India bonds would yield 10 percent. Since they are riskier, I will, as your banker, cover the risk of loss by 80 percent for the first year."

Diana's eyes widened. "You would cover that much?"

Rosalind gave an elegant shrug. "I have plenty of money to spare should the bonds devalue. But I wish to help you and am willing to take on that risk."

"Well, I'm immensely grateful." Diana handed Rosalind the banknotes.

"And other than my husband, I promise no one will know of this arrangement," Rosalind assured her.

"Thank you." They discussed a few more strategies in the meantime to assure that Diana would have some money for living expenses until the bonds began to pay off.

"Now, let's have tea out on the terrace." Rosalind grinned. "The weather is too lovely to be indoors, at least for now. I believe storms are on the way, but we won't have them for a little while yet."

❦

Isla listened quietly to the two women discuss business just outside the door. She had heard lots of business talk since she'd moved into Lennox House. Uncle Ash and Aunt Rosalind seemed to love to talk about such things, and whenever they did, they often ended up kissing. Isla always giggled when they did that.

Uncle Ash wasn't as scary and serious as he pretended

to be. Whenever Papa had to leave, Uncle Ash and Aunt Rosalind would read her stories, take her on walks, and play with her in the gardens. Uncle Ash even let her have extra biscuits at teatime and he would carry her around on his shoulders, pretending to be a giant. Rosalind would let her hold baby Malcolm on her lap and rock him to sleep. She felt like this was *her* family, even though her real mama and papa were gone.

Isla clutched Mrs. Crumpet as she remembered the first time she saw her new papa, when she had been rescued by Uncle Brodie and Aunt Lydia. Her new papa had been lonely. She'd known right away that he needed her, so she'd attached herself to him. That first night he had read her a story to go to sleep, and she'd dreamt of Mama standing in the room watching her with her new papa. Her mama had smiled and whispered, "*Yes.*" Isla knew that her mama liked her new papa very much.

But now Isla was aware that she needed a new mama too. Uncle Ash had told Aunt Rosalind that Rafe, as a papa, needed a wife so that Isla would have a new mother. She didn't understand why Papa needed a *wife*, but Isla would be happy to have a mama again.

But if she needed a mama, she wanted one like the lady who was visiting. *Diana.* She was pretty and kind. She had treated Mrs. Crumpet like a duchess. Maybe she would want to have a daughter? But did she want a husband like Papa? Isla adored Papa, but would her new mama? Would they kiss like Uncle Ash and Aunt Rosalind?

Weighed down with these deep questions, Isla hurried up the stairs at a run and collided with Uncle Ash at the top.

"Well, Isla, you're in a hurry!" He chuckled as he

scooped her and Mrs. Crumpet up in his arms. "Where are the pair of you off to?" he asked.

"To wake Papa. He has to meet the new lady! She can be my new mama!"

"There's a new lady and you want Rafe to meet her?" Ashton's mustache twitched as he realized what else she had said. "Wait, he's still in bed at this hour?" Ashton's brows drew together into a frown.

She nodded and squirmed, wanting to be put down so she could go wake her papa.

"I suppose I should let you get on with your mission, then. Rouse the rogue from his sleep."

He set her down and she ran straight to Papa's bedchamber. She opened the door and crept inside the darkened room. The curtains were pulled closed to make the room dim. Sometimes he was out very late and had to sleep in.

Uncle Ash and Aunt Rosalind didn't know about all the times that he left late at night, but Isla did. Sometimes when she had bad dreams, she would go to his bedchamber, wanting to be cuddled until she fell back asleep, but Papa would be gone. One night, she'd hidden in his wardrobe behind some cloaks, where she fell asleep. She woke a little while later when he returned just before dawn. She'd had to wait until he was asleep before she crept out of the wardrobe and climbed into the bed beside him. She always felt safe when her papa was near. He never seemed to mind when she woke him up at night. Instead, he'd tuck her beneath the blankets and say, "Bad dreams, little kitten? Sleep now. You're safe with me."

And then, as if he'd cast some magic spell, she'd fall instantly asleep.

Now Isla studied her papa. He was sleeping on his stomach, one arm hanging off the side of the bed, breathing softly. With a barely stifled giggle, she tucked Mrs. Crumpet under one arm and then climbed up on the chaise longue at the foot of the bed. Then, with a squeal, she jumped straight onto her papa's back.

"Oof!" he wheezed and woke with a start.

"'Tis a bonnie day, Papa! Ye must wake up!"

"You little rascal," he rasped. He rolled over, sending her flying off him to bounce on the big bed. She couldn't hold in her giggles any longer, and her laughter made him let out a raspy chuckle.

He threw one arm over his eyes as he lay on his back. "What hour is it, kitten?"

"'Tis three o'clock," she declared proudly. She'd been learning to read the time from the grandfather clock with Uncle Ash each morning at breakfast. Papa would usually sit with her and practice reading letters later in the morning. He would write stories about fairies and magical toads and other silly things, and she would sound out the words. She liked to read, especially with Papa.

Her papa let out another displeased moan. "Ugh. I feel as though I've been run over by a coach and four."

"What's a coach and four?" Isla asked.

"A very large coach pulled by four horses," her papa explained. "Now what's all the fuss, kitten?"

"There's a pretty lady downstairs," she announced.

"Pretty, eh?" Her father removed his arm from his eyes to look at her. "*How* pretty?"

She grinned. "*Verra* pretty. Mrs. Crumpet says she could be our new mama."

"Oh, she does, does she?" He arched a skeptical brow.

"Well, tell Mrs. Crumpet that your papa is very selective. He will only consider a new mama if you and I both agree we like her."

"Well, *I* like her," Isla said without hesitation.

"Unless I've been asleep a lot longer than I realized, you can't really know her that well yet, kitten. You must spend time with someone to learn more about them. You understand?"

She saw things in Papa's gaze that she didn't quite understand, but she wanted to pretend that she did.

Isla sat back on her heels, feeling defeated. She thought for sure Papa would want to meet the new lady. He liked pretty ladies, and Diana was the prettiest lady she'd ever seen. When she'd stood up and had a good look at her, something had made her feel very strange, as though she was *supposed* to know this woman. But they'd never met before. At least, Isla didn't think she had. Something inside her had told her that this woman should be her new mama. Now she just had to convince her papa.

"Do ye not want a wife, Papa?" she asked, her voice quiet.

Rafe sat up, scooped her into his arms, and sighed. "It's complicated, little one. But I do. Trust me, I do." He stroked her hair before he kissed her forehead.

"Will ye at least come and see her?" Isla asked hopefully.

"All right. I must get dressed first. Why don't you go downstairs and wait for me?" He gave her a gentle teasing shake and tickled her waist until she laughed. He set her down on the bed and she slid off the side, taking Mrs. Crumpet with her as she left.

Papa would like the new lady, she just knew it. Mrs.

Crumpet had told her they were perfect for each other. Isla wasn't sure what that meant when it came to mamas and papas . . . *Perfect.* But it sounded nice.

She slipped out of the bedchamber, humming softly to herself. Then she went to find Aunt Rosalind and the new lady.

CHAPTER 11

Rafe adjusted his coat, admiring the bottle-green hue and how well it suited him. He wasn't a dandy by any means, but he did prefer to cut a fine figure when he wished to impress a lady.

His hands stilled at the edges of his coat. Did he want to impress this stranger Isla seemed so taken with? He honestly didn't know. Isla hadn't met many women, other than those in his family.

"Is everything all right, Mr. Lennox?" his valet inquired as he lifted up a small brush and ran it over Rafe's back to remove any dust that might mar the coat's perfect appearance.

"Yes, it is, thank you, James." He and James had been together for years, through the leaner times when Rafe had little to his name. James was of a similar age, and while he could have taken his talents as a valet elsewhere, he had chosen to stay loyal to Rafe. He was the only other person who knew about his career as a highwayman outside of Rafe's family, and the only person aside from Will and

Caspian who knew he was *still* working as a highwayman. The valet had guarded the secret well and had earned Rafe's trust completely.

"Sir?" James, as always, could sense something was off with him.

"Apparently, there is a young lady downstairs whom Isla wishes for me to consider marrying."

James's eyes softened. "Ah. The wee mite wants a new mother?"

"Yes." Rafe touched his perfect cravat and then sighed. His valet's gaze met his in the mirror as they shared a knowing look.

"Someday, when 'tis safe, you'll marry," James said, referring to his other life without risking saying the words.

"But not yet," said Rafe. "Not until I have enough to care for a wife and a child."

With a nod, James left the bedchamber, his arms full of Rafe's clothing from last night's ball.

Rafe was still weary from last night, but he could not deny Isla's wish that he meet this "pretty lady," so he headed downstairs. No doubt it was another one of Rosalind's friends. The Scottish hellion was talented at making friends wherever she went, and they often came to visit her at the country house. It was also possible that the young woman was here by design. Ashton and Rosalind were set on getting him married. No doubt those master schemers would be throwing eligible women in his path left and right, hoping he would trip and stumble his way right through the church doors with a marriage license in his hand.

"Rafe, a word." Ashton's voice, cold and hard, made him stumble on the bottom step of the grand staircase. That voice was the way his brother used to sound when he spoke to Rafe, before Isla entered their lives and softened Ashton's heart. His elder brother stood in the doorway of his study, arms crossed, a deep frown carving lines in his face.

"A word?" Rafe couldn't fathom what he'd done to incur Ashton's displeasure . . . unless, of course, Ashton, clever as he was, had figured out Rafe had gone back to robbing coaches. Lord, he hoped it wasn't that.

He stepped into the study, and Ashton closed the door behind him. His brother then went around the side of his desk and stood beside his chair.

"You told me you were finished," Ashton said.

"Finished?" Rafe asked carefully. "Finished with what?"

Ashton pushed a paper across the desk and tapped his index finger at an article. "*This.*"

Rafe read the article's title aloud: "Gang of Highway Thieves Strikes Again. Lord Caddington States He Is Determined to Catch Them." He read the rest of the article in silence, and a chill ran deep through his bones. Caddington was the man who had caused their father's death—not that Ashton knew that. Rafe had done everything to avoid that man since that awful night. The very sight of his name was enough to make Rafe ill. Feeling faint, he gripped the back of a nearby chair so hard his knuckles went white.

"Rafe?" Ashton's voice lost some of its cold harshness. "What's wrong?"

"I . . ." He bowed his head, breathing slowly to calm his racing heart in order to prevent himself from retching all over his shoes. "Sorry, Ash, I feel suddenly rather unwell," he confessed.

His brother ushered him into the chair, then leaned back against the edge of his desk. "So you *have* been robbing again?"

"What? No." Rafe pointed at the article. "Look at the two dates the thieves struck . . . I was here with you and Rosalind." That was not a lie, at least. Whoever had robbed those coaches hadn't been him or his friends. It was someone else using their methods, even their pseudonyms.

Ashton picked up the paper again and seemed to be doing some mental calculations. "You're right. I hadn't given a thought to the dates, only the areas where the robberies occurred. They are in your known territory." He placed a hand on Rafe's shoulder. "I apologize for the accusation."

Rafe nodded. His stomach lurched and he closed his eyes. He tried not to think about the fact that he technically was lying to his brother and that he *was* still robbing coaches. Just not these specific two incidences.

"Rafe, what's the matter? If it's not about the robberies, then what is it?"

"Cad—" The name was a blight upon his tongue. "*Caddington*. The man mentioned in the article. I know him. He's dangerous, Ash. A man best avoided at all costs." He couldn't tell Ashton what Caddington had done. He didn't want to speak of that awful night ever again, nor did he want to remind Ashton that it was Rafe's fault their father was dead.

"I have heard of him, but I've never met him. He is a local magistrate, one with a reputation for meting out harsh punishments. What has he done to you?" Ashton's fingers tightened slightly on Rafe as the brothers locked gazes.

"I met him once, years ago." The memories clawed their way to the surface. "He is a man with no soul. His eyes are empty of all but the need to cause others pain. Promise me—" Rafe grasped Ashton's wrist. "Promise me you will stay away from him." Rafe had never begged Ashton for anything, but he was begging now.

Ashton's eyes widened. "I will avoid him if I can, I promise."

Rafe sighed and fell back against the chair. That horrible name had stolen him back to the past, when he'd been a foolish young man.

I am no longer that boy. I can protect myself and Isla, he reminded himself.

"Perhaps you should take a walk in the gardens for a bit to clear your head?" Ashton suggested.

"Yes, that's an excellent idea." His legs were still shaky as he stood, but he felt better.

Ashton walked with him to one of the doors that led to the gardens. "Do you want me to walk with you?"

"I appreciate the offer, but I will be fine," he assured his brother.

"Very well, but don't stay out too late. It looks as though it might rain this afternoon."

Rafe stepped out into the gardens and looked to the skies. Towering dark clouds seemed to stretch forever. The afternoon sun, in defiance of the coming storm, glowed gold upon the trees and grass. Caspian had always teased Rafe since their university days about being a ceraunophile, a lover of storms. He loved the way the rain covered the earth and tapped upon the panes of glass, how the thunder shook the doors and frames while the trees bent to the might of its winds. Storms could ravage and destroy, but they also cleansed whatever they touched.

Turning toward the garden path, Rafe walked in the direction of those mountainous clouds, feeling stronger with each step. He turned his mind to the matter of this new gang of highwaymen. The thefts had been committed on nights he had been at home, and neither Will nor Caspian would ride without him. The article said three men had been involved in the robberies. Three wasn't an unusual number, but the witnesses had heard the men's names. *Tyburn, Cambridge, and Oxford.* That coincidence could not be ignored. So who were these imposters?

Rafe would find out, but that would take time, and he might even need to enlist Will and Caspian's help. The last thing he could afford was to lose the chance to restart their thefts soon. His highwayman activities were his only source of income at the moment, and he could not put that at risk. He'd already been forced to delay his activities a month, and he'd lost all of the income that he had saved up for months prior to that since Diana Fox had stolen it all.

He circled back to the house, taking his time to walk through the maze of hedgerows, when he heard feminine voices just on the other side of the bushes where he stood.

"I thought for sure Rafe would turn up soon," Rosalind said to someone.

"Rafe?" the other woman replied.

Rafe stilled, his breath halting.

He recognized that voice, because it was a voice that haunted his dreams with sinful fantasies. There was no way he could forget that gasp or how it had been followed by a moan as he'd pumped himself into the wet heat of her body, her legs tight around his waist. Vengeance and lust speared through him, sharp enough to steal his breath. He wanted to seize the woman, kiss her, and then reprimand her in the same breath.

"Oh yes," Rosalind continued. "I forgot to tell you about him. You don't remember ever meeting him?"

"No. I only ever met Joanna. I know that the eldest Lennox is Ashton's elder sister. She married before I came out in society. Thomasina, I think it was . . . But as for Rafe, the name is familiar, but—"

"He's Ashton's younger brother. He's older than Joanna by seven years, but younger than Ash by five."

"So he's thirty?" The other woman chuckled as though she found it amusing that Rosalind would speak of a man's age with such delicacy. "I quite forgot Joanna had another brother. She never talks about him. I met her and Regina in town just recently. And I never had the pleasure of meeting your husband until last night. Despite living nearby, my family wasn't much for dinner parties or balls. The Mertons are the only neighbors I know well."

Rafe was both irritated and amused to think that his little thief didn't know him as his true self, yet she'd been a beautiful, brazen siren in his arms last night.

"Well, I must warn you, he's a determined flirt," Rosalind said. "But he has given up his rakehell ways. Ever since Isla came along, he's been a devoted father."

Diana gave a short gasp. "Oh! Isla is *his* child?"

"Oh yes," Rosalind replied.

"I thought she was one of your brothers' children. She's Scottish, isn't she?"

"Isla was born in Scotland, yes. She only came to England a year ago."

"Oh . . . I see. How very silly of me."

"Nonsense," Rosalind chuckled. "It was quite a rational assumption."

Rafe heard the gravel shift on the path as the two women resumed walking. Then, when he was certain they were coming his way, he sped up, taking the corner at a brisk pace, determined to collide with them. And he did. His body smacked into the nearest woman, and he caught her in his arms, holding on to her.

"Oh! I'm terribly sorry." He now stood face-to-face with none other than his little thief. Her honey-brown eyes were lit with shock, and for an instant he thought he saw a flash of recognition in them. But then it was replaced with confusion and embarrassment.

"Rafe!" Rosalind cried out, forcing him to remember he was playing the polite gentleman. He released Diana and stepped back to a proper distance.

Rosalind rushed to make an introduction. "Diana, this is Mr. Rafe Lennox. Rafe, this is Miss Diana Fox."

"Diana?" He watched her eyes closely but saw none of that first sign of recognition there. Of course, when he used Tyburn's brogue, he didn't sound like himself at all. What a difference an accent could make.

"A pleasure to meet you." Diana ducked her face slightly.

His little fire drake was shy? How interesting. He decided in that moment he didn't want her to know who he was, not yet. Tyburn was her dark shadow lover, but what would she think of Rafe? A gentleman, a father, a former rakehell who was utterly polite to the ladies? Would she like him for who he was, or would she lose interest? It was torture to test her interest, but he needed to know that what existed between them wasn't simply the stuff of midnight dreams and the thrill of danger.

"It is a pleasure to meet you as well. Are you one of Rosalind's friends from London?" he asked. How different she looked now, almost sweetly demure, her cheeks pink, her lashes downcast, when at night she came alive with challenge, her gaze unflinching, her lips insistent, her hands hungry. He wanted to peel off this layer of politeness along with her clothing and carry his little hellion off into the gardens and slake their mutual lust upon the manicured lawns.

"No, I live at Foxglove Hall, the estate just beyond the Merton lands. Do you know it?"

"I believe I heard it mentioned, but I have not visited there."

Rosalind smiled warmly at Diana. "We've only just met, but Diana is certainly a friend."

Diana blushed at the compliment, and Rafe adored the sight of her flushed skin. She was even more beautiful in daylight. The dark fall of her hair was pulled back with ribbons in a tangled tumble of rich color, and her eyes were so bright and warm. Candlelight had adorned her last evening, but sunlight was enraptured by her and made her glow. His lungs suddenly burned as he forgot to breathe. When he realized Rosalind was watching him with wide eyes, he cleared his throat.

"Any friend of Rosalind's can be counted among mine," he said, unable to keep the pleasure out of his voice.

Diana's eyes locked on his as she spoke, her voice slightly airy. "Rosalind said that you have a daughter?"

He nodded. "Ah. Have you met my little kitten?"

"Yes, a short while ago. She is an adorable child."

"She takes after me, winning hearts at every turn," he teased, and Rosalind snorted a laugh.

"She's a better gambler than you, Rafe," Rosalind said, then winked. "At least in winning hearts."

"She'll soon be better than me at whist, but the child has a knack for reading faces. She can always call a bluff."

"We were just about to have tea on the terrace, if you wish to join us."

"I most certainly would." Rafe gestured for the ladies to precede him. Partly because he was a gentleman and partly because he wanted to watch Diana's backside sway in that lovely rose-colored gown.

At the terrace they were met by the nanny, who was introduced to her as Mrs. Chesterfield. The nanny held little Malcolm in her arms, and Isla, who clung to her skirts with one hand.

"Oh, you simply must meet my son, Diana." Rosalind pulled Diana toward the nanny, and she took the baby from Mrs. Chesterfield and showed his little face to Diana.

"Oh, he's a *darling*," Diana answered with honest admiration.

Isla ran to Rafe, and he scooped her up in his arms.

"See? 'Tis the pretty lady, Papa," Isla whispered in his ear.

"Yes, I see," Rafe replied. "What do you think of her?"

"She's verra nice."

"Is she?" He'd only seen passion and fire from Diana before. Now he had a chance to see her softer side. Could she love an orphan he had adopted? If she could not, then he would have to end his obsession with her. He fought to keep the frown off his face at that thought but failed. Isla traced that frown, which made him smile. She giggled in delight and he squeezed her, kissing her forehead, then set her down.

"Go on and have some biscuits," he said, giving her a little push. Isla rushed straight to Diana and tugged on the woman's skirts. Rafe waited to see if she would ignore the child and continue cooing over the baby. But she immediately knelt down and gave Isla her full attention. Isla soon led her by the hand to the table and put her in one of the chairs, along with her doll, Mrs. Crumpet. Perhaps his little dragon had a tender heart after all?

❦

DIANA FOCUSED ON HELPING ISLA WITH HER GLASS OF milk and biscuits and kept her gaze away from Mr. Lennox . . . *Rafe*.

Good heavens, the man was bewitchingly handsome. When he'd grabbed her in the gardens she'd been utterly lost in his eyes. She'd seen what she'd yearned to see. *Tyburn*. Her mysterious lover. But she had to remind herself it was another trick of her mind, just as Lord Lennox had been. This English gentleman was no Scottish rogue. He lived in a fine house. He had no need to rob anyone.

And he had a daughter. A man with a darling child would never risk his life on something foolhardy, like being a highwayman. And a man with Isla in his life could never be lonely the way her wicked highwayman was.

Still, when she looked at Rafe Lennox, something in her became very quiet, very still, except for the wild flutter of excitement in her belly. What the devil was the matter with her? She'd never been fixated on men before, and now she had two men she couldn't stop thinking about.

She accepted the cup of tea a footman had poured for her and glanced surreptitiously at Rafe, who had chosen the seat closest to her. The bottle-green coat he wore made his blue eyes somehow even brighter than the sun, and his pale-gold hair was bronze beneath the sun's late-afternoon rays.

"Isla, kitten, why don't you come and sit on the other side of me?" Rafe patted the seat of the open chair on his other side. "I'm sure Miss Fox doesn't wish to be bothered—"

"She's quite fine, Mr. Lennox, I assure you. I would be delighted to sit with her and Mrs. Crumpet."

Rafe's blue eyes were warm and gentle, full of concern for his daughter. This man wasn't Tyburn. Tyburn had no children, or else she would not have heard that hint of hope when he'd asked if she had become pregnant from their first night together. Rafe Lennox had his child. He had a legacy. He was the farthest thing from lonely.

"See, Papa?" Isla whispered to her father, and she giggled. He made a little grunt that sent the girl into another fit of giggles, and Rafe cleared his throat. Rosalind carried Malcolm across the terrace, cooing softly as she rocked him, which gave Diana and Rafe a few minutes alone.

"So, Foxglove . . ." He seemed to be struggling for small talk, and for some reason that set Diana at ease.

This man was rather too perfect in his looks, and his smooth voice could have seduced a woman out of her clothes in seconds. He wielded far too much sinful power for her not to be affected by him. Diana needed *something* about him that failed to reach perfection so she wouldn't feel so disadvantaged. She prayed he wouldn't notice how old her gown was or wonder at the odd placement of the embroidery that was designed to be patches over the torn and frayed areas of the fabric. But even if he did, she knew he would be a gentleman and not mention it. Still, the idea of him wondering about her circumstances filled her with fresh embarrassment.

"Yes, that's my home. I run the estate now that my father is gone. It keeps me quite busy."

"I offer my condolences about your father." He lifted the little blue-and-white porcelain bowl of sugar cubes and offered them to her. She shook her head. She'd gotten accustomed to denying herself such small pleasures if it helped the cook save money. When they did use sugar, it was for the necessary recipes and not for tea.

"He passed a little less than a year ago. My mother died when I was fifteen. I've become accustomed to being . . ."

"Accustomed to being what?"

"Being on my own," she added, avoiding the word *lonely*. "And you?"

"Me?" He raised a dark-gold brow.

"Er . . ." She blushed and sipped her tea, having realized what she'd just asked, but then she decided to go ahead and ask the difficult question. "Isla's mother, is she . . ."

"Gone," Rafe said quietly. "A year ago in Edinburgh." He looked into the distance, and her heart ached in sympathy.

"I'm sorry, I shouldn't have mentioned it—"

Rafe managed a smile. "It's quite all right. Isla knows her mother is gone and that she loved her very much."

Isla watched them both with grave, silent eyes as she

ate her biscuits. Diana felt wretched for asking such a painful question in front of the child.

"Mrs. Chesterfield, would you mind watching Isla for a few minutes? I need to walk about." Rafe stood and bowed to Diana, just as Rosalind returned to the table. Then he strode away down one of the garden paths.

"Oh dear. It seems I've made a mess of things," Diana confessed to Rosalind. "He must miss his wife desperately."

Rosalind blinked. "Wife?" She cradled Malcolm in her arms as she leaned forward to whisper, "He's never been married."

"What do you mean?" Diana asked in confusion.

Rosalind shook her head again and looked at the nanny. "Would you mind taking Isla to the fountains and letting her play for a bit?"

"Yes, my lady." Mrs. Chesterfield clasped Isla's little hand and led the little girl off into the gardens. Rosalind turned back to Diana.

"Rafe has never been married," Rosalind began. "Isla is his adopted daughter. She was found in Scotland by Rafe, my older brother Brodie, and his wife, Lydia. Isla's mother died of an illness. Her body was stolen by some men who sold corpses to doctors. The men would have killed Isla because she'd witnessed their body-snatching, but Lydia rescued her and brought her home. She took to Rafe like a little chick upon first hatching, and they've been insepa-rable ever since. I'm not quite sure who rescued whom, to be honest."

The nanny and the little girl had disappeared between hedgerows. There was something about Isla that tugged fiercely at Diana's heart. A girl who had lost her family but had found—or rather, *chosen*—another. She was a strong child and would grow into a strong woman. The Lennoxes were wonderful people, the perfect family to take care of such a brave girl.

"I believe you are the first woman to ever ruffle Rafe's feathers like that," Rosalind said.

Diana blinked. "Pardon?"

"Rafe, my brother-in-law, is a rake—or rather, he's in the process of reforming himself from being one—but he's never let a woman affect him before. He always rises to a challenge, and yet at one question from you, he flees into the gardens."

"Affect him? You mean I *upset* him. I asked about a woman who'd died, the mother of the child who is so clearly dear to him. I feel like I stabbed the man in the heart . . ." Diana's face heated with fresh mortification.

"Why don't you go and speak to him?" Rosalind suggested.

"I couldn't. He left us to have a moment alone. The last thing he desires is to have me disturb him."

Rosalind patted Malcolm's bottom as he made soft sucking sounds with his little mouth. "Nonsense. He needs to speak about Isla's parents. He needs to be comfortable with her past so that she may be comfortable with it as well. If you help the man, you help the child."

Diana bit her lip. "You truly think I should go after him?"

"I do. And this little one needs to be fed and put down for a nap. So I shall excuse myself while you seek out Rafe." Rosalind rose, and a footman opened the door to the house for her.

Diana was halfway to the gardens when she realized how scandalous it was to seek out a man on her own.

However . . . this wasn't London, and her married hostess had insisted that she seek the gentleman out. Not to mention that the gentleman in question was her hostess's brother-in-law. Surely it couldn't be that scandalous . . . And it wasn't as though she had a reputation to worry over.

The clouds overhead began to eclipse the sun, and a chill wind rushed through the trees and flowers. She shivered and rubbed her arms. She was thankful she'd worn a long-sleeved gown, but the sudden loss of sunlight was like the unexpected kiss of winter on the summer day. Thunder rumbled, still distant, but walls of sweeping rain could now be seen flowing across the distant golden meadows, turning the grass a dark bronze. She looked back the way she'd come, wondering if she should go back into the house. But no, she still had to apologize to Rafe, and she was no stranger to a little rain. She would find him, and they would walk back together.

She reached a lovely fountain with a stone statue of Neptune mounted in the center, water spouting from his hands and a large carved fish at his feet. She paused to admire the work of art, but there was no sign of the nanny or the little girl she'd expected to see.

"Help!"

A scream tore through the gardens. Diana spun and ran toward the sound, taking turns around bushes until she found the nanny on the path ahead of her.

"What's wrong?" she asked as she reached Mrs. Chesterfield.

The older woman was clutching her chest and gasping, her face red and her eyes blurred with tears. "The baby! I lost the baby!"

"The baby? Rosalind just took him inside for a nap."

"No, not Malcolm. Little Isla. She's gone!"

Diana spun in a circle, looking for any hint of the little blue-and-white dress that Isla wore. There was no sign of her. A moment later, rain swept across the gardens, pelting the earth violently. Thunder crashed ever closer.

"We have to find her!" the nanny cried. "She'll catch her death in this weather."

Mrs. Chesterfield was right. They had to find Isla, and fast.

CHAPTER 12

Diana forced the nanny to sit on the edge of the fountain before the poor woman collapsed. "Wait here. I will find her."

"Oh—but—" Mrs. Chesterfield protested.

The rain came across the gardens again in another violent torrent, and Diana felt her dress grow heavy from it.

"On second thought, go back to the house at once and inform Lady Lennox that I am searching for Isla."

"I should come and help—" Mrs. Chesterfield tried to fix her dampened bonnet. This woman clearly adored her little charge, yet Diana felt the woman should not risk herself in this weather.

"Please go inside. Lady Lennox must know the child is missing. If she is caught in the storm, she will need dry clothes, warm blankets, and a fire in the nursery. Please arrange for those to be ready for us when we return."

Mrs. Chesterfield wiped away rain and tears from her

face. "All right." Once she was on her way, Diana began her search in earnest.

"Isla!" she called as she ran deeper into the garden. She peered under every branch, behind every cluster of roses, and still there was no sign of the child. She reached the end of the gardens and faced a vast rolling hill far below. *There!* She spotted a flash of a blue-and-white pinafore among the gold grass.

"Isla!" She hoisted up her skirts and sprinted through the knee-high grass. The child was so far away. A crash of thunder and lightning sent a spiral of fresh terror through her. The earth shook beneath her with the force of the thunder, and she almost stumbled down the hill. But Diana recovered her balance. The last few years of work with her servants had strengthened both her body and her spirit. She kept going until she found Isla, eyes closed, clutching her doll.

"Mama!" the child wailed. Diana knelt down to put her arms around the child and pulled her close against her chest.

"Shhh, it's all right, darling." The surge of protective instincts she now felt stunned her. She'd stopped thinking about children years ago, around the same time she'd stopped hoping for a love match.

"Mama," Isla whispered again and burrowed into her.

"What were you doing out here?" Diana asked as they hunched down in the grass, trying to find some temporary shelter.

"Mrs. Crumpet told me to take a turn, and I got lost. I couldna find Nanny again."

Isla cried harder after her confession. Diana's chest ached with the need to protect the little girl.

A sudden brilliant flash followed by the crack of exploding wood made Diana dive to the ground, covering the little girl with her body. Her ears felt as though they'd been stuffed with cotton. She couldn't hear anything after, except for a loud, dull ringing. Lightning must have struck a tree.

Her mind tried to process the immediate danger. It wasn't safe to stand, let alone make a run for the house. She'd been told as a child to stay low outside during a storm and never to stand under trees. One of the field workers who'd worked part of her family's lands had been struck by lightning while taking shelter under a tree.

"It's all right," she soothed. Isla had gone very quiet but was trembling hard beneath Diana's body. "We must stay here until it is safe to move."

A deep bellow echoed across the meadow and seemed to shake the clouds above them. "Isla!"

Diana raised her head. A tall figure was coming toward them at a fast sprint through the thick, wet grass. Rafe Lennox.

"Go back! It's too dangerous!" she screamed. If he risked running to them, he might die. As if the storm heard her warning, she felt the air sizzle around them, and the air smelled strange. Another strike was coming . . .

"No!"

His gaze locked on Diana's as he seemed to realize the danger, but it was too late to turn back. She saw his determination to protect his child, which outweighed everything else. He dove forward, his body hitting the slick grass on the steep hill.

A blast of pure white blinded her vision, and thunder deafened her ears once more. Through the haze of her disorientation, she managed to raise her head, afraid to see Rafe lying dead in front of her. But he was running again, no more than a dozen yards away and closing in fast. He had flattened himself just in time, but now—

He slid, feetfirst, straight toward her and skidded right to a stop beside them and threw his body around hers and Isla's. An instant later, another bolt struck part of the gardens far above them. His muscled arms banded around them both like iron.

"Stay down," he commanded. Diana shifted beneath his body, making sure Isla was fully shielded. They lay there, the three of them so flat beneath the raging storm, counting the seconds between the lightning and the thunder for what felt like an eternity before Rafe dared to move.

"The storm's moving north," he said. "I believe we can make a run for it now." Diana raised her head, their noses brushing as she looked up at him.

"Are you certain?"

Rafe nodded. Rain dripped down his nose, and droplets coated his dark-gold lashes. His wet blond hair fell across his eyes, which held such storms as to rival the skies above.

"I've been out in many storms. This one is done with us for now."

Diana wanted to stay where they were to be absolutely sure, but Isla was cold and shaking.

"I think you are right. We must get Isla inside." She kept her tone quiet as she spoke to Rafe. His eyes narrowed as he assessed his child.

"Give her to me. I will carry her." He stood, and Diana uncovered the little girl enough to slide her into her father's arms.

"Isla?" Rafe whispered. His daughter's eyes were closed. She shook hard as she lay limp against his chest. He glanced at Diana then, his face showing clearly what he wanted to do.

"I only wish I could carry you as well." It was beautifully noble of him, but foolish. The child was ill and mattered far more than she did.

"Take her and go, quickly! I'll be fine." Diana shoved at him when he still hesitated. "Go!"

Rafe sprinted back up the hill with Isla in his arms. Diana lifted her skirts and started after him, albeit more slowly. With the benefit of longer legs and breeches, he made it to the house far quicker than she could.

By the time she reached the back terrace, a footman rushed out to meet her, carrying a large white cloth that he draped around her wet shoulders.

"Miss Fox, a bath has been prepared in one of the guest bedchambers for you. I will show you the way now, if you like."

"Thank you, but I would like to see Isla first. Is she all right?"

"The child is . . . not well. Lord Lennox rode for the doctor. He will be back as soon as he can." The footman's face was pale with concern. It was clear everyone in this house adored Isla.

She grasped the footman's hand in earnest. "Please let me see her straightaway."

He finally relented. "I will take you. She is in the nursery." He led Diana up the stairs and down the hall. Towering tapestries adorned the walls, depicting sunny gardens and bright summer days, a stark contrast to the gloom of the skies outside.

The footman paused at a door and knocked. "Mr. Lennox, it's Miss Fox. She is here to see the child."

"Let her come," Rafe's voice called out after a few seconds.

When the footman opened the door, Diana passed into the room and she was startled to find Rafe sitting on the floor with Isla close to the fire. The little girl had been changed into a clean white nightgown and was bundled up in thick woolen blankets.

Rafe held the girl in his lap, his arms wrapped around her as he kept her close enough to the fire for warmth. His blue eyes shimmered with tears as they met Diana's gaze. She eased down onto the stone floor beside him. He was in shock, that much Diana could see. His face was white and his lips parted as he drew in shallow breaths. The child in his hold was quiet, but her trembling had lessened.

"How is she?" Diana asked, her voice barely above a whisper.

Rafe blinked, his gaze seemingly lost on her face. "She is unwell . . . and I don't know what to do to help her."

"I was told the doctor is coming. Lord Lennox is going to fetch him?"

Rafe nodded. "Yes, Ash will bring him back. He will fix it." He seemed to have complete faith in his brother. Diana envied him that unbroken trust in a sibling. She'd thought Eleanor would always be close to her, but when she ran away and eloped, no letters ever arrived, nothing to tell her what had become of her.

Why hadn't she written at least one letter? The thought stung Diana deep, because she could think of only one reason. Her beloved sister *must* be dead. She would not have gone so silent unless something terrible had happened.

Rafe's voice broke through her melancholia. "Thank you . . ."

"Hmm?"

He let out a shivering breath. "*You* saved her. I had just returned to the terrace and Rosalind looked terrified. She said Isla was missing and you went after her. I feared the worst. I . . ." He cuddled the child close, tucking the blankets up under her chin.

Diana tried to smile, but her body ached with the cold of the storm settling in her bones.

"You could've been killed," she replied. "You shouldn't have run down to us on the field like that."

A hard steel look cast his features in stone. "I would never fail my child. *Never*."

She knew then that someone had failed this poor man long ago. Had it been his mother or his father? Diana wasn't sure if it was the weight of her soaked dress or the frightening intensity of Rafe's vow, but a shudder racked her. This child was loved, deeply, *fiercely*. Rafe was a father who would do anything for his child, even surrender his own life.

"May I sit with you and wait for the doctor?" Diana asked.

He didn't answer—he simply reached out with one hand and clasped her fingers in a firm hold, not letting go.

That single touch changed something in her. It almost felt like she was home. For the first time in more than a month, she didn't think of Tyburn and his kisses. She thought only of this man . . . and the ferocity of his love, even though it wasn't meant for her.

RAFE WATCHED THE DOCTOR EXAMINE HIS DAUGHTER, numb in a way he'd only felt once before. Dr. Rainsgate was a spry and hardily built man in his mid-thirties. He wasn't afraid of storms, and he had raced up the stairs to the nursery straightaway upon his arrival. Now Rafe held his breath, frightened beyond imagining what the man would say.

Isla was sitting up in her bed, yet she looked half-asleep as the doctor listened to her heart. He sighed and set his instruments back in his medical bag.

"I believe the shock of the storm is what has made the deepest impact on the child, rather than the rain and chill. Keep her warm, feed her hardy broths with chicken for a day. Do not starve her. If she is hungry, feed her. If she is not, make her eat a little bit. And keep her drinking water. She must not go too long without water." He stood and faced the people who now filled the room. Ash and Rosalind stood behind Rafe, and Mrs. Chesterfield hovered nearby. Diana was at his side, and her presence gave him a strange sense of peace, as though all would be well so long as she was with him.

"Thank you, Dr. Rainsgate," said Rafe.

"I shall return tomorrow to see how she fares," the doctor said.

"Let me see you out, Doctor." Ashton held out a hand toward the door and followed the doctor out of the chamber.

Rosalind gave Rafe's shoulder a gentle squeeze as she left. "I'll speak to the cook and have some broth and milk brought up in a short while. If you and Diana need anything else, just pull the bell cord. The footmen have been notified to be ready."

Mrs. Chesterfield sat down in her chair by Isla's bed and took the little girl's hand as the child lay back down to sleep.

"Rest now, little one," the nanny soothed and tucked the girl in. Rafe's chest tightened, and for a moment he couldn't breathe.

He could have lost her, lost his little girl. That frightful truth held him pinned in place, unable to move, to think. The thought of life without Isla was . . . no life at all. She'd saved him in a way he hadn't known he'd needed, and to fail her as he had, by not thinking of the danger of the storm and immediately taking her back inside? His failure had almost killed his child. And now he had yet another thing to lose if he wasn't careful—the woman standing beside him.

"You should change out of your wet clothes, Mr. Lennox," Diana said, and her voice startled him. "You've been in them too long now, and we cannot have you fall ill."

"*Rafe*—you called me Rafe in the storm." He gazed at the remarkable woman beside him. His little thief, his shining star . . . his fierce, protective fire drake.

Her face flushed. "I'm terribly sorry for the breach of propriety. I wasn't thinking clearly in the moment. But still, I shouldn't have—"

"*Rafe*," he said softly. "I am Rafe to you, *now and always*." He reached for her hand and lifted it to his cheek, pressing her icy fingers to his skin before he kissed them. It was on his lips to reveal that he was her shadow lover, that she could trust him now, just as she had last night when he'd played the part of Tyburn. But something kept him silent. He wanted to earn her trust as himself, not as the wild rogue he'd become out of dire necessity. He wanted to be loved for himself, not for the dangerous life he no longer wished to lead.

Lord, if Ashton ever found out that he was thinking of love like this, he'd laugh himself silly.

"Rafe, then," Diana agreed, and the sound of his name on her lips charged his soul as if he had been struck by lightning.

"You need to change," she reminded him. "If you wish to remain at her bedside, she will need her father fit and well."

"I can't leave her—" he started.

"I will stay here until you return. Between Mrs. Chesterfield and myself, we shall keep her safe."

He hesitated a moment until Diana squeezed his hand. Then he let go of her fingers and rushed to his chamber to change.

When he returned, he found Diana had moved two chairs next to the little girl's bed, and she occupied one of them.

"Are you feeling better?" she asked.

He nodded. "Immeasurably. Now it is your turn."

She shrugged one shoulder as if she didn't care about her soaked state. Damp strands of her long dark hair clung to her shoulders, yet she didn't seem to notice. "I have nothing to change into, and I am quite all right. It isn't the first time I've been soaked to the bone."

No, it certainly wasn't. She'd been drenched the night

he'd abducted her and taken her to the lodge, but he'd insisted on getting her out of the clothes, just as he would now.

Rafe looked Diana over from head to foot. "You and Rosalind are of a similar size. I'm quite sure she would lend you a dressing gown." He began to leave, but she caught his wrist.

"Rafe, please don't trouble her. She's been so wonderful to help me already."

"Help you? With what?"

She hesitated. "It is something of a personal nature. I couldn't possibly ask for another favor."

"Nonsense. You saved *my daughter*. Isla is Rosalind's niece. She would do anything for you, as would I." He meant it. Whatever concerns he'd had about whether Diana could fit into his and Isla's lives had been answered by her valiant actions. He and his family owed her everything.

I shall marry you one day, Diana.

"Wait here. I shall return in a moment." He found a footman in the corridor and instructed him to seek out Rosalind and ask to borrow a spare dressing gown, then returned to the nursery and sat beside Diana in a silent vigil at Isla's bedside.

When Diana returned, she wore a dark-blue dressing gown bound loose at her waist with a white sash tied into a ribbon at the back. Her hair was damp, loose tendrils curling around her face and down her shoulders.

She looked as wild and untamed as the night he'd taken her from that coach. That night he'd had his way with her, and she'd been passionate, wild, out of control. But now . . .

now he wanted only the feel of her hand in his and the promise that her soft brown eyes held if he dared to wrap his arms around her—but as Rafe and not her wicked Tyburn.

He held out his hand. When she took it, he wanted to pull her onto his lap to cuddle her. It was hard to remember that she didn't know that he was secretly Tyburn. Only Tyburn was free to kiss her, to make love to her. Rafe was bound by other rules, and he dared not break them, lest he lose her.

To her, Rafe was still a stranger, and he could frighten her away by pulling her onto his lap and kissing her with the adoration and gratitude he held in his heart. So he contented himself with holding on to her hand as they watched his child sleep.

It was close to midnight when color returned to Isla's cheeks and her breathing deepened. Some of the tension coiled tight within Rafe finally eased.

"Miss Fox is asleep, Mr. Lennox," the nanny whispered. "You should take her to bed. She needs her rest."

He realized Diana's head was now leaning against his shoulder, her arm loosely entwined with his. He smiled. The warmth inside his chest made him feel drowsy with happiness but also a hint of bittersweetness that he could not explain. As though he would lose all this far too soon.

"You're right, Mrs. Chesterfield. Thank you. I will be back momentarily."

"You should rest too, Mr. Lennox. I can stay. You'll do the wee child no good if you are half-dead."

He turned and caught Diana in his arms, then stood to carry her out of the room. One of the footmen was still awake and walking down the corridor.

"Which room did Rosalind have prepared for Miss Fox?" he asked.

"The Garden Room."

"Thank you." Rafe carried his sleeping charge down the corridor, just past his own room. It was one of the prettier rooms, designed for ladies with pale-green walls and lavish flowers printed in chaotic but lovely gold patterns against the green satin wallpaper.

He laid Diana down on the bed, where she roused slightly.

"What's happening?" Diana wiped her eyes and tried to sit up. "Where is Isla?"

"She is faring much better now." Rafe's throat was suddenly tight as he realized her first thoughts had been of his child. "You and I have been ordered by Mrs. Chester-field to rest. Sleep. We will send word to Foxglove about what has happened and inform them that you will remain here tonight."

Diana blinked slowly, then lay back in the bed as he pulled the blankets up around her body, tucking her in as though she were a child.

"Were you truly a rakehell?" Diana asked in a whisper. "You seem far too"—she yawned—"*lovely* . . . to be so dangerous."

Her lashes fell closed, and he knew she was asleep.

She thought him lovely? Why did that make his heart swell and make him want to chuckle at the same time?

His chest clenched as he gazed down at her. This fire-brand of a woman turned into a helplessly sweet kitten when she felt safe, and damn if that didn't make him feel like a hero.

Rafe leaned down and lightly kissed her lips, wanting so much more and knowing he couldn't dare.

"Soon," he whispered instead. "*Soon*."

He put a fresh log on the newly lit fire, secured the fire grate around it, and walked back to his own bedchamber to sleep alone.

CHAPTER 13

Diana's first thought upon waking was of the little girl, how she'd been so cold, shivering and full of terror. She changed into the clean gown that someone had left for her on the foot of the bed and rushed into the hall, grasping a footman's arm as he passed by.

"How is Isla?" she demanded, her heart pounding with dread. The house was far too quiet. In her experience, a quiet house meant death had paid a call.

"She's fine, Miss Fox," the young man assured her. "She slept through the night and ate a hearty breakfast this morning. She is still in bed. The doctor visited this morning and said she was much recovered. He believes it was more the shock from the storm rather than the rain that made her ill."

"Thank you." Diana sagged against the wall, her legs wobbly. A thought occurred to her. "Heavens," she muttered as she felt the world starting to spin. "My staff must be frantic. I didn't mean to stay the night here."

The footman smiled. "Rest easy, Miss Fox. Word was

sent yesterday that you were to remain as a guest after you saved Miss Isla's life. Your butler replied with a thank-you and said to tell you that you should rest. He also sent over a selection of gowns and other necessary things for you to wear."

Peele wanted her to rest? Impossible. They had so much to do. There was another robbery to plan because they had mouths to feed and a house still to run. Paying off their current debts didn't save them from future debts. Her head ached with the sudden rush of anxiety. Diana pressed a hand to her chest as it tightened, and she shut her eyes tight, forcing herself to breathe, praying it would clear her head.

The footman placed a careful hand on her arm. "Miss Fox? Are you unwell?"

A deep, smooth voice cut straight through her sudden panic. "What's the matter?"

Diana lifted her head and saw Mr. Lennox—*Rafe*—standing in the corridor, his eyes focused on her in clear concern. It was a wild relief to see him there, despite the embarrassment she felt at having such a display of weakness in front of him.

"She appears to be unwell, Mr. Lennox," the footman said, which only deepened the flush of shame in Diana's cheeks. She didn't feel unwell, *ever*. She couldn't afford to.

"Thank you, Sampson. I will escort her to somewhere she can sit down." Rafe dismissed the footman and took his place at Diana's elbow. He took her arm, tucking it around his, and she leaned into his body to absorb the heat that emanated from him. He wore no coat, and she could feel his firm muscles through the cloth of his billowing sleeves. He continued to watch her with those fathomless blue eyes. The scent of rain and a faint masculine cologne teased her nose, making her want to lean in closer and inhale deeply.

They stood together until she regained her equilibrium, and he continued to hold her by the waist and let her hold on to his arm. The heat in her face subsided, and the anxiety in her chest eased.

"You look much recovered now, sweetheart. Would you care to join me for breakfast?" He said the word *sweetheart* so sweetly that it brought a tremble to her lips, which she bit to hide before she was able to respond. She gazed into his face, enraptured by those bright-blue eyes, eyes she secretly wished belonged to someone else . . . Yet at the same time, she wanted that man to be this man.

But it was impossible for a man of Rafe Lennox's station to resort to robbing coaches. He was of the landed gentry, gifted with all the creature comforts a man could need, and he had a warm and loving family. There was no need for him to become a highwayman, and that reality pinched at her heart.

But she had to admit that this man was just as enticing to her, just as fascinating and engaging, albeit in a far different way than the mysterious Tyburn. Rafe possessed a wild intensity even as he played the role of a courtly gentleman. In the last several years, she'd forgotten how exciting such feelings could be. She'd had her head down, her body overworked, her mind plagued with fear and anxiety about the future. But whenever Rafe was near, she seemed to come back to the self she wanted to be again.

"Breakfast would be lovely. I believe that should put me to rights."

Rafe's eyes twinkled. "Very well, but you will deprive

me of the pleasure of seeing to your every need if you are no longer unwell."

See to her every need? No one had done that in years . . . no one had offered except that wicked highwayman. The thought was so tempting, to let herself be cared for, but she couldn't.

As if the gentleman could read her mind, Rafe chuckled. "That is twice this morning that the women in my life have indicated I was not needed. Isla was most insistent that she was a lady, and ladies do not need cuddling from their fathers. I think she was a bit embarrassed after all the fuss we made yesterday. I cuddled her anyway, and it is a great pity I cannot offer you the same treatment. Unless you wish it, of course. In which case, I shall place myself fully at your disposal for any and all cuddling you desire."

The man was teasing her most scandalously, and yet the thought of him holding her, kissing her, whispering comforting thoughts . . . It made her chest clench with desperate longing.

They were halfway down the stairs when she suddenly halted.

"Diana?" Rafe said in concern. "What is it?"

She looked once more into Rafe's face as she realized that she had not thought of Tyburn last night or this morning. She'd been thinking of *this* man, Rafe, kissing her.

What a fickle heart she must have to let it wander between two men. Still, a little voice whispered in her head that Mr. Lennox was a man she *could* marry, a man who could offer her a future and security, even friendship. The same could not be said of the mysterious Tyburn. It would be wise to let the fantasy of Tyburn go and think of a possible real future with this man, assuming Rafe would even look at her as a prospective wife. But they'd only just met. It wasn't as if he would propose, or that she would accept such a proposal. She was letting her mind get ahead of itself, as it often did.

"I . . . I'm all right," she said, and he led her the rest of the way to the dining room.

"Would you allow me to prepare you a plate?" Rafe asked. "Is there anything you particularly dislike?"

"Kippers. No kippers, please." She sat in a chair as Rafe removed each lid from the chafing dishes and spooned food onto a plate, then brought it to her. A footman poured her a cup of tea and then stepped into the corridor to speak to the butler, and Rafe joined her once he'd served his own plate. He sat across from her at the table. She was suddenly very aware that it was just the two of them here.

"I want to thank you," Rafe said. "You saved my child's life yesterday."

Goosebumps broke out on her skin as the events of the day before replayed in her mind. The fierce rain, the assault of lightning, and the barrage of thunder. It was a miracle none of them had been hurt.

"You cannot possibly know what that little girl means to me. She is . . ." Rafe's voice grew thick with emotion. "She is my world. She'd saved me when I stood on the precipice of darkness. She pulled me back into the light. The world underestimates the value of a child's love. It is unconditional, held back by no limits. Such a love can save any lost soul."

Diana was moved by his frankness. "You are quite right. When we grow up, we begin to limit everything in our lives, even our love." She stared down at her plate. "I was more than glad to help you yesterday. There is something about Isla that . . ." She couldn't find the words to say what she wished to. "Heavens, I don't know what it is I mean to say, but I feel a *connection* to her."

Some of the worry and concern in Rafe's eyes vanished beneath his natural charm.

"That is the magic of adorable orphans," Rafe said. "One cannot deny the urge to love them and feel connected to them. I never had much time or interest in children before, but the moment I met Isla, she simply stole away any reservations I might have had."

Diana smiled back, remembering how she'd instantly wanted to hug Isla and listen to her chatter on about Mrs. Crumpet. "She's impossible not to adore."

"I was thinking perhaps I could escort you home?" Rafe offered. "When you feel up to it, of course."

Any protest she might have had died upon her lips as their gazes locked across the table and she found herself saying, "Yes."

"Good." Rafe then engaged her in conversation, lifting her somewhat down spirits. He peppered her with questions, everything from her favorite flower to the book she'd been reading lately. She confessed that she had not had much time to read as of late, but she adored novels, and when it came to flowers, she was rather bewitched by the amaranth. Their reddish stems often had spines protecting themselves from being plucked, but they were a wild, exotic-looking bloom that, when planted well, could grow in colorful bracts and dazzle one's senses with showering inflorescences.

"And you?" she asked as they dined.

"Well, my favorite flower . . . How to choose? I mean, there are so many! I'm rather obsessed with flowers, as all serious men must be. It's all we can think of, and you ask me to choose?" Rafe began, making her burst into sudden giggles.

"No, I meant your favorite *book*," she corrected, then giggled again when he gave her a look of mock effrontery.

"You mean to say you do not care what my favorite flower is? You wound me, my dear Diana." He caressed her name with a friendly intimacy she hadn't heard anyone use in a long time. It made her feel like she was no longer on the outside looking in upon a warm, intimate world. That single use of her name had taken her in and rescued her from the cold.

"Well, what is it?" she asked, desperately trying not to laugh.

"*The Sketch Book of Geoffrey Crayon*, by that Irving fellow. Particularly his story 'The Legend of Sleepy Hollow'— magical story. Frightening too . . . What?" He halted when she burst into giggles again.

"Now I meant your favorite *flower*." Diana had to wipe tears from her eyes because she was laughing too hard, probably partly in relief from the stress of the last few days, but also because he was so amusing.

"You change your mind rather quickly. Has anyone ever told you that?"

"I do not!" she insisted. "I suppose I do . . . no, not really."

Rafe chuckled. "Well, 'tis your woman's prerogative."

"Yes, it is. Now about those flowers . . . ," she said, unable to resist teasing him.

"Oh, that . . . well, I like daffodils. The little ones. They are so strong, given their size," he answered quite seriously. "They remind me of Isla."

"I rather agree," she said with a smile. "She is a most darling child."

She finished her tea and ate the last bit of her toast, then licked the marmalade from her fingertips. Rafe's blue eyes grew hot with interest, and Diana self-consciously cleared her throat, which made his gaze lift to meet her own.

"I must thank your brother and his wife, and you for your hospitality and care, but I believe I'm feeling well enough to go home now. Do you still wish to escort me?"

"Of course." He rose from his chair at the same moment she did. "Let me call for my phaeton to be brought around. After I see to Isla, we shall depart."

❦

RAFE HAD HIS PHAETON AND DIANA'S HORSE BROUGHT around while he went up to the nursery to see Isla before he departed. His daughter was sitting up in bed, the color having returned to her cherubic cheeks. She was talking to her doll, Mrs. Crumpet, while her nanny watched, a book abandoned in her lap. Isla saw that he was wearing his coat, hat, and gloves, and her eyes filled with tears.

"You're *leaving*, Papa?"

"What? No, of course not." He rushed over to sit on the edge of her bed. "I am simply escorting Miss Fox home, that is all."

Isla started to push at the coverlet that was tucked up against her little lap. "May I come?"

"Next time, kitten. You're supposed to be resting today." Damnation, it was hard to say no to this child when she sniffled and clutched her doll to her chest.

Isla managed a brave little nod.

"But I *will* tell Miss Fox that you and I shall call upon her for tea soon, if she is available."

Isla brightened at this, and Rafe leaned forward to kiss her forehead. Then he reached above her to retrieve the portraits of her parents from a little bookshelf by the bed and placed them on her lap. He'd gotten them out earlier this morning when he'd checked on her for the hundredth time.

"Now, they will keep you company until I return." He showed her the portraits and then tucked them into her lap so she could look at them.

He sent a silent prayer to the two people who'd brought this child into the world and thanked them for letting him have Isla in his life. Mrs. Chesterfield assured him she wouldn't take her eyes off the girl, and Rafe left the nursery to meet Diana downstairs.

It was strange to be with Diana as himself, not hiding behind a black domino and disguising his voice. But as strange as it was, it was also easy to be with her. She was quiet, it was true, but once he got her talking, she opened up like a blossom after a much-needed rain. She laughed often, the sound delightful and addictive to his ears. Without the danger of his secret identity, she seemed more relaxed.

"Ready?" he asked as they came down the steps to his phaeton. He grasped her by the waist and lifted her into the vehicle. It was certainly forward to touch her so, but after all they'd been through, he simply touched her without thinking. She blushed but said nothing as he climbed into the other side of the carriage. Her horse was tied to the back of the phaeton so it could trail behind them.

"I suppose one of us should comment on the impropriety of the two of us unmarried, unrelated persons traveling together," she said, a hint of amusement in her tone.

"I won't tell anyone if you won't." Rafe flashed her another grin. "It's far from the most scandalous thing I've done," he admitted. "It's actually rather tame compared to some of my past exploits."

Diana shot a glance at him. "I've heard you were quite the rake."

"Has Rosalind been spilling my deep, dark secrets?" Rafe asked with a chuckle.

"More like singing your praises. I think she secretly adores you."

"Truly?" He guided the pair of horses down the road, loosely adjusting the ribbons of leather in his gloved hands. "I never thought she'd . . . Well, we had a bit of a rough start, she and I. Neither of us liked the other upon first meeting."

"Whatever she thought of you before, it has changed," Diana assured him.

"I suppose I've gotten used to others thinking ill of me. It comes with the territory, being the ne'er-do-well brother." Blast, the truth always spilled out of his lips whenever this woman was near him.

"Ne'er-do-well? I see no ne'er-do-well here. We can change who we are, you know," Diana said sagely.

He held her gaze a moment before turning back to the road. "You believe that?"

"I do. Sometimes fate forces us to become someone out of necessity; other times we find the strength within ourselves to do it on our own. I was a silly young creature when I was little, but I changed for the better."

Rafe's mind turned back to the past. "Aren't we all supposed to be silly when we're young? Isn't that the gift of youth? To live without fear of consequences?"

"I suppose it is, but one cannot be young or innocent forever." There was a hint of sorrow in that voice, reminding him of all she had been through.

"I heard about your family. I am sorry," he said after a moment of silence.

"Thank you. It hasn't been easy. I'm just grateful the estate was not entailed to some distant male relative who would swoop in and take my home. My father was wise enough to leave it to me as part of my inheritance."

Diana was ever surprising him, leaving him guessing in the most fascinated sort of way what she was truly capable of. He'd learned much about her over the last day. She'd lived on her own with no family and had earned the fierce loyalty of her servants who had become her new family. She was a brave woman, a clever thief, a woman who would risk her life for a child she barely knew, and she was simply . . . *magnificent*. Ashton had once said that when he looked at Rosalind, she seemed to glow like the sun. He'd thought his brother mad at the time, but now he understood that a woman *could* glow. Even a woman who thought the world had turned its back on her, and she was weary enough to give in, but hadn't. That sort of woman glowed, even if she could not see her own shine.

Rafe vowed in that moment to find a way to show her how simply incredible she truly was. But beyond that, he wanted to be there for her, to help her, to give her shelter in his arms. To cover her face with kisses when she wanted to weep and coax smiles out of her instead. He was puzzled at this sudden change in himself, but he couldn't deny the truth of it. He wanted to think about a future with someone. And not just anyone, but this woman.

"Would you consider marrying someday?" Rafe felt his tongue thicken. This was a question he'd never thought he'd ask, even in a roundabout way, of any woman.

"I . . ." She paused, her eyes roving over the countryside. "If I was certain I could trust the man I married. He would have to be willing to help me take care of my home, my lands, and my servants who have been my family. I would need him to understand that marriage does not make him my master, no matter what the law says. He would be my partner, my equal." She dared to meet his gaze, and he saw a flutter of hope in her eyes, but it was quickly snuffed out by resignation. No doubt because of his reputation she expected him to be like every other man she'd met.

"That, I fear, is a tall order to ask of most gentlemen," she continued. "They believe they are entitled to settle down into my home and my world without proving they deserve to be there. It is a hubris I cannot abide." She smoothed her skirts nervously. "And you? Would *you* ever consider marriage?"

He knew they were both dancing around a very important question that carried the weight of their fates, so his answer had to be carefully given.

"I would. If I found a woman I could trust with myself and with Isla. I know my reputation is questionable, but . . ." He hesitated.

"The right woman will not care about your reputation. Reputation is what others think of you. The right woman would only care about your character, about who *you* are." Diana's words slid directly into the center of his chest, curling up there in a warm ball that made him feel . . . light in a way he hadn't in a long time.

The night his father died, he'd lost his way, but the night Isla had chosen *him* as her father, he'd stumbled back onto the path that would lead him home. And the night he had taken Diana to bed in the hunting lodge, it was as though his home was finally in view. He was so close to finding himself, to being the man he should have been all those years ago. Yet he also feared how much this woman mattered to him. She had slept with him when he'd been Tyburn, and now she was alone with him as Rafe. He knew his little thief's secret, but she did not know his. What if he asked her to choose Rafe and she secretly wanted Tyburn? It was a damned hard thing to find himself jealous of himself. Perhaps he should do what he'd always done and leap into the unknown, trusting to fate, or at least luck.

"Diana . . . I know we've only just met, but I would like to see you more often."

"What are you asking?" she replied, a little breathless.

"I suppose I'm asking, in a frightfully awkward way . . . if I would be allowed to . . . court you?"

Her eyes looked deep into his, and he wished he knew what she was searching for there.

"You wish to *court* me?"

"Is it too soon? I can pretend to wait." He tried to tease her with his words, but he sounded far too earnest.

"Um . . . I . . ." Her hesitation felt like the sword of Damocles above his head.

"Do not answer now. Please take some time to think upon it. For now, let us simply enjoy our ride together. It is a splendid day, and sometimes it's best to just soak in the sunshine and remember to breathe."

They rode in companionable silence to her home, and he had a chance to take it in with new eyes. He'd only ever seen it at night and in the early dawn.

Foxglove was *magnificent*. The old stone manor house was covered with lush ivy on one side, and gardens ran wild on the opposite. It was steeped in character, with its beautiful gables and wild, ancient sort of beauty that only some old homes could manage. The windows winked in the sunlight, as if to welcome him. No wonder Diana was fighting to keep this place. It *was* a home.

Rafe halted the phaeton in front of the steps as an elderly groom came out to meet them.

"Good afternoon, Nelson," Diana said with a smile.

"Glad to see you back, Miss Diana." The old groom gave Rafe an appraising look as he took charge of the horses.

"Will you be staying here, sir?" he asked Rafe.

Rafe looked to Diana. It was her choice, but he hoped she would ask him to.

"Yes. That is, if you would like to?" Diana looked at Rafe, her face flushing a little. "I can offer tea."

"Tea would be marvelous." Even though they just had breakfast an hour ago, he would not turn down any chance to know Diana better and see her world.

"Nelson, would you please see to Mr. Lennox's horses and mine?" She pointed at her own horse, which was tied up to the back of the phaeton.

"Yes, Miss Diana."

A butler greeted them at the door, and again Rafe had the sense that this man was measuring him. Rather than take it personally, Rafe was glad the servants were so protective of his little fire drake.

"Mr. Lennox, this is my butler, Mr. Peele. Mr. Peele, this is Mr. Rafe Lennox, Lord Lennox's younger brother. He was kind enough to escort me home, and I have invited him to stay for tea."

"Mr. Lennox," Peele said gravely and took Rafe's hat and gloves.

"A pleasure, Mr. Peele," Rafe replied. Diana guided him to the sitting room. His keen eyes took in the state of the interior of the house. It was well cared for, but he did notice that repairs were needed. Walls needed repainting, doors needed sanding and re-lacquering. New fabrics were required for furniture. He knew that Diana likely didn't wish for him to see any of this, so he pretended not to. It seemed that even with the debts paid there wasn't enough left over to renovate this home, which made him wonder whether she'd end up in debt again all too soon. The cost of maintaining a house like this in good condition was certainly expensive. He knew that all too well because Ashton so often reminded him of the expenses of their own estate.

It seemed he and Diana had more in common than he realized.

She gestured to a settee. "Please, sit." She pulled a bell cord by the door to summon for the tea service, then sat down in a chair facing him. She adjusted the skirts of her gown, clearly nervous.

"Diana, you need not worry," he said. "I fear I put you in a difficult spot by bringing up the matter of courtship so soon. It's just that . . . after what happened in the field, and how you stayed with me and Isla, I feel as though I've known you for years." Rafe knew he sounded desperate, perhaps even a little mad. But when she spoke, she stunned him.

"I feel the same, as though I've always known you, yet I *barely* know you. I think that is what makes me rather uneasy. I know nothing of your life, nor you of mine."

Rafe took a chance and stood. He grasped her hand and then gently pulled her toward him so that she would sit down beside him on the settee. "Then tell me about yourself, Diana. Let me peer into your heart and you into mine, so that our souls will be satisfied." He clasped her trembling hand in his own.

I am your wicked highwayman. Your Tyburn. You can trust me. He wanted to say those words, but it was too dangerous for her to know the truth, and the last thing he wanted to do was put her in danger. Diana's brown eyes met his, and that flash of lightning zinged from her into him. She searched his face, seeking answers he wished he could give.

"Fate gave me Isla," said Rafe. "And yesterday, I believe fate brought you to me. I am willing to trust in fate again."

She licked her lips, her soft breath escaping in a rush. Her knees bumped his as she angled to face him.

"You would tell me everything? No secrets?" she asked.

"No secrets . . ." The lie was bittersweet and softened only by the fact that someday, when it was safe, he would tell her the full truth.

"Tell me everything, from the beginning. Tell me the story of your life." She squeezed his hands, and something like a wave deep beneath the sea moved through him, filling every part of him with her essence, and all she had done was let him bare his own soul without fear.

He told Diana about his childhood, about the night his father died and how everything in his family had changed as a result. He told her about Caddington and Phelps, and how his father had sent him home, but he'd left the coach and gotten hurt and watched his father get struck by a passing carriage. He'd never told *anyone* else about it. Even though Ashton had been there that night, they'd never spoken of what had transpired. She kept silent until he drew in a breath.

"Did you say Lord *Caddington?*" she asked, her honey-brown eyes swirling with turbulent storms.

"Yes, a man who is both foul and dangerous. I've kept my distance from him ever since that night."

"I believe that is wise," she agreed. "He isn't to be trusted."

Fear spiked in him. "You know him?"

"I've had the displeasure of meeting him once, about a month ago. He interrogated me after I was a victim of a highway coach robbery."

Rafe tensed. "What did you tell him?"

"Nothing. I despised the man so much upon first meeting him that I purposely misled him. Unfortunately, two of the men who were riding in my coach when I was robbed remembered some details that I had withheld. But for my part, I hope those thieves never get caught."

The tension in Rafe's shoulders eased. So that was how Caddington knew their names. That fact had been on his mind since Ashton had shown him the article in the newspaper. Of course, any of their other victims could have shared such information, but now he knew it hadn't been Diana. She had kept her promise to Tyburn.

"Caddington is set on catching them," Diana continued, her voice still quiet. "They've robbed several coaches of his, ones that had money belonging to him."

Rafe's brows rose. He'd had a few lucky nights with Will and Caspian in the last few months where casks of money had been on the coaches they'd robbed, but he'd had no idea they were connected to Caddington. He had to hide the surge of grim pride at knowing he'd wounded the bastard's pocketbook more than once.

"We should speak no more of him," Diana said.

"Agreed. And now it's your turn." He stood and she rose as well. "Shall we walk and you can tell me about yourself?" he offered.

"All right." The door to the sitting room opened, and a middle-aged woman carried in a tea tray.

"Oh, Mrs. Ripley, I'm so sorry," said Diana. "But I think we are going to walk for a bit. We shall drink it when we return."

The housekeeper nodded. "Yes, of course, Miss Fox. So sorry for the delay. I'll reheat it for when you return."

Rafe realized that no footman or maid had brought the tea earlier, and they'd talked quite a long time. It made him wonder how understaffed Diana's house was that even a simple tea service was so delayed.

"This way . . ." Diana led Rafe into the corridor, and when she apologized again about the missed tea, he pulled her to a stop and smiled, leaning down to whisper to her.

"I don't give a fig about the tea, darling. I'm here for *you*. And it's your turn. Tell me everything, and you simply must start at the beginning."

The smile that spread across her face shone with an inner starlight he adored beyond measure.

He could hear the mix of love and pain in her voice as

she shared her childhood with him. They entered a gallery of paintings, and she stopped before one of two small girls.

Diana nodded at the portrait. "That is me and my sister, Eleanor."

The dark-haired one he recognized was Diana. She had been an adorable child, with pink cheeks and a bright-green dress. She was perhaps four years old. His gaze moved to the older girl, and his chest tightened. She reminded him of Isla, or rather what Isla might look like when she was a few years older, when her face turned from a small child to that of a young girl. He was both excited for and dreading that day.

His daughter was going to grow up so fast, and he feared he would miss it every time he closed his eyes. Many parents longed for their children to be children forever, but Rafe's mother had told him when he was young that the joy of children was not keeping them as children, but watching them become the people they were meant to be. It was the journey, not the beginning, that mattered. A parent's true joy was seeing their child at every stage of life.

"She reminds me of Isla a little," Rafe mused as he studied the older girl's features. There was something about the shape of her eyes and her mouth that he found fascinating.

Diana stared at her sister's portrait, smiling sadly. "They both have that same look of mischief, don't they? Eleanor was certainly mischievous when we were young. But as we got older and Mother grew unwell, Eleanor withdrew from everyone. Even though Mother was unwell, Papa still had her. But when Eleanor pulled away . . . I was lost. In some ways, I suppose I still am."

Rafe caught Diana's chin and turned her face toward

his. "You aren't lost. You've made a life here. And I daresay you still have a family." He nodded at the footmen watching her with concern on their faces.

Tears suddenly filled her eyes, and she lifted a hand to brush them away.

"Allow me." With gentle fingers, Rafe brushed the tears from her cheeks.

"I rather feel as though I am but one moment away from failing at everything," Diana confessed. Rafe's heart was pierced with the sharp echo of her pain.

"I know that feeling all too well. My brother and I were close once, but my mother blamed me for my father's death, just as I blamed myself. In the end, I lost her, Thomasina, Ashton, and even little Joanna. I was never good enough. I made no money, only trouble. I never proved my worth, not the way Ashton does."

Diana drew in a breath as he wrapped his arms around her.

"Wouldn't it be a wonderful thing to simply be enough for those we love?" she asked.

He rubbed her back, feeling the stares of the footmen behind him, knowing he was taking too damned many liberties with her. But he had held Diana before, had kissed her tears away before. He had made love to her and known with clear conviction that she wasn't simply enough—she was *everything*. She was a cosmos unto herself, wrapped in mystery and majesty.

He wanted to woo her with words, with flowers, with walks in the gardens, but something inside him warned him that he didn't have the luxury of time. So he courted her with a kiss.

Rafe bent his head, his lips caressing hers, and sweet

agony rippled through him, so hard that he trembled. He'd never thought a kiss could contain the power to save a life, but in that moment she saved his. Diana held every gentle promise of love and passion's fire in her kiss. He tasted an unspoken vow of understanding and acceptance and returned it with his own.

We are the same, my little star. Shine upon me so that I may not fear the darkness within me.

When their lips parted, she gazed at him with wide brown eyes that held the night sky and all the stars within them. She wet her lips and spoke.

"Are you certain we've never met before?"

CHAPTER 14

Rafe, Will, and Caspian waited in the rain-soaked night not too far off from the road, their horses restless as they hid within a copse of trees.

"Are you certain we've never met before?"

Even a week later, Diana's innocent question still haunted Rafe.

He had managed to convince Diana they had never met before the day she came to see Rosalind for tea, even though the lie was bitter on his lips. The way she'd looked at him, those brown eyes still searching for a hint of Tyburn that he was forced to conceal, made his heart clench with pain. Every instinct in him demanded he confess all of his truths to her.

He had never been overly bothered by telling lies, but lying to Diana, even to protect her, seemed to deepen the black stain it laid upon his soul. Yet it was a worthy burden to bear in order to protect her. Someday he would tell her the full truth, when he was done with these raids, when it was safe, but that was a distant, uncertain day.

"Molly promised the coach was coming this way tonight," Caspian whispered as he adjusted his grip on the reins.

Molly, one of their trusted informants who worked in the taproom at the Wild Boar coaching inn, was more than happy to tell what she knew of the passengers who passed through the inn's doorway, so long as Caspian took her upstairs and shared her bed. Caspian, far more reserved than Will, always came back down the stairs after such encounters with his face red from embarrassment but his eyes still half-lidded with satisfaction.

"One of these days, that poor wench will expect you to propose to her," Will said with a chuckle.

Caspian kept his focus on the road ahead of them. "She won't. I told her I cannot marry, ever. Besides, she thinks I'm some poor fellow from Yorkshire." He added this last in a Yorkshire accent, which made Rafe and Will chuckle. Yet Rafe heard the pain in Caspian's tone, which mirrored his own. They led lonely, dangerous lives. He was glad he could protect Diana from it, even though it meant risking his own to find a way to take care of her and Isla.

Unfortunately, the news from Molly hadn't all been good. Molly had warned them that the guard for this coach had been doubled from two to four, so they most likely expected trouble. It made sense, given those imposters working in the same area. More robberies meant more efforts at security. "Is Molly sure about the number of guards?" Rafe asked.

"She's never led us astray before," said Caspian. "Most likely, Caddington is tired of having us steal his money."

This should have worried Rafe. More guards meant they probably had orders to fight back. He should have been focused on Caddington, on the coach they would soon be robbing and how it would be far more dangerous this time. But all he could think about was Diana.

He had visited her every day during the last week, courting her in earnest. She'd had her doubts when he'd shown up with bouquets of flowers, asking her for long walks or rides in the country, but eventually she had agreed. The time they'd spent together had been satisfying in a way that bedding a woman never had been.

His brother had noticed a change in him and didn't tease him whenever he mentioned he was going to see Diana. He would simply smile and nod. Rafe had stopped trying to earn his brother's approval years ago, but now that he had it, he wasn't sure how to react. All he knew was that he needed to be with Diana. Little else other than Isla mattered to him.

He ached to see Diana just as much when he rode away from the house as when he had first arrived. She had become his obsession, but in a quiet, deeper way than anything he'd ever been fascinated with in his life. He'd been able to bare his soul to her, to tell her nearly every secret, save the one that had him wearing his mask tonight.

Twice he'd taken Diana and Isla on picnics. Everything had felt so easy with the three of them, so right. It amazed him how much Isla was like Diana, how she'd turn her head at an angle, or the way she'd nibble on tarts or biscuits. He became overwhelmed with a sense of blissful contentment whenever he looked at these two ladies in his life.

Things were going so well that he was becoming frustrated.

He shouldn't be allowing thoughts of her to distract him from the here and now. Now that he knew Caddington was delivering money to London, he would strike at the man in the only way that could hurt him—by emptying his pockets again and again. And if it furthered Rafe's ability to support Isla and Diana, then it was all the better.

The sound of hooves and wheels could now be heard. "Here it comes," Will hissed, calling Rafe's attention back to the road.

Rafe and Caspian drew their pistols. They each had two more tucked under their cloaks because of Molly's warning. They'd taken coaches with just as many men before, ones ready to fight to keep their purses. Will and Caspian were as well trained as Rafe in the art of swordplay as well as with pistols. They would be able to handle the additional men tonight, but it was important not to be overconfident.

The coach came around the bend of the road. Just as Rafe was ready to call the charge, a crack of gunfire interrupted him.

Impossible. They couldn't already be spotted, could they?

Just then, three cloaked riders emerged from the woods on the opposite side of the road, closer to the coach than Rafe and his companions.

"Who the *devil* are they?" Will snarled as his horse reared up and stomped its hooves down in fury at being held back.

"Wait," said Caspian. "You don't think those are . . . ?"

"I'm afraid so," Rafe growled. "It seems the men impersonating us are no longer content with taking our identities—now they are taking our targets as well."

"The bloody cheek of them," said Will. "Taking what's rightfully ours to steal."

Rafe watched the three imposters circle the coach. Their shouts were lost in the wind, but he knew what was happening. The night was not yet too dark, dusk having only passed an hour before, and rain clouds were only partly scattered across the sky.

Crack! Without warning, the four armed guards opened fire, smoke billowing out through the partially open coach doors, the flash of gunfire seen as white-hot bursts of light. After the imposters were caught off guard, the guards leapt out of the coach and pressed their advantage in the field of battle.

"The fools didn't come armed like we did," Rafe said as he realized what he was watching. He loosened his reins a bit as his horse danced with agitation.

"Pays to have a Molly on your side, eh?" Will said with a sly look to Caspian.

Rafe started to move forward, but Caspian grabbed his arm. "Rafe, you do not mean to help them? Surely . . ."

"I never like an unfair fight. It could easily have been us." Rafe pulled free of Caspian's hand and dug his heels into his horse's flanks, charging out of their hiding spot and onto the road.

The scene ahead of him was chaos. Men were shouting and firing guns, lighting up the surrounding gloom with brief flashes. The rain had caused the coach's wheels to sink deep into muddy ruts. Horses screamed and one of the three imposters fell from his saddle. Rafe halted his horse twenty yards away and lifted his pistol, aiming for one of the armed men from the coach, and fired with a thunderous crack.

The man went down, howling as he clutched his leg. Two others were focused on a second imposter who had come to the aid of the first.

"Get back!" Rafe took out his second pistol and fired

at one of the guards. The imposter, who had crouched over his wounded comrade, whirled and lashed out with a slender blade, forcing one of the armed brutes back a step.

But he was not so easily deterred. The guard moved in and struck the thief across the face with a meaty fist, knocking the man out cold next to his companion. The guard now lunged forward, a wicked blade in his hand, intent on finishing the job.

Rafe removed a third pistol from his cloak and fired into the man's back. The guard collapsed onto the muddy road. There was no time to ruminate on his sins. The thunder of hooves behind him told him Caspian and Will had joined the fray.

Their arrival gave Rafe a chance to see to the wounded thieves. Rafe first checked on the man who'd been shot. The one who'd been knocked unconscious was already starting to come around and groaned, touching his face. The imposters tensed as Rafe approached and slid off his horse, still wearing his mask.

"Ye'd best get him up and on his horse and be off or else ye'll all be dead," Rafe snapped in his Scottish brogue. "I'll help ye."

He grabbed the man who'd been shot and helped him mount his horse. Then he turned to the other man, who mounted his own horse. "Get out of here, now!" he snapped.

The man clutching his injured shoulder whistled sharply, the sound cutting across the road, and the third of the imposter thieves wheeled his horse around and headed straight for them. "Thank you . . ."

Rafe had the sudden urge to reassure the man he'd be

all right, so long as he could get away from here, and prayed the man would.

"Cleanse that wound unless ye wish to die a lingering death. Go!" Rafe smacked his hand on the horse's flank, sending the beast flying into the night. Then he spun and dove back into the fight. He flipped his hold on his last pistol to catch it by the handle and swung it at one of the men's face. The man went down hard, and Rafe punched another man in the stomach, causing him to double over.

"Oxford! Grab the money box!" Rafe shouted to Will, who was closest to the open coach doors.

Will ducked inside the coach and retrieved a box about a foot and a half long. Caspian helped him carry it to the horses and secure it to the back of Will's saddle.

The wounded guard spat at Rafe from where he knelt, clutching his injured leg. "You killed him!" He pointed a finger at the man lying face down in the mud. The man Rafe had shot in the back. "You'll hang for this!"

"Someday. But not today," Rafe said coldly. He felt little sympathy for any man who willingly worked for someone like Caddington. He returned to his horse and mounted up. He met Will and Caspian in the woods a safe distance away.

"Take the money to Lennox House. Hide it in the stables until we can sort all this out. Tell Rosalind anything you like about how I invited you to stay at the house."

"What about you?" Caspian asked.

"I'm going after those fools. I need to warn them off. We got lucky. With Caddington setting traps like this, they'll likely get killed next time. I won't have that on my conscience."

"Be careful," Will said.

"I will." Rafe then turned his horse westward.

It wasn't long before he picked up the trail of the other three highwaymen. In their haste to flee and their need to see their wounded man home, they had ridden together in a straight line directly away from the coach. The rain would wash away their trail in a few hours, but Rafe had enough knowledge of the area to determine the route they were taking. Once he had them in sight, he kept his distance to avoid detection. Trailing them to a wooded area, he gave pause once he realized exactly where he was.

He was on land abutting Foxglove.

Hellfire. Diana had dangerous men living near her. What if those thieves came across her when she was riding alone? Rafe was all too aware that he and his companions were the exception to the rule when it came to highwaymen. She could be in danger if these men couldn't be trusted.

The three riders left their horses in a small stable at the edge of the estate and seemed to disappear into the earth. Granted, the night was growing dark and the rain had thickened, but Rafe was convinced of what he saw. One of the men had pulled up the ground, and they had all vanished beneath. An underground hideout, perhaps? A clever idea, that.

He left his horse in the stable with the others, praying that nothing would happen to his mount while he investigated further.

He reached the spot where the men had disappeared and found a trapdoor. It was covered with mud and grass, but he was able to find the lip of the door with his fingers and lift it up. He peered into the hole, and with a careful test of his booted foot, he found the rungs of a ladder leading down into the dark.

He contemplated following the trio of men right away, but he decided it would be best to warn Diana first. If he came back in daylight, he would feel safer about trailing unknown men into an underground tunnel. Even though he had helped these men escape tonight, he still didn't know or trust them, certainly not enough to approach them by himself in a dark passageway on a stormy night.

He set the trapdoor back into place and retrieved his horse from the small stable, then rode to Diana's stables behind her manor house. They were dark and empty of any stable hands. He slipped his horse into an empty stall, knowing it was a risk if any of the stable hands checked the horses and found one that didn't belong, but it was a risk he'd have to take.

He left the stable and headed for the trellis beneath Diana's bedroom window. With care, he climbed up the ivy-covered wood latticework and eased the bay window open just as he'd done that first night he'd gone to see her as Tyburn. He silently dropped down into the room and glanced around. A rushlight had been newly lit, but there was no sign of Diana. Perhaps she hadn't gone to bed and a thoughtful servant had lit the rushlight.

A commotion in the hall sent Rafe ducking behind the curtains that covered half the window. *Blast!* Had his arrival been witnessed after all? The bedchamber door opened and voices carried over to him.

"Sit her on the chair." Rafe recognized the speaker as Diana's butler, Mr. Peele. "What happened, Matthew?"

"We were ambushed," a man who was presumably Matthew said in a shaky voice. "It was a trap. There were twice as many guards this time. It was as though they knew we were coming. We didn't think . . . Lord, we didn't think . . ."

Rafe's heart stilled. Diana's own servants had been the thieves. But why bring the wounded man to Diana's room?

Then he remembered the butler had asked Matthew to sit *her* on the chair.

"Lift her arm into the light," Peele instructed. "I need a better look at the wound."

It couldn't be.

"Ouch!" Diana's voice jerked Rafe out of his stunned silence.

He flung the curtain back, revealing himself. But whatever effect his shocking reveal might have had upon the room's occupants, it paled in comparison to the shock he felt right now.

Diana sat in a chair by the bed, wearing a black pair of trousers and a black shirt and waistcoat. Her hair was hidden beneath a blond wig that resembled his own hair. Her butler, wearing his dressing gown, and a young man who wore the same black clothing as Diana stared at Rafe, mouths agape.

Rafe saw the bloodied, torn sleeve on Diana's left arm, exposing where she'd been shot. She'd been the one he'd helped onto the horse, the one he'd killed a man to save. The woman he loved more than his own life. And that realization struck him like a bullet. She stared at him with a stunned and pained expression that knocked the breath from his lungs.

"Do ye realize what ye've done?" he snarled at the woman whose very beating heart held the key to his own and charged toward her.

DIANA BLINKED, RAINWATER STILL DRIPPING INTO HER eyes. Tyburn was *here*? How was that even possible? Half an hour ago, he'd saved her life by throwing her onto the back of the very horse she'd stolen from him. Then he had resumed the fight against the armed men who had attacked when she and her footmen had stopped the coach. There was no way he could have gotten to her house so fast, no way he could have known she was one of the thieves who had been posing as him and his accomplices. So how was he here? The question thundered in her head almost as loud as her beating heart. That was swiftly followed by a wrench of pain in her heart. She'd thought she'd never see him again. They were but strangers in the night, and she'd fallen in love with Rafe Lennox, a good man, a *perfect* man, a man who gave her in the sunlight what Tyburn could only ever give her by moonlight.

Her insides fluttered with traitorous warmth at the sight of him, yet a deep sadness swiftly overtook her joy. Tonight must be the last time she would see him. There couldn't be another night, not when she was in love with Rafe.

"Do ye realize what ye've done?" Tyburn roared as he charged across the room toward her.

Peele and Matthew threw themselves in front of her, fists raised.

"One more step, sir, and I'll lay you flat," Peele growled at Tyburn.

Diana tugged at Peele's sleeve with her uninjured arm, but Peele ignored her, focused as he was on the intruder.

Tyburn stopped and his gaze went from Peele to Diana, a silent warning that she understood. She had better make her men move, or else he would.

"It's all right, Peele, Matthew. Tyburn and I know each other."

"Tyburn?" Matthew gasped. "Not *the* Tyburn?" His suspicious gaze turned to one of admiration. "You're really him, aren't you? The true highwayman."

"I am." Rafe brushed Peele and Matthew aside so he could bend over Diana. "What the bloody hell have ye gone and done, lass? I came to warn ye about dangerous thieves on yer lands and find ye're *one* of them. Ye're in over yer head more than ye realize." He knelt on one knee and removed a long blade from his boot. Peele made a move toward him, but Rafe shot the man a look that stopped him cold.

"I willna hurt her." Tyburn cut the stained shirt away and set the blade down so he could examine her wound. His knee brushed hers as he leaned in. The scent of rain still clung to him, reminding Diana of the night they'd first met. She suddenly didn't care about her arm. She only cared that this would be the last time she'd ever see him, ever smell him, ever feel the magic of this man's presence. His fingers explored her arm, and his gaze shifted from her wound to her face. She started to lean into him but caught herself.

"Thank Christ, lass. It only grazed ye." He turned to Matthew. "Fetch hot water, brandy, and clean cloths we can cut into strips."

Peele began to protest but then came to his senses and waved at Matthew. "Do what he says."

Diana winced as Tyburn's fingers carefully examined the skin around her wound. She took in the sight of his blue eyes as they studied her wound, and the way his lips looked so soft and kissable. It was a welcome distraction, and it even reminded her of how Rafe made her feel. It was a curse to long for two beautiful men who were so alike and yet so different.

"Ye canna send for a doctor. He'd ask too many questions. But I dinna think ye'll need stitches, so long as ye keep the wound clean and well tended." He spoke calmly, yet she saw the fear in the highwayman's eyes. A fear for her, because he *cared* for her.

His gaze met hers as his lips thinned, and his anger returned. "What were ye thinking, lass? It wasna enough to rob me blind, ye had to go and rob the whole countryside as well? Ye could've been killed," Tyburn hissed. "Did ye no ken what that would do to yer house, yer staff, *to me?*" Her heart leapt traitorously at the thought that somehow she'd won a place in this mysterious man's heart.

Diana lifted her chin, her pride stung. "We've been quite successful in our efforts, until tonight. This would have been our third robbery."

"Oh, I ken. I read the papers. Imagine my surprise when I read about robberies that I didna even remember committing."

"It seemed a safer way to go about things." She removed her blond wig and sighed as she set it on the table beside her. "I don't know how those men were ready for us, but they were." Her arm ached with an almost numbing pain now, and her entire body was weary.

"Oh, ye dinna ken how they were waiting for ye? Well,

perhaps I can shed some light on that. Put yerself in Caddington's mind. He was used to a certain degree of loss before, but suddenly his coaches are being robbed *twice* as much. How would ye think he would respond?"

Diana blinked. She'd hoped to hide her identity by using Tyburn's, but now she saw that as far as the public was concerned, Tyburn had simply doubled his efforts and become more of a menace.

"It was inevitable, I suppose," said Tyburn. "Caddington kens his coaches are a target now, lass. He was ready for anything tonight."

Diana felt like a fool for not realizing that Caddington would take precautions after so many losses, but her mind had been so full of distractions, delightful ones . . . involving Rafe Lennox. Then she looked to Tyburn and felt the heat of shame for being so glad at seeing him tonight, even when someone else held her heart.

In the last few days, she'd fallen hopelessly in love with Rafe. He'd opened himself to her, revealed every darkness inside him, and she hadn't turned away, because he'd seen that same darkness inside her. They'd both offered themselves to each other without any conditions. That was love in its purest form. To know someone and have them know you, without secrets, and still want to stay.

That was why she could never be with Tyburn. He couldn't know her the way Rafe did, and she could never truly know him. Yet his magnetic presence still stirred something inside her, and it felt like a betrayal to Rafe.

Diana was about to say something, though she wasn't sure what, but the bedchamber door opened and Matthew returned. He gave the supplies to Peele and Tyburn, who worked together in silence to clean her wound.

The brandy poured over the open wound burned like the fires of hell, but Diana didn't dare cry out. She clenched Tyburn's arm, knowing she had to be hurting him. He had removed his gloves, and she was grateful for the warmth of his hand around hers as he gently took her fingers into his and let her squeeze there instead. Peele finished bandaging her arm a minute later.

"Here, drink this. 'Twill numb the pain." Tyburn lifted the bottle to Diana's lips. She took several long gulps, hissing at the burn at the back of her throat, but it worked quickly to make her feel less pain than she had minutes before.

"Is there anything else I can do?" Peele asked her. Diana saw the fatherly love for her in his eyes. Her own eyes filled with tears as she shook her head.

"You and Matthew should check on Luke. He was seeing to the horses. Then you all should go to bed."

"Yes, Miss Fox." Matthew gave Tyburn one more glance before leaving. Peele, however, stood his ground.

"You should not be left alone with this . . . gentleman," her butler said. Tyburn chuckled at that.

"Tyburn and I have an understanding," said Diana. "He will not do anything untoward, I can assure you."

Peele stared at Tyburn. "Harm her and you will regret it. I don't care who you are."

The highwayman nodded in understanding. "If I harm her, I'll put myself in my own grave."

Only then did Peele reluctantly leave them alone. Once he was gone, Tyburn began to lecture her again.

"Have ye gone daft, Diana? Ye canna do this ever again." He tossed his hat onto a chair, then muttered darkly as he paced the length of the room. "'Tis far too dangerous. Caddington desires to catch me, now more than ever."

"If you plan to lecture me, you can leave," Diana said wearily. "You might hunt coaches for sport for all I know, but for me, it is a question of survival." She rose from the chair, but she wobbled as she stood. Between the brandy and the pain, she was still a little unsteady on her feet.

Tyburn caught her up in his arms and carried her to the bed. In an instant she was struck by the familiarity of being in his arms, the maleness of his scent. She wound her uninjured arm around his neck to hold on, just so she could touch him once more before she told him goodbye. Diana ducked her head beneath his chin, shutting her eyes to block out the tears before he saw them. He laid her down on the bed and removed her boots from her feet.

"Ye need out of these wet clothes," he said.

"You always say that." Diana tried for a smile, but it turned into a yawn. She was too tired to move and was perhaps a little drunk with all of the brandy she'd taken on an empty stomach.

With a grunt, Tyburn set about removing her clothing until she was naked as the day she'd been born. If she hadn't been so damned tired and hurting, she might have cared, but at that moment, she didn't. All she could think about was he was touching her again and it would be for the last time.

"Where do ye keep yer underpinnings?" he asked, looking around the room.

"Dresser . . . top drawer." Diana closed her eyes, burying her face in her pillow.

"Ye can sleep in a minute, lass. Sit up for me now," Tyburn commanded. Suddenly the soft, dry fabric of a clean chemise slid over her head. He tucked her arms through the sleeves and tugged it down her body.

"There now, ye can get beneath the covers." He urged her to one side of the bed where he'd pulled back the coverlet, then lifted the blankets up to her chin as though she were a child.

An almost silent sob hiccupped from her lips.

His curse was instant, warm, and it drove another sob from her. "I'll stay the night with ye, if ye want," he whispered, easing down onto the bed beside her.

"*No!*"

The word was ripped from the very insides of her heart. When he heard it, he stilled completely, waiting for her to explain.

"You cannot stay." The drowsiness threatened to cloud her mind. It urged her to lay her head down and sleep, but the flicker of emotion behind the mask made her determined to do the right thing.

"Why not?" Tyburn asked.

"I . . ." The brandy blurred her thoughts and stole her words, but the rightness of what she had to do stayed, even as it tore her heart. "I've fallen in love with someone. And I think I will marry him if he asks me."

Silence, and then she felt the strong grip of Tyburn's fingers around her hand.

"No! I told you, you cannot stay anymore. I couldn't do that to him."

The words cut her like shards of glass, but she didn't dare take them back. She thought of Rafe, the way he'd whispered his dreams to her as they lay beneath a spreading sky, and she knew how vulnerable that beautiful man was, how he feared to say what he wanted from life, because somehow, life had taken so much from him, just as it had from her. She thought of the way he looked at her, as if she was the answer to every question he'd ever had in his heart, as though living one minute without her would destroy him.

"Who is he?" Tyburn rasped, and even as tired as she was, she heard the pain in his voice.

"He's a gentleman . . . a *good* man. He is so wonderful, and yet he thinks he's a scoundrel. He believes himself to be a wicked rake, but with me, he's . . . just himself. There is only truth between us. Truth and desire. Somehow, I have fallen madly in love with him."

She opened her eyes, seeing Tyburn's masked profile as he stared at the rushlight by the bed. She almost took the words back that hurt this man, the man who'd first shown her pleasure and belonging, who'd saved her from a bullet, who'd killed for her. And she had repaid him with rejection. But her soul now belonged to Rafe. Being beside him in that storm, holding Isla safe between them . . . that had changed the very heart of her being.

Tyburn let out a soft breath. "Does he truly ken who ye are, lass? Does he make ye feel as I do?"

"Yes," she whispered. "I didn't think anyone but you could make me feel like this, but he does. He's seen me, all of me, even at my worst."

"So ye are enough for him," Tyburn sighed. "But is he enough for ye?"

"He's everything," Diana confessed. "It all happened so fast, but I feel like my soul and his . . . we've come from the same place. We are the same, he and I." It was something she'd never imagined she'd say about any man, that she could feel so wholly herself and yet a part of another like that, but she did. She and Rachel had often teased each other about mates of the soul when they'd been younger, finding that perfect gentleman. But she didn't want or need a man who was perfect. Rafe was perfect in his imperfection. She wanted Rafe, wanted his misery, his heartache, his joy, his love, his passion. She wanted all of it, wanted all of him.

Tyburn turned to face her. "Will ye miss me, lass?" he asked.

She forced herself to sit up, resting her forehead against Tyburn's shoulder as he tightened his hold on her hand and laced his fingers through hers.

"God forgive me, but I will. I will *miss* you, Tyburn."

"There will never be another in my heart but ye, lass." He lifted her face up and kissed her lips with all the heartache of a final goodbye.

Bliss and misery exploded in the wake of that long, slow melting of mouths in the rushlight. She tasted love in this stranger's kiss, just as she had that first night they'd come together in that little hunting lodge. Tears coated her cheeks as they pulled apart, and she wiped at her eyes.

"Rest now. Ye need to heal." He urged her back to the bed and tucked the blankets up around her again. She watched him through watery eyes as he opened the window. Outside, thunder rumbled, an echo of her soul quaking at this painful parting.

"Tyburn . . . Would you show me who you really are? Or at least tell me your true name?"

Rain pattered on the stones and ivy of the house, which was strangely soothing to her at this moment when her heart felt like it was breaking. Tyburn braced the window open and faced her, the rushlight's glow barely illuminating his masked face.

"I am but a dream, lass. And dreams should never be named. It destroys the magic in them."

And then, just as he had entered her life, her wicked highwayman vanished into the cold, rainy night.

CHAPTER 15

Rafe sprawled out on the floor of the Lennox library beneath the canopy of blankets and wooden broomsticks that formed Fort Lennox.

Rafe and Isla were fierce Highlanders who had taken over the tent fort. They then successfully defended it from the English general Ashton and forced him to surrender his plate of cherry tarts as well as his glasses of punch.

Now they enjoyed their spoils of war in peace while Ashton had retreated to another part of the house to do whatever English villains did when not causing trouble for adorable Scottish children.

Isla sat with her legs crisscrossed as she ate her cherry tart. Above them, the bedsheets that formed the peaked steeple glowed bright with morning sunlight. It was warm and cozy within the blanket fort, and Rafe was tempted to take a nap, but he had matters to tend to, namely broaching the subject of a new mother to Isla without getting her too excited.

It had been two days since that night in Diana's bedchamber. The night she'd been shot. The night she'd confessed her love to him without realizing it. He had ridden back early the next morning to see her as Rafe, but her butler had informed him she wasn't up for visitors, not even him.

Peele had seemed disappointed but assured him that she would send word when she was well enough to receive visitors. Rafe had told Peele that she was welcome to see him at his home any time of the day or night, or to send for him and he would come straightaway. It had been damned hard to get back on his horse and ride home, knowing that Diana was somewhere in her house, hurting, and he could not comfort her the way she needed.

He knew she had to avoid him until her arm was well enough to not pain her. It would be hard to hide that her arm was injured. She would have no way of explaining it to him because he *couldn't* know about what had happened to her. He'd almost stormed back into the house to tell her he was Tyburn, but he'd stopped himself. It was already a huge risk that she was robbing coaches under his name. He couldn't add to that by telling her his other identity.

But now, after just two days, Rafe was restless with the need to see Diana, to make sure she was healing, and that was the very thing he couldn't do. The robbery that night and the attack from Caddington's men had made the papers this morning. It was only a matter of time before the noose tightened. He, Will, and Caspian had agreed not to ride again in this part of the country, but how was he to stop Diana from riding? He knew her well enough now, and his fire drake wouldn't let a bullet stop her from acquiring the money she needed. She was just as motivated as he was to care for what she loved. The second her arm was healed, she'd be right back on her horse and donning a mask. Given that she'd lost the money from the last robbery to his Tyburn persona, she might be even more desperate and take even more risks.

He would have done the same had he been in her position. Which he had. The night Rosalind had shot him when he'd robbed her coach, he'd been badly hurt, but he'd vowed to get back on his horse as soon as he could. Diana had seen his scar from that incident, but she had no idea it was Rosalind who had wounded him.

Rafe frowned as he contemplated the money he'd given Ashton last evening to invest. His cut from that last robbery had been more than nine hundred pounds. A veritable fortune. His brother had raised a brow but didn't demand to know where he had gotten it. Rafe said he had won it unexpectedly from a risk he had taken, which was veiled enough that it sounded like a streak of luck at gambling. That had earned a frown from Ashton, but then he'd gone on to discuss some interesting investment opportunities in certain bonds that he believed would result in profitable returns. The money box they had claimed had been a bigger prize than any of them expected, but he would have traded it all in an instant for Diana to be unharmed.

"Papa, you're frowning," Isla said as she poked his cheek with a cherry-covered finger.

"Sorry, kitten." He wiped the cherry filling from his cheek with a handkerchief and sat up a little. "Isla . . . I have been giving some thought to this new mama business."

His daughter's face brightened. "Oh?" She sounded a

lot like Rosalind, the way she tried to play as if she wasn't all that interested in something while secretly being very interested. His daughter had been spending too much time around her aunt.

"Yes. I don't want you to get your hopes up just yet, but I would like to ask Miss Fox to marry me." He paused to weigh his words. "But she may not be ready just yet. I will ask her when the time is right." Like when she no longer played a highwayman at night. Until she gave up that dangerous aspect of her life, he could not marry her. Of course, he would have to give up his own illicit activities too. Some men would not admit that, but fair was fair, and he knew Diana would need him to commit to the same, especially when she learned he was Tyburn. He and Diana both needed financial stability, but he was damned if he knew how to go about it any quicker than waiting on the investments Ashton was making for him.

"Mrs. Crumpet and I will be patient," Isla said stoically, and sipped her punch.

"Good. Because I—"

"Rafe? Are you in here?" His little sister's voice startled him.

"Jo?" he called out.

Joanna's voice was now just outside the blanket fort's entrance. "Heavens . . . is this a castle?"

"It's Fort Lennox. Isla and I permit you entrance, good lady."

Isla giggled at his imperious tone.

The sheet that formed the doorway of their fort parted, and Joanna crawled in on her hands and knees. Her pale-gold hair flowed down her shoulders, and the blue-

and-gold dress she wore made his sister appear both regal and wild, like some fae queen.

"Is your badger with you?" Rafe asked.

His little sister giggled as she joined him and Isla in the center of the tent. "Of course." The badger in question was Brock, her Highlander husband, Lord Kincade. But Rafe called him badger because his name *meant* badger. And it didn't help that he could sometimes be as moody and grumpy as his namesake.

"And did ye bring yer wee bairn, Jamie?" Rafe teased Joanna in his Scottish brogue.

Joanna sat down beside Isla and picked up a tart. "Yes, Mama met us in London, and we all made the trip here."

Rafe flinched. "Mother is here?"

Joanna watched him, worry in her blue eyes. "Oh, Rafe, she is trying, you know. And she adores Isla."

"Everyone adores Isla," he replied coolly. "It's impossible not to." He didn't want to speak of his mother, certainly not in front of his child. Isla had a good relationship with her new grandmama, and no matter what she thought of him, he didn't want Isla's relationship with her to be affected by his baggage.

"Just promise me you'll try?" Joanna asked. "Besides, Mama heard that you have been courting a woman."

"How on earth did she—*Rosalind*," he growled the name as it occurred to him.

"She may have dropped a letter about it. Mama said you are courting Diana Fox?"

"Er . . . yes." Rafe caught Isla looking and realized this fort was getting quite crowded. "Kitten, it seems Grandmama's here. Perhaps you ought to go see her?"

Isla lifted Mrs. Crumpet up in her arms and let out a soft sigh. It seemed she knew exactly what her father was up to. Did all little girls possess the innate ability to know when someone was trying to distract them?

"I'll join you in a moment," he promised Isla.

The girl rolled her eyes and hugged Joanna before she left.

"My, she's grown up," Joanna observed.

"Yes. And far too quickly."

"Does she know about Miss Fox?"

He nodded. "She adores Di."

"*Di*, is it?" Joanna held back a giggle. "You *are* serious about her."

"I am," Rafe admitted. Joanna was the only one in his family he felt he could be honest with and not fear being judged.

"And I'm *glad*." His sister reached out and clasped his hand in hers. "Diana is quite a wonderful lady. Mama and I were heartbroken when her father died. It was such a pity our families never socialized the way we did with the other nearby families. I would've deeply cherished her friendship growing up. But if you marry her, I shall not only have her as a friend, but a sister too."

"Females and your weddings," Rafe chuckled.

"It's not the weddings we love—it's the adding to our families. Besides, you and Ash always outnumbered me. I was so little that I never had a chance against two older brothers, because Thomasina married James when I was only five and his estate is so far away from here. When Ash married Rosalind I gained another sister, and now I shall have you too." She squeezed his hand and grinned.

"Don't tell Mother that I'm serious about Diana yet,

please. Diana's only just out of mourning, and I do not wish to rush my proposal to her."

"You mean you fear Mama would say something to her?"

"Given that I am her least favorite child, I am always afraid of what she will say. Even something kindly meant could send Diana into a panic, and I don't wish for that. Everything has been moving quickly, even for me."

"Very well. Mum's the word." Joanna mimed twisting a key against her lips and tossing it away, which made Rafe laugh.

"I suppose we need to rescue my little kitten from Mother."

Joanna crawled out of the fort ahead of him and offered him a hand when he exited, then pulled him to his feet.

"That truly is a spectacular fort," Joanna said as she eyed the structure.

"I never do anything by half measures," Rafe said with pride.

"You certainly don't."

They went in search of Isla and his mother, and Rafe braced himself for the meeting. Everyone was out on the terrace. Brock held his and Joanna's son, Jamie. The boy was only a month younger than Ashton and Rosalind's son, Malcolm, who was sitting on Ashton's lap. The men were in deep discussion, and the two babes stared at each other, making sounds as though they were trying desperately to converse just as their fathers were.

Rafe's mother held Isla's hand, and they were walking with Rosalind across the grass of the main lawn, their colorful skirts billowing in the gentle breeze. Regina was still a beautiful woman, one who had refused to let her dowager status destroy her sense of style. She wore no mobcap or silly bonnet with some tame and boring dress. Instead, she wore a bright-green spencer over a dark-blue gown that accented her pale-gold hair.

Despite Rafe's concerns about facing his mother, he was glad she was here for Isla's sake. When he'd first informed his family of his intention to adopt her, he'd expected protests, especially from her. Ashton had been a tad skeptical at first, but it was his mother who had truly surprised him.

She'd come up to him, held his hands in hers, and asked him why he was taking the girl in. He'd answered honestly. "Because she chose me, Mother. She wants and needs me. I could never turn her away, and I believe I need her too."

His mother had nodded and asked to be introduced to Isla once the girl arrived from Scotland. When that day came, his mother had knelt down to Isla's height and opened her arms to the little girl. Isla had hugged her instantly.

She may never forgive me or fully love me after what I've done, but she will love Isla. It was enough for him to know that the child of his heart would never be left alone should something happen to him.

Rafe watched his family from a distance, content to be alone for the moment, when a footman approached.

"Sir? Miss Fox has just arrived. Shall I escort her here?" the young man asked.

"Diana is here? I will come to fetch her, thank you."

He followed the footman to the entryway, where Diana waited. Her hair was unbound except for a ribbon pulling part of it away from her face, and she wore a sensible walking gown of dark purple with pale-pink rosebuds sewn across the patterned sleeves and hem. It had a high neck with a white frilled collar that evoked the fashions of Elizabeth I. The riding boots she wore were black and shiny, but he saw old scuff marks that hadn't quite been buffed out. Her face lit up, and his heart tried to contain the flood of warmth he felt at simply seeing her smile at him.

"Di." He came over and pulled her into his arms, knowing that the servants lingered nearby, but he simply didn't care who saw his forward behavior.

He cupped her face and gently examined her weary eyes. "Are you feeling better?" She still looked far too tired and pale for his liking. He hated that he couldn't tend to her injury himself.

"Yes, I am sorry I could not see you when you came to call." The tightness around her eyes was the only thing that betrayed the fact she was still in some pain. "I hope it's all right that I came to see you unannounced?"

"More than all right," Rafe assured her. He was careful not to touch her injured shoulder, while also hiding the fact that he knew she was hurt. "We are out on the terrace enjoying the day. My sister Joanna and her husband, Brock, just returned from Scotland, and they brought my mother."

"Your family is here? Oh, I shouldn't have come. I . . ."

"Hush." He tilted her face up so he could lean down and feather a kiss over her lips. "You are like family to me, Diana. It would do Joanna good to see you, and Isla has been asking about you all day."

He stole another, deeper kiss, one that teased her as much as it tortured him. He was only satisfied to let her go when he saw how dazed she looked after that second kiss.

Diana laid her palms on his chest. Rafe lifted one of her hands and pressed a kiss to her inner wrist. He felt her pulse leap in response and was rewarded with a splash of color in her pale face.

"Come and spend the day with us." He tucked her arm in his, and they walked out into the sun to meet his family.

❤

A WAVE OF RELIEF SWEPT THROUGH DIANA AS SHE AND Rafe stepped out onto the terrace. She had been worried that he would press her about her "illness," but he hadn't. She'd seen the concern in his eyes, but he hadn't questioned her. Her arm was healing quite well, but part of her weariness came from the dreams she had suffered the last two nights. Those final moments of bidding goodbye to her mysterious highwayman.

She knew she could not be in love with two men, but somehow she was. She loved Tyburn, his fierce intensity, his passion, his dark allure that softened into such tender seductions. But her heart held Rafe's name. His sunny smiles, his sweet ardor, his determination to prove he was *enough* to the world, and to himself, filled her with a deep longing to hold him and assure him he was more than enough.

Most of all, she loved the way he looked at her. He did not stare down at her from a noble height, nor did he raise her upon some pedestal to admire. Rafe saw *all* of her, *knew* all of her, and when he kissed her, she felt both strangely safe and free. He was her shelter from the storm. As much as she was thrilled by Tyburn's midnight visits, Rafe was *more* to her in a way that defied words.

I must forget Tyburn, she reminded herself. Rafe was her future. She knew it in a way that made her blood sing with the promise of the life they could share. Rafe glanced down at her with that half smile of his that did funny things to her knees. She clung tightly to his arm, glad for his strength.

"Ready?" Rafe asked as he led her toward his family on the lawn and by the table. "I swear they don't bite. You've met Rosalind and Ash, of course. And you remember my mother and Joanna. Jo's husband, Brock, is a quiet fellow, but a good man, and a Scot."

"You do love your Scots," Diana teased.

"Lord help me, but I do," he agreed with a laugh. He'd told her of all his adventures with Rosalind's three brothers. It was clear that he cherished those men as friends and brothers. "I hope you don't mind meeting everyone like this . . . with me." His face turned serious, and she understood the implication. For him to introduce her officially to his family would be making a bold statement.

"I don't think I'd mind anything so long as I was with you."

Diana was ready. Ready to start living again. She tried not to think about the money that they had lost in the last robbery or the man Tyburn had killed to save her. Those thoughts would come back to haunt her soon enough, but she could escape for a few hours at least, and she welcomed the distraction.

Joanna was the first to see them. "Miss Fox!"

Diana greeted everyone with a smile as they turned to face her with varying degrees of surprise. "Good afternoon."

Isla pulled her tiny hand free of Regina's and ran toward Diana. "Miss Fox!" Diana knelt and held her arms out, and Isla leapt into her arms a bit too eagerly.

"Isla, wait!" Rafe called out as the girl wrapped her arms tight around Diana. Pain lanced down her arm, and she bit her lip to hold back a hiss.

"Isla, you must let her go," Rafe whispered to the child. "You're hurting her."

"I'm fine, Rafe," Diana lied. Despite the pain, she relished the comfort of holding the little girl. She'd come to adore the child with all her heart, just as she had the girl's father. Love was such a funny thing. One moment she had been determined to be left alone, because she did not desire the weakness that loving someone would create. But she'd forgotten that love could make someone strong too, and Isla's hug was giving her new strength.

Regina and Joanna joined them. "Miss Fox, I'm glad to see you well."

Diana let go of Isla and stood to meet Regina's gaze. The dowager baroness was a beautiful woman who seemed to be made of iron. After all the stories Rafe had shared about his family, Diana believed she understood Regina well. She had shattered when she'd lost her husband but had rebuilt herself on her own terms in order not to break again. It was something Diana was intimately familiar with.

She wished that Regina would find a way to truly forgive Rafe, for Rafe had done nothing wrong the night his father died, and he blamed himself more than anyone else. Someday Diana would convince Rafe to forgive himself, but the person who would set him free of that pain most was this woman. He needed his mother to tell him that he was not to blame before he could ever forgive himself.

Regina's blue eyes moved between her son, Isla, and

Diana. "And how are you faring now that you are out of mourning?"

"Well enough," Diana said. She had her home, her lands, and she was still fighting to keep them. That was well enough in her mind.

"Good," Regina replied. "We are here should you ever need us—*any* of us." She and Ashton shared a look of agreement, which Diana didn't miss.

"Thank you, Lady Lennox."

"Miss Fox, would you like to see the fort Papa and I made?" Isla asked.

"You made a fort?" Diana asked.

"In the library!" said Isla.

Diana looked toward Rafe, intrigued. The rakish gentleman had the good sense to look bashful about his antics.

"Would you mind if I showed Diana the library?" Rafe asked his mother, as if afraid to interrupt his mother's interaction with Diana without permission.

"Not at all." Regina gestured for them to leave and turned toward the table where Brock and Ashton still held her two grandsons.

Rafe gently pulled Diana against his side. "I believe we may now safely make our escape." The heat of his body warmed her clear down to her toes.

"Come! Come see!" Isla stood in the open doorway leading back to the house while a patient footman held the door open for her.

Something about Isla brought back old memories . . . ones that made Diana's heart clench with bittersweet longing. She could see her sister standing there, calling for her to come inside, just as Isla was doing now.

"Are you all right?" Rafe asked as they entered the house. "Perhaps we should find a place to sit down or—"

Diana gave a little shake as the ghost of memory faded away. "I am tired," she admitted. "But I will be all right. I don't want to miss spending time with you today." She leaned her cheek against his shoulder, and Rafe kissed the top of her head. A feeling of blissful safety swept through her.

"How do you do that?" she asked.

The corners of his eyes crinkled as he looked down at her. "Do what?"

"Make me feel safe."

"I do?" Rafe paused in the doorway of the library.

"Yes, you do."

"Good. I always want you to feel safe with me." He leaned down to kiss her again for a long, delicious moment. The pain in her arm vanished, and all her dark thoughts faded away.

"Marry me," Rafe whispered as their lips parted. "Marry me . . . Diana." His blue eyes burned bright, and she lost herself in the color of the summer sky they held. "Marry me when you choose. When you feel ready. I'll take you as my wife the moment you wish to have me as your husband."

Diana's throat tightened. "I . . ." She so badly wished to say yes. "Rafe, you know my estate is struggling. Surely you must take that into account before you ask me to marry . . ."

He smiled and brushed a lock of her hair from her cheek.

"I would take all the struggles in the world as long as I could call you mine."

She saw and heard only truth in his response.

He stroked a fingertip over her lips. "Take your time."

"Miss Fox!" Isla's excited shout reminded Diana of why she was here. "You must see the fort!" The girl rushed over to take Diana's hand and pull her away. Diana glanced back at Rafe as she knelt at the fort's entrance. The look of love and longing in his eyes healed her very soul. How could she refuse him? She held out a hand. Rafe came to her and got down on his knees next to her, one arm sliding around her waist. She tilted her chin up and drew in a soft breath.

"Yes." She whispered the word, and sweet lightning shot through her limbs.

His lips kicked up in a full smile that held the warmth of the very sun in it. "Yes?"

"*Yes.*" She tried to still the wild beating of her heart. She would have to say goodbye to her mask and the midnight rides, but after the last one, she was more than ready. She and Rafe would find a way to save her home without resorting to theft. Perhaps the investments from the deposits she'd given Rosalind would start to bear fruit.

Rafe pressed his forehead to hers and kissed her deeply. After a long, tender moment, they were reminded by a polite cough that they weren't alone.

"Does this mean you'll be my new mama?" Isla asked, clutching her doll to her chest.

"Yes . . . would you like that?"

Isla's eyes filled with tears and she threw herself at Diana, who held the crying girl in her arms and hushed her.

"I'm sorry, I don't have to be your mama," Diana said.

"But I *want* you to be!" Isla said between sobs. "I want a mama . . . I want *you.*"

"Well then, I think we shall both be happy with the

decision," Diana said. She lifted her face to Rafe's as he pulled them both inside the blanket fort to sit.

"It shall be the three of us from now on." Rafe's gaze held Diana's.

"The three of us," Diana agreed. She was ready to open her heart fully and completely to Rafe and to everything that would come from loving him.

CHAPTER 16

"I have news, my lord."

Andrew Caddington glanced up from the papers on his desk with a scowl.

"It had better be *good* news, Phelps." He'd had enough bad news since his coach, protected by four armed guards, had been attacked by highwaymen and his money lost. One of the fools he'd hired had been killed during the struggle, not that Andrew cared, but at least he now had a murder he could hang about that blasted Tyburn's neck once he caught the bastard.

Phelps had been sent to covertly watch Andrew's coach from a vantage point in the woods. When he hadn't returned straightaway with the men who'd been in charge of the coach, Andrew hadn't worried. Phelps was known to go underground while he did his work, whatever it may be that Andrew asked of him.

Andrew couldn't afford to lose much more of his income. Forcing most of the businesses and families in the district to pay for his protection as a magistrate was risky enough, but he'd be damned if he'd let some blasted thieves ruin his plans.

And he had grand plans indeed.

Once he had enough money, he would start investing in the loyalties of influential men in business—and politics. It was time that the power dynamics in London changed. The blue-blooded aristocratic families of old had failed to make themselves useful. They'd grown too dependent on the people who lived on their lands. Andrew had seen to the banishment of his tenants a long time ago. They were a waste of space and a waste of land.

True power lay in a lord's ability to do whatever he pleased, to *whomever* he pleased.

Andrew realized that Phelps had been silent just a little too long. Rarely a good sign. "Well? What is it? You've been gone for two bloody days. I expect you to show results for your absence."

Phelps smiled without humor. "I assure you, it is very good news. I know who your thieves are."

Andrew shoved his ledgers aside and leaned forward. "Who is it?"

"First, you should know you have been robbed not by just one set of thieves but *two*."

"Two? What the devil do you mean?"

"I mean, there is a second band of thieves, using the identity of Tyburn and his men. I believe most of your earlier robberies were conducted by the first band of three thieves. These men were clearly knowledgeable. The last two robberies seem to be the work of a second group of three people. Most of the reports about them match, but there were enough differences that I became suspicious. Two nights ago, it was the second group that attacked your coach first. Tyburn and his men came to their aid once the armed guards made their presence known. I wasn't able to rescue your money because I was outnumbered. The more knowledgeable group of men handled the theft of the money, while the less experienced trio of thieves fled. I chose to follow those three to see what I could learn."

"And where did they go?" Andrew demanded.

"To an old priest hole, which led to a tunnel that took them straight to Foxglove Hall."

"Foxglove—" Andrew's eyes narrowed. "You mean these men work for Diana Fox?"

It had taken him a moment to recall the shabby estate he'd visited when investigating the robberies. That woman who'd lived there had most likely lied to him that day when he'd gone to question her about her supposed abduction. Either she was working directly with him, or they were competitors of sorts. No matter. Now he had another piece of this strange puzzle.

His manservant was still smiling as he took a moment to relish delivering his news. "Better. Miss Fox is *one* of the thieves. I have learned she was shot two nights ago, a simple flesh wound. She'll live."

"A pity," Andrew snorted. He didn't like women and their simpering and lying. They were useless to him.

"Not a pity, as it turns out," Phelps said, far too smugly.

"If you have something relevant to tell me, you'd best spit it out."

Phelps narrowed his eyes, the only hint of rebellion he had ever seen in his loyal servant. That was because Phelps knew just how dangerous Andrew was when he was angry.

"The woman's injury drew the leader of the other band of thieves right to her. I saw him go in through her window.

I believe they might be secret lovers, which would explain why he snuck into her home rather than simply going through the main entrance."

"And who is this other man?" Andrew said impatiently.

"That I learned later. When this man left Foxglove, I followed him back to his home." Phelps paused, seeming to relish his next words. "Lennox House."

"Lennox House? Lord Lennox is harboring these thieves?"

Phelps's eyes glowed with triumph. "No."

"You cannot expect me to believe Lennox *himself* is the leader of the highwaymen."

His manservant was grinning wickedly now. "Not him . . ."

Andrew's breath caught as a sudden, delicious, dangerous excitement filled his veins with the need to cause pain.

"You mean . . . ?"

"Yes," Phelps said. "You finally have the means to catch the one you've wanted."

The web he'd spun to trap a group of bothersome highwaymen had, by good fortune, caught the one man who had eluded him so long ago.

He'd tried over the years to snare the young Lennox in his usual ways, with debts or obligations that he did not realize led straight back to Andrew. But much to his frustration, the boy had never fallen for those cleverly laid traps.

But now . . . now he could feel the sweet vibrations of the struggling of his prey, not even realizing it was already too late. He would finally have Rafe Lennox under his power. He would break the man, take his time and bask in every second of his agony.

"We will need to bait our trap. I trust you will see it done?" Andrew asked.

"With pleasure," said Phelps.

"Good. Get to it. I am no longer willing to wait." He stood and waved for Phelps to leave. There was much to do. He must prepare his private cellar for Rafe's arrival and wait. The anticipation almost made him lightheaded.

Finally, he would have what he'd hungered so long for.

DIANA HUMMED TO HERSELF AS SHE AND MRS. RIPLEY carried the vegetables in from the gardens. They'd harvested quite a few carrots and potatoes this week, as the weather had been good for their small crops. Diana could already taste the stew that their cook would make with the beef she'd acquired from the butcher this morning. Although Diana's arm still twinged, it was more an ache now than an actual pain.

Perhaps it hurt less because she and Rafe were to be married in a month's time, and that fact seemed to make everything *glow* inside her. She wished it could be sooner, but Lord Lennox had insisted upon the banns being read in church and a wedding ceremony with a large breakfast. It seemed most of the Lennox marriages had been hasty matters, and Rafe's elder brother wished to do the thing properly once Rafe had announced the news to his family.

Rafe had given Ashton a most frustrated glare, which made Diana laugh and kiss Rafe's cheek. She had whispered that she would make the wait worth it. He had kissed the shell of her ear and whispered back that he was *certain* he would find a way to see to her needs while they waited out the month. His sensual promise had made her legs wobble as much as some of the famous jellies that the Lennox cook made.

She'd written to Rachel straightaway with the news, since she was back in London again for the next few weeks. Rachel would be delighted; Diana could picture her friend smiling as she read the news.

"We must work on your trousseau, Miss Diana," said Mrs. Ripley. She gave the cook and a scullery maid a grateful smile as the two servants collected the baskets from her and Diana.

"Oh, but I could think of a thousand things that require my attention instead of filling a trunk with fine clothing." Even as she said this, however, a tiny part of her heart sighed with disappointment.

The housekeeper gave a firm shake of her head. "Nonsense. You will have one, no matter what. Now, come with me and let me show you something."

Diana followed Mrs. Ripley out of the kitchen and up into the attic above the maids' and footmen's rooms. Late-afternoon sunlight crept in through the dirty attic windows, illuminating little trails of dust motes but providing enough light to show them a worn path through the old trunks, paintings, and other belongings of more than two hundred years of Foxes.

Mrs. Ripley stopped in front of an old ivory-colored trunk in a dusty corner. She retrieved the set of keys that hung at her waist and knelt in front of the trunk. Diana joined her, curious as to what this particular trunk contained. They had so little time to spend in the attic when the rest of the estate needed so much attention.

"This was your mother's trousseau. I believe everything is still quite nearly perfect inside." The housekeeper unlocked the trunk and lifted the lid. A faint lavender aroma drifted up from the neatly folded garments tucked in thin paper, with a set of letters that had been bound in faded blue ribbon.

"These are love letters from your father," Mrs. Ripley explained. She delicately moved the faded letters aside and opened the first layer of thin paper about the clothing.

"And this was your mother's wedding gown." She held it up so Diana could see. The style was not in the current fashion, but the pearl beading and gold embroidery on the soft icy-blue silk were exquisite and timeless. The gown seemed to shimmer as though some fairy queen had worn it long ago and her magic still clung to the fabric.

Diana's hands trembled as she touched the watered silk. "I've never seen her wedding gown before. It's so beautiful." She could imagine herself wearing it, feeling just as beautiful as her mother had been. For a moment, she felt overwhelmed. She'd long given up hope that she would have a wedding day or a husband. And now . . . She bit her lip to hide a smile as she thought of Rafe's face when he saw her in this gown.

Mrs. Ripley gave a soft grin. "With a few adjustments to bring it up to the current fashions, I believe you could wear this and look as magnificent as your mother did on her wedding day."

Diana bit her lip and nodded. "I wish . . . I wish she and Eleanor were here."

"Me too, my dear. But think of your new family. Lady Lennox, Lady Kincade . . . you will have sisters."

She would have *wonderful* sisters. She scarcely could have imagined that her life could have changed so much for the better so quickly.

"Do you think I'm being hasty, agreeing to marry him so quickly?" she whispered to Mrs. Ripley while they examined some undergarments made of fine satin and Belgian lace.

"If I hadn't seen you with Mr. Lennox, perhaps I would be worried, but I've never seen two people so well suited to each other. The way that man looks at you . . . That is a man who loves deeply, loves purely." Mrs. Ripley paused, her smile bittersweet. "But what matters most is his being here and courting you proper . . . It's undoing the harm of the last few years."

Diana felt a sudden flash of anxiety. "Harm?"

Mrs. Ripley set down the nightgown and took Diana's hands in hers.

"You've always been a force of nature, my dear. More so than your sister. You *shone* as a little girl. It's why that man adores you. You're such a vibrant soul. But these last few years that shine has dimmed. Life has a way of stealing away one's inner light when too much happens to break one's heart."

Mrs. Ripley was usually a woman quite in control of herself, but now she sniffed and wiped away a tear.

"Whenever you are in Mr. Lennox's presence you *shine*, just as you deserve to. Mr. Peele and I have been so relieved and happy to see our little Diana come back to us. You deserve everything good life has to offer, and I believe that man will do anything to give it to you."

She squeezed Diana's hands. "Now, before I become a watering pot, I will have the footmen bring this down today and we will begin work on your wedding gown. We want to make Foxglove proud, don't we?"

"Yes, we do," Diana agreed, her own voice thick with emotion. "Thank you, Mrs. Ripley."

Mrs. Ripley cupped her cheek as though she were a little girl once more. "I never had children of my own, but you . . . I claim you as my daughter in every way I can."

Diana threw her arms around Mrs. Ripley and hugged her.

A FEW HOURS LATER, DIANA WALKED TO THE STABLES TO see how Nelson was doing tending the horses. It was an old habit she'd gotten from her father, who'd liked to check on Nelson, and he'd taken Diana with him more often than not so she could see the horses.

As she stepped into the stables, the aroma of fresh hay and grain mixed with the pleasing scent of leather and horses. She found the old groom in the farthest stall. He was speaking in a soothing voice to the beasts and winked at Diana when he spotted her. She tapped her fingers on the stable door and took a moment to breathe the air and enjoy herself.

"Nelson, don't forget to come in for dinner soon," she reminded the old groom.

"Yes, Miss Diana," he said from behind a tall white Percheron he was brushing.

Diana turned away from the stables and returned to the house. She looked upon her home with new eyes, eyes that didn't feel weary at the thought of caring for it. Now she saw what her life would be, how the gardens would flourish, how there would be Isla and perhaps another child running about the lawns, and she would spend her days with Rafe, basking in the sunlight and living in the way she'd longed for. Foxglove would once more be a shining jewel in the countryside, and her family would have been proud that she'd saved it.

She heard the sudden rush of steps behind her, and pain exploded in the back of her skull. She collapsed on the grass, her hands scrambling in the autumn leaves as she tried to get to her knees.

"You're stronger than I thought," someone hissed, and a second blow sent her into a world of black oblivion.

When she came to, she found herself on the floor of a dimly lit cellar. It took her a full minute to get past the throb in her head as she realized she was sitting in a . . . cell? A lit lamp sat on the floor just beyond her reach through the bars. She groaned and tried to sit up. The world still spun sickeningly, and her fingertips came away from the back of her head with a bit of blood. Where had she been just now? Had she seen Nelson in the stables? Yes, she remembered that she had . . . What happened after that?

Light flickered at the opposite end of the cellar as someone came down a set of stairs and emerged from the gloom.

"Welcome to my home, Miss Fox," Lord Caddington said with a dark chuckle. "I find it amusing that I set the trap to catch a fox, yet I had no idea I would quite literally catch one." He sneered and wrapped his fingers around the iron bars of the cell as he peered down at her.

Diana got to her feet. "You've *kidnapped* me." The green woolen gown she wore was muddy and torn, and parts of her body ached as though she'd been dragged, which was likely given the state of her clothing. Whoever had taken her from her home must've tossed her about with little care to bring her here.

"Correction, I've taken you into *custody*. As the local magistrate, I am within my rights to see justice done. And seeing as how you have been robbing *my* coaches, Miss Fox, I fully intend to do so."

"This doesn't look like a proper jail," she said coolly. "Where are we?"

"This is my private prison, for prisoners I must see to *personally*."

A private prison. No one would know she was here. Diana stayed silent. It would do her no good to argue with a madman.

"But rather than see you hang, I've found a better use for you." His gaze swept over her body, and she turned away from him.

"Oh, come now. I have no interest in you in *that* fashion. No, I've discovered recently that someone I dearly wish to catch happens to have one weakness. You. Quite frankly, I don't see the appeal. However, once I have him, well, I will have no further interest in you."

Rafe. He must mean Rafe. He'd told her about how Caddington had desired him when he'd been a boy, how dangerous he was. She couldn't let Caddington know she knew him or cared about him. She had to protect him however she could.

"You don't wish to know who you have bewitched and inadvertently betrayed? Come now, Miss Fox. Play along with my game or I shall become bored, and you would not like to see what I do when I am bored." Caddington's voice held such ice that Diana was surprised the bars of her cell didn't frost over.

"Who?" Diana uttered the word quite against her will. She didn't want to play his games.

Rather than answer her question, Caddington let go of the iron bars and paced the length of the short corridor in front of her, hands clasped behind his back.

"There is someone I have wanted in my grasp for a very long time. I couldn't take him before because I had no way to keep him. Trapping him in crippling debt wouldn't have been enough, and the man slips through every trap—until now. To have him under my power, to hurt him, make him bleed . . . Ah, what sweet bliss it will be to hear him scream. His life will now belong to me. All I needed was a reason for him to surrender himself to my keeping."

"Who are you talking about?" Diana growled, but deep down a terror like she'd never known before filled her, because she knew the truth. "Just tell me, damn you!"

Caddington, his back to her, bent to retrieve the lantern on the floor and hung it from a hook opposite her cell before he turned to face her.

"Don't act all innocent. You've pretended to be him, after all. The infamous highwayman who has made my life most difficult this past year. I believe you call him Tyburn." The relief she felt that it wasn't Rafe vanished beneath a wave of guilt.

"Tyburn?" Caddington could not catch Tyburn. He was a shadow, a dream. He could not be real, could not be caught.

But he could be lured . . .

"Yes, you see now. I know that he loves you and would risk everything for you."

Diana clenched her skirts, not daring to move or speak. She wouldn't betray Tyburn. She had promised to keep the fact that she knew him a secret, and she would never break that vow.

"Why do you want him? Simply because he robbed your coaches?" Diana demanded.

The evil smile that spread across Caddington's face gave her a terrible chill. He approached her cell and lightly gripped the bars, studying her.

"I have . . . very unique needs, Miss Fox. The need to hurt others. I prefer men, prefer to see strong, virile men fall beneath my whips and my rods. When they beg for mercy, I hear symphonies, Miss Fox."

Her stomach roiled dangerously, and she swallowed down rising bile.

"You're mad," she whispered.

"I am a sadist. I like pain—it is simple enough. And to have a man like Tyburn beg me for mercy, to have him on his knees . . ." He didn't finish, and Diana considered that a small mercy.

"Do your servants know of this?" she asked.

"They do—more than one have been my temporary amusement while I wait for better prey." He chuckled as if at some private joke.

"You're a monster," Diana said.

Caddington stroked his thumbs on the bars and then released them and stepped back, his gaze suddenly full of shadows. "Tyburn will come for you," Caddington said. "Think upon that, Miss Fox."

Caddington walked away, a cruel, victorious smile upon

his lips, and Diana knew that Tyburn was in terrible danger. She sank to her knees, leaning her forehead against the iron bars for a long moment as she closed her eyes. Despair and death were old friends to Diana, and now both specters loomed near her in the gloom of that dingy little cell, whispering to her to let go, to give in to what fate had in store.

All those sunny daydreams she'd had of a life with Rafe and little Isla were vanishing before her, like sand slipping through her fingers. She'd dared to hope, dared to dream . . . and now the loss of those dreams hurt worse than she'd ever imagined because she'd been close enough to touch them, to feel what *could be*.

This was her punishment for daring to desire a fairy-tale life. Cinderella would not be found by the handsome prince. She would be a prisoner of the ashes forever. Diana buried her face in her hands and sank deeper into the dark, praying she could sleep so that she didn't have to face the dawn.

"Diana . . ." The voice was more memory than a whisper, but it stirred Diana awake.

"Eleanor?" She searched the darkness of the cell. She had to be mad to think she felt her sister's presence here.

"Find a way out . . ." The whisper turned into trails of smoke made from the lantern as the candle within burned low and then died, leaving her in total darkness.

"Find a way out," Diana echoed softly. Yes. There was always a way out, if one dared to shine in the dark.

THE SWEET SCENT OF CIGARS STILL CLUNG TO RAFE'S clothing as he left the dining room. It had been a pleasant evening with Ashton, Brock, Will, and Caspian, who had talked and joked and congratulated him. He'd felt younger than he had in years while being surrounded by his brother and his friends tonight. They'd drunk brandy and smoked cigars until long after the ladies had retired to the reading room and Isla had been taken up to bed by Mrs. Chesterfield.

The other gentlemen had gone to bed, but Rafe had stayed where he was, enjoying one last glass of brandy and thinking about how for the first time in years life seemed exciting.

Even though he'd missed Diana at dinner this evening —she'd insisted on returning to Foxglove to see to things— soon they would have a lifetime to spend together. He simply couldn't wait, nor could Isla. They'd spent a long time talking about what their new life would mean, and he was thrilled to see how excited his daughter was about having a mother again. It made him think of Isla's parents and how he wished they could know that she was well taken care of and loved beyond measure.

A footman halted Rafe just as he reached the grand staircase. "This letter just came for you, sir."

"A letter at this hour?" Rafe accepted the slim letter from the footman and went to his bedchamber to read it. Missives that came after dark did not usually bear good tidings. He seated himself in a chair by the fire, broke the red wax seal upon the back, and unfolded the paper.

I have your pretty fox. She will hang for your crimes unless you do exactly as I say. Come to me tonight and tell no one. Surrender yourself to me willingly, and I will let her go unharmed.

There was no signature, but Rafe flipped the note over to examine the wax seal. The crest imprinted into the wax was one he'd seen only once before upon the signet ring of the man who'd threatened Rafe the night his father died.

Caddington.

Caddington had Diana? It made no sense. She had done nothing to—

He remembered how she and her men had fled the road that night when the robbery had gone wrong. They had gone straight back to Foxglove, grouped closely together, and he had easily followed their trail. Had one of Caddington's guards followed them? No, they'd been subdued by Rafe and his men. But someone else could have followed them—someone like Phelps.

They'd crossed paths more than once in grimy taverns near the docks and in the crowded din of gambling hells, with Phelps often speaking to people Rafe had been making wagers with. Each time Rafe had seen him, he'd left the area immediately. Wherever Phelps was, Caddington was likely to be close by.

Rafe wasn't about to chance putting himself in a situation where he and Caddington would have to face each other. The man had unnatural interests. There were rumors about how he craved the pain of others, and more than one person had suggested that he'd killed a few of his servants. Not that anyone dared to challenge him in the light of day. The man was a local magistrate and held a fair amount of power.

And if he had Diana, he could accuse her of being Tyburn and hang her for it.

Rafe clenched the letter in his fist as he cursed his foolishness. He had assumed the storm would cover their tracks. He'd doomed them all.

Rafe stared at the paper he'd crushed in his fist as he tried to breathe.

That sense of urgency that always drove him to reck-lessness, that need to live his life at breakneck speed, came into clear focus now. Some part of him had always known this day would come. For his sins, both old and new, the piper had come to collect his due.

He would not live to grow old with Diana or see Isla become the incredible woman she was destined to be. And he would never get to lie beside Diana in bed and whis-pered to her, "I love you, wife mine," as dawn kissed her face. All his dreams winked out of existence as Rafe's night sky went forever dark.

But there was one shining star he could still save.

He cast the letter into the fire and stood. His hands trembled as he watched the words of his doom be devoured by flames.

"I'm coming, Diana."

CHAPTER 17

Rafe slipped quietly into the nursery and found his daughter asleep in her bed. Her russet curls against the pillow formed a wild halo around her head. Her chest rose and fell as she breathed deeply. She bore a slight smile, as though her dreams were sunny ones. His heart turned in his chest and his eyes burned with tears.

He shot a quick glance at Mrs. Chesterfield, who was quietly reading a book by the fire. She smiled at Rafe and went back to reading. He swore the woman never slept, and aside from Isla giving her the slip right before that awful storm, she was a damned fine nanny. And she would have to be, given what was coming.

Rafe sat down on Isla's bed and she stirred a little, but she didn't wake. He took one of her small hands in his and pressed a kiss to her fingers and drew in a shaky breath.

"You are my world," he whispered, too soft for the nanny to hear. "You saved me that night we met, little kitten. No matter what happens, I will see that you have the life you deserve, even if I cannot be there to see it." He had so much more he wanted to tell her, but he dared not. If he spoke any more, he would lose his will to leave. He had to save Diana, the woman who held his heart and soul. And while he feared he wouldn't survive the night, if Diana did, she would be the one he chose to care for his daughter.

He rose and removed the letters he had tucked into his waistcoat and put them under the gilt frames of the portraits of Isla's parents. They would watch over her while she slept. He tucked Mrs. Crumpet more deeply under Isla's arm and then pressed a kiss, perhaps the last one he would ever give to his daughter, on her forehead.

He left the house without being seen and retrieved his horse from the stable, along with the mask he kept hidden in the loft.

The moon was high in the sky as he tore down the country roads, his cloak flowing out behind him, flapping wildly like a raven's wings. Tonight would be Tyburn's last ride. Tonight Rafe would finish this terrible journey, and one way or another, it would all end.

He was about to face his father's killer, and if he was doomed not to survive the night, perhaps he could take Caddington to the devil with him.

He halted his horse on the gravel path in front of Caddington's estate. There were no lamps lit in the windows, no outward presence of anyone in the house. It was eerily dark and still. He dismounted and let the reins of his horse drop. The horse would stay there as it was trained to. If he could get Diana safely out, she could ride the horse to Lennox House.

He climbed up the steps and rapped the knocker, and

after a moment, the door opened. A familiar face stared back at him.

Mr. Phelps.

The man who had come after him and his father that night, the man who'd set in motion the events that killed his father. His hatred for Phelps was just as strong as it was for Caddington, but he couldn't let the man see it. His suspicion that Phelps had been watching Caddington's coach the night of the robbery was confirmed. Phelps must have followed Diana's men . . . No, followed *him*. It was the only way Caddington could have put all of the pieces together.

"His lordship will be glad to see you received his letter." Phelps stepped back, and Rafe walked past him into the hall. Rafe still wore his domino, yet it didn't erase the feeling that he was utterly exposed.

"Where's the woman?" he said in his Scottish accent.

"Really, Mister Lennox, you may drop the charade," Mr. Phelps said evenly. "That letter was not addressed to some feral Scotsman hiding in a hut in the woods."

"I didna want anyone to know who was riding to your door," said Rafe.

"Yes, but you're *here* now," said Phelps.

The truth was, playing the role one last time was giving him a bit of courage. Rafe was terrified of Caddington. *Tyburn* was not. "Where's the woman?"

Phelps narrowed his eyes. "I will take you to her but only after you sign a confession to your crimes."

"What?" Rafe's gut tightened.

Phelps sneered. "You didn't think that his lordship hadn't thought his plan through? By having a signed confession of Rafe Lennox admitting to being the infamous highwayman Tyburn, he'll have every right to keep you imprisoned."

A terrible, dark chill swept through Rafe's entire body. Of course Caddington would have thought of everything. The man wouldn't miss getting his hands on Rafe, not this time, so he'd make sure to have everything perfectly planned and thought out.

"This way." Phelps showed him to a parlor where a few sheets of paper and an ink bottle and quill were ready for him. "Leave nothing out." Phelps crossed his arms over his chest and his eyes narrowed as Rafe reluctantly sat in the chair and took up the quill. His hand trembled as he wrote out the words he never thought to write as he confessed to several years' worth of robberies. When he'd filled two pages, he set the quill down and stood. Phelps skimmed the words he'd written and nodded in approval.

"Now you may see the woman."

He led Rafe to a hidden door that was concealed beneath a ratty old tapestry and retrieved a lamp that hung on a hook at the top of the stone stairs. The lamp cast dancing shadows on the roughhewn rock walls as they descended, and the air turned musty and dark the deeper they went. Rafe kept a careful distance between himself and Phelps, not knowing what to expect from him.

At the bottom of the stairs, the tunnel opened to a cellar. But rather than containing wine barrels or storage crates, there was a trio of iron-barred cells. In one corner of the first cell sat a huddled figure, more shadow than real until the lamp finally illuminated her.

"Diana!" Rafe shoved past Phelps to run to the cell. The door creaked as he tried to open it, but it didn't budge.

"Tyburn?" She lifted her head from where it had been resting on her bent knees as she stared up at him in wonder and agony.

"Lass," he growled as she stood and ran to him. Her arms stretched through the bars to grasp at his waist. "I'm here," he soothed. *"I'm here now."*

"No . . ." Tears streaked down Diana's dirt-stained face. "You shouldn't have come. It's a trap."

"I ken, lass, but I couldna leave ye here. I agreed to trade my life for yers." He reached through the bars and brushed his fingers over her cheek.

Phelps removed a pistol from under his coat, then took out a set of keys and opened the door of the cell beside Diana's. He gestured from Rafe to the open cell door.

"In you go. The magistrate will be with you shortly."

Rafe didn't look away from Diana as he entered the cell next to hers. Phelps locked the door, sealing Rafe inside, and briefly left them alone.

"Caddington knows I robbed his coaches," Diana breathed. "That horrible man Phelps followed me . . . and he followed you. I'm so sorry I damned us both."

"Hush, lass," Rafe said as he just wanted to hold her a little longer. Once Caddington arrived, he would give the bastard whatever he wanted so that Diana could be set free.

"When he lets ye go, I want ye to ride to Lennox House."

"Lennox House? But why—"

He pressed a finger to her lips. "I ken ye have friends there, people who care about ye. Promise me ye will go to them."

Her sorrowful brown eyes grew wide. "How can I leave you here? I can't—"

"That man ye love . . . He has a wee child that needs ye, lass. I'm not worth yer tears let alone yer life." He couldn't bring the words up . . . the words that would tell her she was losing Rafe too. The pain in his chest was simply too great. It was cruel, to play Tyburn in these final moments, but he couldn't bring himself to face the truth.

"But you are . . . *you are*." She pressed her face against the bars and curled her arms around his neck. To know she loved him, this other side of him, not just as Rafe, this woman was *everything*, and he was about to lose her and his own life.

"Promise me ye'll go to Lennox House."

She shut her eyes tight, then answered with a shaky nod.

"In another life I would've loved ye until death and beyond," Rafe said. "In another life, ye would have been my every dream. A man would die for a love like that."

"Don't be a fool." Diana's face flashed with anger. "You can escape this, damn you. Don't give up. Find a way out."

"Ah, but he can't, Miss Fox. You see, he knows that I, as the local magistrate, have the authority to hang you *both* for your highway robberies." Caddington stood at the foot of the stairs, holding a lamp in one hand and a coiled black whip in the other. "He is counting on my . . . generosity to see that you live. He will stay of his own free will, or else your life is forfeit."

Rafe closed his eyes, stilling his racing heart, knowing what pain that whip would cause him.

"Some traps do not need to be clever or hidden,"

Caddington continued. "Some simply need the right bait and to be snapped shut at just the right moment. I have waited a very long time for this." He came closer as Phelps hung two more lanterns along the walls, lighting the cells more clearly. Caddington wore only a white shirt and pale buckskin trousers. His sleeves were rolled up, exposing thick muscles. He uncoiled the whip in his hands and chuckled as he eyed Rafe and Diana, who still held each other through the bars of their cells.

"It's time you stopped this little charade, boy. Remove the mask. I want to see every minute of agony on your features. And hers."

Rafe blew out a breath as he slowly stepped back from Diana and raised his hands to his face. He slid the mask off and let it drop to the floor at his feet.

Diana's lips parted and her eyes filled with tears, but no words came out.

"Such a cruel trick to play on her," Caddington said with a purr in his voice. "To seduce her as two different men and not tell her the truth. Perhaps you have a bit of sadism in you after all." The harsh sound of Caddington's laugh grated on Rafe's ears.

"I'm sorry," Rafe whispered. Diana's face went from confusion to terror.

"No!" She understood the terrible truth now. She would lose both Tyburn and Rafe tonight. She turned away from him and faced Caddington. "You cannot do this. His brother will come looking for him. Rafe Lennox cannot go missing. If you kill him—"

"Let us speak plainly, Miss Fox. His brother does not care and will not come. Why should he? Rafe got their father killed, isn't that right?" He leaned to look past Diana, giving Rafe a knowing leer. "From all accounts, Lord Lennox has always blamed him for it. No, Rafe's mysterious disappearance will only be of a temporary concern, and then he will be forgotten."

"But he won't be forgotten," Diana insisted. "*I* won't forget him."

Caddington's face darkened. "You seem to forget that the law is on my side, not yours. I have his signed confession upstairs, and Phelps witnessed you robbing my coach himself. You are both guilty of robbery with violence, which is punishable by death. I am the magistrate here, and while it is my duty to hold you until you can be delivered to the Crown Court for trial, well . . . accidents do happen, don't they? And if you breathe a word of this to anyone, Miss Fox, I will see you hanged myself."

Diana's lips parted as if she wanted to speak, but no words came out. Rafe felt invisible walls closing in on him and he dared not move, dared not speak himself.

"But I prefer not to send Rafe to the hangman. No, I far more desire to have him here with me. Of course . . . my toys often get broken. And when that happens, a body will be found, a body with a mask, and Lord Lennox will then hear that his reckless brother met his end while robbing coaches. The book of Rafe Lennox's short and pathetic life will be shut forever."

Diana's face filled with rage. He had to stop her from doing something to anger Caddington, or she'd get herself killed as well.

"Diana, you made me a promise," Rafe said. She stared at him as if he'd gone mad.

"You want me to abandon you?" The fury in her words cut his heart. God, how he loved this woman.

"I want you to take care of my daughter. *Our* daughter. She cannot lose both of us this night. Isla needs you." He knew he'd gotten through to her at last. The fight in her eyes died like flames slowly dwindling into darkness.

"Isla . . ." She said the child's name in a broken breath.

Rafe reached for her hand through the bars. "She needs a mother."

"You aren't fighting fair, Rafe." Diana's fingertips trembled in his hold.

"I'm a scoundrel. We never play fair." He then turned to Caddington. "I want your word that she goes free and that she will be unharmed. Then you will get what you want."

"And what is it you think I want that I do not have already?" Caddington asked, his eyes glinting with hateful desire.

"You have me here, yes, but you do not have my submission," Rafe said. "If I let you do what you will . . . if I agree . . ."

There was triumph in Caddington's face as his fingers caressed his whip.

"Prove it. Bare your back and face the wall."

Rafe reluctantly let go of Diana and unbuttoned his waistcoat, then pulled his shirt off over his head. The pearl necklace Diana had given him was wrapped around his wrist. He'd worn it tonight, needing the strength that little pearl would give him, because it reminded him of Diana's love for him.

He braced his palms against the rock wall, not looking

at anything as Caddington opened the cell door behind him. The slap of leather falling to the floor and the hiss of it slithering across the stones as the whip uncoiled made Rafe grit his teeth.

The whip whistled through the air, and Diana screamed. Her cry hit him harder than the blow of the whip, which set fire to his skin. His face went hot with pain as three more blows cut across his bare back. Caddington paused, breathing hard as he came toward Rafe and grabbed him by the shoulder, forcing him to turn. Whatever he saw on Rafe's face seemed to please him.

"Yes . . . I believe you. You will give me what I want. Your beautiful pain. You and I will have fun together, won't we?"

Rafe's head swarmed like it was full of angry bees, stinging him with memories of the past. His father had known what sort of man Caddington was and what he would want. That was why he'd tried to send Rafe home. He had tried to protect his son and had been killed for it.

"Yes," Caddington groaned in the light. "You see it now. You were always to be mine. Breaking you will give me the greatest pleasure."

Caddington stepped back to the edge of the cell door. "Phelps, dispose of the girl. Break her neck and make it look like a riding accident."

"No!" Rafe turned, ready to lunge, but Phelps raised a pistol, stopping him in his tracks. "You made a promise, Caddington. We had an agreement," Rafe snarled, his back still burning.

"I don't bargain with thieves," Caddington said.

"If you think a bullet will stop—" Rafe surged forward, but Caddington stepped just outside the cell door and slapped it shut an instant before Rafe would have gained his freedom.

"I don't need a bullet to stop you." Caddington pushed the keys into the lock and nodded at Phelps.

Phelps tucked his pistol into a leather belt at his waist and unlocked Diana's cell. She backed up into the corner closest to Rafe.

"Fight him when you are clear of the cellar," Rafe whispered in her ear. "My horse is outside. Take it and go to Ashton. Protect our child."

She turned to face him, her gaze spearing into his. "Then stay alive," she said. "I have waited my whole life for you, and I will not lose you now."

Phelps seized Diana, dragging her away. Her hands remain clasped in his for an instant before her fingers slipped free. She struggled against Phelps. He slapped her hard across the face. She stumbled and went down to the ground limp, her eyes closed as she lay upon the floor.

"Diana!" Rafe roared as Phelps lifted the unconscious woman in his arms and tossed her over his shoulder.

Caddington leaned back against the wall opposite Rafe's cell, grinning like a cat who'd just trapped a canary beneath its paws.

"I knew your pain would be exquisite," he sighed dreamily. "I have fantasized about this over and over, and I feared my dreams would never measure up to the real thing. Were I an artist, I would paint your face a thousand times, a thousand ways, showing the way grief and loss have destroyed your soul piece by piece."

He took a step forward. "You're just like your father. Your weakness is the same. Every time I took his money, I took not only his pride but his self-worth. His love for you, though . . . that I hadn't expected. And watching him see me covet you . . . He knew I would want to hurt you. He died to save you. And now he's failed. And you've failed your own child just as you failed Miss Fox. She will die, and your daughter . . . Well perhaps when she is grown I will take her too and watch her suffer as you do now—unless you comply. And I will tell her what a pathetic fool her father was. Women do have the prettiest tears, don't they?"

Isla . . . in this man's hands. The thought nearly made Rafe's knees buckle. Whatever strength he'd had was gone. He could not stop Phelps from killing Diana. Could not stop Caddington from taking Isla someday. It was over.

With a cold smile, Caddington nodded at the wall. "Face the wall."

Body shaking, Rafe turned to face the wall, listening for the sound of keys turning once more in the lock and of Caddington's boots as he stepped into the cell. He'd finally met his end. The sense of urgency to live fast and furiously had stopped. Rafe was out of time.

"We're all alone, Rafe. There's no one coming to save you now. You will die alone in this dark cell. Unfortunately for you, it won't be fast. I know how to keep my toys alive."

The whip hissed and bit into his back like a viper. Rafe grunted as his skin split beneath the lash and he felt the warmth of blood trickle down his back. Caddington's words played over and over in his mind, but after another two blows knocked the wind from him and he fell against the wall, gasping, his vision blurred. For a brief instant, he wasn't sure where he was—he knew only that he was somewhere else *with* someone else.

Rafe blinked against the sunny light coming into the

room, a room he recognized, the Lennox library, but as it was years ago when he'd been a boy.

A middle-aged man sat before a chessboard, studying the pieces carefully.

"He's wrong, you know," the man said as he lifted his gaze from the board. Rafe stared back into his father's eyes.

"So long as you have yourself, you are never truly alone. Your mother told me that once when we were young and first married. She is a brilliant creature, my Reggie. She always knew that she was valuable, not just to others but to herself. Somehow I had forgotten that I mattered, but there is power in believing in oneself. And it's not too late for you, my boy." His father said this with such gentle affection that Rafe's heart lurched. "Thomasina has her pianoforte, Ashton likes chess, and Joanna has her books, but you, my boy . . . you like risk. Like me." He stood, once more looking at the pieces on the board as if planning his next move. "Do you know what the greatest risk a person can take is?"

Rafe shook his head.

"It's the risk of daring to *live*. That is the greatest risk one can take." He met Rafe's gaze, a sad smile on his lips. "I'm so sorry. That night you found me at that tavern, I should have gone home with you."

Rafe tried to swallow past the lump in his throat. "Why didn't you?"

"I was afraid to face your mother . . . and I had to stop Andrew Caddington from doing what he's doing to you now. I went back into the tavern to kill him, but I failed you."

Rafe took a step toward his father. "No. It was I who

failed you. If I hadn't left the house, if I had listened to Ashton and stayed home . . ."

Malcolm shook his head. "You were a *child*, Rafe. None of this has ever been your fault. The fault will always be mine for leaving that night, for leaving every night to lose our family's fortune, your mother's dowry, all of it."

Rafe shook his head. "But you *saw* me that night. I know you saw me when you tried to cross the road."

"I saw you . . . and I feared you'd been hurt by Caddington while I'd gone back inside the tavern."

"So it is *my* fault," Rafe rasped.

"No," his father said, his tone gentle. "Rafe, one of the tavern wenches hit me in the head minutes earlier—I was unsteady on my feet and should have looked out for coaches. What happened was *my* fault."

The sunny library began to shimmer around them.

"We don't have much time, my boy. You must listen to me. Diana is still alive. Fight for her, for Isla—for yourself." Malcolm's gaze dropped back to the chessboard. His fingers caught on the edge of the board, lifted it suddenly, and the pieces tumbled off the surface, clattering onto the wood floor.

Rafe and his father stared at each other. "Break the rules, Rafe. *Upset the game.* Take every risk."

"Father!" Rafe gasped as the world began to slide into darkness. "I never told you—" He had to tell his father he loved him, but already he could no longer see him.

"I know, my boy. I've always known." His father's last words were a whisper of gold thread, binding the pieces of his shattered heart back together.

Rafe fell to his knees once more, this time on the cold stone floor of Caddington's cell. The sunny library was gone and so was his father—but fire had returned to Rafe's blood.

Fire and rage.

Take every risk.

It was the fear of risk that had held him back. The hope, however faint, that if he surrendered himself to Caddington, the man would spare those he loved. Hope wasn't what he needed. Risk meant not trusting hope or fate. He needed to trust himself. He wasn't alone, so long as he believed in himself.

Even though pain was *everywhere* in Rafe's body and it felt like his back had been shredded, his fury brewed like a violent summer storm just beneath his skin.

"Get up," Caddington snapped in a bored tone.

Rafe rose, a pounding in his ears running far deeper than the blood roaring in his head. It was the ancient rhythm of life that went beyond everything Rafe had understood until that moment.

Upset the game.

He heard the whip lash out, and Rafe swiftly leaned to the side, holding up his arm and letting the leather coil around his wrist. He gripped it and yanked, hard. Caddington stumbled forward, not expecting the move.

Rafe jerked the whip out of Caddington's hands and let it fall to the floor. Then he raised his fists in a fighting stance and waved for Caddington to come at him.

He smiled grimly at Caddington. "My brother was a champion boxer."

"But not you," Caddington sneered as he raised his own fists. "I know. I've followed your every move since your father died. You were never much good at anything, just like your father."

Rafe waited for Caddington to take a swing at him, and then he ducked. The moment Caddington came close enough with that missed punch, Rafe swept his leg out, knocking the man down onto his back. He'd taken down dozens of the best brutes in boxing rings with that very move. He stood over Caddington, his blood roaring in his ears.

"I never fought in any of the fighting salons . . . because I *cheat*."

Then he kicked Caddington square in the face with his boot.

❧

DIANA KEPT HERSELF AS LIMP AS POSSIBLE SO AS NOT TO let that foul man Phelps know she wasn't unconscious. She had taken Rafe's warning to heart. She had to wait for her moment and then *fight*. Nausea filled her belly where Phelps's shoulder dug into it, but she fought the need to vomit. He passed the steps of the cellar and clear, fresher air hit her nose. She saw moonlight cut harshly through the windows as Phelps walked down the corridor.

Any minute now, she would take her chance . . .

Her body swayed as he adjusted her on his shoulder, and she felt the cold handle of a pistol briefly pass by her fingertips. Phelps took two more steps, and when her hands moved again, she grabbed the pistol, pulling it free of his leather belt.

Diana had but one thought as she pulled the trigger and felt the man's body jerk with the impact of the muffled gunshot.

Save Rafe. Save Isla.

Phelps crashed into a wall. One hand gripped a faded tapestry, which he pulled down as his body sank to the floor. Pain crunched through her hip and shoulder as she fell to the floor beside him, knocking the wind from her. The tapestry fluttered down over them, and she fought to get free of the heavy moth-eaten fabric. Phelps lay slumped against the wall, the tapestry half draped over him like a death shroud. He gripped his lower stomach, where blood welled up thick and black in the moonlight. His spent pistol now lay useless next to him. She would have given anything for a second gun so she could charge back to the cellar and save Rafe, but she didn't have time to search for one and did not know who else might be here. She had to do what he'd commanded, ride for help.

"You've killed me," Phelps rasped, a look of shock on his face. "You're nothing but a pathetic woman . . ."

A wave of cold fury burned within Diana as she rose to her feet and stared down at him.

"When a man believes women aren't capable of anything, he is the one who will pay the price for that mistake. Caddington did the same, but I know something he does not." She watched Phelps's lips move as he tried to speak, but his strength was already leaving him.

"Lord Lennox *will* come for Rafe, and I shall be the one to lead him here. Your master will die tonight. I shall make certain of it."

Then she did the hardest thing of her life. She turned and ran away from the man she loved in order to get help. She just prayed she could get back in time.

She felt the hidden eyes of the servants as she moved toward the door.

"You're free to escape this house, but if you are here

when I return, I will assume you are loyal to Caddington and you will face justice."

She wrenched the heavy oak door open and ran out to Rafe's horse waiting on the gravel drive. The beast responded to her as she swung herself up in the saddle and dug her heels into the flanks.

"Fly!" she hissed in the creature's ear. "*Fly!*"

CHAPTER 18

I sla stirred awake, feeling strange and full of sorrow. She'd thought she heard Papa talking to her, but perhaps that was just a dream.

"Papa?"

She pushed back her blankets and found Nanny was reading by the fire.

"Was Papa here?" she asked.

"Yes, a short while ago. He kissed you good night before he went to bed," Nanny said as she closed her book. "And *you* should go on back to bed, dear."

Isla shook her head. "No. I had a bad dream. I want to see Papa!" As she slipped out of her bed, she glimpsed the portraits of her other papa and her other mama on the shelf close to her bed. Beneath them was a stack of letters. Papa only ever put those portraits out when he went away.

"Nanny . . ." She pointed to the letters. "Did Papa go away? He left some letters for me." She loved to hear Papa read letters to her, especially when they were from his family, because he always made funny voices to sound like her aunts and uncles. But the fact that he'd left letters with her parents' portraits made her stomach tighten with fear.

"What are those?" Nanny left her chair by the fire and carefully lifted the portraits to retrieve the letters. "They are addressed to your aunt and uncle . . . What on earth?" She looked at Isla in growing concern. "We need to see Lord Lennox at once." Nanny took the letters in one hand and Isla's palm in her other. They reached Uncle Ashton's bedchamber door, and she rapped her knuckles on it.

"My lord? I'm sorry to disturb you, but I believe it's urgent!"

After a moment, the door opened. Uncle Ashton wore his dressing gown and held a lit candle.

"Mrs. Chesterfield? What's wrong? Is Isla all right?"

"The girl is fine, but Isla found these by her bed. Mr. Lennox came to see her after she was asleep, and I believe he left these for you." She passed Uncle Ashton the letters. "I'm sorry I didn't notice sooner, but he had tucked them underneath the portraits of her parents."

"Rosalind, darling, wake up," Uncle Ashton called over his shoulder. "Come inside, Mrs. Chesterfield." Her uncle stepped back and let Nanny and Isla come into his bedchamber.

Aunt Rosalind was pulling on a pale-pink dressing gown and tying the bright-blue sash around her waist as they entered. When she saw Isla, she held out her arms and Isla ran to her aunt and hugged her as Rosalind knelt down to catch her.

"Isla, dear, what's the matter?"

"I had a bad dream," Isla confessed. "I dreamed Papa left me . . ." She didn't want to relive that dream, of running through the gardens, calling for him and never finding him just as a storm opened up above her. Papa would never leave her forever. Would he?

Ashton set his candle down and opened the envelope with his name. His eyes narrowed, then widened.

"Christ," he muttered. He shoved the letter at Rosalind. She sat down on the floor to read it, whispering the words aloud, forgetting that Isla was right beside her.

Ash,

I know that the last year has been good between us. I wish with everything that it could have continued that way, but my past has caught up with me. The story is too long to tell, but if fate will protect me one last time, Diana may live this night to share it all with you. She is my wife in all the ways that matter; please treat her as such as my last wish. Let her live at Foxglove Hall and raise Isla as her child. See that she has all the dividends from my investments. I know you cannot give me financial support, not after what I've done all these years, but please support them. They are the family of my heart. I wish I could say that I will make you proud of me at least once in my life, but I fear when you learn the truth it will not matter. I love you, brother. I only wish I'd said it more often.

—Rafe

"Ash, what does he mean? It sounds like Diana may be in trouble."

"He also left letters for you, Mother, Thomasina, Joanna, Diana, and Isla," Ashton said as he rifled through the stack of slender letters Nanny had given him. "I fear he isn't coming back."

Uncle Ashton's face went white as he stared at Isla and Rosalind. "I . . ." Whatever it was he wanted to say to her, he couldn't finish it.

"Where would he go? Why did he leave?" Nanny asked him.

"The letter is damnably vague on those points . . ." Uncle Ashton sank into his chair and buried his face in his hands. Isla pulled free of Rosalind and hurried over to her uncle, setting a hand on his knee.

"Mayhap Papa's friends know where he is?"

Ashton looked up. "Will and Caspian?"

Isla nodded.

"Kitten, you're bloody brilliant." Ashton kissed her forehead and rushed from the room, leaving Rosalind to be in charge.

"Mrs. Chesterfield, wake everyone up and have the cook prepare some food and brew some tea." Rosalind stopped by the bassinet near her bed and kissed her child's head before adjusting his blankets. "Ashton will need to be ready for whatever we must do."

❧

DIANA SAW A GROUP OF RIDERS COMING TOWARD HER IN the distance. Dawn was an hour away, and the skies were a faint purple at the edge of the horizon. There was enough light for her to see the horses as they thundered toward her, but not enough to know whether to expect friend or foe. When they were close enough to be recognized, a sob of relief choked her throat.

It was Lord Lennox, followed by three other men. She halted her horse upon the road and waited for them to reach her.

"Diana?" Ashton gasped. He slowed his horse, causing

it to snort and toss its head. "We feared something had happened to you. Where is Rafe?"

She glanced at the riders behind him: Brock Kincade, the intimidating Scottish brother-in-law, and two other men Diana thought looked familiar but could not place. One was fair-haired and the other dark. Each wore a worried look as they waited for her to speak.

"Lord Caddington kidnapped me, and Rafe exchanged his life for mine." Diana pointed back the way she'd come. "We must hurry. Caddington will kill him!"

Ashton nodded and she turned her horse back down the path. Now she led the charge to Caddington's home. She'd been afraid they would ask a thousand questions, questions she didn't have time to answer truthfully, but Lord Lennox had trusted her brief statement and followed her.

For the first time in the last hour she had hope, feeble though it was. She couldn't get the image of that whip striking Rafe's back out of her mind, nor could she stop reliving the moment when he'd removed the mask. *Rafe and Tyburn.* The two men she loved were one and the same. She hadn't been angry with him, nor did she feel betrayed, no matter what that devil Caddington had tried to convince Rafe of. She had been relieved, even overjoyed at that moment, only to become terrified when she realized she was going to lose both of them.

He won't die, he wouldn't dare.

She tried to argue with herself, but she had seen that he'd given up when Phelps had been given the order to kill her. He couldn't know she was still alive, and if he didn't . . . Surely he wouldn't give up on her and his daughter like that. He'd made it clear while courting her that she had become his world, that he had nothing left but her and Isla to fight for . . .

She turned back from the dark path where those thoughts were leading her, and suddenly tears blurred her vision too much for her to see the road ahead of her. Her horse was lathered with sweat and foam dripped from its mouth as they reached the gates of Caddington's home. As they approached the house, she jerked the reins, halting her horse, and threw herself from the saddle so fast she nearly tripped over her torn skirts.

Ashton and the others were on her heels, pistols raised as they entered the house, expecting trouble. Phelps's body lay where she'd left it. His dead eyes stared into nothing, the tapestry still partially draped over him.

Lord Lennox looked between Diana and the body of the man she'd killed, his brows raised in a silent question.

"He tried to kill me—" Diana pointed to the pistol that lay abandoned on the floor. "But I was quicker."

One of the men who had come with Lord Lennox and Brock looked around with uncertainty. "Where is everyone?"

"Yes, it's far too quiet," the other man agreed.

"Aye." Brock passed the stairs, his pistol still ready.

"Before I left the house, I told the servants to flee. It seems that they did."

They searched the hall, and Diana caught sight of a body that hadn't been there when she'd fled.

"No," she whispered, her heart suddenly freezing. "No . . . no . . ."

"Rafe!" Lord Lennox bellowed as he ran to his brother's body. Rafe's back was slashed to ribbons. The sight turned

Diana's stomach so violently she nearly tossed her accounts.

Lord Lennox turned Rafe onto his side, and Rafe's closed eyes fluttered.

"He's alive!" Lord Lennox said. "Thank God. Rafe, damn you, hold on." Lennox glanced around. "We need to bind his back, to stem the bleeding as much as possible. Will, go to the stables and see if they have a wagon we can use to transport him home. Brock, ride for the doctor in the village at once. Have him meet us there."

Diana crouched beside Rafe, brushing her fingertips over his face. A lump formed in her throat when she saw her mother's pearl necklace wrapped around his wrist. He truly was both her beloved Tyburn and her darling Rafe. He was *everything* to her. She couldn't lose him now.

"Rafe, fight for me—for *us*," she said, tears falling now, blinding her to all but his face. His eyes finally won the struggle, and they remained open as he looked up at her.

"Di . . . ," he rasped. "You came back . . ." He choked on the words, a shocked look in his eyes.

She could scarcely breathe. "I'll always come back for you."

His lips twitched, but he didn't have the strength to smile. "Father told me . . . upend the board . . . break the rules . . ." His eyes drifted to his brother's face. "Ash?" he whispered in shock.

"I'm here." Ashton's usually controlled voice broke as he held Rafe's face in his palm. "I'm here, little brother."

"Ash . . . No . . . He'll kill you . . ." Rafe's body shuddered. "Can't let you face him."

"Haven't you learned by now that I would do *anything*

for you, you fool?" Ashton asked. Diana put a fist to her mouth to hold back a sob.

"My fault . . . Father . . ." Rafe's gaze began to drift into the distance.

"No, it wasn't!" Diana said, then turned to Ashton. "What happened to your father wasn't his fault, Lord Lennox. Caddington met Rafe and wanted your father to give him over for his debts. Caddington wanted to hurt Rafe as he'd done to many young men in his care. Your father saw the danger he posed to Rafe, so he tried to send him home. What happened to your father, that coach hitting him—it wasn't Rafe's fault. You can't blame him."

"Is that the truth?" Ashton asked her, his blue eyes swirling with storms. "Caddington wanted my father to give Rafe over?"

"Yes," Diana said. "Even your mother doesn't know, but Rafe has carried that guilt all this time, guilt that he stayed when he shouldn't have, but he couldn't leave your father and you behind. He was a child, and he only wanted to help you bring your father home."

Sudden tears dripped down Ashton's face as he bent and pressed his forehead to Rafe's, his body sheltering his younger brother's as he drew in a ragged breath.

"I didn't know. Forgive me—*I didn't know*. I should never have placed the blame upon you, but I was a coward."

"No . . . ," Rafe murmured drowsily. "You were . . . my hero . . . *always*."

"Ashton, I have a wagon ready out front!" Will shouted from the doorway of the house.

"Caspian, help me lift him. Diana, be ready to assist us if we start to fall," Lennox commanded.

Lennox and Caspian got Rafe to his feet. They were halfway down the hall when something clattered behind them. Diana retrieved Ashton's pistol from the floor and spun to face the threat.

Caddington stood in the doorway to the cellar, his face a mess of blood and dark bruises. One arm clutched his chest as if protecting broken ribs. It was clear he and Rafe must have fought before Rafe had escaped the cellar. In his other hand, he held a gun, pointed at Rafe's back.

"Stand down . . . Lord Lennox," Caddington wheezed as he approached the body of his dead manservant. "Your brother is wanted for . . . so many crimes. I have his . . . signed confession to it all. He is *mine*."

Diana raised the pistol. "He will never belong to you!"

Lennox gently took the gun from Diana's shaking hand. "No, my dear. You've been brave enough this night. I will not have you shedding any more blood."

Ashton now faced Caddington, who seemed to be enjoying the agony he was causing.

"Careful, Lennox," he said, still shuffling forward. "Helping two murderers escape? Assaulting a magistrate? You will be ruined."

"On the contrary. The Lord High Chancellor is a good friend of mine. If I were to suffer you to live, he would see you removed from your position and charges brought against you. It is *you* who will be ruined, Caddington."

For a moment, Diana saw doubt cross Caddington's face. He looked at the pistol that lay beside Phelps's body and lunged for it. He grabbed it and took aim. Diana turned her body to shield Rafe as much as she could.

Crack!

Diana flinched at the gunshot, expecting pain. But

none came. When she opened her eyes, she glimpsed Caddington slumping to the floor, dead, Ashton's bullet having struck the center of his evil heart. Ashton slowly lowered his pistol, still staring at Caddington for a long moment as though to make sure the man breathed no more. It was only then that Diana remembered the pistol Caddington had tried to use had been spent when she'd killed his manservant.

"They say revenge doesn't bring any satisfaction," Ashton said quietly. "But they are wrong. I am quite satisfied knowing that man shall never hurt another person ever again."

Diana agreed. She found that justice was only for someone who could be redeemed. A man like Caddington had no chance at redemption. She let out a shaky breath, her legs feeling like they just might give out beneath her in sheer relief that it was all over.

For a long moment Diana stared at Caddington's body, almost unable to believe he was dead, that this monster who'd haunted Rafe's nightmares was finally, truly gone.

"Come on!" Caspian said. "We must move."

The three of them carried Rafe down to the waiting wagon.

Diana sat in the hay beside Rafe, who was lying upon his stomach. Will drove the horses in a half circle until they were back onto the road and away from that dark and awful place—away from death. Lord Lennox sat on the other side of Rafe in the back of the wagon. The slow light of dawn illuminated his face.

"Tell me everything—please. I need the truth, all of it," Lennox pleaded with Diana. She let out a shaky breath and told Ashton everything.

"I met Rafe when he held up the coach I was on. He was pretending to be a Scotsman named Tyburn . . ."

She left out nothing, not even the fact that she and Rafe had made love more than once. She confessed that she had also taken up robbery using Tyburn's identity to save her family home, learning about the story of Malcolm Lennox's death, and how Caddington had formed an unnatural fixation on Rafe all those years ago.

"My father must have gone back into the tavern after trying to send Rafe home," said Lennox. "He must've known Rafe was in danger and wanted to stop Caddington. But he was attacked by one of the wenches and robbed. That blow to his head left him disoriented when I found him. He wasn't thinking clearly when he saw Rafe across the street from us. I tried to stop him from crossing, but . . . I couldn't. What happened that night could *never* be Rafe's fault. I never truly believed Rafe killed him, but in my grief and anger I told him I did, and shame kept me from taking back those words. Christ, he was only a child, though in truth I was not much older. It was easier to put my fury and blame on him." He dragged a hand over his weary face.

"How old were you?" Diana asked.

"I was fifteen, a young man, I . . ."

She put a hand on his arm. "You were a child too. I believe it's time for the Lennox men to stop blaming themselves, and each other, for what was an accident."

Lennox smiled then, the expression fond. "No wonder my brother is madly in love with you. I'm glad for it. He deserves someone to be his champion after so long."

His unexpected praise hit her heart in a most tender place.

"What will happen now?" Diana asked after a moment. "Now that Caddington and Phelps are dead? We killed them." Diana met his weary gaze. She didn't want to think about the legal ramifications or the emotional ones of having taken a life, but it was something neither of them could avoid.

Lennox took a moment before replying. "I learned a long time ago that sometimes the only way to stop evil is to remove its pieces from the chessboard. Then it cannot make any more moves against you and it cannot hurt you. I will speak to the king as well as the Lord High Chancellor and tell them what happened. George will listen to me. I have not worked all these years without the means to garner his favor and have something like this go my way. If it helps, I will take Phelps's death on my own as well."

"No, my lord, you mustn't—"

Ashton held up a hand. "Let me do this for you, for the woman my brother loves. The woman who will cherish both him and his child. You are now under the protection of the house of Lennox." In that moment, the already striking lord became a knight of old, his vow moving over her, leaving goosebumps on her skin.

They looked down at the bloody ravaged stripes on Rafe's back, and Ashton's face hardened.

"I wish that I could strike that devil down a thousand times over for what he's done."

Diana, who would never have considered herself a bloodthirsty creature, agreed. He was right. Evil did not belong on the chessboard.

"If . . . *When*," Ashton corrected himself. "When Rafe is feeling better, I shall let you marry straightaway by special license, no more delays. Lord knows you've both had enough challenges in your lives. I won't add one more to the list."

"Thank you," Diana whispered. Though in truth she didn't care about the wedding. She only wanted Rafe to be all right, to see him smiling at her, to let him tease her and feel his lips on hers and his body wrapped around hers at night. Neither of them would ever be alone again if only he would be all right. She stroked Rafe's sweat-dampened hair and silently urged Will to make the horses go faster.

Hold on, my love . . . hold on.

CHAPTER 19

All of Lennox House was awake when the wagon rolled to a stop. Half a dozen footmen ran down the steps to meet them. Diana watched anxiously as Rafe was carried inside. Joanna, Regina, and Rosalind were at the entryway, along with Mrs. Chesterfield, who held Isla's hand. The little girl watched her father with tear-filled eyes as he was carried past her up the stairs. She clutched her little doll to her chest and made not one sound.

It was the child's silence that broke through the state of numbness Diana had drifted into, pushing her into action. Isla shouldn't see Rafe like this, bloodied, broken, fighting for his life. She rushed over to the child and hoisted her up into her arms, turning the girl's face away and cupping the back of her head with one hand. Isla trembled in her arms, just as she had that day they'd been trapped in the storm.

"It's all right, my little darling. It will be all right, you'll see," she promised the girl. She would do whatever she had to do to keep that promise, for both of them. "Mrs. Chesterfield, would you get some warm milk and biscuits? I'm taking Isla back to the nursery. She should be in bed, resting."

"*No!* I want to stay. Please?" The little girl curled her arms tight around Diana's neck. Such a strong protective instinct surged up within Diana, as though this child was truly hers to love and protect forever.

Diana brushed the girl's curls away from her face. "I know, my darling. But this is not a memory you should have of your father. I'll make sure you see him the moment he feels better."

She carried Isla to the nursery and had just reached the top of the stairs when Brock and the village doctor raced past them. Neither man said a word as they passed, hurrying instead to Rafe's room.

When Diana reached the nursery, she set the girl down next to her bed and pulled back the covers. She patted the bed, and Isla crawled into the center of it.

"Will Papa be all right?" Isla asked, those sweet doe eyes so full of trust. This child had known so much darkness, so much loss. How could she ever bear to lose her father?

In an instant, Rafe's words came back to her like a lightning strike: *"I would never fail my child. Never."*

"Yes," she whispered. "He will get better, I promise." Though her mind knew it was not a promise she could make, her heart told her that Rafe would not let Isla down. He would break every rule there was to come back to them.

She saw Rafe so clearly now, more clearly than ever

before. Her mysterious highwayman, her teasing gentleman, her prayer in the dark to once more find the light. He was as multifaceted as any jewel he'd ever stolen, as beautifully complex as the night sky without a moon to hide the stars.

She brushed a hand through Isla's soft russet curls and kissed the girl's head. She froze as she found herself staring at something that nearly stopped her heart.

Two portraits sitting up on a shelf beside the bed came level with Diana's eyes. Time seemed to stretch outward into an infinite moment before she snapped back to herself again. Diana sucked in a shocked breath. It was *impossible*. It made no sense.

"Miss Fox?" Isla turned to see what Diana was fixated on.

"Isla, who . . . who are these people?" Diana asked. She lifted up the set of portraits and sat down on the bed beside the child. Isla crawled over and touched the gilt frames in a familiar way, as though she'd done it a thousand times.

"That's my mama. My *first* mama. And this is my other papa," she whispered. "They died."

Diana felt her head spin as fractured memories and dreams about mirrors in a world she could not join her family in came crashing in around her. It was as though the mirror in her mind had shattered, sending glass shards in a hundred different directions, and at last she saw the truth she'd been too afraid to face in her dreams.

"Isla, what was your mother's name?"

The little girl stared at the woman's portrait with soft, sad eyes. "Papa used to say, 'Sweet Ellie, love of my life.'"

Diana stared at the woman in the frame. "Ellie . . . Was that short for Eleanor?"

Isla shrugged. "I dinna ken," the little girl said.

Diana's elder sister's pleasing countenance gaze back at her through layers of oil paint. Eleanor looked young, vibrant, beautiful, and *wonderful*.

She pointed to the portrait of the handsome young man. "And what was your papa's name?" She'd never met the man Eleanor had danced with on that fateful night of a long-ago Merton country ball. She'd only known the man had been Scottish and they'd run away a few days later. Eleanor had left a note saying goodbye, saying that someday she'd come home to her family. Only she never had. Diana, brokenhearted though she was, had understood that the house had been too lonely without their mother.

"She called him Angus."

Diana rubbed her thumb gently over the pair of frames the way Isla had. Eleanor had died . . . as had her husband. Isla was their daughter.

Isla is my niece. That truth was both sweet and heartbreaking. She'd never wanted to believe her sister was dead, but now she knew for sure. And yet her sister's daughter had come into her life like a tiny miracle. It was equal parts sad and wondrous.

"Isla." Her voice broke as she tried to speak. "I think . . . your mother was my sister."

The girl stared up at her with surprise, and Diana wondered how she'd been so blind to the truth for so long. Isla was so much like Eleanor. She might favor her father in hair and eye color, but her face, her expressions, they were *entirely* Eleanor. The answer to that last painful mystery in her life had been right in front of her all this time.

She replayed every conversation she'd had with Rosalind and Rafe about Isla's parents. They had died of an illness, and Eleanor . . . Oh God, Eleanor's body had been taken to be sold to a doctor, and Rafe and his family had saved Isla from the body snatchers.

She wrapped her arms around Isla and pulled her even closer as tears fell freely down her cheeks. The last bit of her stubborn strength failed her at last, and Diana broke, truly broke as everything she'd held on to since her mother's death clawed its way to the surface. Isla cried too, and they held each other fast until they both cried themselves out.

"Will ye still be my new mama?" Isla asked in a quiet voice. Diana smiled past her tears.

"Yes . . . you've always been *mine*. You are my niece, and now you are my daughter. I will never leave you, sweetheart." It was likely Isla didn't fully understand just what Diana had vowed to her, but someday she would. She would learn that destiny had brought Eleanor's daughter home, because Rafe Lennox's heart was made of gold.

❧

"How is he?"

Rafe heard his mother's voice through the fog of pain.

Another voice came through more clearly. "The damage to his back is severe, but I have cleaned and stitched the wounds that pose the greatest danger. The bandages must be kept clean and changed daily to prevent a fever. He will need to sleep on his stomach, and

I would recommend a diet of beef to help with the loss of blood. I imagine he will have to rebuild the muscles of his back from the damage done by the whip, but he is young and healthy, so there is every hope he will recover. Once his skin has healed, he should practice his usual movements else his muscles will never regain their strength."

"Thank you, Doctor," he heard Ashton say.

Rafe wanted to move but had not the strength to do so.

"Ash," he whispered. Even that single utterance scraped every nerve in his throat.

A comforting hand settled on the back of his head. "I'm here, little brother. Don't try to speak."

"Diana . . . " He hissed as pain shot up his back from the effort of speaking.

"She's safe. She is looking after Isla for you. *Everyone* is safe, do you understand? Now be quiet. You need to rest."

It was as if his older brother knew what he needed to hear the most. Rafe relaxed and drifted to sleep.

He was unsure how long he had slept when he woke again, but when he licked his chapped lips, he felt the presence of someone nearby.

"Water," he said.

A glass was carefully brought to his lips and he drank slowly, grateful for the assistance. When he found the strength to open his eyes, he saw his mother held the glass. Her blue eyes watched his face, and he saw dried tracks of tears covering her cheeks. His mother had been crying for *him*?

"Drink a little more for me, dear boy," she whispered, as though he were a child. "The doctor said you must drink."

"I'm sorry." He let out a breath and fought off a cold shudder.

His mother's eyes flashed. "You're *never* to say those words again, not to me. *I* am the one who is sorry." She bit her lip, and tears streamed down his mother's usually controlled face.

She set the glass on the table and smoothed a cool hand over his brow, brushing hair out of his eyes. "Ashton told me everything."

"He told you?" What had his brother said? He was too afraid to ask.

Regina nodded. "You didn't cause your father's death, Rafe. You were a little boy who wanted to bring him home. His choices were *never* your responsibility. He chose to leave our house that night, and he chose to put himself in that position. He stepped onto the road after he'd been injured and his balance was unsteady. None of these things are your fault."

Her fingers trembled as she sucked in a breath. "It is I who failed you, my darling boy. I never asked Ashton or you what happened. I assumed that you'd done something because Ashton blamed you. But he was a boy too. What does a lad of fifteen know about grief except that one can, temporarily, avoid it with anger?

"But I shouldn't have made the same mistake. I knew Malcolm's vices would someday lead to this. I just didn't think it would be so soon." She covered her mouth with the back of her hand, yet she didn't look away from him as she wept. "The years I've wasted . . . the years I should've had with you . . . my beautiful boy who only ever tried to be a son any mother would be proud of. And I am proud, Rafe, so very proud of you."

"Mother . . ." It felt like every rib was breaking in his chest as he absorbed her words and the love that layered them.

"I will spend the rest of my life missing your father, but I will not miss a moment more with *you*. If you'd let me, I wish to start again, to be the mother you deserve."

"I should've done something," Rafe confessed, his voice breaking. "If I'd only gone home as he'd wished, he might not have seen me and tried to cross the road."

Regina shook her head. "He chose to cross the street, Rafe. You must stop believing you could have done anything differently to change his actions."

Rafe blinked away thick tears and tried to regain his shaking breath. "But I am not the son you should have had."

His mother stroked the backs of her fingers over his cheek, her eyes bright.

"Nonsense. I would change nothing about you, Rafe. Even if you could turn back the hands of time and fix every mistake you've made, you wouldn't be *this* Rafe. I would never erase the man you've become, not even to have your father back."

Rafe moved his arm, carefully reaching out to clasp his mother's hand.

"I've done a great many things I regret . . ."

A twinkle sparkled in his mother's eyes. "If you mean those nocturnal activities involving masks and pistols, well, they brought you to Diana, didn't they? I know it might not be the most conventional method of courtship, but since when have any of my children ever done things conventionally? Thomasina was compromised by a notorious rake—thank God he's made a marvelous husband.

Ashton blackmailed his lovely wife into marriage. Joanna ran off to Scotland to elope with her charming Highlander." She grinned at him. "What's one more wild story to share with one's grandchildren?"

The tightness in Rafe's chest eased as he realized his mother was right. If he had never stopped that coach, if he had never met Diana, then he would never have found the star in the night sky leading home to his family.

"No more regrets," his mother said soothingly. "Do you understand? Not for any of us."

His eyes drifted closed once more as his mother continued to stroke his hair.

When he woke next, candlelight illuminated the room. Ashton sat in a chair close by, his fingers steepled as he watched Rafe. His blond hair was a little tousled, as though he'd tugged too hard at the strands. He seemed to be contemplating something.

"That's not a look I like," Rafe muttered. "I always get lectured when you have that look."

Ashton's lips twitched. "On the contrary, it's not a lecturing look, it's a look of . . ." Ashton paused and said slowly, "Deep clarity."

"Deep clarity?"

"Yes. I was thinking about how things would've been different if you hadn't been a part of my life. Part of this family. We wouldn't *be* a family."

Rafe moved to look more clearly at Ashton's face. "I'm afraid I don't follow."

Ashton lowered his hands. "You see, if you hadn't robbed Rosalind's coach, she never would've walked to this house in the storm and never would have fallen ill."

"Are you saying that I almost killed your wife?" Rafe

chuckled, but it hurt like the devil. "Because if memory serves, she almost killed *me* when she bloody shot me in the shoulder."

"What I am trying to say is that when Rosalind fell ill, I fell in love with her. But even then, I wouldn't have married her . . . not until you tricked her into that chess match against me and I won her hand in marriage." Ashton let out a slow breath. "I wouldn't have my wife—or my son, for that matter—without you."

A lump formed in Rafe's throat. He'd never thought of it that way. His eyes burned and even the tip of his nose tingled. *Damnation.* If his brother made him cry, it was going to hurt like hell.

"Joanna and Brock would never have made it to Gretna Green without your help, because you concealed their trail from me and my friends when we chased them. And let's not forget that time when Joanna saved Brock's life because *you* taught her how to fight."

At this, Rafe grinned. "She was an excellent pupil. Knocked the wind out of me more than once."

"Then there's Isla. She never would've found her home and her life without you." His lips curved in a fuller smile. "She would never have come home where she belongs." There was something about the way Ashton said *home* this time that puzzled Rafe. The word seemed layered with more meaning, but Rafe was too tired to consider what.

Ashton leaned closer. "What I am saying, little brother, is that you are the *heart* of this family." He placed a hand over Rafe's and squeezed it gently. "And it is my turn to care for you the way you've always done for us. I will see that Foxglove has a full staff, and all repairs shall be done at once. You will have an annual income befitting your role in this family. Any dividends you earn upon your investments will be yours to do with as you wish."

Rafe was stunned for a moment but soon recovered. "You know that money I gave you to invest was stolen, don't you?" He didn't want Ashton to rethink this later on. It was better to have the truth out now.

Ashton chuckled. "Yes, I am aware. But as I understand it, you never stole from those who couldn't afford it, and a good portion seems to have belonged to the man I consider most responsible for our father's death."

Rafe's smile died. "Caddington is truly dead?" He had only hazy memories, hearing Caddington's voice as they tried to flee and Ashton firing a shot.

"Yes, thankfully," Ashton replied. "I made sure of it."

"I didn't want you to carry the darkness of his death. I should have—"

Ashton silenced him with a shush, as though Rafe were a child. Lord, he'd been treated more like a child today than he ever had in his life. He wasn't quite sure he liked all the cooing and fussing.

"You carried your darkness long enough. It's time I take the burden for a while. It is what brothers do." Ashton's words brought back memories of the pair of them when they'd been young, before their father died. He'd followed Ashton everywhere like a young pup, tail wagging, waiting for any sign of affection, and Ashton had given it to him freely. He'd ruffle Rafe's hair and let him in on whatever adventure Ashton was involved in, and he'd always say, *"Come along, Rafe, I'll watch out for you. It's what brothers do . . ."*

This golden memory was buried so deep that Rafe had almost forgotten they'd once been so close. Could they be again? He dearly hoped so.

Rafe searched Ashton's face.

"You let me grow into my strength, Rafe. You suffered while I became the man I am. It's time I put that strength to use now." He cleared his throat. "I know you are still feeling wretched, but there are two ladies who are quite desperate to see you. Are you willing to have visitors?"

"You had better mean Diana and Isla, although I admit I'm terrified they shall weep at the sight of me."

"I think you're well worth the tears, little brother." Ashton walked over to the bedchamber door and opened it.

"He's ready to see you, but no climbing on him, sweetling. He's still hurt," Ashton counseled as Isla came into view where Rafe lay on the bed. Her face was shining with fresh tears, which broke his heart. He never wanted to make his child cry.

"Kitten, I'm all right." He held out a hand and she clutched it, holding on to him as though he were the only thing that mattered. And if that didn't make his own eyes fill with tears . . .

Diana now entered the room. "Rafe," she whispered, and he lifted his gaze to hers.

"I love the way you say my name—like a prayer."

"That's because it is." Diana held up the two small painted portraits of Isla's parents. He stared between her and the portraits, confused.

"All these years I prayed for answers, and *you* were the answer." She held the portrait of Isla's mother next to her own face. "Don't you see?" she asked, her voice wavering with a wave of emotions he didn't understand. He looked from the portrait to Diana.

Diana put a hand on Isla's shoulder. "My sister Eleanor is Isla's mother Ellie."

"Diana is my aunt *and* my mama," Isla said, noting how Rafe was slow to grasp the revelation he'd just been given.

"Your Eleanor is *Ellie?*" He stared between Isla and Diana, his heart stretching, filling with grief and love all at once. "How did you discover this?"

"I knew in my heart the moment I saw this portrait," said Diana. "But while you were resting, Mrs. Chesterfield showed me the bag you brought back from Scotland. It held Eleanor's clothing and letters—letters that she addressed to me but had never sent. I read them all, Rafe." Diana's voice shook. "After her husband, Angus, died, she was going to come home to Foxglove, to bring Isla to our estate, only she never made it. You fulfilled my sister's wishes and brought her daughter home to me."

"Those letters were for you?" He'd briefly read through a few of them when he'd first met Isla. But he would have remembered if one had been addressed to Diana, and none had been. "The letters held no name for whom they were intended."

Diana pulled one letter out of the pocket of her dress. She unfolded the paper and held it out to him so he could see the little symbol that was in place of a name.

"Yes, she always drew a little cat's face," Rafe said. "It's one of the reasons I call Isla 'kitten.' It made me think of her mother."

"It's a kit, actually, not a kitten. A baby fox. Eleanor always called me 'little fox' because I was the youngest member of the Fox family."

Rafe stared at the letter, thinking of how a strange

twist of fate had put those letters and that child into his path.

All this time Rafe had held Diana's past and Isla's future in that bag he'd carried all the way from Edinburgh. It was as though fate had pulled him toward Diana, their meeting inevitable somehow.

Isla looked between Rafe and Diana. Her tiny fingers were still tucked into Rafe's hand. "Will she still be my new mama?"

Diana bent to kiss Isla's forehead and placed her hand over Rafe and Isla's joined palms. "Of course. It's the three of us from now on," she promised. "*Always*." She echoed the vows they'd made that day in the library when she'd agreed to marry him.

Rafe felt like he could fly. Despite the pain, anything felt possible now.

"I may fall asleep," Rafe said. "But I'd like for you both to stay."

Diana lifted Isla onto the bed, and she lay down and promptly fell asleep.

"Huh, she beat me to it," he muttered.

Diana lingered near the edge of the bed by Rafe, unsure of herself.

"I need to return something to you." Rafe lifted his wrist that still bore the pearl necklace as a bracelet. "This belongs with you." He sensed her hesitation. "You said it was your mother's. It belongs with you."

"I'd almost forgotten," Diana admitted. "It seems so silly to have worried about such a small thing when we first met." She undid the clasp of the necklace and slipped it off his wrist with great care before she fastened it around her neck. "And to think, all this time you held my *true* pearl—Isla."

"I saw how much it meant that night when you left it in my care," Rafe said. "I was careful with it, just as I will always be careful with you. You're *my* treasure, Diana."

Her eyes filled with fresh tears. "You must stop being so wonderful. I cannot cry anymore."

He chuckled, ignoring the flash of pain it caused. "As long as they're happy tears, I won't apologize."

"Rogue," she admonished with a little smile.

"*Your* rogue," he said. "I love you, my little fire drake. I vow to love you with every breath in me, with every bit of my soul."

She knelt by the bed, bringing her face close to his. Her brown eyes were bright with heat and shone with the light of the vast and beautiful universe that Diana held within her.

"I love you, Rafe. I love you with all that I am and all that I will be. You *saved* me—you gave me back myself. I'd got lost somewhere along the way, and you brought me home." She leaned in and kissed him, then looked over at Isla beside him. "You brought us both home." Then she kissed him again, and for far longer.

There was something exquisite about being kissed by the woman he loved even as his body burned with pain. But it was a pain he would endure again in an instant if he had to. It reminded him of how precious life was, how terribly short but infinitely sweet, if only one was brave enough to take the risk to live. To love.

His father had been right. He loved to take risks. And loving this woman and this child . . . they were his chance to live.

"God, I love you," he whispered. She threaded her fingers into his hair and smiled, her lips moving over his in a way that gave him his old strength back.

"Sleep, my fair prince. You've slain your dragons and have earned your rest. Isla and I will be here when you wake. We have years ahead of us to do all that we desire."

"Yes, we will." And then, with her touching him with tender fingers, he did as she commanded.

After so many years of struggling to find his way alone in the dark, Rafe Lennox followed the light of love shining from Diana, his beautiful star, and found his way home.

Rafe finished tucking the carefully wrapped gifts under the tree as Diana waited in the doorway of the Foxglove library. The once-empty library was again full of books, which Rafe had insisted on buying when he'd learned she'd sold nearly every book to pay debts. As always, her husband knew the exact way to make her fall even more in love with him. Tonight, garlands hung from every surface and more than one doorway held sprigs of mistletoe, creating delightful trouble among some of the servants, who seemed to take every advantage of the chance to kiss.

A beautiful yew tree had been felled and brought into the house by Rafe and the male servants four days ago. When she'd questioned the presence of a *tree* inside their house, Rafe chuckled and said it was a tradition from the royal court, which had started putting trees in the palace for Christmas as far back as 1800 when Queen Charlotte brought the first yew tree into Windsor.

Diana found that the large tree decorated with apples,

dried berries on strings, and colorful paper garlands was the most beautiful thing she'd ever seen. Rafe said it would only be a matter of time before the tradition caught on everywhere. Now that she'd seen the tree at its finest, she rather believed he was right. Someday, all of England would wish to have such trees in their homes.

She smiled as he carefully adjusted the stack of gifts beneath the tree. He had taken the matter of gift-giving most seriously. Every servant in the house had one under the tree from him and Diana. Isla had a small mountain of gifts just for her, of course.

Diana could scarcely believe how easily she and Rafe had settled into her home after their marriage. They had waited for him to heal and decided together to have a proper wedding breakfast, which had pleased Regina and Ashton beyond measure. Will and Caspian, who she now knew were the real Oxford and Cambridge highwayman, had even chosen to stay at Foxglove and had assisted with the repairs. They'd also taken Ashton up on his offer to invest their own money from their adventures, and both men were able to leave the life of highwaymen behind them.

Rafe had moved into Foxglove only a week after that awful night, well before they were properly wed. No one had protested, and what little town gossip had circulated had been brief and lacking any sting to it. As Ashton had explained, Rafe had suffered a terrible accident and needed rest and quiet to recuperate, and Lennox House was far too bustling and full to allow Rafe the rest he needed. It seemed that the neighbors were all quite pleased with the marriage and the knowledge that Foxglove, a once-majestic house, would regain its glory through the union of the Lennoxes and the Foxes.

Ashton had taken care of the situation with Caddington. They'd learned that Caddington's frequent deliveries of money to London, which Rafe and Diana had both robbed, were to be payments securing the loyalties of various aristocratic families. What had infuriated Ashton and Rafe was when they'd learned the money Caddington had been sending came from local merchants and small businesses in the countryside who'd been forced to pay for "protection." When the king had learned of this, he'd seen to it that Caddington's estate was stripped of its title, and the house and land were gifted to a man who'd recently done the Crown a favor and earned himself a title. Caddington's death had been listed officially as having been caused by a fight with Mr. Phelps, his manservant. None of the servants who'd worked for Caddington came forward in his defense.

Rafe had been quiet whenever Ashton visited them and gave new information on the situation. When it was finally resolved, Rafe had pulled Diana into his arms on a settee in the library and held her for a long while. She'd burrowed into him and kissed his cheek and held him in return, giving him her silent promise that he was safe at last. It was then they could truly turn their thoughts to the future.

Although she trusted Rafe, her experience with men had left her concerned that he might wish to assert himself as head of the household, making all the decisions. To her relief, this did not happen, though he freely offered his advice when he felt she needed it. He'd done exactly what he'd promised and became her partner, not her master.

With this new confidence in herself, she'd found that life truly could be magical when one found the right man.

Rachel came to visit every few days and delighted in Diana's newfound happiness. Diana wondered if life was *too* perfect. Whenever she voiced such concerns, Rafe would kiss her furrowed brow and remind her that she'd had a far from perfect past and perhaps she was due a more perfect future. So she'd stopped worrying and simply embraced all the good that had happened of late.

They continued to make repairs to the home, and they'd examined the account books and worked side by side with Mr. Peele and Mrs. Ripley to bring Foxglove back to its former glory. Some days, it was as though she'd stepped into a story and found fairy tales were, in fact, true.

Diana turned her thoughts back to her husband, who was still kneeling at the base of the tall, lushly decorated tree. With the last gift placed, Rafe stood proudly and brushed his hands on his trousers, then faced her with a twinkle of mischief in his eyes. "There. I've seen to everyone . . . but you."

"Me?" Diana laughed. "Whatever do you mean, *husband?*" She loved to call him that, to tease him and know that he was hers, *all* hers. He, in turn, seemed to delight in calling her *wife* just as much. They said the words as though it was a private joke between them, two people who'd given up on love and spouses only to have found each other.

"I still have to give you *your* gift." He stalked toward her in a way that sent butterflies fluttering in her lower belly. She so adored it when her husband showed that leopard-like grace whenever he came toward her with lust in his eyes.

"You bought me a wardrobe to fill two bedchambers," she reminded him. She had one more present of her own to give him, though it was quite impossible to wrap.

"Those were *necessities*, not gifts," he said. "And I used the money that Ashton invested for me because it's been paying back most handsomely."

Diana laughed. "And so did mine from Rosalind. Can you believe they put our money in the same India bonds without realizing it? Those two truly are made for each other."

"Sickeningly perfect," Rafe agreed, grinning.

It had stunned them both to learn that Rosalind and Ashton had taken their stolen fortunes and made the exact same investments, which had resulted in excellent returns. Those funds would continue to perform, and with Rafe's yearly income, for the first time in years Diana felt the fate of her home would be secure.

Rafe gently grasped Diana's waist and leaned in to nuzzle her cheek. "Back to the matter of your gift, *wife*." Excitement zinged from her cheeks down to her toes. This man's touch would always make her dizzy.

"What about yours?" she countered.

Beneath the tree, she had half a dozen presents with his name upon them. She'd purchased waistcoats to accent his hair and eyes, a new pocket watch, a signet ring with a fox's head upon it, and several other items. But the one she couldn't wrap was the one she wanted to give him most.

"Why don't you visit the nursery and see that Isla is finally asleep?" Rafe asked. "Then meet me in our bedchamber."

"What are you up to?" Rafe could be a delightful tease most of the time, and she loved his surprises.

"Nothing, my wife. Now, off you go." He turned her around to face the door and gently swatted her backside. She obediently left the library, unable to deny her curiosity. She did wish to make sure Isla was sleeping soundly. They had spent Christmas Eve at Lennox House, had a fine Christmas dinner, and played enough parlor games to wear the child out.

Isla's new nursery held the bed that Rafe had chosen for her. All of her toys and clothes had been moved from Lennox House after the marriage. Even Mrs. Chesterfield had agreed to come to Foxglove with them. Right now she was at her usual post by Isla's bed, but her book was abandoned and she was asleep. Diana crossed the room to stoke the fire with the poker and adjust the fire grate, then tucked Isla's covers up and readjusted the doll in her arms. A memory came back to her quite suddenly and vividly.

Diana and Eleanor had just opened their presents one year when Diana had been five and Eleanor was seven. Diana had been given a beautiful brunette doll who wore a lovely green gown. The doll had dark hair and brown eyes just like Diana. She thought it was the most beautiful doll she'd ever seen.

"What's her name?" Diana had asked her parents. They told her it was her duty to name her doll, but she then looked to her older sister as always for guidance in such crucial matters. "Eleanor, what should I call her?"

"Why, little fox, she's Mrs. Crumpet, of course. She's a duchess, you know," Eleanor had declared so confidently that Diana had accepted the name without question.

As quickly as her memories had led her away, she returned once more to Isla's bedside.

"Mrs. Crumpet . . . a duchess, of course." Diana's voice wavered as she whispered the doll's name. It was such an old memory, one that she'd quite forgotten . . . until now. A brush against her shoulder had her turning, expecting to see Rafe behind her, but no one was there.

Except perhaps there was. Diana felt the silvery presence move through and around her, and her soul glowed with a quiet, unshakeable joy.

"Thank you, Eleanor. Thank you for coming home."

It might have been a whisper of wind against the panes of glass from the snow flurries outside or the whistle of sap from the logs on the fire. It might have been her imagination or wishful thinking. Whatever the source, she heard the words and felt the *love* they carried with the magic of Christmas.

"Love you, little fox . . ."

Diana kissed Isla's forehead, and the little girl smiled in her sleep the same way Rafe did. She truly was the daughter of his heart. Diana's life had been upended at the loss of her family, and a deep well of grief had opened within her. Now that well was filled with love for her new family.

Before she had met Rafe and Isla, she'd had a family, the people at Foxglove who had stood by her and cared for her. More than once, Rafe had reminded her that even during her bleakest moments, when her shine had dimmed, she'd had the light of others to burn for her in the dark. And now her family at Foxglove had grown with the addition of Rafe and Isla. He had given her back so much of herself, and she could never stop showing him how much she loved him. She heard Ashton's words that day they'd rescued him from Caddington: *"Rafe, you are the heart of this family."* And he was right. Rafe was all heart, and he'd chosen to love her with that heart.

She lingered a moment longer in the nursery as sunny dreams danced in her mind's eye, promising a wonderful future for her growing family. Then she headed for her bedchamber, where Rafe was waiting for her.

She paused when she noticed a lone candle someone had left unattended on a little table between two tapestries. She lifted it and blew out the candle before setting it back down on the table. The smoke curled up in the moonlight, and she felt a cold whisper of wind behind her.

Something hard and circular pressed against her lower back and a gloved hand suddenly encircled her throat, holding her firmly without squeezing. She sucked in a shocked breath as a hard, hot body held her immobile from behind.

"Easy, lass. Ye wouldna wish to wake the house," a cool, seductive voice murmured in her ear. "Now take me to yer bedchamber."

"Why?" she hissed.

"Because ye owe me, little fire drake, and I've come to claim what's mine." Warm, silken lips caressed her ear before the wicked intruder nibbled on the lobe, making her moan.

The man forced her to guide them to her bedchamber door, and he ushered her inside with a wave of his pistol before he closed the door behind him, smiling at her from behind a black domino. The piercing blue eyes of her beloved, wicked Tyburn stared back at her.

"Stand and deliver . . . *wife*," the highwayman commanded as he waved his pistol at her dressing gown. "I want my prize."

Heart hammering, she unlaced the front of her dressing gown and let it pool at her feet. She hesitated with the ties of the chemise at her collarbone, and he growled for her to continue as he leaned back against the closed door, blocking her escape with his lithe, muscled body.

"I'm afraid I have nothing to give you," she whispered, excitement racing along her skin.

"Yer body is all I need, but I'll steal yer heart too since I'm a greedy man." The masked man pushed away from the door, tossing the pistol aside and seizing her. His gloved hands roved over her body as he rid her of her chemise and bared her naked body to his gaze. He stroked the leather-covered tips of his fingers over her hard nipples and cupped each breast, kneading them, without ever taking his eyes off her.

His eyes narrowed. "Ye seem more sensitive than I remember," he mused as he tugged on one nipple.

She gasped and arched into him. "Perhaps because . . ." She stifled her words, catching herself before she said too much.

"Because what?" he asked, his voice sinfully dark and dangerous. He tugged at one breast almost roughly, just the way she liked it.

"I forget . . . oh Lord . . ." Her body was almost shaking with need for him now. "How did you know?" He stroked one hand over her bare bottom, caressing it while somehow making her feel deliciously owned by him.

How could he have known that she loved Tyburn as much as she loved Rafe? That they were two beings who

belonged together in this world within the same man—
her man.

"Because I love ye, lass, and I ken what ye need, that when the moon is high and the wind whistles down the lonesome roads, ye need to see me, need to be claimed by me."

"Yes," she agreed, writhing in his arms. "Please . . . *Please . . .*"

"Tell me how ye want it, sweet little lass," he crooned against her ear.

"I want it wicked."

He cupped her face, his mouth slanting over hers, his tongue ruthless between her lips as he showed her what he soon would do, and it melted her insides in the most wanton way.

"Then ye'll take me as I wish," he warned with a dark laugh. Suddenly she was turned around to face away from him, and he bent her over the bed. He tossed his gloves aside and trailed his strong, elegant fingers down her bare back, then under her to cup her breasts. She braced herself on her elbows, moaning as he played with her. He moved closer behind her, and she heard him unfasten his trousers.

"Now, little fire drake, take me. Make me burn." His cock thrust into her as he grasped her hips, his fingers digging in. She was full, so full of him, and she whimpered at the sheer pleasure of that all-consuming feeling of belonging to this man. She pushed back against him, meeting him thrust for thrust.

"Yes," he rasped in dark victory. "Yer mine, lass, mine . . . always."

"Always," she echoed as she was struck with a climax with the force of a lightning bolt. She couldn't make a single sound as pure, blinding pleasure shot through her. Diana collapsed limp on the bed as the highwayman continued to slake his lust upon her, and she reveled in his hoarse cry as he came a few moments later. He held still, deep within her, breathing hard, and her body held him, still pulsing with faint aftershocks.

He slowly withdrew and gently settled her upon the bed. He shed all but the domino before he returned to her side with a wet cloth. She shyly parted her legs as he wiped her clean, then crawled into bed beside her, taking her into his arms.

"I have something else to give you," she said as she lay on his chest and stared up at his masked countenance.

"Oh?"

She slipped the mask from his face and saw Rafe's eyes crinkle with love and mischief.

"The problem is," she said with a little smile, "I couldn't quite manage putting it under that beautiful tree."

"Big, is it?" he teased. "*How* big?" He was like a child ready to tear into his gifts.

"Actually, at the moment, it's rather small," she admitted. "But it will grow, and I think Isla will be quite excited about it too."

Rafe's eyes suddenly glowed in the candlelight. "And what could be small but grow, that Isla would like? You didn't buy her a kitten, did you? I was thinking of giving her one of the barn cat's kittens in a few weeks, when it's old enough."

"No," Diana laughed. "Although it will want milk and it will cry, just as kittens do."

The look on his face, the shock followed by joy and wonder . . . how she had longed to see that. The wonder of a man knowing he would become a father a second time.

He grasped her, pulling her even closer to him. "You speak the truth? You are with child?" His voice was breathless, and his excitement made his smile dance.

"Yes, quite sure," she promised him. "I shall give you what I've given no other man."

He cupped her face with one hand, brushing his thumb over her lips.

"You already gave me something you've given no other man—you gave me your heart."

"Then you are twice blessed," she teased, but his deep gaze, so intense, stole her smile and her breath.

"I am *forever* blessed, Diana."

Diana saw the heart belonging to her wicked highwayman, Rafe Lennox, shining like the gold of the coming dawn of a *perfect* Christmas morning.

THANK YOU SO MUCH FOR READING *HER WICKED Highwayman*. The next book in the series will be about Thomasina Lennox, in a fun flashback tale! Be sure to follow me on Social Media and sign up for my newsletter to be alerted when it releases!

Turn the page to read a fun note where I discuss the inspiration for Rafe's story, the emotional journey of the Lennox siblings and share some fun historical tidbits!

A NOTE FROM THE AUTHOR

Hello my lovely readers!

I am so grateful that you just finished reading Rafe Lennox's story. As you may have noticed at the beginning of this book, I included a piece of *The Highwayman* Poem by Alfred Noyes. Alfred truly captured the rich allure of the elusive highwayman, showing us just how these figures captured our imagination. If you haven't listened to Loreena McKennitt's song version of this poem, definitely go listen! You will hear what helped inspire me while writing Rafe and his persona of Tyburn.

When I started writing Her Wicked Highwayman, I was astonished to see how much my characters had changed between book four *Wicked Rivals* and this one which is book nineteen in the series. Rafe had appeared in Ashton's story as this wild creature in the night, robbing Rosalind's coach. I had never imagined then that he would take on the shape he had, or how he'd sneak into so many books (*Wicked Rivals, Never Kiss a Scot, Never Tempt a Scot* and Escaping *the Earl*).

He continued to surprise me, appearing at every turn when I least expected him. But perhaps what surprised me most was when he and Isla had an instant connection. I didn't know then who his heroine was, or what his fate would be. I only knew that I had to wait, that the story would reveal itself at the right time. However, I did know that Isla was the key to Rafe's destiny, that by choosing him, rather than Brodie and Lydia, I knew that something magnificent would happen.

I don't know how other writers hear their stories, or if they hear them like whispers on a moonlit night like I do, but Rafe kept whispering to me, telling me that he was coming, even as I wrote other stories, he refused to leave my head. Still, I did not know his story yet. Until one summer day in 2024, when I finished writing *Dukes and Diamonds*, it was then I heard him say he was ready. And yes, for me as a writer, I hear and see quite clearly, like a waking dream, what happens in my stories. I saw Rafe and a woman together on a dark road, felt her pain, felt her loss and when her face came to me, I saw enough of Isla in her features to know that Rafe's heroine would be related to the little girl. It was then I knew that Isla was and always would be the key to Rafe's fate.

This story was painful and yet it was beautiful too, because I was able to reexamine that awful night that Malcolm Lennox died from his other son's perspective. In Ashton's story in *Wicked Rivals*, you see Ashton's life and how he viewed the night his father died. But it wasn't until this book that you see the fuller story. I thought it was a fitting commentary on life. We always think we know the full story, but the truth is, other people out there hold other memories of the same things, they have different information and different reactions and consequences. It was emotionally difficult to show the strained relationship between Rafe and Ashton, but I want readers to remember that my heroes are and never will be perfect people. They are flawed but no less loveable.

With Rafe's story, I was able to examine the relationship between Rafe and his family. As I was writing, I was stunned to realize that is Ashton is quite right, Rafe has always been the heart of the Lennox family. He took every beating on an emotional level, took every pain into himself and kept going, helping his family without a thought for appreciation or reciprocation. In his own mischievous way, he was being rather selfless, despite his insistence otherwise.

I hope you enjoyed reading Rafe's happily ever after! The next book in the series will be a flash back of sorts to when the eldest sibling, the mysterious Thomasina fell in love. As Ashton's elder sibling by two years, she isn't often mentioned, because she married so quickly and moved into her husband's home, as all women of those periods did. She had a wild and exciting romance that I cannot wait to share with you!

Now, I thought to end this author note with some fun historical information. As my copy editor Jessica and I were discussing edits, she suggested that I include some fun information for you. When I get deep into writing, I often forget that readers don't have access to my head and can't know everything I've read as research over the years. So I thought I'd share some of it with you!

Women Bankers

When I first wrote Wicked Rivals, I read an amazing

book called ***Women Who Made Money: Women Partners in British Private Banks 1752-1906*** , by **Margaret Dawes and Nesta Selwyn.** In this book, the authors explain how women could become either through inheritance or investment, owners of banks. Usually these were smaller banks or country banks, but they were legitimate financial institutions. Despite the law requiring a woman's property to become that of her husband's, there were quite a few interesting loopholes that allowed women to retain ownership, have it in a trust or inherit it. Many of the woman who became bankers in this period were middle-class but there were some upper class. So it was quite possible for Rosalind to run her own bank and be able to handle investments and accounts for others.

The Green Baize Door

This was only briefly mentioned once in the book but my copy editor raised an interesting query when she asked if I was talking about baize, like the felt on a billiard table. I was then able to share the fascinating history of the green baize door with her and she thought you would love to know too.

This door was the entrance to the servant world in the majority of English homes. The baize fabric wrapped around the front and back of the doors and was sealed on with brass tacks. It helped keep the door "quiet" because it was constantly being opened and closed for the servants to pass through into the main part of the house to do their duties. The use of baize dates back to 1525 and it was used on a variety of surfaces from nursery doors to writing desks and gaming tables including billiard tables. The cloth, aside from absorbing sounds could also absorb kitchen odors as well. The green baize door became an iconic symbol for the divide between the working class and the residents of the house. I often write it into scenes where I am discussing the servants because the visual of a large oak door covered with green baize fabric is quite interesting to picture.

Christmas Traditions

There is a common belief that Christmas trees and Christmas gifts weren't around in the regency era. We often solely connect that with the Victorian period. But Queen Charlotte actually brought the first Christmas tree, a yew tree, into Windsor palace and she and her children decorated it. When Prince Albert came along in the early Victorian period, he made the tradition more popular and he used a fir tree rather than a yew. But Christmas trees did exist before Prince Albert.

The act of giving gifts was also occurring in the Regency era. It depended upon each family's particular tradition but presents could be given on Christmas Eve, Christmas Day, Boxing Day, Twelfth Night and New Years Day. Landowners and well-off people would often give gifts to the poor or the struggling people in their communities. They also gave favors to the tradesman, servants and tenants they patronized. Between people of equal social standing, the gifts were between family or close friends. Women took this time as a chance to show off their needlepoint skills, drawing or other ladies' interests. Children also received gifts at this time. They were not necessarily put under the three, but I couldn't resist working in that tradition for Rafe, because I rather picture him as the type of father who would stay up until three in the morning putting together toys for the children if he lived in the modern age.

I hope you enjoyed these interesting tidbits! Thank you again for reading Rafe's book. I would love it if you shared the cover, your favorite quotes or pictures of your favorite pages from the book (yes you can absolutely share a screenshot of your kindle or reading app with quotes highlighted!). If you belong to any reader groups, please recommend this book to fellow readers and tell them why you love Rafe! And of course, reviews are deeply appreciated! Even just a few sentences about what you loved is all a review needs!

Thank you for being such a wonderful supporter of my characters and stories!

ABOUT THE AUTHOR

Lauren Smith is an Oklahoma attorney by day, author by night who pens adventurous and edgy romance stories by the light of her smart phone flashlight app. She knew she was destined to be a romance writer when she attempted to re-write the entire *Titanic* movie just to save Jack from drowning. Connecting with readers by writing emotionally moving, realistic and sexy romances no matter what time period is her passion. She's won multiple awards in several romance subgenres including: New England Reader's Choice Awards, Greater Detroit BookSeller's Best Awards, and a Semi-Finalist award for the Mary Wollstonecraft Shelley Award.

To Connect with Lauren, visit her at:
www.laurensmithbooks.com
lauren@laurensmithbooks.com

facebook.com/LaurenDianaSmith
x.com/LSmithAuthor
instagram.com/Laurensmithbooks
bookbub.com/authors/lauren-smith
tiktok.com/@laurenandemmabooks